ELLA PRUITT

I0537356

Doug Cooper Spencer

DEDICATION

To Laura Estella Bell-Cooper for showing me just how high a person can fly with imagination and for loving without fear, and to my daughter Courtney and my husband Greg who continue to stand by me when times are rough. Love knows no condition but love.

OTHER BOOKS BY DOUG COOPER SPENCER

This Place of Men

People Like Us

Leaving Gomorrah

A Letter to a Friend

Gather the Bones

"Some choices we live not only once but a thousand times over, remember them for the rest of our lives." ~ Richard Bach

Acknowledgements

'We'll Understand It Better By and By', by Charles Albert Tindley, circ. 1905

'Through It All', by Andrea Crouch, Copyright 1971, Manna Music

CHAPTER ONE

Ella shivered in the gray morning light as she slid her feet from her house slippers and planted them flat on the cold floor. She needed the bite of the cold to push away her exhaustion. Then she pulled her robe close around her neck, sat back in her chair, and stared out into the room, the memories holding her almost motionless. She sipped a cup of ginger tea to calm her stomach. Even now, years later, she held the odor of the lake that day in her nostrils and still, it sickened her. The odor came to her every now and then as a sign that once more, what happened back then was asking for recognition. The putrid smell of dirty water, the pungent aroma of weeds, the mud around the lake and the odor of rotting flesh would rise around her and she would become nauseated. Then there were the nightmares, sometimes so startling they would awaken her and remain with her for days afterwards. The dreams happened a lot, but usually they were cut into small portions, an image appearing here or there perhaps in a totally unrelated dream as a symbol, enough to remind her of that time. But every so often the dreams and the memories would take hold of her, making her relive her past. Last night the dream was of that day at the lake. Again, she saw his face as his body was lifted from the water and she felt the kick in her belly. The dream must have startled her, and in her desperation she must have awakened her husband because when she woke the next morning he was sleeping in another room.

Now she sat in the den with the cup of tea in her lap, seeped in regret and an abiding fear. In the distance, her husband moved around in the kitchen as he prepared for work. She could hear him closing the refrigerator door and the clack of dishes as he fixed himself something to eat. He blew a frustrated breath and pulled a chair from the kitchen table, allowing the sound of the dragging chair to rattle throughout the house.

Ella understood her husband's frustration, but things were the way they were. The journey had been hers and it would be hers. The journey started before she met her husband. It had been her journey since the day she first saw the young man, since the nights she let the young man slip into her bedroom and lay with her while her father slept down the hall. It took shape and meaning when she stood in the crowd of onlookers and watched as they pulled the body from the lake, since the days when she walked the streets of New Home looking for the young man, since the day she had the baby, and the night she bundled the baby up and slipped away from New Home on a Greyhound.

The night she ran away from home Ella had fixed three bottles of baby formula because it was all the food the baby had left, and she made her way to the bus station. She had an idea of where she was going when she boarded the bus that night, but it was just that, an idea, because at the age of fourteen most of what she figured about life was a collection of images and observations she had gotten from magazines and TV and the stories the young man had told her about the places he had been, the things he had seen and things he knew to be true. That was pretty much what she knew about life until that horrible day at the lake and the day the baby came. They were all reasons why she had to leave town. She hadn't been back to New Home since that night she boarded the Greyhound and her family never looked for her. The journey had been and always would be hers.

Her husband stopped by the den to check on her before leaving for the church. "You want something to eat?" Milton's question was more of an inquiry into her disposition than anything else. Being a minister, he was always concerned with disposition.

"I'm fine," Ella answered. "I'm going to start getting ready for work soon."

He looked at her for a second more without speaking. Then he walked into the room and gave her a peck on the forehead.

"I'm sorry," she said.

"You have to turn it over to God, Ella," he said. He looked pitifully at her, shook his head and left.

Twenty minutes passed after Milton left before Ella got up from her chair. It was twenty minutes more she had used to go over her life, the assemblage of incidents that created it and how the story might end. She was always told that God would never give you more than you could stand. She hoped they were right.

She went into the kitchen and turned on the TV that sat on the counter as she always did to have the voices fill the space that grew inside of her and the somberness of the space around her. She cleaned up after her husband, running water in the sink where he had left his dishes, and began washing them as she looked out the window into the back yard. In the far corner of the yard the gazebo sat, graying in the December light, and all around it winter was there: the dull grass of the lawn, bare trees with thin, gnarled branches that moved slightly in the breeze like bony fingers scratching at secrets, and large gray clouds that lumbered across an even grayer sky. For her, winter brought calm. Unlike summer, with its overwrought expectations and often-disastrous results, winter slowed things down and it was these slow times she needed. She had come to respect winter because it didn't scream at her the way hot summer days did.

Gathering up the last crumbs of toast from the kitchen counter into a dishcloth, she rinsed them down the drain and went to get ready for work, passing the bedroom where her son used to sleep, stopping to tend to his bed, fluffing the pillows and smoothing the covers, though the bed hadn't been slept in for years. She would call him later to make sure he was okay. The dreams were occurring more often causing her to worry more about her son. After all, the words had been written: *"The Lord God, merciful and gracious, long suffering, and abundant in goodness and truth, keeping mercy for thousands, forgiving iniquity and transgression and sin, and that will by no means clear the guilty; visiting the iniquity of the fathers upon the children, and upon the children's children, unto the third and to the fourth generation."*

They had been written.

She turned on the shower and waited for the water to heat, then she disrobed and as she had for so many years, she ran her fingers over the scar along her abdomen before feeling the ache in her groin. Hanging her robe on the back of the bathroom door, she got into the shower.

That afternoon Ella made her monthly visit to check in on a client. She talked a bit with the security guard as she signed in at the desk in the lobby. She then made her way across the lobby, passed under a large chandelier, got on the elevator and headed up to Mrs. Wexner's apartment. Two elderly women and a younger man were on the elevator plus a young lady who Ella figured was probably the day nurse of one of the women by the way the young lady held onto the woman's arm, steady in the way a professional does, but less intimate than a family member. The middle-aged man, about Ella's age, stood with his arm crooked to aid the other old woman as she held onto him. The man had a beard and was dressed in a black suit, wore an open collar white shirt, and a black fedora typical of the Jewish men Ella often saw in the building. By the care the man took with the woman, Ella assumed he was the woman's son. They smiled and nodded to Ella as the elevator moved to the floors. The elevator stopped and the man held the door open as the nurse slowly led her elderly client off. Then it closed and continued until it came to the floor Ella had requested. She said goodbye to the other elderly woman and the man and exited.

Ella was met at the door by her client's attendant, a tall, stately woman dressed in an unassuming skirt and blouse with a soft coral colored sweater with its sleeves pushed up. She greeted Ella as she stood back to let her in.

"Hi Ella."

"Hi Madelyn. How are you?"

"I'm well."

"That's good. Is she doing okay today?" Ella asked, as they walked through the foyer of the large apartment.

"She's fine. Just a bit feisty at times. But at least she's that."

"Yeah. It shows she still has drive."

They came to the den where Mrs. Wexner sat watching TV. Her face lighted when she saw Ella and she raised her hand and took Ella's hand in hers. "Ella."

"Hi Mrs. Wexner. How are you?"

"Oh, wonderful. Just watching TV."

"That's good."

Ella sat beside Mrs. Wexner and watched the show, a travelogue on Borneo. "How are you feeling, Mrs. Wexner?" Ella quietly asked.

"Oh fine." Mrs. Wexner answered without taking her eyes off the TV. Ella smiled at the elderly woman's enjoyment. She looked at Mrs. Wexner to assess her state of mind, but in a silent way so as not to disturb her mood.

"Karl never wanted to go there," Mrs. Wexner said, her eyes still on the screen. "He always wanted to go places that were cold. I used to tell him I was tired of going to cold places. We came from a cold place. Why go back?" She ended her comment, this time turning to Ella. "Some people never want to try new things. Karl was like that."

"Some people are like that," Ella replied.

Mrs. Wexner sighed, "Well," then turned back to the TV.

Ella put her hand on top of Mrs. Wexner's hand that rested on the arm of the chair in which the elderly woman sat. Ella saw the numbers on Mrs. Wexner's forearm. Now a faded blue on her pale, loose skin, they were part of the woman's story just like the many photos on the table across the room. Some of the photos were of a young Mrs. Wexner, standing beside her husband in front of a large automobile, a fox stole around her shoulder. They had broad smiles on their faces and the car was loaded with luggage. Ella always wondered if they were about to go on vacation, or fleeing what they knew was to come. There were many photos of Mrs. Wexner and Karl and of other faces Ella had been told were family members, most of them lost during the war, but there were just as many photos of Greta, her best friend. They were taken after Karl passed away. The two of them became roommates after years of friendship and after Greta lost her husband. There were photos of Mrs. Wexner and Greta traveling to places Karl refused to go to, and her smile was just as bright as when she was with Karl. And now Greta was gone. Ella knew just as much about Mrs. Wexner's story as she did her own.

It was late afternoon when Ella finished visiting with her clients. She looked at her watch and decided her son should be up and that she would call him. The late hours he kept and the people he ran with bothered her to no end and was another reason she was often concerned with his safety, but she wasn't surprised that he would turn out the way he did, because his father had lived the same way. To this day she had no idea if Danny's father was still alive. Damon was his name, and at times she felt she needed to find him, to let him know he had a son and to get him to go back to New Home with her and face the people there. But she knew if she ever found Damon and if she ever went back to New Home, she would lose so much of what she had gained. Still, the conversation played out often in her head, to the point of keeping her up some nights.

Ella had so much to lose if she went back to the town she grew up in, but there were times she felt she might lose even more if she stayed away from it. She dialed her son's number and pushed thoughts of New Home out of her head.

CHAPTER TWO

"It's going on two-thirty Danny and you're not up?"

Danny lay in bed and listened to his mother over the phone. His body still ached from the night before. Cortez had told him his ribs were probably just bruised but they ached like the rest of his body as he reached for the phone that afternoon.

"No. I'm not up." He was bothered that his mother woke him and he was irritated by her question.

"This is ridiculous. It doesn't make any sense, that life you're living. I don't know anything about it and don't want to know anything about it--"

"Then leave it alone, Mom."

"Boy, don't talk to me like that."

Danny caught himself. "Just leave it alone, Mom. I'm ok." He assured her of this, though he knew his mother never believed him when told her he was fine, but what else was he going to tell her?

They talked a while, with Ella asking Danny if he needed anything and why he hung around the people he hung around. But it was when she asked him how he felt that Danny heard something different. His mother's voice seemed weighted with concern, as if she needed a real answer instead of one that might simply assuage her.

Yet the reply Danny gave was the same, that he was fine, but just sleepy. And with that, Ella knew there was nothing else to say, so she told him she loved him.

"I love you too, Mom."

"Danny."

"Huh?"

"I want you to come to the house for Christmas."

Danny didn't reply. The two of them sat silently by for a moment, both of them caught off-guard by Ella's sudden request. He hadn't been to the house for Christmas dinner in years. In fact, he rarely went to his parents' home since the fight he had with his step-father some years ago, a fight in which he almost killed the man.

"Ok", he said to his mother's stunned silence. He could hear her gather her breath before replying, "Good." Once their conversation was over, he pulled the covers over his head and went back to sleep.

After sleeping well into the evening Danny finally got up. It was dark outside. He looked out the window to nearly empty streets. A man walked down the avenue under the streetlights, hunched against the cold with his collar up and his hands tucked deep in his coat pockets. Danny would be out there soon and he would be gone until the next morning. He was feeling better now; the ache in his body had eased so he was ready for more work.

He fixed himself something to eat, then went over to the closet in his bedroom and pulled out a dark brown satchel that he kept in the corner on the floor of the closet. He sat at the kitchen table and placed the satchel alongside his meal and undid the clasp. In the satchel were two books, a couple of old notebooks, a photo of himself as an infant in his mother's arms, in front of a building, and some newspaper and magazine clippings. He pulled out the two books and one of the notebooks and placed them on the table. And there, in the quiet of his apartment, he began to eat as he read one of the books. Every once in a while he would lift the book to his face, peering at the page as if by bringing the book closer to his face he could make more sense of the words. He knew the meanings of the everyday words in the book, but it was the arrangement of the words, not so much the meanings of singular words, that he couldn't grasp. He knew the thought behind the words was important because such an author as the man on the opening page with the distinguished look that people associated with greatness, the man who wrote the book, wouldn't have put them on paper if they weren't important. The thoughts of the writer had to have meaning, and Danny wanted to know them.

He continued to study the page, concentrating on unfamiliar words that at the moment seemed only like an arrangement of symbols. He had never been good at reading, but he was too proud to let anyone teach him, even though it was something he wanted to do so badly.

He moved his mouth, forming various shapes as he pronounced what he thought were the sounds of the words, slowly, and in parcels of consonants. His voice whispered in the quiet of his apartment and he listened to himself as he spoke each word. He had found the book in a store; it was a store four stories high, with nothing but books and magazines, mostly used. Every so often he passed the bookstore and with each passing he wanted to go inside but he was intimidated from crossing the doorway. Yet there was an attraction to the place, something about the warmly lit aisles, the shelves of dark wood and the collection of books that always caught his attention. He had always found fascination in finding things, of knowing about people and places and things outside of himself, and possibly even finding out more about himself. It was a place where secrets were unclothed, and all he had to do was to learn how to read the wonderful leather binderies along the wall.

One day he managed the nerves to go inside of the bookstore and he came out with two books: Descartes' *Discourse on the Method of Rightly Conducting One's Reason and of Seeking Truth in the Sciences*, and a dictionary. The first book caught his attention because of the long title and the words 'reason' and 'truth' connected things in him that he felt were discordant. He purchased the dictionary because he knew he would need it to understand the meanings in the first book.

After he finished dinner and after a while of studying the book Danny looked at the clock and saw it was almost time to go. He slipped the folded piece of paper that he used as a bookmark between the pages of the book and put both books back on the floor of his bedroom closet underneath two cardboard storage boxes. He walked back to the living room and began warming up: light stretching, a few sets of eight count body push-ups, pull-ups, and finished up by shadow boxing. Once he was done he took a shower, then put the rest of his dinner in a small container and headed downstairs to the first floor of his building. He placed the container of food on the floor outside of the first apartment, knocked twice on the door, then turning the collar up on his coat, he went out for the night.

~~~~

The bus moved through the night along the highway, passing fields that appeared as dark, woven carpet. Every once in a while the light from a distant house would dot the darkened landscape, like a waking eye, before closing once again as the bus continued. The young lady rested her head on a pillow that she had fashioned from her sweater and her coat and stared out the window of the bus, counting the lights along the highway. It was well past midnight and most of the passengers were asleep, but the young lady couldn't sleep; she had tried, but she couldn't because there were so many thoughts moving around in her head that she would jolt awake each time she tried to rest. Now she found herself simply staring out the window of the bus, counting the streetlights in hopes that the counting would replace her thoughts. Fifty-three seconds. That was the time it took for another light to pass by the window.

The woman who sat in the seat next to her slept with her face away from the young lady and snored in soft notes. The bus was mostly quiet except for the low roar of the engine and every now and then the young lady could hear whispered conversations from a few seats behind her, but other than that most of the passengers ended another long day of their trip in sleep.

Alongside the young lady, tucked between the seat and the wall of the bus, was her large purse. It contained things she needed, including a spiral notebook and a few photos. When the sun rose she would write more of her thoughts in the notebook, because the thoughts she had about what she had been told would serve her once she got to her destination. She pressed the back of her fingers against the window to feel the cold outside and watched as another light passed by.

Outside the bus, the highway opened before the travelers, concrete passing through the beams of the headlights and moving beneath and beyond the bus, a trail of the memories of the riders onboard. There was no one to slow them as the bus made its way through the night. The road was empty and it was silent except for the bus that roared along in the dark towards Cincinnati.

Another light along the highway passed by. 'Fifty-three seconds,' she counted.

CHAPTER THREE

Milton headed to his office, passing the two small rooms that were used for Sunday school classes. He had been in the basement to check on a leak in the plumbing, and to check on the workers the church had hired to fix it. He couldn't tell how successful the workers were, a middle-aged man and his young journeyman, but it appeared as if they were solving the problem. For the most part he was pleased by what little he saw of the work, but not by the appearance of the journeyman. The young man's pants hung below his behind and his hair was twisted instead of combed. Milton didn't like that. He made a mental note to not hire them again if the young man couldn't work on his appearance.

But the plumbing was actually just an excuse for Milton to go downstairs and piddle around while he got his thoughts together for his next session. He wasn't sure how to handle the couple that was coming to see him. As he walked to his office he told his secretary to not make any future contracts with the plumber if he couldn't have his assistant dress respectfully.

Mrs. Hargrove nodded. "He look a mess, don't he?"

"Yeah. Very disrespectful." Milton looked at his watch, "Give me a little more time if the Nixons get here sooner than they're scheduled."

"Is it that bad?" Mrs. Hargrove attempted to look concerned. But Milton could see that she was licking her chops for some gossip. He didn't answer her.

When the Nixons arrived, they sat on the couch close to each other but their expressions were far apart. Milton could tell by the expression on the husband's face that the challenge the couple was going through had left him bewildered. His name was Derrick and he sat quietly by, his body loose, and he blinked and looked at Milton with the eyes of someone who had been taken on a ride and was pleading for a way to get off, while his wife, Cecily, sat erect with her hands clasped in her lap.

"Why don't you want to keep the baby?" Milton had intended to approach the question in a more subtle way, but now that the three of them were in the room and he sat across from the couple he felt it was best to simply come to the point.

The wife wasn't fazed by Milton's abruptness. She had expected it, considering the nature of the subject. "I don't want to have children, Reverend Pruitt. I never intended to get pregnant."

"But you're married. It happens," Milton said. "People get married and they have children."

"Not for me," she said. "We agreed on that before we got married. Me and Derrick both said we didn't want to have any kids." She looked at her husband, who moved his head slowly up and then down, in feeble agreement.

"That's true," the husband said. "We had talked about it when we were dating and we decided to not have kids."

"Oh. I see…" Milton considered the news.

"But I've changed my mind," the husband continued. "Now I do want to have children. And since this happened, well, it's like God intended for it to happen." His wife let out a light exasperated breath and looked away from her husband.

"You can't change what God intended, Sister Nixon. You shouldn't." Milton looked at her knowing what was on her mind. "This is your chance to start a family."

"Reverend Pruitt, I… I do not want to have this child." She looked down at her hands that had loosened from the iron-like clasp they had been held in and she continued. "I'm not the motherly type. I don't have those maternal instincts like I hear most women talking about. I don't have it, so it wouldn't make any sense to have a baby."

"Things might change after you have the baby," her husband said, taking his wife's hand in his.

"As the baby starts growing inside you, those maternal feelings can start to grow too," Milton said. "That's what I've heard a lot of women say. And I believe that. It's God's way of forming that bond that creates family. Just give it a chance and let it all happen the way God wants it to be."

"Be fruitful and multiply," her husband half-whispered.

After the session, Milton sat alone in his office. He knew the woman didn't want to have the child and that she was aware that she had a small window of time to discontinue the pregnancy. They had sat in the office, the wife, her husband and Milton, and had talked all about how giving birth was the right thing to do. She said she had used contraceptives to prevent getting pregnant and was surprised when she found out she was expecting, but the news only served to make her determined to not go through with the pregnancy. All the justification Milton could use, he used, but nothing seemed to sway the woman. To his and her husband's declarations that she would be taking a life by ending the pregnancy, she insisted that it was her body and that she should not have to go through something she didn't want to go through. The session ended with neither of them changing her mind.

Milton thought how lucky the woman was to be able to even have children. He had always wanted to have a child, a son who looked like him and had the fire to follow in Milton's footsteps to carry out God's word; but that would never happen since Ella could no longer have children. This fact that Ella wasn't able to give him a child was something that came to him every now and then during those times when he thought only of himself. Equally disturbing was that the only child Ella had she had it when she was only fourteen years old. It sickened him to imagine her conceiving a child at thirteen, lying there with her legs open, legs no larger than a child's legs, with a man on top of her. At the point of him imagining the man moving inside of her and how her face, a girl's face, must have appeared during the act, he would clear his mind of it all. But he never forgot what he knew. Ella not giving him a son, but having brought in a child to their marriage she had by another man, a wandering stranger, left Milton with a feeling of estrangement and it sometimes left him wondering just where he was in the picture.

He had never felt that he was a part of the bond Ella had with her son. Just thinking about Ella's attachment to Danny bothered Milton because he had always felt she was holding onto Danny's father by coddling Danny. She had told Milton when they were dating that when she had boarded the bus up in New Home that she didn't know where she was going. She said something pulled at her to head west, as if Danny's father was somewhere out there waiting to see his son. She said she had gotten off the bus in Cincinnati only to change her and Danny's clothes and to find something to eat, but for some reason she ended up staying. She told him she didn't know why she decided to stay, but she did.

Milton never forgave Ella for telling him that story. That she was running across the country to look for a man. That was something he didn't have to know, just like there were things about him she didn't have to know. By his way of thinking, that was the best way to manage things: if past actions have no direct bearing on the present, then a person should simply ask for God's forgiveness, forgive oneself for any misdeeds one might have committed and leave the misgivings behind as a lesson and to not revisit them. That was all that was needed and it was something she could have done. No one had any need to know about her and Danny's father. Especially Milton.

The story around Christ The Redeemer Baptist Church was that Ella had been abandoned by her husband when he ran off with another woman, leaving her alone with their baby, and that Milton, who had gone so long without a wife because he couldn't find a righteous woman, met Ella at a church picnic and they instantly fell in love. As the story was told, when he found out she had a child, it caused him to hesitate, not because she had a child, but because he wasn't sure of the circumstances that led up to her having the child. He needed to find a woman who was pure, if not of body at least of soul. Not someone who had gotten herself pregnant because of her loose ways and then was dumped along the way like so many of the women out there in the streets. Once he heard her story, he literally cried. Then she cried. Then he promised to take care of her and her son. Then, so the story goes, he asked if he could pray that the love they had for each other would continue forever, and that was how they became a family. That was the story that went around Christ The Redeemer Baptist Church, and Milton and Ella never disputed it. They allowed everyone to think they hadn't caught wind of it from Danny, who had been told by a classmate in Sunday school of the story of his life. Back then even Danny believed it, but over time that story began to fade the more Danny looked into his stepfather's eyes.

~~~~

Service had always been a part of Ella's life. It was something she learned from her father, Emmanuel. Emmanuel Stallworth was one of the wealthiest men in the small all-black town of New Home and he gave a lot of himself to the community, though some of the folks of New Home resented it, seeing instead his brand of benevolence as little more than a practice of stewardship over the lives of those who were less fortunate than him.

It was nothing for Emmanuel to give money to the truly unfortunate, the circumstance of their misfortune being something he alone determined before making his decision to give the money away rather than lending it out; and during the summer holidays it was Emmanuel Stallworth's deep pockets that funded the hog roast in the park by the lake and the Thanksgiving and Christmas dinners in the basement of the church he attended.

Emmanuel understood that much of what was considered the 'misfortunate' circumstances of the people of New Home was due to their skin color. Emmanuel knew this very well because he remembered riding in the cab of an old truck as a child along with his sister, his mother and his father as his family made their way north from Georgia. He remembered looking out of the window of the truck that was burdened with as many of the things his family could carry, and with his uncle and cousin riding in the back atop the stacks of crates and sacks, watching the long fields of green, white and brown roll off into the distance. They had sought a place where they had been told they could find respectable work and would finally be free of discrimination only to find themselves relegated to a square of land that the citizens of the nearby all white town of Stratford had found suitable for the Negroes that were arriving, everyday it seemed, threatening the state of mind of the citizens of Stratford with their presence. The Negroes were given the square of land, a little over seven hundred acres, and the Negroes named it New Home. Emmanuel understood these things, but he had been able to wriggle through the tiny portal allowed only to a few Negroes to achieve success. But it was black success, and it was never on par with the success of some of the people in Stratford. It was something Emmanuel never forgot, but still, he was one of the successful men in New Home and he used it to his advantage. So in return for what he called benevolence, he never let those whom he helped get away without service to him and his family. From cleaning the gutters of the house to simply running errands, there was always one of the truly less fortunate who was on call.

Ella remembered hot summer days and her mother answering the door to a woman who would arrive to do housework or a man who would stand on the other side of the screen door and tell her that Ella's father had 'asked' him if he would help out by mowing the lawn, or by washing the second car that Ella's mother drove to and from her salon; the faces of the men and women who responded to the benevolence changed weekly and sometimes even daily.

The salon was just one of the businesses Ella's family owned. Even though Ella's mother Victoria knew nothing about taking care of hair, other than what she did to her own hair in terms of styling it, the salon was just another venture for a disillusioned aspirant to engage in, and it was a whim her mother had answered by Ella's father who went to great lengths to keep his wife entertained. Their main businesses, however, were insurance, Stallworth's Funeral Home, and rental properties in New Home.

Ella's parents had met when they both were students at Howard University. Emmanuel had majored in accounting. Victoria, in world languages and anthropology, before finding that she was more interested in hair and fashion than language and culture. To her, hair and fashion only made sense for a woman of her light complexion and less than kinky hair to pursue. After Ella's father completed his degree, he moved his wife and their first child, Ella's brother Ren, short for Rendall (a name Emmanuel found odd and always believed it to have been the name of a previous boyfriend of his wife since she wouldn't come clean about how she came up with such an odd name and which caused Ella's father to never allow his wife to go back to Baltimore to visit her family unless he accompanied her. He was never able to prove the source of the name, but held a deep disgust whenever someone called his son by his full name), back to Ohio, where they settled in the town Emmanuel grew up in, New Home. In later years, after he had achieved financial success, he tried to buy a home in Stratford, but the purchase was blocked. Black folks were to live in New Home. The fact that there were suddenly no homes available for Emmanuel to purchase in Stratford left a bitter taste in his mouth for the rest of his life. But instead of taking it out on the people of Stratford, he took it out on the people of New Home, calling them niggers and never expecting much of them. Still, it was home.

Victoria despised New Home as well and she despised the people of New Home even more than Emmanuel did. He at least had experience with them. Victoria didn't. Except for the family in the house to the right of theirs, and except for Emmanuel's older sister Bernice, Victoria found the rest of the people of New Home so lacking in vision and so languid in presence that she often had few words to say to them except for courteous exchanges, but even those words fell cold and uncaring before they reached the ears of the people she addressed. Having been raised in Baltimore, she regarded the people of New Home as backwards and with little ahead of them, in terms of a future, other than working in one of the mills of nearby Stratford or washing dishes in Stratford's restaurants. It was why, even after adjusting to life in New Home, she held no reservations when it came to some of New Home's residents mowing her family's lawn or doing her laundry, because it freed her to go shopping in Stratford with Bernice. It freed her to sit at one of the nicer restaurants in Stratford, one that didn't tell Negroes looking for a table that they were booked, and she and Bernice would talk of how life could be if so many things were different. It also allowed Victoria time to tend to her second love outside of the salon: designing and sewing outfits. She would spend hours in her sewing room, bathed in the afternoon sunlight that streamed through the large windows, and by lamps at night, surrounded by fabrics of various colors, especially hues of reds, blues, greens and yellow on large bolsters laying on tables and sometimes spread out along a table cut in different angles. It was there that she would spend much of her time, sketching and fitting and pinning fabrics to mannequins, then sewing the garments with the intention of sending them back east and one day having marketed them enough to possibly get her and her family out of New Home. She never was able to get her husband and her children out of New Home so she left the night when she refused to wake up.

The passing of Ella's mother took its toll on her family. The house fell into a silence that it never recovered from. Bernice came over to help the family through its grief, but she wasn't able to dispel the grayness that had descended on the household. She had taken charge of things after Victoria died. She came over with the same resolve she had when she was told that her sister-in-law had passed, the will to move on. Bernice had come to the door the day Victoria had died with the sense of having prepared for it all. It was as if she was privy to her sister-in-law's passing before it took place, but was sworn to keep it between Victoria and herself. She immediately went to Victoria's closet and picked out the dress to put on Victoria, knowing where to find each accessory for the outfit as if she had prior knowledge of where to find them, and then she began telling her brother what Victoria wanted from him after Victoria left. But Emmanuel was too broken to hear her. He only knew that he had lost the best friend he'd ever had, so his grief was almost unbearable.

While Emmanuel had always been a man who preferred to talk about business with outsiders than talking to his children, he would, at the behest of his wife, engage in small talk with them. He talked more with Ren than he did his daughters because he felt that it would be Ren who would one day take over the family business. But with Victoria there was constant conversation with the children, mostly about things she felt they might never learn living in New Home. She would tell them stories of traveling overseas with her parents, and of her days as a young model (something, that if you had asked anyone who knew her, they would've told you they had no notion of that fact); the rest of the time she would either read to them from one of the many books she and Emmanuel had in the library or tell them her family's history. All of that ended when she decided to leave. From then on there was little movement in the house that bespoke joy. Even the very air in the house seemed to lay like a long heavy sigh and the few sounds that were made within the walls of the large bright house were the sounds of footsteps of what was left of the family walking from one room to another, followed always by the sound of closing doors, then silence would claim the space once again.

It was the doors that Ella recalled from the days following her mother's passing. They were almost always closed. The door to Ren's bedroom had usually been closed but now he had even turned to locking it. Miriam, her younger sister stayed for a while in her bedroom but a month after they buried her mother Miriam became fascinated with sewing and began using her mother's supplies to thread her way through her days. She started with sewing buttons on her father's shirts and his sport coats, then she offered to stitch tears in the clothes of family members before starting to make clothing for her dolls. One dress, then another and another until she ended up spending long hours in her mother's sewing room behind closed French doors, bathed in sunlight, and dotted by lamps at night, humming and sewing.

But it was her father's door that mystified Ella the most. It was the door to the bedroom he had shared with his wife, and it was the room from which Ella would hear him talking to his deceased wife.

"That's what I told them, Victoria…"

(Laughter) "Now you know that ain't right…"

"But why, Victoria?"

Ella would hear him talking into the silence of the room when she would walk by, his voice lively or sometimes full of despair coming from behind the door. It wasn't until months had gone by hearing her father talk to her mother that she sometimes heard her mother's voice come from the room as well, answering him. At first she thought it was her imagination, until she got Ren to vouch for her. She got him to come from his room and stand by the door. They listened to their father go on for a while. "Girl, he always does that. He's just missing momma," Ren had protested. And then it came, their mother's voice as clear as a bell: *"Emmanuel, put on a different pair of socks. Those are wearing thin."* Ella looked at her brother, who stood with his mouth hanging agape. He turned and went to his room, shutting his door, and never spoke of the moment again. A few years later, having tired of hearing his father talk to a dead woman, his youngest sister sewing deliriously day in and day out, and Ella walking around the house measuring the absence of what used to be, carrying a child that her father despised, that Ren begged his father to send him off to boarding school. It took a few months but Emmanuel gave in after Ren convinced him it would benefit him in running the family business, but also Emmanuel feared that if he kept his son there, Ren might die from despair like his mother had.

Still, when she was alive, Emmanuel had taken delight in seeing his wife and her various endeavors, but he never knew her desire to use them to escape the small, backwards town he had brought her to and he would only see his wife donate some of the outfits to the less fortunate of New Home without understanding that they were given as rejected designs. To Emmanuel and his children, it was another example of the more blessed helping those who had been less than blessed.

This form of service from her family was something Ella, her brother and her younger sister had become accustomed to; they had seen it for most of their young lives and never questioned the integrity of it. It wasn't until one day when Ella walked in on a woman doing the laundry that her understanding of her parents' benevolence became clear. Ella had been upstairs in her bedroom talking with her dolls as she usually did before going out to play, telling them she would be going outside for the day and that she didn't want them being bad children while she was away. It was her routine. On her way outside she went into the kitchen to go out back where she would cross over to the neighbor's yard and play with her friends. As she walked through the kitchen she passed the room where she heard the rolling and rumbling sound of the washer and dryer, and while it was never that important to check in on the help, this day was different.

Usually she was already out and about when the laundry was being done and she would come home to find clothes cleaned and neatly folded in a basket so her mother could take them up to their rooms, but that day she heard the wash being done and it caught her attention. She stopped at the back door and decided she wanted to see the person who created this magical act before she headed outside. Stepping lightly with the intention of not disturbing the person, she crossed the kitchen to the doorway of the laundry room and looked in. There was a woman busily sorting out their soiled clothes. She had her back to Ella so Ella couldn't see her face, but Ella figured by the woman's wide square hips and the stockings she wore rolled up her plump legs to her knees the way Ella had seen older women wear their stockings, that the woman was a bit older than both of Ella's parents. Ella watched her for a moment, listening to the heavy breathing of the woman and trying to make out the mumbling that came under the woman's breath. She wasn't used to talking to the help since they changed ranks so often and she had never had a chance to get to know them, so she decided to quietly leave the woman to her work when suddenly the woman stood up with a basket of clothes. She saw Ella and glared at her. "This what you wanna see, huh," the woman said to Ella. Ella looked into the eyes of the woman and saw the hatred there, and it was then that she understood the meaning of her parents' benevolence. Ella backed away from the doorway and ran to her room where she stayed until the woman left. From that day on she stayed in her room whenever someone came to help out around the house.

In Milton's case regarding acts of service, growing up it would have been his family that would have been considered as one of the unfortunate ones and that was in need of service. His father never held a steady job and drank up much of the money he did bring into the house. Milton's family suffered greatly, leaving Milton with an aching sadness whenever he remembered his childhood. His mother did all she could to make ends meet; she cut corners everywhere except during her children's birthdays and for the Christmas season. During the day she cooked for a wealthy family that would often let her take home leftover food to her own family, which was both a blessing and a curse because Milton's father expected this and therefore brought home even less money. Everyone knew about the problems Milton's family faced. It was obvious. They saw his father stumbling from the bars, they knew of the other woman whose belly was swollen twice from the affair he carried on. They knew these things, but while they didn't like it, they left it alone, minded their own business and simply tried to be the best neighbors they could to Milton's pitiful mother and her pitiful children.

But pity wasn't something anyone needed to expend on Milton because Milton had the gift of illusion. He was one of those persons who could walk into a room and make people see things about him that weren't necessarily true, and needless to say, they were usually great things; and when he spoke he had a tendency to say what a person needed to hear, so with that effect he was able to move easily within the circle of friends who had influence in the neighborhood. So in spite of his problems Milton led a reasonably normal life outside of their home.

But he couldn't escape the poverty and the violence that met him whenever he crossed the doorway to their home; the smell of poverty met him at the door. It was stale. And then there was its matted texture, and its muted color. The acts of violence his father committed against him, his mother and his sister when he would come home drunk were burned deep into Milton's memory, but most of all it was the sadness that lingered. He was never able to escape the sadness. When his mother passed away he cried uncontrollably, not because of her passing, but because she had never had a good life. Those were the things that stayed with Milton.

In Milton's eyes, his father was vile. He had been a man who took pleasure in embracing everything he thought was wrong and had the audacity to laugh at his vile ways all the way to his grave. Milton didn't want to be like that. Living under his father and seeing the harm he caused is what moved Milton to the church.

Milton couldn't understand this virus that gripped some people and turned them bad. He felt everyone was born good. If not, then there was no God, and there was one. But what would possess some people to become evil? In spite of preaching about the Devil, he really didn't know whether or not he believed the Devil had that much license over lives, but he couldn't understand the nature of evil and it was this search for an answer that had led him to the church. People like his father and the misery he caused Milton's mother and the rest of the family had left an enduring scar. Milton wanted to understand why his father lived the way he did and even more, why he, his mother and his sister had to suffer through the evil. He needed to understand these things and how he could move beyond it, so for Milton, service to those in need was threefold: it was surely a way of living a good Christian life, but it was also a way of easing the pain of others who might be going through what he went through, and most of all, it was to appease a god he knew could, at any moment, take him back to the misery he once knew so very well. So service to others had become so much a way of life for him that he rarely gave thought to it.

There was one thing, however, that Milton never acknowledged and that was the resentment he had for people who allowed themselves to fall into the type of disrepair he saw in some of the people who came through the lines at the pantry where he and Ella gave service and who he saw on the news at night, their faces, many of them like his own. He resented them and had only enough room in his heart to change them, not love them. Those were the things that gave him substance, but would never be named.

The food pantry was a large hall with concrete floors and aisles of foldup tables and chairs; some of the tables were wooden picnic benches painted a deep, red clay color, almost brown, the benches having been donated to the pantry by the Park Commission. Milton came in a side door that led to the kitchen, carrying a crate of vegetables from a truck in the dock area. He was part of a chain of men who unloaded the food from the trucks. He enjoyed the physical work because it gave him a chance to work his muscles and it sometimes led to a night of intense lovemaking, mostly on his part, with Ella, something that happened infrequently, with sex rarely even being telegraphed between the two of them.

Age and familiarity had quieted the sexual desire they had for each other, and though neither of them discussed the matter with the other, both of them wondered if after having Danny and the surgery, Ella had lost much of her sexual desire. For Milton that thought only made him dislike Danny even more because not only could Ella no longer pleasure Milton the way he desired, he could never have a child of his own.

There was one thing both of them did know, and it was that Danny's father, Damon, still came to Ella's mind. They both knew this because Milton had heard her mention Damon's name in her sleep and over the years he confronted her about it. She told him that whenever Damon's name was mentioned that it was a nightmare and not a dream, but it bothered Milton nonetheless. Conversation about Damon had occurred so often over the years that Milton had given up trying to replace him, but never reconciling the fact that he had to share her with the memories she kept of another man. With each year he became more and more distant to Ella when it came to sex and she asked him about it one day. They were in the car and a heavy silence had fallen over them. In the heavy silence Ella could feel that there were things on Milton's mind and that, given their marriage, they had the capacity to be things that didn't include her, so out of the heavy silence she asked him, "Milton, we don't have sex that much anymore; what do you do?" He drove on in silence for a few seconds more, keeping his eyes straight on the road before answering her. "I take care of myself," he said. Then he mumbled, "Just like I'm sure you do." There was nothing more to say so she never brought it back up again and simply waited for those infrequent moments when he would make love to her.

The pantry manager moved through the kitchen, telling the ones unloading the truck where to store the food since the pantry was now becoming overstocked with donations. It irked Milton that he was taking orders, but only slightly so. Still he was the one used to heading a body of people, not taking orders, not since his childhood. His father had given orders. But he acknowledged his mission at the pantry as rendering service for God and it was with that understanding that he followed the orders of the pantry manager, but he knew he could never work in such an environment in which he took orders instead of giving them. It would be too much like his childhood.

CHAPTER FOUR

Danny climbed the stairs to the third floor of the building. A strong wind rattled the panes of the old windows, conquering the glass and cutting the air with bitter cold in the dimly lit hallway. A young man passed by Danny on the way downstairs. He looked suspiciously at Danny.

"What the fuck you lookin' at?" Danny growled. The young man's look of suspicion turned to a look of fear and he hurried down the stairs, glancing back once more before disappearing from the second landing. Danny hoped no one else would come into the hallway. He turned the corner and walked down to the apartment. He knocked on the door and listened as the man walked across the floor and came to the door. Danny hoped the man wouldn't ask who was at his door. He didn't. As he unlocked the door Danny pulled the ski mask that had been rolled up to his head over his face and as the man opened the door Danny pushed it open farther causing the man to jump back. "Fuck!" the man exclaimed. The man swung but Danny weaved and caught him with a right to the side of the head sending the man stumbling backwards. "Oh you gonna swing on me? Huh nigga?" Danny closed in on the man as the man recovered his balance, but it didn't help because Danny hit him square in the face. He caught the man by the front of his jacket to keep him from falling and hit him one, two, and then a third and fourth time to the man's face, causing the man to finally collapse.

For a second Danny stood over the man to see if the man was about to get back up, but the man didn't move. Kneeling over him, Danny smacked his face to bring him around. "Yo. You know why this happened to you, don't you?" He called out to the man but the man was unconscious. Danny looked at the bloodied face of the man as he lay in the middle of his living room. 'Shit', Danny said to himself. He didn't know he had beaten the man that bad. Suddenly the man began to choke on his own blood, making a harsh gagging sound. "Shit." This time Danny said it aloud as he realized what was happening and turned the man onto his stomach and pushed on the man's back to clear his air passage. After a while the man began to breathe again with labored breaths. "Pay up, nigga," Danny said to the man as the man slowly gained consciousness. Then Danny stood and walked out the door.

His body had heated during the altercation but now cooled as he walked through the night air. Snowflakes chased by the wind rushed from the darkness into the light of street lamps then disappeared back into the blackness as Danny continued through the night.

He walked to where he left his car, feeling the heat of his body dissipate with each step. Another job was done and once more there was no sense of definition, no satisfaction, just a job done. A few men moved past the darkened buildings along Burnet Avenue. No one approached Danny. It was as if by his very presence, a sharp menacing presence, they knew to avoid him. They moved slowly in their hooded sweaters and jackets, convening every now and then under the street lamps before heading back into the shadow of the night. None of them knew what had just happened, just like Danny didn't know of their crimes.

When he got to his car he peeled off his gloves and felt the sting of broken skin on his knuckles, adding more scarring to skin that was already callousing. He got in his car and started the engine. The stereo instantly came on. He turned it off and sat quietly listening to the purr of the engine and feeling himself disappear from nothing to nothing into the night. Outside the window he watched a hooded man pass under the light of a streetlamp; as Danny watched the figure fade into the darkness he shivered, not from the cold but from the fear of uncertainty.

That job done, Danny went back to the bar where he worked. The bar was called 'First Down', a throwback to the years the owner played in the NFL. Another member of the security staff, Littlejohn, sat on a stool at the door talking with a customer as Danny came in. He looked at Danny to see if everything went right, then, feeling assured, he greeted him. It was still early on a Thursday evening so things would be slow for another two or three hours before Danny would get to work. The owner of the bar, whose name was Cortez, sat at the bar with a few other men and two women, one of whom clung to Cortez's arm. They were watching a football game on TV and discussing what went wrong with a play with most of the patrons listening to Cortez since he played for years in the NFL, while one or two of the men argued with him just so they could show him up.

Danny walked up to the bar, "I don't know why y'all arguing with this negro when you know he ain't gonna let y'all be right." He said this about Cortez mainly to let Cortez know he had returned.

Everyone started laughing. Cortez turned to Danny. "What's up? My cat!" and slapped him on the shoulder with massive hands that felt like they weighed pounds instead of ounces. He squeezed Danny's shoulder and studied his face for a brief second, just as Littlejohn had done at the door. Danny ordered a drink, light on alcohol since he had to work the shift, and leaned at the bar next to one of the women. "Hey Danny," the woman smiled. He smiled back, "What's up Lauren?" The other woman was busy touching Cortez's biceps, which Cortez would flex into hard black boulders every once in a while as he continued talking with the guys. Danny looked at Cortez and the woman for a long minute then threw his drink back in a quick swallow and ordered another one before turning his attention to the woman who sat beside him, watching her fingers trace the large veins on hands. When she came to his knuckles she lifted them. "What happened? Look like you been fightin' or somethin'."

Cortez turned a bit towards him, his ears picking up the conversation.

"Nah, I was just at the gym, boxing." Danny answered her before taking another swallow. "Gotta warm up before I come in this mothafucka." The lady laughed and kissed the back of his hand. "I got a lot more veins you can kiss," Danny said, sultrily causing a burst of laughter in the room.

Around ten o'clock the bar began to fill up and Danny took his place with Littlejohn as bouncers, leaving an attractive, but stern female attendant, Minnie, who was also Cortez's business partner to work the door. Security at 'First Down' was a pretty easy job. Most of the nights went smoothly. Danny and Littlejohn would walk around the bar to make sure things were right. First Down was a bar that had two floors and often it was the second floor, overlooking the first one, that needed the most patrol because that's where drug deals had been known to take place, or women would loudly object to men

touching them improperly in the VIP section. It happened sometimes, but not often because the patrons knew they would be
roughed up by Danny, Littlejohn, or Cortez and ejected from the
club. As far as the drug dealing went, while it wasn't allowed, what
often transpired was drug dealers who needed some spot money to
buy a shipment would come to Cortez for a loan. Danny could tell
when something like that was going down because Cortez would tell
him or Littlejohn to watch his back while he took the guy into the
office to do business. It's when the money wasn't paid back as agreed
that Cortez would send Danny or Littlejohn to collect, or to leave a
little reminder.

"The nigga actually swung on me," Danny said as he lifted his
drink.

"You didn't fuck him up too bad, did you," Cortez asked as he
leaned back in his chair and put his size fifteen feet up on his desk.
The bar was closed and Danny sat in the office with Cortez and Littlejohn. "You know you have a tendency to overdo shit, man. Why do
you do that?"

"For real tho'," Littlejohn said, laughing. Littlejohn's first name
was Julius, so, given that, he chose to go only by his last name. "I
know when to stop, but you…" he continued, laughing even harder.

Danny shook his head. "I don't know. I get carried away sometimes."

"You damn right, you do," Cortez said. "So you didn't get carried
away this time did you? I mean, I can't get my money if the nigga
can't work."

"Nah, I think he'll be alright."

"Good. Practice some restraint."

Restraint had always been something Danny found difficult.
Growing up, he heard his mother ask it of him. She would take him
by his arm, gripping him hard, and tell him to settle down. But it was
the look in her eyes, he recalled, that said even more; it was a look of
desperation. It took him little time to figure out that she feared he
would become like his father, or even worse, would be taken away like
his father had.

Even though Danny had never met his father, he knew two
things about him: that he was a bad person and his bad ways was why
he disappeared. Danny knew this because at times when he would act
out he would hear his mother bemoan that he was going to be like his
father, and it was those words that made him want to know more
about his father. Yet her lamenting was also enough to make him hate

his father, the man he never met, for making Danny the way he was. Growing up, Danny only knew himself as being bad, or somehow not wanted by anyone except his mother. He saw it in his stepfather's eyes and the way he spoke to Danny and he saw it in the faces of neighbors as they turned their faces from him. He wasn't sure what he was doing that made people regret him, but he blamed his father for it, the man who was inside of him and made him do things that made people turn away from him and that made his mother fearful. He would sometimes spend his days trying to figure out how to rid himself of his father and purge himself of the thing his mother regretted most about her son.

Danny wasn't sure exactly what it was that frightened his mother, but he knew that whatever it was it had to do with his father, so one day it came to him that if his father no longer existed that maybe he, himself, would become a better person and that both transitions would put his mother's mind at ease. So one afternoon, Danny, then only a boy of seven years, walked into the kitchen and stood behind his mother who was preparing dinner, and told her he wanted to kill his father. His child's voiced announced it with such pride that it stopped his mother cold, stunned, her back still to him. Turning around she looked down at her son with a terrified look on her face. Danny stood looking at her with an expression so innocent that it made no connection to the words he had just uttered.

Ella's eyes were widened with fear not only of the words, but of the innocence as well. "Don't say that!" She stooped in front of him, drying her hands on a dishtowel. "Where did you get that idea?"

"I don't know."

"Don't ever say that," she demanded. "Do you hear me?"

Danny looked at her and dropped his head in shame. "Yes ma'am." He apologized even though he was unsure why she was upset. He thought by offering his father's death his mother would be happy since she seemed to regret him so. But she wasn't happy and it only confused him.

"You should never want to kill anyone. You hear me?" She held him by his shoulders and looked closely in his face with even more desperation. "Do you hear me?" She shook him firmly.

"Yes ma'am," he said as he watched the fear in her eyes. He walked away more confused than ever because his mother had him by a man she regretted having known and now he was living under another man who regretted having him around and neither of these men did she want to die. Had his mother gone to the corner of the backyard where her son usually played she would know where he got the idea of killing his father. Along the fence, under the tree lay a grave of wingless insects: butterflies, moths and grasshoppers, their wings torn off.

"Just hit him once, or twice so he gets the message," Cortez advised.

"Maybe three. That's the most I go for," Littlejohn added.

"Three," Cortez agreed. "But that's it unless I tell you to fuck him up."

"I know, I know," Danny said. He always wondered what they would do if Cortez didn't get his money from these guys? What then?

Littlejohn looked at the clock on his phone. "Well, I'm getting ready to head out before ol' girl starts trippin'."

"Yeah man. You know Azhure got you on a timer," Cortez said, laughing. "Ding! Time's up nigga. Come on home."

"Yeahhh… Littlejohn pursed his lips. "She got me on a timer."

"You keep that dick in your pants and she won't be on you."

Danny laughed and nodded in agreement.

"Hey. It's just sex," Littlejohn said. He threw his drink back and looked at Danny. "You comin' or you gonna hang around?"

"Nah, I'm gonna hang around."

"Alright," Littlejohn said, glancing at Cortez. "I'll see y'all tomorrow."

~~~~

There hadn't been much snow the weeks heading into Christmas and what little snow that had fallen had melted or had been blown deep into the grass. Ella held out hope that a nice snowfall would come just in time for the holiday; she wished even more for a fresh snow so it would be full and white in time for the Christmas party she and Milton were having. Last year's party was dry with no snowfall, unlike the party before that. During that season the snow rose in white mounds, reflecting the holiday lights around their house. Nights like that made her Christmas parties even more successful because everyone's mood were especially festive.

She stood by the ladder, holding strands of Christmas lights, handing them up every few feet to Milton as he put them around the trim of the house.

"I hope it snows in time for the party," she said.

"Maybe it will. They say it's supposed to be a worse than average winter," Milton replied half-attentively. It really didn't matter to him, but he knew his wife wanted it. The two of them differed when it came to Christmas: she wanted Christmases that reminded her of her childhood back in New Home. Her father would have grand dinners and parties at their house and the house would be done up with all the trimmings that spoke of having gone from being a poor black boy who grew up in the Jim Crow era to a man of considerable wealth. It reminded him that he no longer had to cow-tow to white people like he did growing up and that he had more money than many of the ones who used to spit when he would walk by as boy. The holidays were times when he would be especially generous to the citizens of New Home, sponsoring a Thanksgiving dinner at the church and then a Christmas party where he would give out gifts. Ella, her mother and her two siblings would stand at a table, behaving with a sense of privilege, and hand the gifts out to the townspeople who passed the table and took the gifts with hateful expressions veiled behind their smiles and words of gratitude. Nonetheless, it was the parties Ella remembered most and it was a time she tried to re-capture as an adult.

Christmas was different for Milton when he was growing up. Since his family was dirt poor they rarely had much of a Christmas unless the family his mother worked for gave them extra food, which it usually did along with a gift for Milton and one for his younger sister, Charlotte. Sometimes his father would pick up extra money and they would have a little more to eat on the table and he would bring home gifts he had gotten them, though they were never what Milton and his sister wanted but it was understood that their father didn't give much thought to them anyway to ask them what they might want for Christmas. Sometimes the gifts would come from his father's girl-friend, someone named Miss Samuels. Milton figured that was who Miss Samuels was because his mother would become angry whenever Milton's father would tell them Miss Samuels sent the gifts to them.

He remembered one day, it was on a Christmas Eve, his father put him and his sister in the car and began driving. It was cold and Milton and Charlotte sat huddled up in the back seat of the car watching the back of their father's head as he drove along through the dying evening light. They weren't sure where they were going, but they knew not to ask so they just watched the back of their father's head as he hummed and sang along to the radio. In a while he stopped and went inside an apartment building, leaving Milton and his sister in the car. "Where's Daddy going?" Charlotte asked partly out of curiosity and partly out of concern for her and Milton's safety. She was used to her father's incendiary behavior, and she saw the frightened look on their mother's face when he told her he was taking the kids with him. Their father had left the car running and the radio playing. He told them to crack one of the back windows so the car's exhaust wouldn't build up and he left them. Milton remembers sitting there in the chilly car holding Charlotte and wondering if they could get away. The man on the radio continued to sing 'merry Christmas, baby'. To this day that's all Milton could remember of the song. In time his father came back out with a woman clinging to his arm. She got in the car carrying two gifts; she was dressed up as if she was going to a party and wore a fragrance that reminded Milton of roses. "This is Miss Samuels," their father said as he got in the car. "Hi kids!" Miss Samuels cheerfully called out. Milton and his sister quietly greeted her. "I got presents for you," she said and handed them the gifts. "What do you say?" Their father turned around and looked menacingly at them. They responded meekly. "Thank you." After leaving Miss Samuels' apartment, his father stopped by a liquor store and brought a bottle that was in a brown paper bag, then he took them back to the house, dropped them off and left with Miss Samuels.

That's how Milton remembered Christmas and it left him with a cautionary tale more than feelings of joy. Once he went over to the Lord he understood that Christmas was to give thanks that the Lord Jesus had been born and that by coming to Jesus as Lord there would be no more Christmases like the ones he endured as a child. Now he only prayed that Charlotte would find her way to Christ.

"I saw 'Johnny Mathis' today," Milton said as he hung the lights. He laughed knowing his wife understood who he was talking about. "He can't wait for the party. Said he has his songs all ready."

"Oh my," Ella replied with a smile.

'Johnny Mathis' was the nickname the members of the church had given to one of the lead singers of the men's chorus. LaShon Treadwell was his real name, but he sang with a vibrato that was reminiscent of Johnny Mathis so they called him that, and he gladly accepted the name.

Personally, Milton didn't much care for LaShon because of LaShon's effeminate ways. While Milton wasn't one of those ministers who railed often against homosexuals he knew there were some in his church but he figured they knew that they were up against God and he would let them settle their affairs with Him. Only once did Milton confront one of the gay members of his church, but that was because the deacon had the nerve to bring his ways to Milton's home. As a result Milton gave the deacon a choice to quietly leave Christ The Redeemer Baptist Church or face humiliation. The deacon agreed to leave the church.

"The evening wouldn't be the same without LaShon," Ella replied.

They were about finished with putting up the lights. They had made it to the back of the house when Ella looked across the yard at the gazebo. This year she wanted to adorn it as well.

"Why?" Milton asked. "No one will be out there."

"I know, but it looks so lonely just sitting there unadorned while the house looks so festive. Anyway, I think it would be a great conversation piece. Nobody talks about it because no one ever notices it in the dark." She looked at Milton for a reply before continuing, "I think it would make a great conversation piece."

Milton hesitated as he stared at the gazebo. Finally he replied, "If you want to." He sighed and gathered up another strand of lights.

Once the gazebo was done they stood back and admired it. "You were right," Milton said. "All it needed was a little light. It's been in the dark for too long."

Ella put her arm around her husband's waist and he wrapped his arm around her shoulder. "Yeah," she agreed. They walked back towards the house.

Ella didn't mention to Milton that she had asked Danny to come over. She knew he wouldn't be pleased but she knew that in spite of his order that Danny never step foot in their house again, he had enough sense not to confront Danny, just as he did whenever Danny decided to stop by to see his mother. Ella had done all she could to make Danny and Milton like each other but they never had, from the first time they met she sensed distrust between them. It was as if they knew something about the other and it brought the taste of bile to their mouths.

She never understood the bitterness they had for each other. Danny was only nineteen months old when he first met Milton and his contempt for him was immediate. Danny cried and reared back in Ella's arms whenever Milton came near him and screamed in anger from the time he would open his eyes and find Milton in the small room Danny and Ella lived in back then, until the time he went to sleep or until Milton left.

Ella always thought it could have been something Danny sensed about how Milton felt about him. The first time Milton laid eyes on Danny he fell into a questioning stare, watching the little boy lying asleep on the large bed in the single room of the house Ella shared with Miss Leonard, the woman who had taken her in. When she lifted the sleeping child in her arms and sat by Milton he continued to stare at the baby, never asking to hold him or even to ask what was his name. Later Milton explained to Ella that he wasn't sure how to handle a baby that small but that he would get used to it, and Ella accepted his explanation thinking in truth it was probably because he was startled by the fact that she wasn't much older than her baby.

Miss Leonard told Ella that wasn't it. Miss Leonard didn't care for Milton the first time she laid eyes on him. She told Ella that Milton was just "one of those self-righteous persons. Always wanting to judge somebody." She said she saw it in the way he carried himself, stiff and aloof, "his head held so high he could sniff an angel's ass", and the way he was always looking around, his eyes studying people and situations, assessing. No, he was nothing more than a judgmental man, is how Miss Leonard saw Milton.

Miss Leonard had taken Ella and Danny into her home after she had seen how much Ella was struggling with Danny. She had been on the same bus as Ella on her way back from Michigan and she spent the night watching Ella, a girl, struggling to care for an increasingly irritable child. When they stopped in Cincinnati and Ella went into the restroom at the bus station, Miss Leonard asked her if she was doing ok, to which Ella replied that she was.

"Where you on your way to," Miss Leonard asked.

"Los Angeles."

"That's a long way. You don't have many diapers left. You got enough formula left? You're talking at least another day or so before you get to L.A."

That's when Miss Leonard invited the helpless girl into her home for a few days, and those few days became a few years until Ella was on her feet.

Over time Milton made true on his promise. He began to get accustomed to the child. After he and Ella married he would take Danny out for walks. He would take him by the hand and the two of them would go to the store, or just out in the neighborhood. But no matter how much Milton tried to connect with Danny, Danny never reciprocated. He would look at Milton in silence with a mix of curiosity and suspicion, something that he never stopped doing even as he got older, and when Milton would take him out with him, Danny would remain respectfully silent, and would only look at Milton long enough to discern what was happening at that moment before turning his attention to other people and other things, never turning his attention fully on his stepfather.

As he became older Danny became more rebellious; he would oppose almost everything Milton asked of him, giving in only enough to please his mother, because like his stepfather, he also loved Ella, and it was the love both of them had for her that made life tolerable for all of them.

But eventually even the tolerance fell apart. Danny was becoming a man and the bad blood between he and his stepfather grew. Danny and Milton argued almost everyday. And when they weren't arguing they barely spoke to each other, but even in their silence there was a hatred that boiled just beneath the surface. The tension kept Ella on edge until it all finally came to a head in the back yard one day.

It was while Milton was building the gazebo. Ella had told him she wanted one and he had decided to build it. Milton was able to build the gazebo alone, but he agreed to let Danny help out in an attempt to reach out to him. When they began Milton and Danny worked together, but as the days went on, something went wrong and Milton began to take over the project by himself as his stepson disappeared into the background.

Each day the two of them would go out back but Danny would stand with his hands in his pockets or lean against the fence and watch Milton work. To this day Ella could only assume what might have led up to what happened in the backyard because it wasn't long after the incident. But all she could remember that day was hearing a sudden crash and the sound of raised voices and harsh scuffling. When she ran to the back door Danny had Milton half bent backwards over one of the railings. His fists gripped Milton's collar and their faces were only inches apart from each other as they stood in the midst of scattered tools. Ella stood in the back doorway with a look of horror on her face; she ran through the yard, feeling the unevenness of the ground beneath her feet as she rushed towards them. When she got to them she saw the expression on Danny's face. His expression was hard and dark but his mouth had a slight grin to it as he stared at Milton jammed against the railing. She saw her son's face and flashes of his father's face came to her, then she heard Milton saying over and over 'I want you outta this house.' Then there was the sight of the hammer by Danny's feet. She saw it and knew she had to stop the fight. Stepping closer she moved the hammer to the side with her foot and began pulling at Danny's hands trying to pry them loose from her husband. She called Danny's name over and over to get through to him, but her mind was on the hammer that was still within reach. Milton was glaring at Danny, telling him to leave, and even though he was the one at risk he spoke with authority. Ella was finally able to bring Danny around. That night Danny packed his things and left, but before he left he walked through the house to find Milton. They met in the hallway that led from the den to the living room. Danny walked up on Milton. Ella called to him to stop, but he didn't. He walked past Milton, brushing hard past him, knocking Milton against the wall. And in passing he left one final message: "If you ever do something to hurt my mother, I'm gonna fuck you up."

That was the last day Danny was allowed to live in the house but what happened that afternoon in the back yard would continue to resonate through their home. It wafted through the air like a bad odor and rode on whispers in the silence. It was the blame that made it even worse because even though that afternoon was never spoken of again, Ella knew Milton blamed her for everything: the way Danny was raised, the incident that had occurred the weeks before and anything else that made Danny who he was because Ella was always defending Danny and she was the one who kept him around when he should've been shipped off somewhere to a relative.

Ella always denied her husband's accusation that she was defensive when it came to how Danny was treated, but it was true that she didn't allow Milton to spank him. Maybe it was because of the way Danny's real father had been treated and the way she had been treated when her family and the townspeople of New Home discovered that she was pregnant by him. Maybe it was the way everyone waited for Danny to arrive in the world so they could declare all the things that was wrong with him. Maybe that was it. All she knew was as long as she lived no one would put a hand on Danny without dealing with her.

CHAPTER FIVE

The choir sang joyously as the water covered Ella, enveloping her in its womb. From beneath the water she could still hear the voices. The words were muffled but she knew the song well: *Temptations, hidden snares often take us unawares, and our hearts are made to bleed for a thoughtless word or deed; and we wonder why the test when we try to do our best, but we'll understand it better by and by...'* and she sang it in her head as the hands cradled her beneath the water. She cried from joy, silently, her tears mixing with the waters of the lake as she felt the heaviness in her heart lift upward to the edges of the waters, past the minister and the choir, up towards the sky that shimmered like blue crystal to God where she knew she would be forgiven. But as she stared at the sky she soon realized that time had passed. It had passed and she was still underneath the lake so her heart began to race. She tried to raise her head but she couldn't, the muscles of her neck wouldn't answer her demand. She turned her head violently from side to side, lashing beneath the water as she fought to make it to the surface of the lake but she couldn't. The hands that had been cradling her were now on her chest holding her down, pushing her deeper and deeper into the depths of the lake. The choir continued to sing: *By and by, when the morning comes, when the saints of God are gathered home, we'll tell the story how we've overcome, for we'll understand it better by and by...'* and now they clapped their hands and moved from side to side, their images wavering through the water. Suddenly she opened her mouth to scream with the last of the air she had in her but nothing came out except the bubbles formed by the final exhaust of air from her lungs. Then she was alone. Her eyes were wide with fear and she couldn't move as she slowly sank, down, down, deeper into the lake. The hands that had been on her chest were no longer there; the voices were gone, leaving a heavy silence and there was an approaching darkness as she sank downward further from the sun and the sky above. Around her flotsam floated by as pieces of wood, and leaves and vines. She cried as she watched them, understanding that she was now part of them forever floating beneath the dirty waters of the lake.

She no longer sought to leave the lake because she knew why she was there; then from the shadows of the water a clump of vines came towards her, the vines reaching for her like bony arms and they wrapped around her, curling her up into the heart of their entanglement, curling her up, up into the center until she was bound to them, and there in the bowels of the entanglement she saw him. His eyes and mouth were opened wide, left there by the terror of his death. The belt was still around his neck and the vines pulled her closer and closer to him, and she screamed silently in the inaudible water as their faces closed in together, she and the young man, touching, face against face, cold wet horror, cold wet flesh to cold wet flesh, one against the other, both of them bound forever beneath the waters of the lake.

Ella scribbled notes onto her pad as she sat with her client. Her mind kept drifting back to the dream so she only heard part of what the woman was saying, yet her hand continued to write, scratching along the pad as if her hands themselves knew what to write. The disturbance of sleep had left her feeling tired. She closed her eyes for a second for relief.

The dream the night before had worn on her and left her lying awake for the rest of that night. She knew she had to go back to New Home.

Throughout the day she questioned herself:

'Why don't you go back?'
'Because I'm scared.'
'What are you afraid of?'
'Of losing things. I'm afraid of losing things.'

Ella left the client she had been attending and headed on to the next one. As she drove through the streets things seemed unfamiliar to her. The people and the city seemed so distant to the place she knew though she drove the route every week. She moved along the streets as if everything she knew was unknown, moving forward not with the understanding that where she was headed was there, but that it might be there. Finally she pulled up to the home of her next client. It would be the last one of the day. She turned off the car and put her keys in her purse. Gathering up her notebook she got out of the car and went into the building.

After she had finished with her visit she closed her notebook, patted the man on the hand and gave him assuring words that made him smile. She stood to leave and reached for her purse and saw that she had left it in the car. She rushed out of the apartment and hurried down the stairs of the building. She hurried to the car, looked inside and saw her purse there, still closed. Once she was in the car, she pulled out her keys and started the engine, then sat a while as the engine idled. Her mind was becoming so polluted with memory and it was beginning to affect her days more and more. She sat for a few minutes to catch her breath and to relieve her heart that was still racing. She sat quietly, staring out of the window. The streets were damp and gray. People walked along under the pewter colored sky while just above them the naked branches of trees crossed over their heads. She watched this and thought about New Home, and of what happened, and of the dreams and she wondered how long it would be before something worse happened. She opened her purse and got out her phone and called her son. She wanted to hear his voice. They talked for a few minutes. She told him she was just giving him a call to see how his day was going. He told her he was at work and that his day was going well. They continued to talk a little bit until her son was interrupted by one of his co-workers. She could tell that he was busy so she told him she would let him go and that they should see each other soon, before Christmas dinner. He told her that would be nice, but for now he had to get back to work. She understood. He was busy and she felt better. She only needed to hear his voice.

When she got home Ella began fixing dinner. It was the middle of the week and usually she and Milton would have something light for dinner like a salad and a deli sandwich one of them would bring home. But that evening she decided to make a Sunday meal.

She turned on the stereo that sat on the kitchen counter to keep her company as she moved around the kitchen pulling out a knife, the cutting board, pots and the roaster she used for big meals. She cut up onions and peppers, and poured them into the ground turkey, and she crumbled up crackers, watching the yellow-brown fragments fall from her hands. Finally she cracked open eggs and put them in the meat; she sang along with a song on the radio as she pushed her hands deep into the mixture, turning it and mixing it. The softness of the meat and the sliminess of the yolk that slid between her fingers, the vegetables disappearing into the mixture and the rhythm her hands made as they moved through the mixture relaxed her, the movement of her hands and her body reminded her that what she was doing, now at that moment, was real, and not the dreams.

After she finished cooking she sat at the dining room table and went over her notes, putting them into her laptop as she waited for Milton to come home. Eventually she fell asleep in the middle of her work at the dining room table and was awakened by Milton when he came in.

They ate dinner and talked about their day, both of them telling only what they had become accustomed to telling and afterwards they watched TV until Milton suggested they go to the prayer room in the house before going to bed.

Ella slept well that night, sleeping close to Milton and to the words Milton had prayed that evening in the prayer room. He had told God that he knew God understood how frail humans could be, and that they were prone to error, bound to it. But that God's wisdom knew this, and that He understood this about His children. Milton then went on to ask God to relieve those who might have committed sin to be forgiven and to lift the burden of memory from them so that they might go on, relieved of their burden by walking in the ways of the Lord.

The next day Ella woke up with a calm mind and she and Milton sat at breakfast for the first time in weeks, talking and laughing and watching the light in each other's eyes.

CHAPTER SIX

For as long as he could remember Danny always felt he was in the wrong place. All of his life he felt that most of the people around him and the events that occurred around him were out of place with where he was supposed to be, yet he wasn't sure where he was supposed to be and that was what bothered him, and it was what led him to drift through life, settling into one event after another for the sake of convenience or the promise of reward. Even his associations with people had been fragile: uneasy negotiations like with his stepfather, or carefully constructed dealings with strangers who might become no more than acquaintances, or only sharp, quick engagements for sex or violence.

It had even been a fragile encounter when he first met Littlejohn while the two of them were in jail. Danny had been given ninety days for assaulting a man in a bar. The man had continued to mouth off at Danny over something inane—because Danny always drank by himself, something the man took as Danny thinking he was 'too good' to associate with the others who came to the bar. The man had been warned by Danny to mind his own business and when the man didn't Danny beat him up, but it wasn't just a beating, Danny almost killed the man and it was the extent to which he beat the man and his kiss-my-ass expression that made the judge sentence him. The ninety days locked up was supposed to give Danny time to think about what he had done so he could correct himself, but to Danny it was only another sentence until he could find the next event to take on.

He and Littlejohn were both in jail for the same type offense, but Littlejohn was in for a longer sentence because he had a history of assault charges. He had also been convicted for damaging property after he kicked in his former girlfriend's car window. Most of the other men who were locked up with them avoided Danny and Little-john because even for the other prisoners Danny and Littlejohn looked like they would be more than the other inmates could handle. That gave Danny and Littlejohn time to get to know each other and they remained friends even after they got out.

Littlejohn was the first person Danny had ever met who understood him. Littlejohn understood Danny's anger because he himself had been around it most of his life. He understood Danny's anger and his capacity for violence just like Ella understood it, yet unlike Danny's mother, Littlejohn didn't become alarmed by it but worked with Danny to keep it under control, like he himself had learned to do, and to use it when it was necessary or convenient. And now, working for Cortez they were given a chance to employ all of their skills and make money doing it. But Littlejohn wanted more.

"Hey. You talk to Cortez about making us business partners?" Littlejohn asked the question as he knelt inside of the SUV. He pulled a case of vodka into the back of the truck.

"Nah man, I ain't brought it up," Danny said as he put another case in the truck.

"How come? I thought you was supposed to talk to him about it. Or at least introduce the idea to him so the both of us can talk to him together."

"I'm not sure if I want to be a business partner."

"See? There you go again. Why you always backin' out of things like that? I mean, you and me done talked about this and you were like 'cool'. Now you switchin' up again." Littlejohn climbed down from the back of the SUV. "We been workin' for him goin' on five years now," Littlejohn continued, "doin' everything for him: security, runnin' errands, sometimes bartendin'. We even do his dirty shit," he whispered as he leaned in to Danny. "He knows we got his back. Hell, we the only ones besides Minnie who done been there with him for a while. He done made Minnie a business partner so why not us?"

"Minnie bought into it," Danny said as he went over the inventory sheet. "She gave up part of her salary. I don't know if I wanna do that."

"We talked about this."

"Littlejohn, man I know we did. But I told you from the start I had reservations."

"You plannin' on leaving ain't you?" Littlejohn started up the engine, watching Danny as he closed the door. "You still on that 'findin'-your-father' shit."

"I don't know. I just have a feelin' I might not stay here."

They pulled out of the lot.

"I still can't understand why you need to find out who your ol' man is. What difference is it gonna make?"

Danny didn't answer so Littlejohn went on: "I know who my father is and it don't mean shit except that now I know he's out there doin' the same shit I am. Just another nigga tryin' to make it, and I ain't nowhere in his plans."

"It ain't that," Danny said. "I just don't see myself stayin' around here."

"Where you gonna go? You always talkin' about leavin' but you never say where."

"Shit I don't know."

"Look, between the two of us, you the one who can talk to Cortez. You can talk to him when y'all are together and shit. He listens to you. I ain't got it like that. So why don't you do this, man? If not for yourself, do it for me. Put the word in for me. I mean, shit, nigga got all that money from when he played football and he got other investments, and I know First Down is bringing in cash, we see it."

"Ok, I'll start talkin' with him."

Danny's reply didn't convince Littlejohn. "You a nigga without conviction, you know that? You ain't got no aspirations."

"Look, I said I'll talk to him."

"I hope so. For the both of us, because we both deserve it. And I hope you decide to stay around."

Danny had that evening off. After dropping off the inventory to the bar he met his mother for dinner. He watched his mother as they sat in a restaurant. He had always thought his mother was a good-looking woman. Even when he was a boy he would say to himself that his mother was his girlfriend because to him she was just as beautiful as the women he saw on TV. Now, as a man he watched his mother's face as she spoke to him, the graceful lines that were forming on her face and the wisps of gray hair that were forming on her head. But having lived with his mother he saw more than the graceful lines and the graying hair. He had seen his mother during those times when she struggled to keep her thoughts focused to quiet her memories. He saw those memories in the expression on her face and in the movement of her hands or the way she held her head. Sometimes they would speak of memories she would rather not have. In her face it would be the way the light in her eyes would sometimes dim as if she had suddenly gone somewhere else in her mind, then light again, struggling to come back to the present; the way her hands would pause in thought then begin to wring themselves from a painful memory, or the way she would turn her head sometimes as if she were listening to something far away. Those were the expressions Danny had come to notice about his mother. In time he became used to her expressions, but the thoughts of what his mother might be carrying in her head always left him feeling uneasy because he knew he was part of the memories that haunted her.

"Can you believe it? Folks out there jogging in the middle of winter." Ella made the remark as she looked out the window of the restaurant at two women running along Fifth Street. "You'd think they would at least wait until it got a bit milder outside."

"They're dedicated," Danny said.

"I guess so."

"Yeah. They're dedicated about being healthy and lookin' good. Ain't nothin' wrong with that."

"Vanity," Ella mumbled as she shook her head and watched the women head past Fountain Square. Then she looked at her son. "You look like you work out. You always look so fit."

"Thanks." Danny knew his mother was fishing for an opening to find out more about his life, to draw a connection between his working out and possibly his occupation. She knew he worked at a bar doing security, but he knew she always felt there was more to it than what he was telling. It was the crazy hours he sometimes kept and the times when he wouldn't answer her phone calls right away that conjured up suspicion. He also figured it had something to do with his father that caused her to worry over Danny since she never wanted to talk about his father.

"It's something me and your father have to do more of," Ella continued, speaking of Milton instead of Danny's biological father.

"How is Milt doing," Danny asked. He had stopped calling Milton his father after the fight. He had wanted to stop calling his stepfather 'dad' when he became a teenager, but he knew it wasn't what his mother wanted.

"He's doing fine. Just busy like always."

"Some of the church family still got him goin', huh?"

Ella shook her head. "Like children, some of them. Can't manage their own lives. Always some drama going on."

"That's because they know they got people like Milt to handle things for them."

"You're right. And he knows that too."

"But it keeps him in a job," Danny said as he ate.

"How is your job," Ella asked.

"It's fine. I like it," Danny said. He wanted to kick himself for giving her that opening. "Good people and nice money, what else can you ask for?"

"A career? Do you plan on doing that for the rest of your life?"

"I don't know."

"There's not much money in security. At least in the kind of security you do."

"I know."

"Well time waits for no one. You need to start pursuing something you know you're most likely to continue for a while."

Danny nodded in agreement.

After a while Ella mentioned that she was happy that he was coming to the Christmas dinner.

"Yeah, it should be nice," he said.

"Some of the members of the church will be happy to see you."

"It has been a while."

"You're going to ask me why I insisted you come this year?"

"Nope. I just figured you felt it was time. But I do wonder why Milt went along with it."

"Because it's been years since that stupid fight the two of you had, and I think he knows it's time to put it all behind him and that the both of you should start acting like men."

"It was more than the fight, Mom."

"Doesn't matter. Your father has grown now. He understands that the world isn't going to be like he thinks it should be."

"Well, we'll see how it goes," Danny said.

Ella didn't respond to Danny's comment. She wondered herself because Milton wasn't too pleased with Danny coming to the dinner. He was willing to get over what happened between he and Danny, but he felt Danny's presence in their home only invited evil.

As they were ending dinner Danny ordered another meal. The server thanked him and walked away.

"Why did you do that?"

"It's for an old man who lives in my building. I usually get him something to eat."

Ella took his hand in hers. "Oh Danny. That's good. God will bless you for that."

"Yeah. Well, it's not why I'm doin' it."

Ella steadied herself before speaking. "But he'll bless you for it nonetheless."

"Ok," Danny said.

When Danny got to his place he set the meal outside of the neighbor's door. He could hear the gospel music playing from the stereo inside of the apartment. His mother had said God would bless him for bringing the man dinner but Danny knew it wasn't why he did it. The old man's loneliness reminded Danny of himself. Danny knocked on the man's door then started up to his apartment. As he made his way up the stairs he heard the music stop and a few seconds later he heard the man open the door, pick up the bag, and close the door back and the music started to play again.

Once he got inside of his apartment, Danny undressed and sat on the couch watching TV as he thought about his conversations with his mother and with Littlejohn. The one thing both of them seemed sure of about Danny was that he didn't seem to have any plans for his future, and as bothersome as it was to Danny he wondered if they were right. He knew he needed something to aim for but he wasn't sure what. Everything that seemed to matter the most to him was hinged on him understanding who he was and why he was. He knew most people would probably do what Littlejohn suggested and let it go. It was what his mother wanted too. But Littlejohn didn't have to look into his mother's eyes and see the secrecy there and know that he was part of something so painful that his mother didn't want to speak on it. And Ella, she didn't know how much the fettered thoughts and the shackled memories she kept pulled at Danny as much as it did her.

Danny turned off the TV, went to his bedroom closet and pulled out the books. Then he sat down at the kitchen table and opened them where he would sit for rest of the night.

CHAPTER SEVEN

Some people said the hats of the churchwomen looked like lilies, but in Milton's eyes they lacked the beauty and the peacefulness of lilies because he knew the faces beneath the hats. He knew the eyes that would cut others who were not like them, or the words that moved so light from the lips of many of the women beneath those hats, words that lighted softly in the air before leaving an acrid sting once they were taken in. He knew these things not only of the women, but of the men as well in his church because he had to contend with them. To him the hats showed a certain arrogance to it all that he felt shouldn't be a part of worshipping the Lord, an arrogance that bordered on the obscene when compared to the humility of the Christ they professed to serve. Yet he understood the need of a people with a history of privation to feel special at least one day a week. It was a fragile matter that he handled with care.

It was Sunday afternoon after services had ended and many of the members from different churches would gather for Sunday dinner at some of the restaurants. Christ The Redeemer Baptist Church had tried to have Sunday dinners at the church, but that lasted for only a few months because the women saw no sense in spending their own money on members who rarely contributed and just as well they couldn't see standing over a hot stove on Sunday after having done it for most of the week; and the fact that some members of the church just weren't cut out for cooking put the strain on others while the inept ones suffered from humiliation. It was too much, so just like other churches, the members of Christ The Redeemer Baptist Church met at a restaurant for Sunday dinner, and it was enough to satisfy Milton. He had never had that experience growing up since his father was hateful towards the church and forbade his wife to create even a semblance of an after church dinner. He allowed her to attend church every so often (mainly as insurance towards his not going to hell if there turned out to be one after all, though he doubted it), but afterwards, if she would suggest they have a roast on Sunday they would end up having grits and fish. So for Milton, the dinners had special meaning for him.

Inside the restaurant, members of his church and other churches moved around the tables and along the buffet lines, their eyes and smiles meeting and greeting those who came their way. It was a social event that strengthened their community and that held at bay the evil that moved outside their circle, and sometimes in their own heads.

Social events like these were easy for Ella because she was granted the grace and the genuine interest it took to enjoy these types of settings. Milton, on the other hand, quietly struggled with it. All of the joking and the laughter. None of that came easy to him. He had seen life and he knew it was nothing to joke about. He saw his seriousness as the tool needed to fix life, far from the tendency he felt people had of using levity to dance around problems. Yet he understood that most people weren't like him and that they might never understand what he had gleaned out of life. So he engaged in light banter like everyone else, but in his mind it was only to get along with others, not something to actually relish in for the sake of pleasure. And that was why most of his attempts at lightness came across vapid or even incisive.

From the center of the restaurant LaShon, the church's lead male vocalist, could be heard greeting a woman who had just come in. "Sister Eldridge!" he called out, his voice floating through the air, "Now you know you are carrying on in that hat!"

Sister Eldridge thanked him, her face beaming with pride at the compliment just as all the women did when they received LaShon's praise.

Milton cut his eyes at LaShon then pushed him out of his mind. Milton and Ella then began making their rounds, visiting the tables of those who held status from both their church and other churches that were there, as it was incumbent of them to do so. Now it was expected of all the others to greet the pastors and their spouses, or at least to acknowledge their presence even if with nothing more than a smile and a bow of the head. It wasn't that Milton required this ceremony but he understood the value of it for those who needed to be recognized by those they considered as their superiors, and in those terms human nature prevailed. Ella took her place alongside him.

Later into dinner LaShon came over to their table; he was smiling broadly as he led a young lady by the hand. "Reverend, First Lady. We have a visitor today who didn't stand up when you asked for visitors to stand."

By the look on the young lady's face, she was clearly embarrassed and, it appeared, a bit nervous, but LaShon held her close, his arm clasped firmly in hers, forcing her to stand at the table.

Milton shook the young lady's hand. "We're glad you visited with us. What's your name?"

"Natasha," LaShon blurted out. "Not Tasha, but Na-Tasha," he enunciated as he thrust his hand into the air. "Isn't that a fabulous name? Mysterious like a secret agent, or a femme fatale, but we know she's not that," he laughed.

"Let her talk, LaShon," Ella said as she shook the young lady's hand. Ella was immediately struck by the young lady's poise and her attractive smile, a soft smile that showed just enough of her teeth in the manner Ella's own mother had told her a proper lady should smile, anything more was the grin of women in bars or other lowly places. "I'm sure she can tell us her name," Ella said with a smile.

"Natasha," the young lady repeated.

Milton hesitated for what would be two or three heartbeats before he continued his greeting. "Well Natasha, we're glad you could make it and please come back. And the next time don't be so shy about letting us know you're here."

"Thank you Reverend Pruitt. I enjoyed the service."

That done, LaShon ushered the young lady back to the table where they had been sitting.

"LaShon," Milton exhaled as he shook his head.

"LaShon," Ella repeated with a smile. "Always a sucker for beautiful women."

"Now if only he knew what to do with one," Milton whispered as he leaned in to his wife.

"Milton!" She scolded, laughing softly as she hit his leg beneath the table. She watched Natasha a bit longer and thought how attractive she was, and how, if things were different, how much of an attractive couple she would make with Danny. Looking out across the restaurant at the Sunday diners in their suits and large hats, the men stiff in their Sunday best, Ella thought how Danny should be sitting at one of the tables chatting with the friends he knew, the ones he grew up with in Christ The Redeemer Baptist Church. Danny was once a part of the family but was lured away by the streets. She didn't even know much about the people he associated with. Every now and then a name would come out, 'Littlejohn', or 'Cortez' or some nonsensical names that she didn't care to recall. And they all seemed to sleep like vampires, down during the day and up all night.

Ella and Danny were drifting apart and this bothered Ella. She couldn't afford to lose another person in her life, even more so that person being her baby. If only Danny and Milton hadn't had that fight, if Danny hadn't done what he did, if he had stayed in the house. Things would have gotten better. She told herself that and she felt it. But all of that mess happened and drove him away, and now it appeared as if he had found another road. Ella was far less than pleased. As Milton drove from the restaurant that night they talked about their day in church, but it was Danny and his father, Damon, who were on Ella's mind.

"We ain't got no business over there. Those people ain't done nothin' to us. And especially black people. Why should we fight over there when we still strugglin' here?"

Ella walked arm in arm with Damon as they read the Jet Magazine together. They walked along the path to the spot in the woods where they met almost everyday since the few weeks after he first spoke to her at the store. He had been stocking the shelves that day when they first met. She had seen him around town and had heard about him as everyone talked about the new boy in town who was staying with old lady Hogan. They had said he was strange, just like old lady Hogan. That he never looked at folks, but that he watched them, like he was looking into them. It unnerved some folks and they kept their distance from him. Mostly it was the folks who had the most to hide who despised him because it was as if he could see what they had done.

It was grocery day and Ella, her father and her sister Miriam were stocking up for the week. Her mother had died two years earlier, so their father had become dependent on Ella and Miriam to help him get the things that were needed at home. That day at the grocery store Ella saw Damon when she passed the aisle for jellies and jams. He was on his knees stocking jars on a lower shelf. His quiet demeanor and handsome face caught her attention so she hurried to the aisle of canned goods and got the few items she had forgotten, then came back to the aisle he was working in. This time he stood, quietly placing stock. He looked even more beautiful, the way his store apron wrapped around his lean waist and the long arms and strong hands as he placed the jars on the shelf. Ella had to get a closer look at the strange young man who she had only seen in passing as he walked along the back roads that led out to the small shack he shared with Old Lady Hogan. He was usually by himself, or with Buddy, another guy who worked at the store and lived on the outskirts of town like Damon, but when Damon walked alone he always seemed to be in another place in his head other than New Home. It was when she reached for a jar of preserves that they finally met. He told her he would get the jar for her, and from that moment on they came to know each other day by day with each of her visits to the store until they began to meet each other in secret.

Meeting Damon brought light to the gray in Ella's world after her mother left. For the two years since her mother's leaving Ella had found herself stumbling around trying to satisfy herself with things like cooking and cleaning the house and making sure her father had his clothes laid out and his briefcase ready for work the next day. The little things that she had seen her mother do. But it wasn't enough to fill the sadness Ella felt, just as it hadn't been enough for her mother.

"Aren't we trying to keep them from becoming Communists? That's what my father says," Ella said as she looked at the photos in the magazine.

"If they wanna become Communists, then they can become Communists. It ain't none of our business."

She looked at Damon in the summer afternoon light: his lean face, his dark brown complexion and the shape of his head which had a slight hook in the back that fit right in the palm of her hand. She knew this because sometimes she would place her hand right there whenever they were playing and mug him. He would laugh, and tell her she was doing it too hard and that she almost broke his neck. Then he would mug her lightly upside her head, and they would laugh and enjoy the little time they had together before she would sneak back home before her father left work. They both knew that they had to keep their relationship secret because of how much the townspeople distrusted him and that her father would have him skinned alive if he knew this young man, some four years older, and much older than that in experience, was spending time with his daughter whom Emmanuel had all but beatified since his wife's passing.

Ella and Damon continued to walk along the path. He had had a fresh haircut that day and she could still see tiny clips of hair on the collar of his shirt and smell the flowery fragrance of the oil that the barber put on his head. Damon said where he came from, the Muslims all cut their hair short and even though he wasn't Muslim, he thought it was cool.

"We just want to control them so we can show the Chinese who's boss," Damon went on.

"Oh you think you know so much," Ella said.

"I do."

"Welll... do you know that with sea horses, it's the males who become pregnant?"

"Nah. Really?"

"Yep."

"Damn. Well, I'm glad I'm not a seahorse." He studied Ella's face. "You sure?"

"Look it up."

They walked a little farther in silence before she pressed closer to him. "You don't think they'll call you up for service in the army, do you?"

"I don't know. I hope not."

Now Ella looked out the window of the car as Milton drove them home. Snow began to fall.

CHAPTER EIGHT

A sharp cold wind cut through the streets that morning as Danny left a diner carrying two breakfasts. He was tired and his eyes burned from lack of sleep. He looked up at the sky. It was deep and gray and still. It was early and only a few cars passed by. One car looked like Milton's car but it wasn't. He knew his stepfather wouldn't be out this early anyway unless there was an emergency: a sick and shut-in needed last rites or something like that. And his real father? Nobody seemed to know. Maybe he was someplace warm and comfortable or maybe he was out in the streets like Danny was, but his father would be coming home from a long night in some distant city. Danny couldn't imagine his father being dead. Sometimes when Danny thought of his stepfather, his blood father would cross his mind. He felt as long as his stepfather was alive then his blood father was too, that was how invincible Danny's imaginings of his birth father were.

The only thing Danny knew for sure about his father was his first name: Damon. Everything else was assumption built on snatches of phrases and random conversation. Danny didn't know Damon's last name because his mother never told him. In fact, he really didn't know his mother's maiden name because she even refused that bit of information, which, in turn meant since he didn't know his father's last name or his mother's maiden name, he didn't know his surname. His mother told him his last name was Pruitt, the name she changed it to after she married his stepfather and that was all that mattered.

But it wasn't. The unspoken things and the reasons they went unspoken were the things that mattered. Those were the things that made him angry and the things that made people call him 'a bad boy' when he was growing up.

His only memory of a father was of his stepfather. As a young child he thought Milton was his real father, but later he was to hear that that wasn't so, which answered why Milton always looked past him instead of at him. In time he came to understand that it was his mother who his stepfather wanted and that he came along as luggage.

More than knowing his father, Danny never had much of a sense of bloodline. There was no blood family to which he could connect; his mother refused to talk about her family, leaving only Milton's family, an adopted family, as the family Danny could refer to. And they were more like visitors than family since most of them were still trying to rekindle a relationship with Milton that had been estranged during the hard times under Milton's father.

To make matters worse, when Milton's family came around, the way in which they would relate to Danny was often awkward. They would smile awkwardly and touch him awkwardly on the head and speak to him with few words. When he would be told to go outside and play with his cousins, even they would just stand and stare at him, and he at them.

The only person in Milton's family Danny felt even a semblance of kinship to was Milton's sister, Charlotte. She didn't come around when she knew other family members would be at the house because they hadn't figured out how to accept her. They considered her to be crazy, so when she came over she came over alone. Danny liked Charlotte because he felt she knew what it was like to be unwanted, and he liked her because she would laugh and grab him in her arms. She was the only member of Milton's family Danny liked, and then she left.

Danny knew there were ways he could find out more about his past, but given his mother's efforts at keeping it secret he was afraid of the answers he might find, so he settled on living his life with a choice of either to be sad over the circumstances of his life, or to be angry. He chose anger because of the two emotions it was anger that propelled him forward. Sadness would have been a drag on him. It would have held him in places where he would have felt powerless, in a place where he pled for help and where he turned his life over to others for safekeeping like so many of the people he saw in church, powerless. He wasn't built like that. He could never see turning his life over to someone else; he could build an agreement with someone else, but other than his relationship with his mother there could never be a sense of propriety. So the way he saw it, anger had served him well.

He pulled up to his building and went inside. He stopped at the first apartment and placed the bag containing one of the breakfasts on the floor outside the door, knocked twice, then went upstairs to his place.

~~~~

Milton gathered his pillow under his head. The house was quiet except for the faint hum from the furnace turning on in the basement. Mornings when he didn't have to be at the church and after Ella left for work and the house would settle in silence were the only time Milton had to himself.

He stayed in bed for a half hour or so, separating himself from duty and work. Being a pastor took up so much of his day, tending to financial matters, listening to congregation members and the mess they would get themselves into, mediating disputes, comforting the broken hearted and correcting the broken; early mornings were his balm. He relaxed a little more because he knew he would soon be getting up. He had an important meeting that day with other pastors over a certain matter in the community. Not to his surprise, they had implored that he attend the meeting because they knew that as an activist he had a career much longer and more admired than many of the other ministers even before he became a minister.

But these mornings alone were his mornings, his time to himself, and he ended them all the same; he would move his hand down into his boxers and stroke himself, letting thoughts and memories come until he would spill the white fluid over his stomach. Milton had struck an agreement with God that He would allow Milton those moments needed to relieve himself so Milton wouldn't become the kind of man his father had been. Milton knew he still had a lot of work to do to become the man God wanted him to be, but until he was fixed he was sure God was understanding.

After he was done he got out of bed and took a shower and started his day.

The postman arrived. Milton heard him whistling as usual and the barking of the dogs along the street, then the opening, thump, and closing of the mailbox as the postman left the mail. Sipping on his coffee, Milton got up from the table and got the mail. Among the small stack of envelopes was a handwritten letter. He instantly recognized the handwriting of his sister Charlotte and the inked stamp of the Ohio Reformatory for Women. He didn't open the letter at once because he knew it would be like the other letters she had written him. He put the letter in the pocket of the overcoat he would be wearing and went on with the beginning of his day.

She said she found her there under her blanket. She said she came to when she heard her favorite game show was on the TV. It was noon and she never missed it. She said she looked at the TV and then, over to the doorway where her baby girl lay with the blanket over her. She doesn't know how it happened, but it happened.

Milton went over the story in his head. He recalled his sister, Charlotte, sitting behind the glass at the jail as she told him her story. She looked much older than her actual age. Drugs and alcohol had seen to that. She told him the story and asked him why. That was six years ago. She had asked him 'why'. He knew from the look in her eyes she wanted to know more than the reason her child was murdered and she was serving time for it; the 'why' she asked carried more. It questioned the reason she had been dealt the life she had. Milton had understood her question but he couldn't give her an answer because he just didn't know. Instead he told her things would get better for her, even though he figured she would be in prison for much of the rest of her life, and he told her to trust in the Lord and then he promised her that he and Ella would be there for her if she needed anything. But he simply didn't know the answer to her question. It was the same question he often asked himself: why did they have to go through such pain growing up when they did nothing to deserve it? All he knew was he had to find a way out of the pain, so he turned to God while his sister fell to the streets.

Milton touched the envelope inside of his coat as he walked up the street from the dry cleaners to the church. He hadn't held to his promise to visit Charlotte often once she was shipped off to prison. He went twice in the six years since she was sent up to Marysville but found he couldn't go anymore. Charlotte only wanted to talk about how horrible their lives had been growing up and to ask him 'Why?' He decided he couldn't stand to listen to the stories anymore and he didn't have any answers so he stopped visiting her. Now she wrote him every so often asking him to please come visit her, but it never failed, even in her letters she would mention their past and pose the question.

Milton entered the church and stopped by Mrs. Hargrove's office to greet her and to pick up his messages. He would read the letter once he got to his office.

"There's been a change on your calendar, Pastor," Mrs. Hargrove said.

"What now?" Milton widened his eyes and smiled. Sometimes he felt overburdened, but he realized that it only meant he was valuable.

"Nothing big, now. So don't get all up in a bunch," Mrs. Hargrove said. Mrs. Hargrove laughed and shook her head. "You always getting so stressed. It's just a change of date and venue for lunch," she said.

"The meeting?"

Mrs. Hargrove nodded her head in bemusement. "Look."

Milton grunted as he looked at her computer screen. Mrs. Hargrove grunted back in affirmation.

"Figures," Milton said. "Well, I'll be there."

"Of course you will. You have to be there." Mrs. Hargrove went back to work.

Charlotte's letter opened as her letters always did: *'Hi, Big Brother. I hope you, Ella and Danny are doing well.'* Milton sat at his desk and read the letter. He didn't anticipate much unexpected news to come out of the letter but he always held hope that maybe somewhere in the narrative he would find glints of his sister's peace of mind. The rest of the letter went on as usual with Charlotte recounting her days at the facility and the progress she felt she was making. Then, as always, she would veer off into ruminations about their life growing up. This time she brought up the first time she and Milton stood in line with their mother at the Department of Human Resources. *'Do you remember that morning?'* she asked.

Milton remembered that morning very well. He especially remembered the stench of alcohol and sweat as men passed along the street on a hot August morning all those years ago. But most of all he remembered the visit his mother had received a few weeks before that morning.

His mother had held Charlotte by the hand as she moved single step in the line leading to the front door of the building. She would tap a curious Milton, who was too old to have to hold his mother's hand, to keep up. The men he saw in the doorways of buildings and who wandered along the streets reminded him so much of his father.

Milton recalled how he stood in slight fascination and despair that there was an actual world in which people like his father lived out their lives. He watched the men and even women, which was even more fascinating because the women were so unlike his mother, and he wondered 'why?' He looked at Charlotte, who was only around six at the time, and then at his mother and the marks on her forearm which were close to Milton's face as he moved step by step alongside her; the marks had become a dusty rose color, the scabs having fallen off revealing little of the violence from that night. In time they would turn the color of her natural complexion and the story of the horrible night would be gone from view but not from the memories of the children who had to bear witness.

He still recalled how his father went over the edge that particular night. His mother had been ironing. Milton and Charlotte were sitting on the floor watching TV when his father came home. His father stumbled into the house with an awful smell. Even now Milton could still recall the smell that he now recognized as the stench of old sex, sweat and alcohol that seemed to combine with the ardent stench of anger. His father stood over Milton and his sister and tried to play with them, but he was too drunk to make sense of his intentions. He tried to talk to them, but his words wouldn't come so he simply stared at his children, his body rocking back and forth as it sought a center of balance. Milton was afraid for himself and for his sister so he slid his hand into Charlotte's hand and held it. His father mumbled something and went to the kitchen where his mother was. There were words exchanged and the crash of metal onto the floor. Charlotte pulled her hand away from Milton and jumped up in fear. Milton stood and looked into the kitchen to see the iron on the floor. His mother backed away from his father with the most terrified look in her eyes that Milton had ever seen. The look was unlike the look she usually had when her husband hit her; the look she usually had when her husband's hand came to her face or to the back of her head was a look of expectation, but that night her eyes were a strange red, as if fear had pushed all the blood in her body to the spaces in her eyes and that her eyes had stretched to a point that seemed beyond her face as she backed into the corner of the kitchen. Milton's father was yelling at her, then he reached over and grabbed the clothes hangers that were on the table and began telling her something- - he was telling her something as he twisted the metal of the hangers together, and then he began to whip her. Milton and Charlotte began to scream. With their screams he remembered hearing his mother moan with each blow and pleaded for her husband to stop. Doing the only thing he could do, Milton pulled his little sister to him and covered her face. To this day Milton blamed himself for sending his father into a rage. If only he hadn't insulted his father by taking his sister's hand in his… That would be the last time their father would beat their mother like that. The next day Milton's mother received a visitor. The woman that lived a few doors from them showed up on their doorstep. At first Milton's mother talked to the woman through the screen door. He recalled the woman telling his mother that she was worried about the safety of Milton's mother and he and Charlotte. He remembered his mother telling the woman that everything would be fine but that the woman was persistent as she held something in her hand. After a while, Milton remembered his mother slowly opening the screen door and taking the small brown sack from the woman. Only a few weeks later Milton's father would pass out at work and would suffer from what would be the beginning of a string of illnesses, leaving his wife and public assistance as the family's main support.

Milton finished the letter and returned it to the pocket of his overcoat.

The meeting Milton attended that day was with other ministers who were dead-set against what they had learned of the school board's decision to fund a support group for gay students at one the city's high schools. It was a small but vocal group of ministers that found support of gay folks in any way to be insufferable but that had decided to address the matter as an issue of funding with taxpayers' money rather than their dislike of homosexuals. It was a select group of male ministers that convened the meeting because for this group, its feelings towards female ministers as decision makers or leaders in the community was just as conservative as its views towards gay folks. Their views were such that it would've been no surprise to anyone outside the group that the ministers came to the conclusion that the funding situation needed to be addressed. While Milton wasn't sure of the impact of standing in favor with the move of the ministers, he knew equal rights was a subject he would have to face sooner or later, so taking a public stand at that time was the right time. He would figure out how to navigate the issues in his personal life later. It was decided by the ministers that a news conference would be called and the meeting was adjourned.

After meeting with the ministers Milton headed out to a lunch he had planned.

He met Mr. Nixon at a café, this time without Mrs. Nixon and away from the church. Ever since their session the husband stayed on Milton's mind. He knew the wife had decided she was going to go through with the abortion, and it left Milton concerned over the husband's state of mind. But it wasn't only Mr. Nixon's state of mind Milton was concerned with, he was equally bothered by the position the husband had been put in, unable to take a stand against the wife, and even more, a wife who used her authority over her husband. Though Milton told himself it was the act of the possible abortion itself that was the main area of contention, it was these other thoughts that stood in his mind just as well, and as the days went on, even more.

Mr. Nixon walked into the diner and looked around. It was a bright day and Milton could see him against the noonday sunlight that poured through the windows of the eatery. He waved at him just as Mr. Nixon was telling the waitress he was there to meet someone. They shook hands when Mr. Nixon came to the table.

"How are you, Pastor," Mr. Nixon greeted as they shook hands.

"I'm well," Milton said as he sat back down.

Mr. Nixon removed his hat and coat and laid them across the booth.

"I just wanted to check on you," Milton said.

"Thanks. It's been crazy, but I think I'll get through it."

"Are you sure?"

The waitress came over and took their orders.

"Not really," he said. "I want the baby."

"And that's what I'm concerned about," Milton said. He sat a little back in his seat. "Seems as if Sister Nixon has made up her mind."

Mr. Nixon nodded his head a few times, his eyes cast down at the table.

"So what about you?"

"What do you mean," Mr. Nixon asked.

"How are you going to deal with this?"

Shaking his head, Mr. Nixon answered. "Don't seem like there's nothing I can do."

"There's always something you can do."

Mr. Nixon looked at him suddenly. His face was a mix of curiosity and surprise. "What—what do you mean?"

"I'm saying there's always something you can do in any situation. Look at your options. You do have options, you know. Look at them and present them to her."

After a long silence, Mr. Nixon asked, "Those options. What are they?"

"You'll know," Milton said. "And you have just as much right to them as she has to hers. Now I'm telling you this because you're just as much a part of my flock as Sister Nixon is. But she's put herself in control of this situation without much regard for you or the baby." He paused and looked closely at Mr. Nixon before continuing, "Or to God." The server brought their orders and left. "I'm looking out for you as well as honoring what I know the Lord wants from us," he continued.

"Choosing between my wife and a baby I don't even know…" Mr. Nixon said, shaking his head. "At this point we're not even sure if you can call it a baby."

"Don't say that." Milton spoke sharply. He didn't realize how much he disliked the wife. Calming himself, he continued. "You might find some things uncomfortable in your final decision, but if it's the right decision, one based on scripture, then you have to live up to it in spite of the pain it might cause."

Mr. Nixon looked at Milton shaking his head in disbelief. "I'm not going to destroy my marriage over this."

"It's not about destroying your marriage. It's about honoring what God wants. Brother Nixon, I think you'll be honoring God. If she wants to destroy a life, then she will. But what about you? Are you going to give her the 'go ahead'? You need to make sure you're the one who honors God." Milton looked down at his hands that were clasped in front of him on the table. "Now I try very hard to keep marriages together, but in this case your wife has made up her mind to do something that's immoral. And if she had no problems committing that sin, then…" He looked at Mr. Nixon. "But this time you don't have to eat of the apple."

Mr. Nixon looked at him and smiled. "Pastor," he said, with a knowing expression on his face. "I'm not going to leave my wife because of her decision."

Milton walked back to his car after he and Mr. Nixon finished their conversation. He hurried along the streets under the bright winter's sun, a surge of emotions boiling up in him. He was bothered that Mr. Nixon would give up so much authority to his wife. And then for Mr. Nixon to give in to that particular woman! So arrogant the way she sat in his office the other day, her head held high like an empress, and proclaimed her decision. Arrogant. Milton had seen this type of arrogance before in so many others, decisions made of their own desires instead of conviction to God's laws that were designed for their own good. They were ignorant of God's love for them and much too arrogant to see otherwise. Caught up in their search for selfish comfort it would only bring about their downfall, he told himself. He had seen it happen time and time again. But there was something that stung Milton more than all else, though he wouldn't admit it, and that was how he had been insulted at having been reduced to a laughable figure in the husband's eyes. He wouldn't stand for it.

That Sunday Milton, preached from Ephesians 6:10 through 6:24. He reminded the church of the need to engage in defiance of evil and the need to commit to spiritual warfare. Milton leaned on the lectern as he spoke. He reminded the congregation that man is at constant odds with evil, and that evil, by its very nature is insidious and also far-reaching. Milton's eyes looked over the congregation, watching the faces caught up in his words. He went on telling the congregation, which looked with rapt attention at him, knowing that his words would take them from whatever hell they were in, that sometimes evil came in the most unlikely personality. His hands tightened on the sides of the lectern as he reminded the congregation that it is to the church, the body of Christ, that they must give thanks, and to seek a better life because Jesus had given his blood that they would be without sin.

Out in the congregation, heads nodded in agreement, the lily field of hats weaving to quiet whispers of 'amen'.

He paused and looked over the church, allowing his eyes to ride across the faces looking up at him, allowing them to hear his words.

Ella sat up front and watched her husband. She didn't nod her head in agreement as the others did, but stared at him not so much hearing his words as feeling his emotions. The passage he had decided to preach wasn't the one he had discussed with her. He always ran his sermons by her for effect, before putting them before the church. This sermon was not the one he had spoken to her the night before.

In a final exhausted voice he instructed, "Put on the whole armor of God, that ye may be able to stand against the wiles of the devil."

Then, raising his eyes towards the heavens he began to sing 'We've Come This Far By Faith'. The organ roared in and the choir stood and joined, bellowing to the God they knew understood them and all of the pain they endured.

It wasn't until later that evening that Ella brought up the sermon. She had put off asking Milton about it that afternoon because she was mulling over in her head why he had preached that sermon and who it was meant for. By that evening she had decided to ask him. They were sitting in the den. Milton had built a fire in the fireplace and the two of them sat, watching TV.

"Why did you do a different sermon today?"

"It came to me that it was needed. God told me it was needed today. You know the Nixons?"

Ella thought for a second and nodded, "Yeah."

He told her about what they were going through.

"But why?" Ella asked. "Why would two people come together and not want to start a family? It sounds so selfish."

"I don't know," Milton sighed. "It's crazy, if you ask me."

"I'm surprised Sister Nixon would want to do that." Ella had never gotten to know Sister Nixon. Any conversation with her had been the type of cordial exchange that was expected of a pastor's wife: pleasant and full of blessings. Rather it was the fact that any member of the church would make such a decision that surprised her. "I guess it's her decision though, what she wants to do with her body, but... it just doesn't seem right."

"No. You're wrong, Ella. It's not her decision."

Ella looked questioningly at Milton.

"It really isn't, Ella. You see that's the problem. People think they can do what they want with their bodies when they can't. God gave us these bodies. They belong to him, not us."

"But Sister Nixon would be the one who would have to live with the pregnancy. I don't know," Ella said as she looked at the fire in the fireplace. "I have to admit that I'm torn over the subject. I would never do it."

"And Brother Nixon has decided to go along with it," Milton added.

"Then that was the evil you were talking about." Ella spoke with relief.

"Yeah. Why? What were you thinking?"

Ella was hesitant to reply, but Milton stared at her waiting for a reply. "I thought, maybe you were talking about Danny. And my inviting him to the house."

"That wasn't it," Milton said, shaking his head. They continued watching TV for a few minutes before Milton asked, "Why did you do that anyway? I mean, why would you invite someone, anyone who lives the kind of criminal life he lives into our home? Ella, he's a criminal and more."

"You don't know that, Milton."

"Oh come on Ella. He's out there in the streets. He's bound to be into some stuff. All kinds of stuff. And it's really not just about Danny, it's about the--"

"Yes it is, Milton. It is about Danny." Ella cut Milton short but her remark wasn't meant to be sharp, it was more a statement of resignation than indictment. Defending Danny had been her burden since the day he came into the world.

Milton put the TV on mute. He looked closely at Ella. "Do you remember the first thing we did when we bought this house? We had Reverend Stewart come by and bless it. We had him bless it that it would be free of the kind of mess Danny carries with him. The evil he seems to relish in. Ella, this is a sanctified home," Milton said as he took Ella's hands in his. "A house that has been cleansed in the name of God."

Ella looked down where Milton held her hands. "What do you expect me to do, Milton? Do you expect me to just turn my back on my child?"

Milton looked at her, unsure of saying what was on his mind.

"Well I'm not, Milton. When we moved into this house it was the three of us, not just you and me, it was the three of us; and no matter what happens, this will be his home as long as it's mine."

They sat in silence for a while, Milton continuing to hold Ella's hand, each one holding onto their thoughts and the words woven in those thoughts. Finally Ella spoke. "I know you don't consider Danny to be your son, Milton."

"You can't say I haven't tried."

"To be honest, Milton, I can't say that at all."

"I can't believe you just said that," Milton said, watching her.

"Yes you can, Milton. Yes you can. Tell me," she continued quietly, "What would you do if you had a child that went astray? Would you turn your back on it?

Milton didn't answer.

"Would you? You can't even answer, can you?"

"I don't know. I guess I'll never find out."

Ella pulled her hand from her husband's hands and stood up. "Even Jesus worked with those who needed him most, Milton. Maybe you need to remember that." She left the room.

~~~~

The sun headed towards the edge of the sky when Ella set out to find Damon. She knew the way to Damon's house and she knew that what happened the last time she was there wouldn't happen this time. But it was just that thing, that thing that wouldn't happen that bothered her. It had been three days since they pulled the body from the lake and four days since she last saw Damon. Her father had forbidden her to leave the house; he knew she would go looking for the boy and locking her in was all he could do to keep her from leaving. Over those days Ella mostly sat in her room watching the colors of the room change in shades throughout the day, thinking about Damon and feeling the baby move in her belly. She didn't bathe for the first few days until her sister came into the room and smelled the odor and told their father, and for all the days spent she didn't eat enough to feed two mouths.

She was still a month from her due date but the baby proved it was ready to come much sooner. It moved a lot and seemed to kick more, sometimes, it seemed, in fits of rage. Her sister was locked away in her sewing room and her brother was out of the house that day as Ella listened to the loneliness, which seemed to have multiplied since she was unable to see Damon and it was all she could stand. She got up from her chair and went into the bathroom where she ran water in the tub and filled it with rose scented bath oil, then, after soaking for a while, she got out, dried herself and dressed; she combed her hair and wrapped it into the bun style that Damon liked and went downstairs. Her father had locked all of the doors and had instructed her brother and sister to do the same if they left the house, which they did. It never dawned on him that a fourteen-year old pregnant girl could still climb through a window.

Once Ella was out of the house she stood in the backyard and looked around for prying eyes. It was late afternoon and quiet. Anyone who led responsible lives in New Home was either at work or away on errands so she had none of the neighbors who would ask why she was standing, full of child looking about in the yard behind the house like someone who was lost or had lost her mind.

The store where Damon worked was the first place Ella told herself to look for him. It was one of the few places where she always found him since there weren't too many people in town who associated with him. Other than that it was the small house in which Buddy lived, who was the only friend Damon had in town; but she knew since they found Buddy's body in the lake, Damon wouldn't be there, or it would be the shack in the woods Damon shared with his aunt.

The store was in the center of town along Langley Street, which was the main street that ran through New Home before the name changed as it left the black part of the county and into the county seat. Ella began walking through the streets on her way to the store. Along the way the people of New Home slowed to stare at her. She walked quietly with her head held high, not out of pride, but out of shame. She couldn't bear to look at anyone because she knew what she had done was on everyone's lips and in the shake of everyone's head so false vanity was all she had left to hold onto. It was something she learned from her mother. Most of the folks who looked at her did more than just look, they watched her; some of them watched, afraid to approach her because she carried Damon's baby, and the fact that she carried a murderer's child in some way made her complicit if only because she chose to lay with him and let him between her legs. There were others who watched her walking through the hot streets who worried over her and felt ashamed for her father, that a thirteen year old girl would have given herself to an older boy, and that now at fourteen this little girl with the small frame walked with a belly swollen almost the size of her entire torso in the searing August heat. They would be the ones who would get her father if they didn't have second thoughts about getting involved. But in the minds of others, ones who despised her father for his arrogance, ones who had been pressed into service by her father, they hoped she would lose the child and maybe her life before she made it to wherever she was headed.

When she made it to the store she saw one of the young men who worked there sweeping the sidewalk in front of store. He told her to sit down on a bench a bit away from the store. He knew the owner wouldn't want her near the store itself, and he went in and got her a cup of water and a sandwich he had in his lunchbox. He stood by the bench as she drank the water and ate the sandwich and asked her if she was looking for Damon. She told him she was. He told her how stupid it was to think Damon would be there after what he had done then he asked her why she would look for him. She didn't answer him. Then he asked why did she think Damon would kill Buddy. This time Ella paused and looked down at the sandwich in her hand. "I don't know," she said.

"Well look, I gotta git back to work," the young man finally said. "You need to go back home and forget about him." He started to put his hand on Ella's shoulder but stopped as if whatever she was would affect him. Then, considering more he gently placed his hand on her shoulder. "Go on home."

After the young man left, Ella got up from the bench, looked at the cars that had slowed under the watchful eyes of drivers, and continued along the streets.

Langley Street continued past the edge of town with tributaries that veered from it into the backwoods, to the shacks and dead or dying farms between New Home and the county seat of Stratford. It was where the Negroes who were either too ignorant to fit into city life or those who were too obstinate to fit in lived their lives in small shacks, making a living trying to create the life they had in the fields of Georgia and Mississippi or by working for wages that didn't afford them to live within the city limits. The U.S. Census Bureau and the people of nearby Stratford considered them to be citizens of New Home, but New Home didn't claim them. Ella walked off the main street onto the road that led to the house where Damon lived with his aunt.

Her stomach full and water in her, she easily made her way along the trail through the woods. Before, the verdant fragrance of the trees and the heavy smell of wet earth would have caused Ella to smile as she thought about Damon, but now she wasn't sure how she would find him. An image of him sweating and hiding in the shadows of the little shack where he lived came to her, and he would whisper 'you gittin' big' and she would sit with him, holding him, his body shivering as they made plans to run away together to California like he had once suggested, but she pushed that image out of her mind. All she knew was she had to see him so they could talk about what they had done.

But when she got to the clearing he wasn't there, so she went farther along the path to his house.

The small shack where he once lived sat in a pool of silence in the woods. The dogs that were usually tied to the post were gone, and the '56 Mercury that usually sat rusting on blocks was gone as well. She walked over to the small house and looked through the windows and saw that everything was still there, but that the beds had been stripped and the old refrigerator had been unplugged, its door left open and all of the food gone. Ella felt her body weaken. Her knees began to shake as she realized Damon was gone. She stumbled back, taking deep breaths as she tried to adjust to his absence. She walked over to an old washtub that had been turned upside down and sat on it, and there in the blood red evening she cried. The baby began to kick and along the sides of the tub a stream ran from between her legs as red as the evening.

CHAPTER NINE

The sermon that Sunday had shown Natasha just how moving Milton could be. She had visited Christ The Redeemer Baptist Church again and had witnessed Milton in full splendor; it was as if he could bend light with his hands or part the waters of the Red Sea themselves when he stood in the pulpit. And his voice, she had come to realize over the visits to the church that his voice wasn't loud like she had expected, instead it was low as if it was encumbered by the weight of compassion; it was a voice that wasn't strident, but it was heard because of the promise he presented to those who listened to him. She now understood the effect he probably had on her mother, especially at the impressionable age her mother had been when she first met Milton. Like a lot of black folks her mother had been taught to respect pastors. Black ministers had, after all, been given the license over the lives of Black folks when they were at their lowest point as a people in America, so black ministers would command the respect of anyone who came into their presence. No matter the nature of the animal beneath the clothing. Natasha understood this, and she figured her mother had been no less different than many others in the presence of a man of the cloth. Now that Natasha had met the man, she would let him know how much more wisdom she had than her mother had all those years ago.

Those were the thoughts that wove through Natasha's mind as she walked from the campus to her apartment, climbing the hill to the street where she lived. The landscape of Cincinnati was so unlike that of Oklahoma, especially Tarpley where she grew up, which was flat and expansive, the expanse being held at bay by the crystal blue skies that sat just at its edge. Instead, the streets of Cincinnati rose just to the east outside of her apartment, just as it did in the west and north, its urban landscape of brownstones, and buildings of turn-of-the-century German and Italian influence jutting up towards the horizon on either side before plunging downward towards the down-town area and the riverfront. She had never lived in a place with so many hills.

She wondered how her mother had dealt with the constant climb-ing and descending of the hills of the city. Had she cursed them as Natasha, did or had she taken delight in their majesty? Questions like these pulled at Natasha's thoughts.

Natasha could have gone somewhere else to continue her educa-tion, but tracing her mother's footsteps was just as important as her college education, it was the education she needed to connect the lines of who she was and where she had come from, and it was the search for that education that brought Natasha to Cincinnati. The story her grandmother had told her had become a part of her life, and exploring it in all its finite or infinite possibilities had become her quest.

It was a story that unfolded years ago and that concluded with her mother lying on the edge of death as Natasha came into the world gasping as if she, herself, had only barely escaped a similar or-deal. Granny was to tell her many years later that Natasha's mother had intentionally given the last breath she had to her daughter so that her daughter might live.

That was why all her life the little girl had taken on such curiosity of the workings of the thing called life. To her it was mysterious; graceful in its fullness, yet respectful of boundaries. But just what those boundaries were was what enticed Natasha the most.

Natasha's mother's name was Abigail Lynn, but most of the resi-dents of Tarpley had simply called her Abilyn, and for a good part of her early years that was all Natasha had known of her, that the folks of Tarpley had called her mother by an abbreviated name.

Everyday as Natasha helped Granny clean the house, Natasha would look at the picture of Abigail Lynn that sat under a lamp on a table graced with a large pink and white doily. She knew it was her mother. Granny had told her so one day when Natasha had asked who was the attractive young woman who looked out at her everyday. At first she thought it was a youthful Granny, but something about the face, the eyes that twinkled from the frame and the broad smile, seemed to speak to her as someone quite different. The way the woman in the photo held her head, with an air of insouciance. Granny would never be so daring. Natasha didn't know who the young lady was, but she knew the young lady wasn't her grandmother so she had asked and her grandmother told her. At first Natasha was surprised because Granny had been the only mother she had ever known, but now, there was someone else who had been just as instrumental to her wellbeing, someone who needed to be known.

Natasha remembered that day so well. It was the day she came of age. She would no longer sit alone on the porch and look out across the backyard onto the outskirts of Tarpley and wonder what lay just past where the earth and sky met. It was the day Granny and Abilyn invited her into the story.

Granny rarely spoke his name. As far as she was concerned there was no need to bring him up. But there were times when Natasha would overhear her grandmother in conversation mention his name. "Milton Pruitt," she would say, and then with much indignity, "And he call hisself a minister."

That was how Natasha found out who was her father. When Natasha came of age, Granny sat her down and told her the whole story. She told the story, glancing every now and then at Natasha's grandfather who sat just across the room reading the daily paper, of Abilyn who had always been full of spirit, hard to hold down, and how she had always wanted to move far from Tarpley. At that point Natasha's grandfather grunted, "And you see where that got her," before getting up and leaving the room. He was unable to bear the retelling.

Granny continued. She told how Abilyn had always wanted to sing and to travel the world on the concert stage. "Whenever people would hear her voice," Granny said, "They would say, girl you got to get away from here. Make it big." And that was what Abilyn decided to do.

Abilyn's talent had taken her to The University of Cincinnati because of its prestigious College Conservatory of Music. Granny and Natasha's grandfather, PawPaw, had been overjoyed with Abilyn's acceptance into the school once they learned of the school's alumni, but PawPaw had always had reservations about his daughter being so far from home. Abilyn had never been the healthiest girl, having been born with a weak heart. But with both Abilyn and Granny's coaxing (at this point, Granny's eyes welled with tears), he gave in and the two of them rode halfway across the country to see their only child off to college.

That first year in school went especially well for Abilyn, but that second year things began to change. Her correspondences became less frequent, and when Granny and Paw Paw did receive one, they noticed how less lively and chatty they became. Instead, Abilyn's letters and phone calls had become more refined in concept and language, and her feelings about many things she once held simply vanished. She no longer talked about Tarpley, or of missing Granny's cooking and kidding around with her father. In fact, she rarely spoke of coming home at all. Her change in personality had all been a part of her growing up; that was what Granny and Paw Paw had concluded, but they couldn't turn away from the fact that they missed their little girl.

Finally, Abilyn did return. It was the summer of her third year, and she brought with her the news that she was pregnant. She had met a man, considerably older than she and he had seduced her with promises that he would always be there for her. But when she had broken the news to him of her pregnancy, he had turned his back on her, giving her money to leave Cincinnati, and to 'take care of the situation', and he was gone. Abilyn took the money, but she took care of the situation on her terms. She came back to Tarpley and had the baby.

And now Natasha had come to Cincinnati to find the man whom she would call father.

Getting to know her father hadn't been foremost on Natasha's mind. She never felt a need to know him since, in her world, he never existed and by all accounts he never even intended for her to exist. She only wanted to see him; to view him close enough to see who helped make the skin and the hair of her body, the bones in her hands that she was often told were so beautiful, and the eyes that would look at him. Seeing him along a street is how she had always imagined it.

The things Granny had told Natasha about Milton, what little Granny knew, had been told to her as a cautionary tale, as a moral in which Natasha's father was the villain who was to be avoided. But it wasn't in Natasha's nature to see things simply; instead she saw things with fascination so it would have been correct to say Natasha was fascinated by the story that led to her becoming. Once she saw Milton she realized she needed more, how much more she wasn't sure.

But it was when she heard Milton's voice and watched the light in his eyes as he spoke to her that things began to change, thoughts and emotions that were now becoming words and phrases; but most of all it was when he touched her, when he took her hand between his hands that day at the restaurant that the emotions and the thoughts rose above fascination, moving in her head and flushing her body, causing her to want to remove her hands from his palms because palms mean so much more than just a mere touch. Palms were warm, welcoming and inviting, and she didn't want to feel either, yet at the same time she did. These were the experiences that bothered her and yet attracted her to this place and to this man.

Natasha moved thoughts of Milton from her mind and brought her attention back to the one she was having with her advisor, Dr. Nash, who at the time was eviscerating Natasha's writing style.

"Where are your notations," Dr. Nash asked. "You should've at least learned how a formal research paper should look before you even decided to attend grad school." Dr. Nash continued to look at Natasha's paper then put the papers on the table. "This is a last minute job, Natasha," she said, removing her glasses in frustration.

Dr. Nash had taken special interest in Natasha when she found out Natasha was Abilyn's daughter. Abilyn had been one of Dr. Nash's students and the events surrounding Abilyn leaving school and her death was something the professor never forgot.

Natasha had found out about Dr. Nash after she had decided to attend the same university Abilyn had attended. The day she told Granny and Paw Paw of her decision to attend the university both of them became silent, neither of them answering as they sat in the kitchen that morning. Natasha figured they probably wouldn't be in agreement with her, but she thought they would at least understand. Finally Granny looked at Paw Paw and said, "I told you." Paw Paw got up from the table and put his plate in the sink and walked out the back door.

The next day Granny told Natasha to help her go through some of Abilyn's things. She had Natasha drag a trunk from the corner of a storage closet into the kitchen and the two of them began looking through the trunk. They were looking for a sympathy card they had gotten from one of Abilyn's professors. Granny couldn't remember the professor's name, but she knew she would recognize the card when she saw it. She had had time to think about Natasha's decision and had come to understand it.

Natasha sat on the floor in front of the trunk and Granny sat alongside her in a chair she had pulled out from the kitchen table. There in the morning light that filled the kitchen, the two of them brought Abilyn back through cards, photos and keepsakes. With each item Natasha lifted from the trunk: an open envelope, a folded letter, a scarf that draped across Natasha's hand, Natasha called her mother back to life and she knew she wanted to open the door to her mother's life that had been shut long ago. Paw Paw stayed away from the kitchen that morning, deciding to work with a neighbor on the neighbor's truck. "I don't know why y'all so hell-bent on going back there," Paw Paw said that morning as they had breakfast.

"Because she wants to go, Ernest," Granny had replied. "And it's her life that has to be satisfied."

"Crazy," Paw Paw said. "Crazy. Just bringin' on mess that don't have to be." He shook his head. "Baby Girl, I hope you ain't asking for more than you need," he said as he kissed Natasha on her forehead. "And you. You should know better," he said to his wife. He kissed her on her cheek. "Just crazy," he grumbled as he left.

"Here," Granny said as she pulled the card from a large envelope. "This is a card we got from one of your momma's professors." She adjusted her glasses. "Melvine Nash. Let her know you want to come to the university and see what she says." She handed the card to Natasha. That was a little over a year ago. Since then both Granny and PawPaw had passed away and now Natasha sat across from the woman who had made Natasha's move to Cincinnati an easy one. The woman who Natasha knew would expect her to achieve what Abilyn hadn't.

That evening Natasha worked on her project then closed out the program on her computer and went to take a shower as she prepared for LaShon to pick her up. She had accepted LaShon's invitation to go shopping with him. She hadn't ventured out much from the university neighborhood where she lived and worked since she had arrived in Cincinnati to do her studies, except for the two times she attended Christ The Redeemer Baptist Church and LaShon, having laid eyes on her, had taken a strong liking to her. He had moved swiftly into her life after the day he met her. Since that Sunday they had talked on the phone a bit and even met up for lunch. She felt a kinship with LaShon because she believed both of them were people navigating a secret life that they felt would end in rejection if things came to light.

She figured LaShon was gay but never asked him because she thought it would be rude. She had had gay friends in the past and had learned to let them declare their identity in their own way. After all, there was no need to ask him; he was definitely not there for romance or sex.

"Did you go home for Thanksgiving," LaShon asked as they walked through a shopping mall, weaving in and out of the crowd that was building in excitement over the holiday season.

"No."

"Why not?"

"I really don't have anyone there except for cousins. Traveling that far to spend holidays with cousins… that's a bit much."

"Oh." LaShon didn't want to press the conversation further. "So what are your plans once you finish school?"

"My grandparents thought I should go into teaching—they raised me. And when I told them my plans they were like, 'not teaching?' I told them I most likely will. That or work for the State Department."

"It'll be teaching," LaShon assured her.

They continued to talk as they walked on looking in store windows and at the people.

"That's that old school way of thinking," LaShon said. "My parents wanted me to go to school for business, but I didn't want that. I like design. Graphics, photography. I dropped out of school but I'm going to go back."

"Good. And maybe you should get a minor in business or something. It's always good to have that."

A group of guys passed and looked at Natasha.

"Damn, girl," LaShon said. He and Natasha laughed and she elbowed him. "And they were good looking too. Cincinnati got some fine brothas, you know," LaShon confessed.

"That's what I'm finding out."

"A lot of 'em too," LaShon said as they continued on.

"So you're not going home for Christmas either?"

Natasha told him she wasn't because she had too much to do.

"It must be something to be so far away. Oklahoma, huh?" LaShon laughed. "Girl I still can't imagine any black folks living in Oklahoma."

"Well, we're there."

They went into a few stores, mostly looking around and buying a few things. It was when they were in a department store that LaShon brought up Ella and Milton's party.

"You know, since you're going to be here, why don't you come to Pastor's Christmas party?"

"I don't know…" Natasha said, shaking her head as she looked at a perfume display. "I'm not really a part of the church."

"You've attended twice, and you've met him and sister Pruitt so they know you, so why not? You can be my date."

His words hit her, *'they know you'.*

"I'd rather be invited."

"Well I can make that happen. Now you know that, don't you?" LaShon looked at her with eyebrows raised. "I mean, I am the reigning diva in the choir. They wouldn't turn me down. Besides, they wouldn't anyway. They're not like that. Come on. Please?"

Hesitantly conceding, Natasha agreed. "Ok. As long as you really don't think they would mind."

"They won't mind. Now come on, let's go shopping for this party."

An hour or so later they stopped by the food court to get a bite. They sat at a table that allowed them to have their backs towards a wall, giving them full view of the shoppers. By then they had both agreed that man-watching was one of their pastimes.

"What kind of folks are Reverend Pruitt and his wife," Natasha asked.

"Nice people. Especially sister Pruitt. She's really nice. Pastor though? He's nice, but he can be stern."

"Like what?"

"Well, you know, pastors have to be stern in order to lead their flock, and he can be more than stern; he can be hard—but in a tough love kind of way. You know…" LaShon looked at a guy passing by with his girlfriend.

"How is he to you?" Natasha asked.

LaShon unfolded the paper on his pretzel. "He's alright with me. I like him."

"Oh," Natasha replied with a nod.

After a few seconds LaShon continued. "If you're asking about my being gay, we don't discuss it. I'm pretty sure he knows. Shit, everybody knows, I'm sure. We just don't talk about it. But he can be pretty stern, his son can tell you that."

"His son?" Natasha hoped she didn't come off too surprised. She tried to contain herself. "I didn't know he had any children. I mean, I haven't seen them at church or anything."

"And you won't either," LaShon chuckled. "He has a son, well, it's his stepson. I think sister Pruitt might have been married before, but from the looks of it, I think she just had a baby when she was younger because she don't look old enough to have a child his age."

"What's his name?"

"Danny. Fine as hell, girl, but crazy as fuck. At least that's what I hear. Him and pastor didn't get along at all and one day pastor had enough and kicked him out."

"Really?"

LaShon nodded his head. "Sister Pruitt wasn't too happy about it, but she knew pastor was right."

"How old was he when they kicked him out?"

"Pastor kicked him out, not sister Pruitt. I think he was like seventeen or something like that. Kind of young, though."

"Then he must've really done a lot to cause that to happen. Either that or Reverend Pruitt isn't very forgiving. How old is their son now?"

"He's older than you and me, so I'm guessing early thirties. He used to come to church with them. Grew up in the church like me. I can remember seeing him. He was nice and all, but something about him was weird. Kinda dark, really. Like he was angry. You could see it in his eyes the way he would watch people and not say much only until somebody spoke to him. I think it used to embarrass sister Pruitt that he would act that way, but hey," LaShon said, hunching his shoulders, "it's who he is. Fine as hell though," he reiterated. "But I always wondered what was the last straw that broke the camel's back so that pastor finally kicked him out."

~~~~

Danny never put much stock in things because he had learned not to. He had tried it, like trying to make his mother happy but ending up having only a skim of happiness come to her in return, before having the happiness fill up once again with regret; or like trying to believe that his stepfather could save souls. From what Danny saw in his home, in the way the members of Christ The Redeemer Baptist Church acted and from what he garnered from his mother's regret, souls went their way in spite of what anyone else said. There had been a host of things Danny had tried putting stock in and for the most part all of his efforts were answered with little, if any reward, so he had learned that to make it through life he only needed to ride events to their end before jumping off and on to the next event. It was a simpler way to look at life and it made life easier for him because he wouldn't have much expectation of anything or of anyone.

That's what Danny told himself. But in reality it wasn't that way at all for him. People were bound to have expectations and Danny was no different, regardless of what he told himself. That was the thing that caught him up as he listened to Cortez sleeping beside him that morning. Even though he had told himself nothing would come from sleeping with Cortez a few years earlier when Cortez had called him and asked him to come over, the night Danny drove down to Cortez's apartment and they sat around smoking weed and talking in looping conversation that wound itself back to the two of them and they had spent the night in Cortez's bed, that same night Danny felt something come alive inside of himself. In spite of that night Danny had told himself that nothing more would come of it than working for Cortez. Yet, some years gone by, he and Cortez were still spending nights together. In that tiny space in the mind that refuses to be filled with anything but expectation there is always the smallest speck of hope, and the same was true with Danny. Still, putting stock in people and things was something Danny chose not to do.

The early morning sun illuminated the dingy walls of the gym. The double doors had been opened and held in place by cinder blocks on both doors as a brisk wind moved into the large old room. Danny stood in front of the gym's owner, Mr. Fletcher, getting his gloves laced up. Better known as Fletch, Mr. Fletcher was a man in his early seventies. He was short with a frame that once had the muscled leanness of a fighter, but was now slight, with a protruding belly that strained against the jacket he wore. On the walls of the gym were autographed photos of fighters and posters of Mr. Fletcher from his younger years as a boxer. One of the posters was yellow with a black and white photograph of him from nineteen fifty-eight, crouched in a fighter's stance, his gloves up and his face looking out half romantic, half menacingly from the photo and large red letters emblazoned across the top of the poster proclaiming 'Dynamic Action Slugfest'. Danny stared at the poster as he lifted his other hand to Fletch.

"I don't know why you won't just go ahead and get into the game, Danny. You got the fire in you," Fletch said. He pulled quick and hard at the fasteners as he spoke.

"I don't have the discipline," Danny said, still looking at the younger Mr. Fletcher. "And I'm too hot-headed."

"That's something you need to think about son," Fletch said as he walked Danny to a corner of the gym. Fletch had been hired to keep Cortez's men in shape. Not only were the security team, which consisted mostly of Danny and Littlejohn, members of the gym but so were the male bartenders since they were sometimes called into service to help Danny and Littlejohn eject rowdy patrons from the bar. Cortez paid Fletch a little extra to give individualized training to Danny and Littlejohn. Fletch had an idea why Danny and Littlejohn were given special treatment at the gym but he chose not to talk about it with anyone. He simply took the money and dished out the knowledge.

So far there was only one other person in the gym: a guy working out on a speed bag. Most of the other members would come later, because, as Fletch put it, 'they didn't have the fire.'

Danny put the workout bag in motion, pushing it slightly to get it swinging, then he began to dance rhythmically on the balls of his feet around the bag: in, out, from side to side, weaving and ducking as he imagined the foe.

"Lead out with your back foot," Fletch reminded. "There you go. There you go." Fletch's eyes gleamed as he watched Danny's work. He had said from the first day he met Danny that Danny was a natural. Danny listened to Fletch's wisdom and went through his paces.

When they were done Fletch sat in a chair that he kept beside the shower and talked to Danny as Danny showered.

"That anger ain't gonna get nowhere if you don't understand it," Fletch said.

"I know," Danny said. "My mother always got on me about it." He called out to Fletch over the sound of the spraying water.

"She was right," Fletch said.

"Yeah. I know." Danny answered the man as he let the water run over his face and his chest. He understood why Fletch kept a chair by the shower so he turned full-front to Fletch to let the old man have his look. All of the special members of the gym knew their role in giving Fletch pleasure.

"It's an energy," Fletch continued as he watched Danny. "Learn how to use it. Use it as a way of handling a skill and it'll come out as just that, a skill. It becomes art."

"Anger as art," Danny chided.

"Yeah. It's just energy and art is how you express it, just like any feeling. But when it comes out in art people respect it. When it don't, well, people don't respect it and it'll only mess you up."

Danny took Fletch's words with him as he left the gym, but only as something amusing to tell others.

Ella came to Danny's bedroom and climbed into his bed. It was late at night. She pulled the blanket over them and wrapped her arms around him and pulled him close to her.

Danny awoke. "Mom? What's wrong," he asked, half asleep.

"Nothing. Go back to sleep."

But Danny knew something was wrong. He felt his mother's arms tighten around him, holding him close to her. He felt her breath against the back of his head. Her breathing was fast and he felt her heart beating rapidly against his back.

"Mom?"

"Go to sleep," she said quietly. "Go to sleep."

Danny tried to obey his mother but he couldn't go back to sleep so he lay staring into the dark night of his bedroom feeling the pounding of his mother's heart against his back.

The beating of his mother's heart and the confusion he felt as he stared off into the darkness that night was something that continued to visit Danny every so often just as it did this day. He sat in a coffeehouse after he left the gym and looked out onto the street as that night came to him again. The coffeehouse was close and warm, womb-like against the weather outside. People spoke softly and intimately at tables along the wall while some sat quietly reading books they had taken off the large bookcase that ran along one of the walls. The books and sense of quiet were why Danny came to the place. Sometimes he took a book from the bookcase but he would become embarrassed and put it back because he felt he probably looked like he didn't understand much of what he was reading. He would glance at the other readers and see the absorbed expressions on their faces as they read. This would cause him to gently close his book and put it back on the shelf. Sometimes he would write down on a napkin the title of a book that he saw someone reading and fold the napkin in his pocket or he would take one of the magazines he found at the coffee shop and put it under his coat or in his shirt and take it home.

Rushes of cold air came into the shop whenever someone would open the front door to enter or leave, bringing a reminder of the weather outside. Danny felt a crumb crumple beneath his elbow as he rested his arm on the table. He brushed off the crumbs and rested his arm once again on the table and stared out of the window before turning his attention to his lunch. The events of that night had become such a presence in Danny that it had bound itself to him in such a way that it was really no longer a memory but a piece of who Danny was, as much a part of him like the hair on his head or the skin that covered his bones. It was just one of the many events that joined him to his mother and to the history that she kept from him. His mother's dilemma was his even though he didn't know the nature of it. That was why putting stock in things didn't come easy for Danny, because of the uncertainty that he knew hung somewhere in the darkness of that night.

~~~~

In spite of what Ella thought about Milton's relationship with Danny, it wasn't that Milton didn't want Danny around. It was the trouble Danny brought with him whenever he came around that was the problem. That was the thought that ran through Milton's head as he walked to the hospital to visit a sick member of his congregation.

Milton felt he had given Danny more chances to prove himself than he deserved. Yes, he understood that he and Danny just never clicked, he never really understood why. It was just the way chemistry can be between people. But Milton was convinced that he had given Danny more than a fair shake at making things work and each time, Danny failed. Sometimes chances run out and God knows Danny had had enough of them.

What bothered Milton even more was that people like Ella and Sister Nixon were given the privilege of having children and they couldn't appreciate it. And though he was reluctant to speak ill of his sister because he understood what she had gone through, it was the same for Charlotte. Her child was lying in a grave because Charlotte wouldn't care for it like she should have. None of them deserved to have kids and still, they did. In the case of Sister Nixon, she was blessed by being pregnant. It was more than something that bothered Milton, it insulted him, but he knew that to feel insulted about something like that would be an affront to God's wisdom. Still, there was the stab of insult that Milton felt whenever he would think of it.

Ella's way of constantly defending Danny was just as much of a problem as Danny's behavior was, Milton continued to think as he came into the lobby of the hospital. He greeted the woman at the reception desk who was familiar with Milton from his visits. What was going to happen when Danny fell all the way—and it was something that was definitely going to happen—what then? Ella would stand crying and wringing her hands saying how much of a good person her son was like the mothers Milton saw on the news when they knew how much of an ass their sons were. He knew he wouldn't be there by Ella's side when she said those things. That was for sure. He didn't know much about Danny's birth father, but the guy, from what little Milton had learned of him from Ella, couldn't have been any good to have done what he did with a thirteen-year-old. People having babies who shouldn't. And yet, here he was. Willing, but unable.

Milton entered the patient's room and greeted her with a blessing.

CHAPTER TEN

There was a time when Danny thought his stepfather was the tallest man on earth, though he was never sure given that he rarely looked up at his stepfather because of what he saw whenever he did. Milton picked him up from school everyday, since he passed through the area where the school was located on his way home, and bending to Ella's wish that he and Danny would grow closer in their relationship he would pick the boy up, but it never brought them closer.

Danny would stand beside Milton on those days, the crown of his head just at his stepfather's waist. He would stand beside his stepfather watching his classmates as they left with their parents. Some of them would be skipping as they held their parent's hand, the 'skitch, skitch' of their shoes across the pavement would pull his eyes to their feet and he would watch the excitement in the movement of their feet and listen to the joyous sound of the skipping. He would stand beside his stepfather while Milton talked to a teacher or an administrator. They would talk about things Danny didn't understand, so he would watch his stepfather's legs, silently measuring the length to pass the time. But he was never sure just how far his stepfather rose in height. Danny was never able to brag about how tall his father was like the other boys did because Milton wasn't his father. He knew this because Milton never looked at him like a son. And he was never sure whether or not Milton might be taller than his classmates' fathers because of Danny's reluctance to raise his head and look up at Milton. Not unless he had to. It was why Danny could only wonder how tall his stepfather was.

On those afternoons when Milton would pick Danny up from school, they said little to each other, if anything at all. Milton would take Danny by the hand after Milton had finished talking with the school's staff and lead Danny across the street to the car. He would never speak to Danny and Danny never spoke to him. The both of them would get in the car and head for the house in silence. Danny would sit in the back seat looking out the window at the houses and cars passing by, at people walking together and children holding onto their parents as they talked to them. The children would look up into the faces of their parents as they talked. Then Danny would sit quietly back in the seat of Milton's car and study his sneakers on his feet, watching the light and shadows moving across the canvas of his sneakers and how his laces would hang down from his shoes, dangling.

~~~~

Murder for the folks of New Home wasn't rare, but the way this one was done was different. Usually a killing was done out of sudden rage, with the assailant found standing nearby weeping and saying how sorry he or she was. But this murder was different. There was something especially heinous about it because whoever committed it had taken his time with the victim and then had moved the body. It was a killing that had a lot of thought behind it in a way only something evil could make happen. Ella could still remember the thick wooly hair, like a dark cloud, so full that it poured water back into the lake as they lifted the body from the murky waters. Someone, possibly a boy who had come to skim stones, had discovered the body and had run back into town calling for help. Soon the bank of the small lake swarmed with people, some who had come to help and others who simply wanted to watch, and still others who stood on the shore with knotted bellies and a need to know.

Ella was one of those with a need to know. It had been a few days since she had seen Damon. Even though her father had forbade her to see the unnamed father of her child again, Ella and Damon met whenever and wherever they could. Sometimes Damon would be so bold as to come into Ella's bedroom long after the rest of Ella's family had gone to bed. She would let him in and they would lie together and he would explore her body in ways that were new to her, and she would gush with pleasure as Damon would peer up at her from between her legs and then would turn her on her side and cuddle her, spoon fashion, and enter her, moving slow and gentle until his release. And the two of them would lie like that for an hour or so before he would slip back out the window. This went on for months, quietly, his arms around her growing belly in the moonlight, neither of them speaking, neither of them wondering.

But after days of not hearing from Damon or hearing of him, Ella had become concerned. And it was this concern that brought her to the lake and the body.

When the news of the discovery hit the street, one of the first persons contacted had been Ella's father. He was always the one who folks contacted when potentially unmanageable situations arose. Emmanuel's skill at decision-making and the respect he had with the white citizens of Stratford was both appreciated and despised by the folks of New Home, but his sense of responsibility for his people took precedence over any ill feelings the citizens might have towards him.

Upon hearing the news Ella's father immediately jumped in his car and was about to pull out of the driveway when Ella ran up to the passenger side. "Daddy, I have to go with you."

He looked at her, surprised at her sudden appearance and offset by her growing belly. "No."

But she wouldn't let go of the door. "I'm coming Daddy," she said in a stern tone, "Or I'll walk there if I have to."

Her presence, the firmness of her resolve as well as her grip on the door caused her father to take a second look at her. Staring, he saw the young woman who opted to forego adolescence; and to this decision there was nothing more to say.

Once they arrived at the lake, her father turned to her. "I want you to stay in the car. I'll signal you if it's him." Then he got out and strode over and through the throng of onlookers.

But as soon as her father disappeared into the crowd, Ella jumped out of the car and hurried to the bank, and that was when she saw the body being lifted from the waters.

The men dragged the corpse from the lake. Their hands were cupped under its arms and the water rushed from the body onto the ground and back into the lake. They turned the body over so it lay face up. And it was then that Ella saw. It was a young man. A belt had been tightened around the young man's throat and bore deep into his skin that had been softened by the water. The crowd gasped as the face, gray and wrinkled from the submergence, looked towards the afternoon sun as if its last spark of hope had vanished. Suddenly, his name traveled through the crowd. "Buddy. Buddy. It's Buddy!"

Ella covered her mouth. Like the others of the small community, she knew Buddy. Her father looked up from where the body lay and came over to where she stood. "I told you to stay in the car," he said with a calmness that opposed the horror. He grabbed her by the arm and ushered her through the crowd. She could feel the intense pressure of his grip but she felt no pain. Her head was racing much too fast to feel anything but the dizzying ride of confusion. *Buddy. Damon. Where is Damon?'*

Once at the car, her father yelled at her to stay put. As her father walked back towards the lake Ella felt her legs weaken and she fell to the ground on all fours and began to cry. There was something about seeing Buddy lying on the shore. Something more than his death that gripped her. The very air around him, the expression left on his face seemed to speak to her, to tell her that this thing that put him there was not death, but conclusion. And it was this sense of conclusion, the act of abandonment and suddenly, the feeling of utter loneliness that caused the tears to stream down her face because she realized that Buddy was dead and Damon was gone and that all of it was her fault.

Four months later Ella had the baby. It would be the last child she would give birth to because her father told the visiting doctor to fix it so she couldn't have any more kids. In her father's eyes she was ruined because giving birth at fourteen meant having a man in her at thirteen, and this told him that she was undoubtedly a girl with a ruined spirit who would probably have more men inside her and more bastard children like the grandchild she gave him. She wouldn't know what had been done until the nurse who assisted the doctor explained to her the reason for the pain she had days after having given birth to her child. Then the nurse apologized, gave her pills to dull the pain, and left her in the stillness of her bedroom.

Ella's father had decided that she would have the child at home to escape prying eyes. And once the baby had come into the world, she looked at the dark soft face swaddled in her arms and thought of Damon.

The baby's arrival was problematic from the day it came out of Ella. The cord was wrapped around its neck and it struggled in the doctor's hands as no child had ever done before. Ella's family took to the baby each in their own way: Ren was disgusted by what his sister had done, but he enjoyed having the child around; Miriam found more reason to make clothes, and Emmanuel, well, he just looked at the child and walked away. In fact looking at the child and walking away was all he ever did over the baby.

Ella named the baby Daniel because it was the closest she could get to naming him Damon without giving away the name of the father. Within weeks little Daniel's name had spread throughout New Home as the townsfolk became enthralled with the unfolding drama of the child and the baby's daddy. Who was the father? Was the baby dark-skinned or light-skinned? Was it ugly or pretty? And just as important, would it survive Emmanuel's hatred of it.

At first Ella paid little mind to her father and the people of New Home. She would hold Danny close to her bosom and walk proudly up the street. However, after months of such foolishness, Ella, young and full of pride, had had enough. And that was when she bundled up her little boy and left her home, the hatred and the stares, and the prying eyes.

Since Ella left New Home, she had written only one letter to her family to let them know that she and the baby were fine and were living in Cincinnati; she gave them her mailing address, a post office box at the time, but no one ever wrote her back. It was enough to tell her that she was alone now with Danny and that it was up to her to make a life for the both of them and it was what she had done and had been doing, for all of the years since, with her son.

CHAPTER ELEVEN

"What are you writing now?" Mrs. Wexner asked impatiently, looking away from the TV to Ella.

"I'm filling out some health care forms for you and trying to get some of my notes done." Ella was sitting in the living room of Mrs. Wexner's apartment, scribbling out her notes as she and Mrs. Wexner ate lunch. She wanted to get some of her paperwork done because she knew she wouldn't be going back to the office. She had taken the rest of the day off so she could spend some time with Danny. She needed to see him. She had been having more of the dreams about New Home, the murder and about Danny's father. But this time she also dreamt about Danny. She dreamed that the doctor who delivered Danny took the same knife he used to sever her insides and quietly drew the knife across the baby's throat.

The dreams were beginning to come frequently and the memories of the past were lingering. Ella's nights were now half spent with restless sleep and the other half with sleeplessness. Usually the dreams and the memories would have subsided as they often did, or even diminished until their usual return months later, but this time they hadn't; in fact the dreams had risen to such a height that they no longer appeared as dreams, but as distant signals, a forewarning and it was why she needed to see Danny. It was time to tell him about his father.

Ella's head ached from another night of half-sleep as she looked at the pages of her notebook, and looking at the old lady sitting near her, her eyes felt raw. She reached down and lifted the cup of coffee to her mouth and took another sip, then a larger swallow.

The colors of Mrs. Wexner's living room seemed more brilliant than usual in the afternoon sun; the red, ivory and gold colors of the carpet and the furniture made the room radiate with light just as radiant as the heat the elderly woman had filling the apartment. In the background, Mrs. Wexner's aide moved around the large apartment busying herself with chores, stopping to answer some of Ella's questions about Mrs. Wexner's care, which would sometimes cause the elderly woman to quip that she was able to answer questions about her own life, thank you, but they both knew she couldn't.

"After I leave here I'm going to visit Danny," Ella said.

"Oh! Danny! How is he?" Mrs. Wexner turned to her again holding the TV remote. She had met Danny once many years ago when he and Milton came to pick up Ella. He was nine years old at the time and in Mrs. Wexner's mind he was still the same age.

"He's fine."

"Such a nice boy. We have to give you something sweet to take home to him, some candy, or cakes... Madelyn," she called out to her aide, "Do we have any cakes for Mrs. Pruitt to take home to her little boy?"

"Yes, we do," Madelyn replied in an attempt to assuage Mrs. Wexner.

"Well get one ready for Mrs. Pruitt to take with her."

"I will."

"Oh, and I'll give him some coins to put away in his bank."

"Thank you, Mrs. Wexner," Ella replied. It was the usual thing. Mrs. Wexner would give her the coins and Ella would return them to the aide before she left.

Ella went back to her paperwork and Mrs. Wexner turned back to watching the TV.

Suddenly Mrs. Wexner spoke. "Milton Pruitt." She turned to Ella. "They said his name. Milton Pruitt. Your husband, Ella." The elderly woman continued watching the news. "A foolish man, your husband," she said, her pale wrinkled hand wavering before the TV screen.

Ella looked up from the notebook in her lap to the TV screen. Milton was on the news with a group of ministers. He stood just behind the spokesman of the group.

"That is him, right?" Mrs. Wexner questioned.

"Yes," Ella mumbled.

"To think he should deny a people their right to live."

Ella hesitated before replying. "He's not denying anyone their right to live, Mrs. Wexner." Milton had told Ella about the meeting and they discussed whether or not he should be a part of the opposition. Until then they had lived quietly on the subject of same-sex rights because there had been no need to come out on it, pro or con. The matter only came up at home because of the incident with Danny and Deacon Samuels.

"Tell me then, what are they doing?"

"It's about funding," Ella hesitantly replied, aware that she was about to embark on a conversation she was unwilling to engage in. She had only slightly prepared herself for what she and Milton knew would be long discussions, even arguments with people about the stand the ministers had decided to take. "They're not saying the schools can't have groups like those, it's that they shouldn't be funded with taxpayers' money."

"Ah! It's more than that," Mrs. Wexner declared. "I've seen it before. People like your husband. They contrive messages to mask their true intent. I've seen it before," she repeated, "back in the old country." She turned to Ella. "I believe even if the funding was done through other sources they would still object. You know this, don't you?"

"I don't know that."

"Yes you do. You're married to him and you know of his intentions." Mrs. Wexner clicked her tongue. "Never mind," she said shooing Ella aside, "I think I now understand your position."

In fact Ella didn't know where she stood on the matter. She had told Milton that when he told her he wanted her to be at a meeting that night with the ministers and their wives as they met with the community. She told him it would be in conflict with her role as a social worker, but he insisted and she gave in. She would be there but she would remain quiet on the subject. She would much rather have preferred to not give any consideration to the subject even though it had been a bane in her life. She only knew it had caused her so much heartache and that maybe if it didn't exist things in her life might have been better. Those are the thoughts that crossed Ella's mind as she left Mrs. Wexner's apartment, past the photos of Mrs. Wexner and Greta.

After she left Mrs. Wexner's apartment, Ella called Danny to let him know she was on her way. She stopped by and got take-out for the two of them and headed to his apartment.

She pulled up to Danny's building and parked behind his car on the street. This would be her first time going inside of his apartment. Whenever she came she would wait outside for him to come out to the car, or if she was dropping him off she would do just that, but she never went inside. She was never sure what she might find if she went inside of her son's apartment. There were things she had learned over time to not see.

The building Danny lived in was an old Tudor style building whose paint had faded over the years and whose windows looked equally worn with the broken putty around the panes. The street Danny lived on was a long avenue that always seemed quiet, or maybe, given the shady activities that appeared to take place at either end of it, maybe his street was silent. That's what went through Ella's mind as she turned off the car. She sat for a moment to allow a young lady pushing a child in a fragile looking stroller whose wheels wobbled relentlessly over the sidewalk to pass, then she got out and cautiously looked around before locking the car door and walking up the uneven walkway to the front door. Pushing a bit to unstick the door, Ella opened it and stepped into the foyer. It was dimly lit and smelled of old mop water that had been hastily smeared over the dirty tile of the floor, leaving grit beneath her shoes. The building was more still than she had imagined. She had expected to hear the screaming of babies and yelling parents like she would hear when she visited some of her clients, there was nothing like that, nothing except for music coming from the first apartment. She recognized it as an old gospel song sung by Mahalia Jackson, 'How I Got Over'. She felt relieved to hear the music, thinking at least there was some-one there who was like her.

Danny appeared at the top of the stairs and called to her. "Hi Mom," he spoke as he came down to meet her. "I saw you drive up."

"Hi baby." She kissed him on the cheek then she nodded towards the apartment where the music was coming from and smiled.

"Oh, that's Mr. Stiggers," Danny said as he led the way up the stairs. "He's the old man I told you about. He just stays in his apart-ment all day and plays music. I think he's lonely or something."

"Is it always church music?"

"Yeah, pretty much," Danny said, giving it some thought. "I don't think he has a family or anything," Danny continued. "Or maybe they just forgot about him, you know, maybe he lived too long and they forgot about him. He's the one I usually drop off something to eat to make sure he's eating right."

"I still say God will bless you for that," Ella said as she climbed the stairs.

"Alright," Danny replied as he unlocked the door of his apartment.

Ella didn't respond.

"I'm heating up some soup," Danny said, opening the door and letting his mother step through. "I figure we could have some with the sandwiches you bought."

Ella looked around the apartment. It was cleaner than she had expected and much more orderly than she would've imagined. "This is nice, baby."

"Thanks," Danny said.

After the soup had heated, Danny brought her a bowl and sat it on the coffee table. Ella had found the couch more comfortable than the two rickety chairs that sat at the small kitchen table. He then made them coffee and brought in two steaming cups and sat them alongside their meal.

Their conversation tended towards general talk: how they were doing, friends of the family and such since Danny had no siblings to ask of and no family gossip about near relatives, and they tended to avoid talking much about Milton.

Ella continued to notice how quiet the building was. "Your neighbors seem respectful. I'm used to a lot going on when I visit buildings."

"Yeah, they are. It's a pretty cool place. Everybody's at work right now, but even when they're here it's still pretty cool."

"Why is your apartment so quiet," she asked, looking around.

"What do you mean? It's the way I like it."

She thought more about her question and realized that it wasn't the quietness of his place that called her attention, but rather a tugging absence of something that left his apartment mute, void of sound. It was a silence borne of emptiness.

"You don't listen to the radio or TV?"

"Sometimes, but not too much."

"Baby are you sure you're ok?"

Danny looked at his mother with surprise and laughed, "Yeah I'm ok. But it don't seem like you are. What's the matter?"

"It's you. I just worry over you." Even though she had told herself that this would be the day she would tell Danny about his father, she found herself once again unable to go through with it.

"Look I keep tellin' you not to."

"But I do. I can't help it."

"Yeah, but it's kinda insultin', you know?"

"How?"

Danny sat back on the couch. "It's like you just know I'm gonna get into trouble. Like you don't have faith in me."

"No, it's not that. It's just that…" her voice trailed.

"It's just what? That I'm going to be like my father, whatever he did. Because whatever he did I don't think it's right for you to judge me based on him."

"I know, I know. You're right." Ella sat in brief silence then she continued. "Danny, look, I know I've never told you about your father."

"No, you haven't. But I can tell how you react whenever he comes up that it's not good."

"Yeah," she said, nodding in agreement. "I never wanted to speak on your father. What he did."

"What are you talkin' about?" Danny locked his eyes on his mother. Ella wouldn't go on. "You have to tell me, Mom."

Ella breathed in and spoke the words as she exhaled. "Danny, your father…" she looked at her son as she gathered her words. "Your father killed a man."

"What?" The revelation made Danny sit up.

"He murdered someone."

"Shit," Danny whispered as he sat back once again on the couch. "Really?"

"I didn't want to revisit any of it," Ella said. "I wish I could… we could just go on and never have to talk about it."

Danny raised his eyebrows, still stunned by the revelation.

"He killed a man," Ella repeated. "He didn't just kill him. It was a brutal act. Something I never thought he could do. And then he ran."

"Brutal like how?"

"The man was beaten really bad and then," she stopped, her eyes welling with tears as she looked out into the room. "Your father, he put a belt around the man's neck and drug his body through the woods into a lake, and just left him there." She looked at her son sitting stunned on the couch and took his hand. "Danny, it's something I wish hadn't happened and I just wanted to keep it away from you."

"But why? Why would you keep that from me? It's something I need to know."

"You were so young—"

"That's when I was a little boy, Mom. I'm a man now and I need to know things like that."

"Would it have made much of a difference?"

"I don't know, but it was my right to know. He was my father."

They sat in the living room, the sunlight slowly leaving through the windows, neither of them speaking for a while.

"What was his full name?"

"Damon Scott. Your father's name is Damon Scott."

"He didn't have a middle name?"

She shook her head and fell back into silence. Then, "It's why I worry over you," Ella finally said. "I don't know… sometimes I wonder if you're going to be punished for something that your father did."

"That's crazy."

"I don't know. I just don't know. I've thought that for so many years, in the back of my mind. It's only when I would have dreams and memories of what happened that I would think about it more, but usually the dreams and all of the memories of those days would leave, they would go away for a while and I would feel fine. But now…"

"Now what?"

"Now, Danny they just keep coming. The dreams and the memories of what happened back then just keep coming. It's almost like they're trying to tell me something. Like they're demanding something." Ella squeezed her son's hand.

Danny pulled his hand from his mother's hands and stood up. "Mom, don't come in here with that mess. I'm fine. And all that karma shit, well, me and it ain't got nothing to do with each other. That's something he did, not me." He walked across the room and turned back around. "Where is he?"

"Your father?"

"Yeah."

"I don't know. He had to leave town after what he had done. And then, not long after he left I had you and then I had to leave."

"Why?"

"Because people were looking at me for, well…"

"Having a baby by him?"

She nodded her head, her eyes looking down to her hands. "That and they saw you as being nothing more than the baby of a murderer."

"Your family too?"

"Yeah."

Danny walked back over to the couch and sat down beside his mother. "Look, all I can tell you is I'm fine, Mom," he said putting his arm around her. "And that I can take care of myself."

"Would you let me know if you can't," Ella asked.

"Yeah. I would let you know if I can't."

The sun had gone down as Danny walked his mother downstairs. They had moved on from talking about his father and what happened back in New Home because spending too much conversation on it would only have made her visit deplorable. As they got to the first floor they heard the music coming from Mr. Stiggers' apartment, another gospel tune. Ella smiled as she looked at Danny then at the door of the man's apartment. "It's good what you're doing."

"Thanks," Danny said.

As they walked up to the front door the music stopped suddenly in mid-song. The hallway fell into the same dreadful silence as Danny's apartment. Danny put his arm around his mother and walked her to her car.

The minister council's meeting with the public had to be moved from a neighborhood community center to a private hall because the city decided it didn't want them to use city owned property for such a meeting, even though the ministers had named the meeting 'A Night Out with The People'.

The night had become chilly as people walked to the hall. The moon sat in a distant pocket of the sky and the air was still. The hall was already filling as Milton and Ella arrived.

Milton's eyes brightened as he watched the procession of interested citizens. He had been telling Ella on their way there to be ready to field questions. She said she expected as much but wondered what she would say.

"Just tell them the facts, that taxpayers' dollars shouldn't go towards funding gay rights. Just tell them the facts," he repeated.

The night turned out to be a fiery one with protestors as the ministers made their case. Milton stood before the microphone and railed at the audacity of a government body that would lend its support to something that he said was clearly not of the voice of the people of Cincinnati. He raised his hand and pointed towards the doors of the hall. "How many of our citizens are comfortable getting up each morning to go in to work and then to have to pay part of their hard-earned money to fund something they don't even believe in? Not many," he assured. "Not many."

Camera's flashed rapidly as he gestured.

Ella watched her husband, a brown, handsome man, as his face brightened and dimmed in the bursts of light.

"For some they see it as 'furthering equality'," he said with disdain. "But to many of those hardworking taxpayers, they see it as the moral decline of our society."

The crowd broke into applause amidst the flash of lights.

Afterwards the attendees mingled during the meet and greet. Most of the press had left with only some from a few newspapers remaining. Most of the ministers being interviewed were men. The women ministers, though few, were left to mingle with the wives of ministers.

Ella greeted people and engaged in lively conversation, but she made sure that she kept the conversation away from the topic that the ministers had addressed that night. It went well until one reporter, a woman who clearly wasn't a minister's wife or a person who might be interested in furthering the cause of the ministers approached her. The woman was the only person there in worn jeans and old, paint-splattered tennis shoes, and on her tattered sweater she had a button of Angela Davis and another one that had the words 'equality' written beneath a fist. The woman came to Ella with her notepad in her hand.

"Hi," she greeted.

Ella returned the greeting with some reservation. The two of them began to talk. The woman asked Ella some pointed questions.

Finally Ella ended the conversation by telling her, "Look, I'm a social worker. My job is to see that everyone gets a chance."

At that moment Milton walked upon the two women and immediately took over the conversation.

On the way home Milton spoke angrily to Ella.

"Why would you say something like that, Ella? Is that what you meant by agreeing to tell them the facts?"

"I didn't want to come to this meeting, Milton. You wanted me there. And yes Milton, those are the facts."

He turned on the radio and drove without speaking for a moment.

"You could've simply told the woman you had no comment," he finally said.

"But I did have a comment and I gave it."

"Well next time, don't."

CHAPTER TWELVE

The gravel crackled beneath Milton's shoes as he made his way to the gravesite. He raised his shoulders against the wind and climbed the hill to the small plot. On the other side of the cemetery, about forty yards or so away, his mother was buried, and somewhere else in the same cemetery his father was buried, each plot sitting alone, apart from the other. Milton had spent part of the morning trying to write a letter to Charlotte, but each version of the letter seemed less adequate than the one before. He needed something to incite in him the right words to say to his sister, something different than the ones he had written before or the words he spoke when he visited her. What he had said then were words that he knew couldn't address the pain his sister felt. He realized it as soon as he spoke them, telling her to turn her life over to Jesus and then how he had used words that artfully disclaimed her worth in the eyes of upstanding people. They had been words that came from his learning, but not from his heart. Looking back, he admitted that he had hoped, if anything, the words he had spoken to her would suffice, if only to allow him to move on from policing her and to distance himself from the narrative of his past. But the letters continued to arrive at his house every few months as his sister waited for a visit from him, or even a reply. Ella had told him that he had to give his sister something more substantial and it was why he came to visit the grave of Charlotte's little girl. He needed to understand everything that had happened. Everything. From Charlotte's birth to the death of her child.

The stone at the site was small. A square of pink granite polished and engraved with the baby girl's name, 'Taniya' with the middle name, 'Pauline', which was Milton's mother's middle name; a long graceful carving of ivy bordered the stone, and at the top of the stone, in the right hand corner a baby angel lingered with flowers in its hands.

Milton didn't know too much about the child because he wasn't given enough time to know her, but from what he could remember she was given to extreme anxiety. She cried a lot in agitation of things, yet she could also be extremely happy, always ready to laugh with a giggle that shook her whole body, and she took a special liking to Danny. Seeing Danny and Taniya together were the only times Milton could recall feeling good about his stepson.

Yet there was always a danger that surrounded the little girl. Charlotte had gotten deeper into drugs and alcohol and men who weren't good for her; the door to her apartment swung open constantly with men coming and going, crashing on her couch because they had no place to stay or sleeping in her bed because they needed someone into which they could release their confusion. He had watched his sister grow up. He watched her as a little girl as she would look with bewilderment at their father, and with wonderment at their mother; how she would hide behind Milton and cry as their father would abuse their mother and then, in the blink of an eye go back to playing with her dolls when the confrontations ended, all as if nothing had ever occurred. So it was no surprise when he saw her drift away from their mother and Milton after their father passed and she became a young lady. She hadn't become immune to what she had gone through, but she had learned to anesthetize her pain with distraction.

What bothered Milton more than anything about his sister's behavior was that his mother had to live to see it. She had to witness her daughter's slow descent and realize that the daughter was becoming like the father.

His mother died with a heart that had rare occasion to rejoice over much in her life. She was content because she never gave up on faith that there was something greater than the morass of a life she lived, and in her final days she smiled, her smile weakened by the toll of the cancer in her body, but Milton knew she never rejoiced.

Even at the funeral, Charlotte came with a man whom neither Milton nor his family had ever met. Both Charlotte and the man were worn, their skin like aged leather and their breath smelling like a concoction of alcohol and breath mints. The man lead Charlotte to the casket, where she cried and told the corpse that she was going to do better. The man nodded his head in agreement and whispered, 'yes', though both of them knew better than to trust their own words, they were just words of guilt sprayed on a dead body.

There was a time when Milton and Ella considered adopting Taniya. Charlotte had the baby some years after she and Milton's mother had passed. No one was ever sure who was the father. Milton and Ella sat at the dining room table a few months after the baby was born and discussed if they should adopt her. Danny had passed by and overheard them. "Yeah, I think you should adopt Taniya," he said as leaned in the entrance. "Aunt Charlotte, I love her but… I don't know…" he said as he shook his head and walked away. But they didn't and now the little girl lay in the ground beneath the polished pink stone with an angel holding flowers over her head.

How many of the people lying under the many stones in this garden languished while they were on this earth? A few yards away his mother lay; Milton knew her story, and here, at his feet, his niece lay. He had told Charlotte to give her life over to Jesus, but standing in this garden of stones and bones he wondered if it really mattered? His mother always had love for Jesus even throughout her suffering, even calling on Him under the fists of her husband; and poor Taniya, she never had a chance to give her life over to Jesus, having it taken instead by someone with more authority. Those were the thoughts that made Milton who he was. It was the pain and the anger that set him on his journey to understand God, and, if he would never understand God, maybe at least he could strike a bargain with Him; but as it were, what he had to do now was to make sure that what happened to his mother, his niece and his sister never happened again.

CHAPTER THIRTEEN

Abilyn came home that summer of her fourth year in college. She had broken the news to Granny and PawPaw. She was pregnant and she needed to come home. Abilyn's belongings had arrived at the house the day before she arrived, brown boxes with her handwriting across them. PawPaw had stood for a long while looking at the boxes on the porch, staring at them and the white labels with Abilyn's script before moving the boxes to her bedroom. Granny and PawPaw had driven the sixty miles to the airport to pick Abilyn up. When she walked through the gate she looked smaller than when she left. And darker, dimmed, as if the light in her the day she waved goodbye to them as she left for school had been extinguished. The three of them hugged, each one cautious to not linger too long in their embrace because they didn't want to show the fear and the disappointment they each felt.

The ride home from the airport was long and with few words. Granny and PawPaw sat in the front seat and Abilyn sat in the back watching the vast Oklahoma plains roll by.

Over the days after Abilyn's return words finally started to come back between Abilyn and her parents. Abilyn and Granny talked about what had been going on in Tarpley since Abilyn left and Abilyn and PawPaw mostly talked about the news he heard on the radio and watched on the television. For the most part they hadn't spoken about the pregnancy until a few days had passed. Abilyn hadn't started to show and she was early in her first trimester so there was still a chance to make a decision about keeping the baby. The news of her pregnancy was devastating to her parents not only because of her leaving college but because of the risk of her having a child. No one had ever discussed her having a baby before, with all of the visits to her doctor when she was growing up, because she was just too young for any talk like that. All they knew was she had a heart condition and shouldn't overtax it.

Every now and then PawPaw would interject something about her finishing school, but he never spoke about the pregnancy. He left that to Granny and Abilyn. As far as PawPaw was concerned the man who got his daughter pregnant was nothing more than the fluids he left in Abilyn and the money he had given her to make sure the baby never came into the world.

Granny and Abilyn spent time alone in Abilyn's bedroom behind closed doors, talking about what Abilyn had been through. That was when Granny first heard Milton's name. She took an immediate dislike to his name and even more to him when she heard about the affair. He was older than Abilyn and he was married. This made Granny feel even more disappointed in Abilyn, to be the other woman. Milton became even more despicable to Granny when she found out he was a minister. It was something that set PawPaw off when he found out because he had never trusted ministers. He always took ministers with side-eyed skepticism. Abilyn confessed though, that the relationship she and Milton had was just as much her decision as his. In fact, Abilyn still held that it wasn't a decision to have the relationship because it just happened. It was the decision not to call it off that she didn't make sooner. She told her mother how the relationship started off as friendly and how it just somehow became more. Granny sat on the bed with Abilyn as she listened to her. She listened to her daughter all the while looking out of the window just beyond the bed watching the leaves on the tree outside Abilyn's bedroom and the blue sky, so blue and deep, and the two clouds that spread across the sky as if they had been combed into wisps across the blue, looking at nothing at particular, listening to her daughter, understanding her, and not wanting anything her daughter was telling her to be true. After she had listened to Abilyn's story Granny turned back from the window and the green tree and the bluest of blue skies with the two clouds swept across it and she asked, 'Now what?' What was Abilyn going to do? The question took grit for her to ask of Abilyn because Granny wasn't sure what her daughter should do. Abilyn had sighed and told her mother she didn't know.

Weeks of not acting to end the pregnancy answered the question Abilyn's parents had asked of her. She would have the child. Granny and PawPaw accepted their daughter's decision and spent the rest of the nine months worried. Since the pregnancy Abilyn's doctor had confirmed the challenge she might have giving birth, but Abilyn stood firm. She told her parents she had faith that everything would turn out fine and that they would have a grandchild.

The months that followed Abilyn's return home she went back to work at the job she had left when she headed off to school. Things were going well. She told her parents she would continue her studies at the University of Oklahoma once she had the baby and things would be fine. She had come around to choosing names for the baby. If it was a boy his name would be Ernest, named after her father, and if it was a girl she would name her Nadine, after her mother. Granny told her Nadine sounded too old so they decided on Natasha. There was never any mention of Milton being in the baby's life and he would most likely never know that the child he didn't want to exist did.

That was what Granny told Natasha and it was what came to Natasha's mind as she listened to LaShon give his reason for standing behind Milton and the ministers against the school board. She listened as LaShon declared the ministers to be men of God. She listened to him while the two of them were sitting in a bar where LaShon usually hung out, a bar down a side street where he prayed that he would never be found by anyone in his church. She listened and she thought about Granny's telling of Milton. She thought about how absent Milton had been when Abilyn took her last breath. There was no sign of him except for the fluids he left in her mother and the money he had given her mother to make sure Natasha never came into the world. She listened and she remembered the story.

Everything looked fine the day Abilyn went into labor. Her visits to the doctor had been with concern, yet the doctor had said she looked to be in good health other than her heart, and even her heart was doing as well as could be expected.

It was a little after three in the morning when Abilyn went into labor. At nine-ten that same morning her little girl came into the world, the same time Abilyn left.

~~~~

Longing for companionship is the mark of a lonely soul. That was never the case with Danny. He was usually alone when he was growing up but he was never lonely. He never yearned for friendship or was ever in need of a companion of any type, and aside from his mother, he spent much of his time by himself. But instead of being a lonely boy, Danny was simply a solitary figure. He never had the feeling of being connected to anyone other than his mother. And though he preferred things to be that way because it made navigating his solitary world more reasonable, still the notion of having no one else he could feel connected to spooked him.

Ella told him that Milton was his father, but he knew from the distance he and Milton had whenever their eyes met that the man he called 'daddy' simply wasn't. Besides, Milton looked out of place whenever he stood beside Ella and even more awkward in the photos Danny would see of the three of them together in portraits that sat on the tables and that hung from the wall. In the photos Milton would be sitting, shoulders squared and strong eyed and Ella would be sitting alongside him, with a grateful smile, and behind them stood little Danny, with a smile that was disconnected by the blank look in his eyes.

Danny's life had disembarked long ago from that place of relevance, where folks told you who you are, where you knew them as grandparents, or as aunts and uncles or as cousins or even your father. Instead, long before he could recall, Danny's life had been set adrift in uncertainty, enshrouded in secrecy and it was the uncertainty that turned into confusion and it was the confusion that turned into the anger that fed him and pressed him into becoming a solitary figure.

The thing about living in solitary spaces is that the solitary space becomes a canvas, open to one's own imaginings, and it takes a unique disposition to fill that space. Danny had just the disposition needed to fill solitude; there were things he did that were kind and generous, and other things that were horrific, from creating 'I Love You' cards to give to his mother to the things he did with the insects. His interest in disassembling insects started when he captured a butterfly one day. He held the butterfly by one of its wings and watched it as it struggled to free itself, its one wing beating violently against the air. Danny watched the bug, its brown body and its wings that were a brilliant white with light green trim around the edges. He felt triumphant that he had captured the butterfly, but the butterfly's relentless struggle challenged him, threatening to escape if he let it go, diminishing the sense of victory Danny felt. So it came to him that capturing the insect wasn't enough, that to truly feel victorious he had to win over the butterfly's threat to escape, to stop the battering of the lone wing that beat against his fingers. He had to stop it to claim victory over the animal so he brought the bug to his face, took hold of the free wing of the butterfly and then moving the butterfly to his ear, he pulled until he heard the snap of the wing, disengaging it from the butterfly's body. Mortally wounded, the butterfly lashed violently about from the one wing until finally, it stopped, and hung lifelessly by the limp wing Danny held between his fingers. A sense of accomplishment rose in Danny and he smiled. The single act he had just committed not only bestowed upon Danny the role of victor, but it also bestowed upon the limp insect hanging from his fingers the unfortunate status of becoming a trophy, a symbol of Danny's accomplishment, and that being the case the insect was too special to just toss away. So Danny respectfully laid it in the grass along the fence in the far corner of the backyard. In time he would have so many of these accomplishments over butterflies, grasshoppers, and dragonflies, that he had to make a small clearing alongside the fence in which to place his trophies.

No one knew of Danny's secret except his aunt Charlotte, his stepfather's sister. One weekend Charlotte had been asked to watch over Danny while Ella and Milton were away at a church convention. It was a time when Charlotte had only just begun to decline, so her descent was barely noticeable and subtle enough for Ella to trust her with Danny.

Danny had always liked Charlotte because he saw the wounds she carried in her that expressed themselves in the nervous, almost constant movement of her hands, the quick sharp laugh she would elicit at the slightest form of humor, and the incessant arguing she engaged in with Milton or anyone who she felt might threaten whatever long-term thought she entertained. Danny saw these wounds and he understood them, even if he couldn't explain them. That weekend Danny and Charlotte laughed a lot and played games and watched shows on TV that he wouldn't have been allowed to watch if Ella and Milton had been home, and they ate food that he knew his mother and his stepfather wouldn't have approved of. He liked Charlotte and because he did he felt he could show her his collection.

"Charlotte, I wanna show you something," he said that Saturday as they were eating hot dogs and watching a film about a woman who ripped through bodies of the men who had raped her in a bar. At first Charlotte didn't want to go with him because she was engrossed in the movie, but at his insistence she stopped the videocassette and went with him to the back yard. When they got to the site, Danny stood back and pointed at the ground. "Look," he said, grinning with pride.

At first Charlotte couldn't tell what Danny was pointing at, but as she bent over to get a closer look her face changed from curiosity to shock. "Boy what are you doing? You can't be goin' around doin' that to no animals. I mean, even though they're just bugs, still you shouldn't be doin' that." She looked at the wings spread along the ground. "And you even killed butterflies! How could you kill something so pretty as butterflies?" She made Danny promise not to kill any more butterflies and he promised. He would never again kill another butterfly.

The snap Danny heard the first day he took the wing off the butterfly now came as a muffled pop as he pulled the man's shoulder from its socket. Littlejohn held the man down and gagged his mouth so no one could hear the screams. They left the man in a field in the trunk of the man's car.

"See? That's the kind of shit we do for Cortez and he don't even give us anything extra," Littlejohn said as they sat in a bar afterwards. They had finished the only job Cortez had for them so they had the rest of day off. Littlejohn spoke low enough so they wouldn't be overheard by the men and women at the next table, "And this is why I think we should be more than just employees, y'know man. I mean, who else would do the kind of shit we do for him?"

The ski masks they wore for the job had been tucked in the pockets of their coats. Danny self-consciously put his hand into the pocket of his coat that hung on the back of his chair to make sure the mask wasn't exposed. "I see your point," he said as he nodded his head slightly.

"That's why you have to talk to him. You goin' over there tonight?"

"Maybe. I don't know."

"You should. That way you can talk to him." Littlejohn grinned and tapped Danny on the arm. "Do it when y'all 'bout to get busy. You know." He grinned again and nudged Danny.

"Man shut up."

"For real though. That's when you should talk to him. It's when I talk to old girl and she does the same shit to me."

"I'll talk to him."

"Good. Because we deserve more."

Danny understood where Littlejohn was coming from. They had been through a lot together. He remembered the apartment they shared after they had gotten out of jail. Neither of them had a place to go when they got out. The woman who Littlejohn had lived with no longer wanted him around and Danny had lost the apartment Ella had gotten him after Milton kicked him out of the house. He and Littlejohn had been staying in a home run by an urban gospel mission whose only requirements were that they look for employment, attend church service and sell candy and bottled water on the streets to raise money for the church. It wasn't until Littlejohn remembered a man he knew who owned a few apartments that their situation changed.

"I know this dude, this white man, who owns some apartments in Over-the-Rhine," Littlejohn said, waving a bottle of water in the air. He and Danny walked along the median of a busy boulevard hawking the bottles of water and candy.

"For real?"

"Yeah. Me an' him was talkin' and he told me he had a place we could stay in for almost nothin'."

"Where at in Over-the-Rhine?"

"Why you care? We ain't got no place and this selling shit for that preacher ain't doin' nothin' for us."

Danny laughed. "You wrong about that. I'm gonna become a CEO *and* make it to heaven with this shit."

"C'mon man. We need to get the fuck outta that church. Ol' Rev is just pimpin' us."

"Ok. How much dude askin'?"

"A hundred twenty-five a month."

They took the man up on his offer and moved into the tiny apartment. It wasn't until they had been there for a week that Danny discovered the owner, who lived on the first floor, had frequent visits from Littlejohn. After one of the visits Danny asked Littlejohn what was going on and it's when Littlejohn told him he was letting the man suck his dick every once in a while to keep the rent down. Then he opened a bottle of beer, kicked off his shoes and sat on the couch to watch a game on TV.

"But now he wants me to fuck him. I told him about you."

"What?"

"Shit, I figure you probably better at that than me."

With Danny fucking the man their rent was reduced and even overlooked some months. That went on until they met Cortez.

Yeah, Danny thought, they did deserve more.

"My mom told me who my old man is," Danny said, changing the subject.

"For real?"

Danny nodded, "Yeah. His name is Damon. Or was. She don't even know if he's still alive."

"So she don't even know where he is, huh?"

"Nah."

"Just did his thang and cut out, just like my old man did." Littlejohn shook his head as he took a drink.

"It wasn't like that with him, though. Or at least it don't seem that way. He had to leave."

Littlejohn looked at him in anticipation of the rest of the story. Danny leaned over to him, "He killed a man so he had to leave town."

"Oh shit," Littlejohn exclaimed quietly. "Then you got it in your blood, man."

"I guess so." He looked at Littlejohn, then over to the people at the next table, before turning back to his buddy who sat grinning. "I guess so," Danny repeated.

"Damn," Littlejohn said, feeling proud to be his friend. "A real gangsta."

They drank a bit longer, listening to the music coming out of the jukebox and watching the other people in the bar before Littlejohn continued. "So I guess that means now you really wanna know who your old man is, huh? This ain't - - I mean, you ain't gonna let that get in the way of you askin' Cortez about makin' us partners are you?"

"Uh uh. I don't think it's that important to know that much about my old man."

"Right," Littlejohn goaded. "They all alike so why bother? I mean you got a father, well a man who raised you and took care of you and your mom—real good care, so why should your real father matter?"

"Yep," Danny agreed as he raised the glass to his mouth and took a swig.

They threw back a few more drinks and headed from the bar.

"So you gonna talk to him, right? Littlejohn wanted more assurance as they stood beside their cars. They talked as they watched people walking along the street to make sure no one would recognize them for the work they did.

"Nigga, you got one more time to ask me that. I said I would."

"You goin' over there tonight?"

"I don't know." He looked at Littlejohn, who cocked his head. "Okay. Yeah. I'll go over there tonight."

"Cool," Littlejohn said.

CHAPTER FOURTEEN

The first time Ella did it she was in the bathtub. It was a Saturday night and she was taking her third bath of the day. During the summer she took more than one bath because of the perspiration from the sweltering Ohio summers and because there wasn't much more for her to do. Since her mother died she found she didn't have anyone to talk to; her sister was younger than her and her brother didn't seem to care about what she thought about so her days in summer were spent straightening up the house, rearranging small things around the house, like vases and curios and an occasional chair because the stultifying days took on something new when she would place a vase in a different location in the house and fill it with flowers. Her father understood what she was doing and why so he would smile and tell her how nice things looked. As far as friends she had only one, Sarah, who lived several blocks over. They would see each other from time to time in the summer when they were away from school, or whenever Sarah's parents would let her venture the several blocks to visit Ella because everyone knew Emmanuel wouldn't allow Ella to go farther than the street they lived on. He knew Ella was growing and it frightened him. He didn't have a wife to calm him with an explanation of the ways of a girl's growth into womanhood so all he felt he could do was to protect her from the noses of the boys her age who were beginning to sniff around.

The days of summer went lazily by for Ella and that Saturday had been no different so she took her last bath of the day before going to her room and reading before falling asleep. She sat in the tub soaking in the warm water that had turned an opalescent white from the bar of soap that sat at the bottom of the tub. Ripples glided along the water from a drip from the faucet and disappeared around her body. She could hear her father watching TV as the sound of the music and the voices rose through the floor. It was around ten o'clock so he was watching his favorite detective show, 'Mannix'; he had stopped watching shows that made him laugh after her mother died. In one of the bedrooms down the hall she heard her sister's radio playing. Her brother was most likely in front of the TV with her father. The window of the bathroom was open just over the tub and Ella listened to the crickets singing and every once in a while she could hear a car roll down the quiet avenue in front of their house.

Her body was beginning to shape itself in a way that excited her: her breasts were rounding out and her hips had become slightly wider than before but not near as wide as some of her classmates because she had always been a small girl, but they pushed at the sides of her jeans to the point that soon she would have to start buying jeans that were made for girls her age. She understood why her father was becoming unsettled with each day that he saw the changes in her and she felt sorry for him when he would sometimes look at her and turn his head away in sadness but for her it was a joyous time in her life even though she didn't know what she would do with what she was discovering about herself.

The water had become even more clouded and had begun to cool, so Ella took the bar of soap from the bottom of the tub and began to bathe, moving the washcloth over her skin, stopping to take her soapy fingers and gently rub her nipples that stood erect from her touch. It was when she began to wash between her thighs that her interest piqued. Before that night she hadn't had much interest in what was beyond the outer layer of skin between her legs except for the need to wash herself, but this night thoughts filled her head and gently suggested that there was more to this body of hers that was changing, so she began to explore, guilelessly moving her hands between her thighs and it was that night that Ella discovered the secret that would make her father turn his head in sadness.

But Damon's hands were different than hers. They were larger and rougher and they filled the space between Ella's legs much more than her own that afternoon as they lay on the blanket in a clearing in the woods near the house Damon shared with his aunt. The two of them lay half clothed, Damon with his shirt open and his pants and shorts halfway down his legs and Ella with her blouse undone, her skirt lifted and her panties around one of her ankles. She watched Damon's face as it hovered over hers and heard him talking to her. A bug flitted past Damon's head as he whispered to her and behind him there was a canopy of green and spotted sunlight. He was gentle with her that afternoon just like he told her he would be and that he only wanted to touch her, nothing else. They had been meeting secretly for a little over two months with Ella telling only her sister about him and her sister promising not to tell their father about Ella having a boyfriend. To Ella and Miriam it was romantic that Ella would have a boyfriend, but over the weeks Ella had begun to realize that her feelings had become deeper than merely romantic.

Damon kissed her softly and then sucked on her nipples that had until then only been touched by her own fingers, and he kissed her again, holding his mouth to hers as he moved his large finger in gentle circles between her legs, moving his penis along her thigh. As she shook in his arms he held her tight to his chest then neither of them said anything else. They only smiled and looked into each other's eyes.

After lying together for a while longer she told him she had to go. She knew her brother would be returning from a day out with his buddies and would tell her father if he found out she had been leaving the area of the street that had been set for the girls.

Ella and Damon walked silently along the path that led to the edge of the woods, holding hands and looking at each other every now and then. Finally, as they got to the spot where they would separate Damon told her, "I want to see you tonight."

She looked questioningly at him. "How? You can't."

"I need to."

"My father... how?"

Damon shook his head. "I'll figure it out."

"No. I don't want to get in trouble. I'll be back tomorrow."

He looked at her for a moment then nodded, "Okay."

That night Ella couldn't sleep. Everyone else was asleep and the house was quiet except for the soft chime of the grandfather clock in the vestibule. A night breeze came through Ella's bedroom window and she watched the curtains softly dance on the breeze. She thought about Damon and what happened that afternoon. She had gained a knowledge she never had before. It was as if she had suddenly become someone different, no longer the little girl her father wanted her to remain but the other person he tried to keep her from finding.

She felt both privileged and frightened because she wasn't sure what to do with what she now knew. But she had confidence in Damon. He was older and larger and more wise than she was, and most of all he loved her just as much as she loved him, so she felt he would be the one who would guide her and protect her. She rolled onto her side and thought about seeing Damon again the next day.

It was about an hour later when Ella thought she heard something in the yard below. She wasn't sure, but it sounded like the rustling of grass or maybe it was the rustling of clothing. Then the sound stopped but her ears had piqued and she heard what she thought was breathing. At first Ella thought she was imagining things, because surely she wouldn't be able to hear breathing from such a distance. Then she realized it was in her head: the sound of movement, the breathing, and now she heard a beating heart and she felt the closeness as if Damon was standing near. She held herself for a moment and thought about him and how awful it was to have to wait to see him again the next day. But the breathing and the beating of his heart continued in her head so loudly that it caused her to sit up and look towards the window. Getting out of bed she walked over to the window and looked down into the backyard and there he stood, Damon, half-hidden behind the large maple in the back yard. The moon caught his dark skin and made it shine against the night.

Ella covered her mouth in shock. "Damon! What, what are you doing here?" she whispered.

He stepped from behind the tree and walked to just beneath her window and whispered, "I need to be with you."

"You're going to get both of us in trouble."

Damon didn't say anything, but just stood looking up at her.

"Oh my God," Ella whispered as she left her window.

Ella's legs were weak from fear as she tipped through the hallway past her father's bedroom and down the stairs where she let Damon in through the back door. "My father will kill both of us," she said as Damon stepped inside.

They walked quietly through the house and up the stairs to Ella's room. Ella's heart beat wildly with fear thinking that at any second one of the bedroom doors would open as someone went to the bathroom and she and Damon would be spotted, but she couldn't let go of Damon's hand.

"You can't stay the night," she told Damon as she closed the door to her bedroom and locked it.

"I know," he said as he kissed her. Then he lifted her pajama shirt over her head and smiled. "I know," he repeated as he continued to kiss her and went down to her nipples, sucking them softly. She held his head to her chest, feeling the soft wooliness of his hair and his face press harder against her body. He slid her bottoms down and she stepped out of them. Then he raised his arms and pulled his tee shirt over his head and undid his belt and slid his pants and underwear down and stepped out of them. It was Ella's first time seeing Damon naked. She looked at him, tall, long and dark standing against the moonlight, and she walked up to him and held him close.

That was the night that Ella let Damon enter her. She was a bit scared at first because she didn't know what to expect, but at the same time she wanted him inside of her because she felt he belonged there. At first it hurt a little, but Damon was gentle, firm but gentle, and in a while Ella relaxed as the pain left and she gasped as Damon made his way inside of her, his fullness filling her in a way she had never experienced.

Afterwards they lay with Damon holding her in his arms. She wasn't sure what she felt about herself. In just a few minutes Damon had taken from her the girl she once was and had given her something she wasn't sure she was ready to receive. She wasn't sure of this new person who was lying in Damon's arms, and she wasn't sure what to think about this transformation of her body that lay on twisted wet sheets. She wasn't sure what to think, but she knew she felt secure in Damon's arms. The feelings she experienced of having Damon deep inside of her, filling her up, the movement, slow and deliberate, of seeing Damon's eyes gaze into her own and of hearing the heaviness of his breath in her ear, the whispers, the both of them moving together in her bed, slowly, determined to become one with each other because they loved each other. Yes, they loved each other. *He loved her and he belonged to her. He was hers and she was his.* All of this excited Ella and she would continue to lay with Damon for months to come.

Those were the things Ella didn't tell Danny about her and his father, but of what she did tell Danny, Ella hoped it would make his life better. Until now, the incidents that led up to his birth weren't stories she shared with anyone, and to her knowledge no one outside of New Home probably knew the story, and if time served her well even the people of New Home might have forgotten. Maybe. She had hoped that moving away from New Home would allow her to start her life over, and even though she had wanted to start it over with Damon, settling in Cincinnati and meeting Milton was the blessing she hadn't expected. She couldn't imagine where she might be now if she had stayed on that bus heading west. Probably holed up somewhere in a small apartment in Missouri or some small town in Kansas, looking out over the city wondering what Damon was up to. Damon had proven he was no good for her, yet her insides still fluttered sometimes when she thought about him.

"Lord have mercy," Ella whispered to herself. "Everything's going up." She walked down the aisle of a grocery store picking out what she would need for the Christmas dinner. It was just two weeks away. She was grateful that Danny agreed to come to the dinner. And she was pleased that she had begun to invite Danny into the story they shared.

Ella had always known that she would tell Danny about his real father but she wanted to wait until Danny was older before she told him because she couldn't figure out how to tell a young child that he was born out of wedlock. She couldn't understand how other mothers did it. In her line of work she saw it all the time; these women did it and went on with their business but she wasn't like that, she had character, her father had given his children a sense of character, which was why she knew how it must have stung her father when he found out she was pregnant and it was what led him to have the doctor do what he did to her to make sure she wouldn't become that way again. No one had asked her if she wanted to have it done because she was just a girl and had no say in the matter. She wasn't even aware of it until she awoke. Even though she was just a girl, she felt her father had made a decision over something that was hers, not his, not the doctor's or anyone else's. Now, though decades later, she could still feel a dull pain in her abdomen where the men had acted against her.

But what's done is done. That's what Ella had to tell herself in order to move on. It's done and there was nothing she could do to undo it. Now her attention was on the only child who would ever come from her. It was his life that she had to salvage.

She wished she had been more forthcoming with Danny when he was younger, not in the way those other women do with brutal honesty, but in a way that he would have understood and that would leave him feeling fine with himself. Maybe if she had told him sooner he would have felt like he belonged somewhere and wouldn't have been that boy she saw growing up: alone, dark and full of venom.

Telling Danny only part of the story satisfied Ella and she hoped it would satisfy him as well because he needed to feel satisfied so he could come back into the fold and be the son she hoped he would be. She was relieved to finally invite someone else into the story.

When she finished shopping she headed out to her car. The evening was cold and damp and the sky was dark with a ribbon of gray at its edge as the remaining daylight slowly disappeared from the city. She walked across the lot, pushing the shopping cart across the wet pavement, and wondered what Damon might be doing, or if he was even still alive.

CHAPTER FIFTEEN

Milton thrust the cup into the bag of ice melt and began spreading the particles along the path he had cleared to the house. He waited until late into the afternoon to shovel the snow because the forecasters had predicted another fall by evening, but now they were saying it would only be flurries. Ella was getting the kind of evening she wanted, he thought, as he walked along the driveway. She was running around the house right now cooking and prepping the rooms where the guests would be.

Milton grunted disapprovingly as he walked along the driveway spreading the mixture. He wasn't pleased that she had asked Danny to come. Even though he was ready to bury the hatchet with Danny, he still wasn't happy with him being at the dinner or even in the house. It was as if Ella actually expected him to buy into that "love the sinner, but hate the sin" mess, just because he was a minister. The mantra itself was bothersome and even more if he was expected to live by it.

As he got to the street, Milton looked back at the clearing he had made to the house and in the distance he saw the gazebo sitting in the far corner of the backyard. It sat finished with its slate roof angling skyward and a necklace of glass bulbs draped along it that would be lighted for the dinner that night. He shook his head slightly as he looked at it. He knew that Ella was right to let go of what happened, but it was difficult to forget, and seeing the gazebo sitting bejeweled in the backyard made it even harder to forgive.

Milton knew Ella liked gazebos, he figured it was probably flamed by romantic memories she had of New Home, and it was why he decided to build a gazebo for her in the backyard, to help her adjust to the fact that she might never return to her home. It was his gift to her and to make it even more of a gift he had included Danny in on the construction. That spring he and Danny worked tirelessly putting the structure together. For a while the work on the gazebo brought peace to the home. Overjoyed, Ella would bring sandwiches and freshly squeezed lemonade out to Milton and Danny, her face glowing more from seeing Milton and Danny working together than the gift of the gazebo itself; he and Danny would talk and sometimes even laugh as they lifted boards and hammered nails. Milton showed Danny how to use certain tools and Ella watched them from the kitchen window, Danny watching Milton and nodding his head as he listened to Milton's instructions.

It was about a month into the building of the gazebo when Milton came home to pick up some papers he had left that he saw it. The gazebo had been built, and all it needed was the lattice work along the ground and painting. As he went into the kitchen to get something to eat, he noticed Danny standing at the bottom of the gazebo on the far side in the shadows of the trees. Milton stood for a second and adjusted his sight as he looked out of the window across the large backyard to make sure it was the back of Danny's head he saw and it was, and he was talking to someone. 'The boy's skipping school', Milton thought to himself. Milton opened the back door and called Danny as he made his way across the lawn. Danny turned, startled to see him and there was sudden movement on the other side of the gazebo. "Milt," Danny called out as if to caution Milton from approaching, but when Milton got to where Danny was standing he saw Danny buckling his pants and there on the ground with his pants half up was Deacon Samuels. Deacon Samuels began to cry, "Oh Lord! Oh Lord," as he crumpled in a ball on the ground. He begged Milton and God to forgive him. He covered his face with his hands, sobbing and pleading for forgiveness. The sight of the man, older than Milton, lying in a ball in the grass, his flabby ass hanging out, sobbing like a child with his hands over his face was a pathetic sight that disgusted Milton so much that Milton yelled at him. "Get up! Get up now, dammit!" Deacon Samuels slowly uncovered his face. "Pull up your goddamned pants," Milton instructed. He turned his head away as the deacon stood before him uncovered and began to pull up his shorts and his pants. "Pastor, I'm sorry. I'm sorry," Deacon Samuels said. "Just shut up and go," Milton instructed. Deacon Samuels walked from the yard like a child about to face punishment.

He adjusted his clothes and wiped his face so as to appear decent before he made it to the street. All during the confrontation Danny had been standing there watching without intervening, not even with a single word, but watching; then, with cool calm, he walked back to the house.

Ella cried when Milton told her what happened and she confronted Danny, who had little to say as if there wasn't much to say beyond the obvious, but for Ella it meant much more and for some days afterwards she shut herself in her bedroom for hours at a time, not wanting to talk to either Milton or Danny. In time she and Milton talked about what had happened and she told him she didn't know what to do but pray, but Milton felt Danny had defiled their home and since Danny showed no remorse-- for god's sake he didn't even apologize for his behavior or who he was found out to be-- Milton figured it was best that Danny leave as soon as he graduated from school that year. He told Ella that Danny's attitude was the very nature of sin coming in search of destroying things God had set forth, but Ella wouldn't hear of it and she told Milton that she wasn't going to put her son out into the streets with no place to go.

For weeks the gazebo sat unfinished until Milton decided to complete it. He had begun to work on it again and soon Danny went out to help as if the events that had occurred hadn't, but things weren't as they had been when the two of them first started on the gazebo. It was only a day later that Milton and Danny had the fight and Danny left home.

Milton closed up the bag of ice melt and put it in the corner of the garage. Only a few neighbors had shoveled their walkways. He was glad he had gotten it done before the next snowfall. He closed the garage door and went into the house.

Only a few flurries fell the night of the dinner. Each flake drifted on a solitary quest to join the flakes that had fallen before it and they settled along the blanket of snow on the ground as the guests made their way to Ella and Milton's house.

Natasha walked from the car with LaShon. The both of them carried dishes that Natasha had made. She had been told she didn't have to bring anything, but the days leading up to the dinner had compacted itself into a ball of nervous energy until she had to cook to ease the tugging in her chest. As she turned from the street and started up the walkway to the house, a thought illuminated in her, it was the thought that had been working its way up in her all of the days since she found out she was invited to the dinner, *'You're not supposed to be here,'* it said. It was the word 'here' that rang the loudest in her head because she knew it didn't mean 'here' at Milton and Ella's house, even though she held some reservation about coming, but it meant she shouldn't even have lived at all if Milton had had his way. Before, that understanding that she hadn't been meant to live had been acknowledged, but only in the way something long accepted is acknowledged, as an impression that never demanded much consideration. Before, she had Granny and PawPaw to render any such thoughts inconsequential. They had provided her with the life those who are loved needed, a life that tells them that they are wanted, that there's a place in that circle of family that was reserved for them, but in the last few days that understanding had begun to ask for reckoning, yet Natasha had covered that request with work, school and baking so it never took hold until now.

The house sat only steps from her, with bright windows glowing in the night and tiny Christmas lights that blinked around the trim of the house all reflecting off the soft down of snow. Through the windows Natasha could see guests in the warmly lighted rooms, talking and moving about. She searched the heads framed in the windows for Milton's presence and she saw him. Suddenly the cobbler she carried in her hands began to shift as her hands began to tremble. As she came closer to the house she slowed her pace to allow LaShon to walk a bit ahead of her.

Noticing this, LaShon looked back. "Girl, come on. I told you you're invited. They know you're coming."

Taking a breath, Natasha walked with LaShon to the door.

Ella greeted LaShon and Natasha at the door, pressing her cheek to theirs. "You know you didn't have to make anything," she said to Natasha. "There's way plenty food here tonight."

"I just wanted to bring something. I love to cook anyway," Natasha said.

LaShon handed his dish to Ella. "I told her," he said as he looked into the living room towards the guests.

"The kitchen's right here," Ella said as she led Natasha through the foyer past the living room and dining room.

Natasha gave a quick sideward glance and saw Milton sitting on the arm of a sofa listening to a man who was talking to him and a few others. She saw Milton look her way. "You have a lovely home," Natasha said, turning to Ella, searching for conversation.

"Thank you. It's about time to do some work on it. We've been here a long time."

"How long?"

"Almost twenty-three years."

"Old houses are built to last. My grandparents' home was almost a hundred."

Two women came into the kitchen carrying platters and began working with the food. Ella introduced them to Natasha.

"Where are you from," Ella asked. "You might have told me, but I forget."

"Oklahoma."

"Oklahoma," one of the women repeated. "I've never known any black folks from Oklahoma."

Natasha chuckled, "I hear that a lot out here. But if you lived out west you wouldn't think that."

At that moment Danny came into the kitchen carrying an empty bowl. "Mom we're out of dip." He sat the bowl on the counter.

"We just put that dip out there," one of the other women declared. "We better hurry up and get this food out there before they fill themselves up on appetizers."

"Yeah," Ella agreed. "Oh, Natasha, this is my son Danny. Danny, Natasha."

Natasha and Danny shook hands. "Pleased to me you," Danny said.

"Me too."

Ella filled another bowl and Danny left the kitchen. Natasha watched him walk away and again thought of her place in this family.

"Seeing that boy here is such a surprise," one of the women said. The other woman nodded in agreement. "I wish he would come on back to church. Too good looking to let all that go to waste out there in those streets."

"Let all what go to waste, Patsy?" the other woman asked mischievously.

The women in the kitchen laughed.

"I bet you could get him back in church," one of the women said to Natasha. "You see the way he looked at her?"

"Mmhmm," the other woman agreed.

"You just might be the one to get him back in church," the woman said, aiming an acknowledging eye at Natasha. "Right, Ella?"

Ella didn't respond to the question. She opened the oven and took out a casserole. "We better get this food out there."

Natasha helped Ella and the other women in the kitchen and then began setting up the food on the dining room table. She looked out into the living room at the gathering. A large group had shown up. Guests were laughing and talking among themselves. LaShon sat at the piano with a woman caught up in what seemed like a disagreement over a musical composition, LaShon lightly striking a key on the piano, and the woman shaking her head while shooing his hand away before striking a key of her own.

She saw Milton, who was still sitting on the arm of the sofa studying a man who was engaged in a lively discussion with other members of the church. She watched Milton and understood what her mother most likely saw in him. Even now, some twenty or so years later he was still a handsome man with eyes full of laughter. He was a man who commanded attention by his mere presence, as opposed to someone who felt they needed to make their presence known through imposition, yet she could tell by the way he received the recognition of others that he expected the attention. But also, watching him she saw a man who wouldn't abandon her if he knew her and wouldn't wish that she hadn't been born the way she knew some parents did of their children. Those were the ones who regretted having their children but whose sense of duty compelled them to continue on with the regrettable offspring. It was the way Miss Pauline was back in Tarpley. She regretted marrying her husband and 'letting him fill her up' with all those children. That's what she would tell Granny over coffee. She would talk endlessly of unfulfilled dreams and wondered aloud if she would ever be able to start her life over. After Miss Pauline would leave, Granny would tell Natasha, "It took two to make all them babies. I don't know why she trying to take it out on those children." To Natasha, Milton didn't seem like that type of person.

There was one person who wasn't in the living room when Natasha came in and that was Danny. He sat in the den with a few other guests watching TV. He didn't have a need or desire to mix with the members of the church, especially his stepfather. As far as Danny was concerned he came to be near his mother.

If there was one thing Danny learned about life it was that stories tell stories. Nothing happens without another tale that preceded it and nothing happens without a tale that will speak of it. This was something Danny learned from his mother's refusal to talk about their past. There seemed to be too much ugliness in the stories to tell.

It was this refusal to speak on the stories of the way Ella held the stories so tight in her that they became secrets that affected their lives. The weight of the secrets drifted like an odor suffocating any attempt at happiness in her life and in the lives of those who tried to love her. And the secrecy held a stench because it was assumed by Danny (and known to some degree by Milton) that it came from a place that was lodged in ugliness.

There was a cost that came with the secrecy as well, and part of it was that it made everyone in the house skeptical of each other. In Danny's case it was far more than doubt, it was hatred and most of that hatred was directed at Milton because somewhere along the line Danny had allowed the concoction of the things his mother kept from him to form a hatred that made it difficult for Danny to even be near his step-father. He told himself that it was Ella's desperation to hold onto Milton, with all of Milton's self-righteousness, that caused her mouth to close so tight when it came to her past and for that fact, Danny had always put much of the blame on Milton.

But now that Ella had opened up to Danny, even a little, it made Danny's visit home more bearable because of the tiny bit of hope he had. He knew he could have looked into parts of their past with the things he knew, like the place of birth printed on his birth certificate, but he had always been too afraid of what he might find and how, depending on the ugliness of what he found, it would affect his relationship with his mother. So he needed her to tell him and now it appeared as if she was beginning to do that.

What Ella had told him a few weeks earlier as she sat on the sofa in his apartment came more as a surprise than a shock, because the crime his father was said to have committed actually spoke to Danny's own life, and that was the surprise, that he might be continuing in his father's footsteps. It was a surprise, but not something that shocked him. But still, there were other things he knew she needed to tell him because he knew it only made sense that there were events that came before what she chose to tell him. In fact, there seemed to be other stories in her as she sat there that evening telling him what happened. Her hands had come together that evening, prayer like, and her fingers had chosen to interlock themselves, still moving in small, sifting motions as she spoke. That was enough of a sign to Danny that there was more that she needed to tell.

Since that evening when Ella told Danny about his father, a new affinity had grown between Danny and his mother that was apart from the familial love they had for each other. But this new bond hinged on Ella telling the rest of the story. Danny knew that being at the Christmas dinner would send his mother the message that he was ready to know more of who they were.

It was time for dinner. A circle was formed around the dining room with everyone holding hands. Milton stood at the head of the table with Ella holding his hand and Danny holding hers. Natasha stood along the circle and listened to Milton say blessings. Every now and then she would raise her head slightly and peer at him across the room, taking in his voice and his mannerisms: the tilt of his head as he prayed, the moments when he raised his brow and the furrows that formed along his forehead, the gentle squeeze of Ella's hand, all of the things that helped her form more of the signature of the man.

The evening continued on with most of the members in the living room, eating and listening to LaShon in concert. Everyone laughed and talked and joined in at times with the songs, while Danny went back to the den.

It was around eleven o'clock when the last of the guests left, except for the women who had helped in the kitchen and Natasha and LaShon, who helped clean up. Natasha removed dinnerware from the buffet and the table alongside Ella. She liked Ella. She could tell that Ella was a genuinely kind person, which gave Natasha some relief, yet there was a sense of regret she felt that Ella had no idea of what had happened between Milton and Abilyn and who she, this young lady who helped her clean off the table, was, and she wondered would she even be allowed in this house if Ella knew? She wondered if she would even be allowed near the family if Milton knew her. She continued to clean up, watching her father every now and then working alongside Danny and LaShon to get the house back in order.

The sisters of the kitchen had done their work and called it a night. Now Ella and her family and LaShon and Natasha sat in the kitchen. Milton put on coffee and they sat around the kitchen table and talked about the evening.

"Well, another year done," Milton said. "And I'm bone tired."

"Once my energy level dies down I'm going to feel the same," Ella said. "I think everyone enjoyed themselves," she added.

"Yeah," Danny said. "I think so too."

"It was a great time, Sister Pruitt," LaShon said.

Ella smiled. "Thank you. You know I always enjoy doing it. Me and my helpers," she said, looking at Natasha.

"Didn't this year's dinner seem larger than usual?" LaShon went on.

"Yeah, it seemed like it was larger than the ones I remember," Danny said. "At least since the last time I was here."

"It was." Ella answered quickly, cutting through the awkwardness of Danny's statement.

LaShon glanced at Natasha, who self-consciously raised a cup to her mouth.

"I'm glad you came," Milton said to Danny. Milt spoke haltingly as he studied the sincerity of his words.

Danny responded with some hesitancy. "Yeah. Me too." Then, "It was nice seeing all those crazy folks again," he said with a laugh.

"I filled Natasha in on some of the messiness." Ella shook her head, looking at Natasha.

"She did," Natasha said with a smile.

"Trust me, I've been filling her in, too," LaShon added. "Messy."

"Well look, Christ The Redeemer's family is just like any other family, crazy, but loving, so don't dissuade Natasha from joining us," Milton said. "We're always open to having new family members."

Danny cut a quick glance at his stepfather.

"You're right, Pastor. Believe me. It's the same in any large group," Natasha said.

"See? We can use some new thinking at church," Milton said.

"I told her she should go on up front next time you open the doors to newcomers," LaShon said.

"Let me apologize for them, Natasha." Ella laid her hand on Natasha's arm. "Not one time did they ask you if you already belonged to a church. You might already have a church back home."

"Bethesda AME. That's the church I went to."

"See?" Ella said, looking at her husband and LaShon.

"But I'm not sure if I'm going to move back there after school."

"Good," Milton said.

LaShon grinned, "I hope you decide to stay here."

"Where are you from," Danny asked.

"Oklahoma." She made the reply as she attempted to keep her eyes from Milton but she couldn't help glancing at him.

Milton pursed his lips and nodded his head slightly. "Well, if you do decide to stay on in Cincinnati, you know you have Christ The Redeemer as a home."

"And while you're here I hope you keep attending," Ella said. "As a matter of fact, let's keep in touch."

They continued to sit around the kitchen table, laughing and talking. No one noticed, though, how Milton spent the rest of that night studying Natasha's face.

CHAPTER SIXTEEN

Danny pulled up in front of his building after he left the dinner. He looked around the street before turning off his car. It was something he had learned to do. In the night his street looked like a dark vein arching outward into the darkness. Furrows of dark snow blackened by grime lined the street and the sidewalk, and ice clung to trees, giving them a despondent appearance. After a few seconds he turned off his car.

The streets were quiet as the cold and the late hours had pushed everyone inside. The buildings that lined the street were dotted with lights from the apartments of people who were still up or apartments that were dark except for holiday lights that blinked lonely in the night. He saw light coming from Mr. Stiggers' apartment, it was a dim light that spilled around the edges of the heavy draperies that were never opened, but only lifted every now and then so the old man could peer out, then lowered once again. Danny expected him to be up. There was only one more unit lighted in his building. It belonged to the lady who lived on the other end of the building facing the street. Her name was Gloria and she lived there with her kids, two boys and a girl. Danny talked with her every once in a while, mostly about how she thought Mr. Stiggers was doing, and Danny spoke to her kids whenever he saw them, but he never took the time to really get to know them.

Danny looked around the streets once more, then picked up the two containers of food from the front seat and went into his building. Ella had fixed two dinners, one for him and one for Mr. Stiggers.

As Danny stepped into the vestibule he heard someone crying. It was Mr. Stiggers. Danny closed the front door and walked up to Mr. Stiggers' door. He leaned close and listened to hear that the elderly man was sobbing uncontrollably. Every now and then Mr. Stiggers would mumble something between the sobbing.

Danny knocked softly on the door. "Mr. Stiggers? You ok?" He listened for a second to the crying then knocked once more, "You ok, Mr. Stiggers?"

Suddenly the crying stopped and a gospel song came from the stereo, filling the apartment. Danny listened closely for a few seconds more then he set the dinner in front of the door and went up to his apartment.

~~~~

Milton pulled a box from a corner of the basement and opened the lid. It was full of sundry items, even though it was marked 'Christmas decorations'. He had been promising Ella that he would clean out the basement come Spring, but he decided to start sooner out of a need to occupy his mind. On the other end of the basement, past the furnace and the water heater, was his workroom. Aside from the tools in his workroom was a large toolbox that was always locked and inside of that toolbox were a few items he kept to remember Abilyn by. But he never opened it.

It was late February and in the two months since the Christmas dinner he found he couldn't keep his mind off the time he spent with Abilyn. Though it had been over twenty years since their affair, at any moment during any day memories of Abilyn would come to him, sometimes as a soft movement in the white silk blouse he had always liked seeing her in, or in the sound of someone's voice that would remind him of Abilyn's voice, or it could be just a momentary vision of her turning her head away to look at something and how her eyes appeared as she would turn back to him.

He had never tried to get over Abilyn because he didn't want to desecrate his feelings for her, so instead, he counted on his thoughts of her to dissipate with the passage of time. It was the best way to honor what had been. After all, he had concluded that it was neither of their faults that they fell in love. He hadn't gone out to find someone to fall in love with and he always knew from the conversations he and Abilyn had that she had no intentions of falling in love with him either.

No one can explain why people fall in love, it just happens. But Milton was an upstanding man who couldn't carry on with the relationship because he was already married, so he went to Abilyn about ending the affair. But that evening when he went to see Abilyn was the evening she broke the news to him. She told him she was carrying his child. Milton recalled how she looked when she told him. They had been sitting in her apartment with the early evening sun filling the room, lighting Abilyn as she sat on the sofa with an expression on her face that was at once of disbelief and indecision. She was apologetic as she told him the news. Milton jumped up from where he had been sitting beside her and cupped his forehead. It was as if someone or something had shoved him hard in his chest, and he began to breathe rapidly, "No. No," he kept saying as he looked down at Abilyn, who sat quietly on the couch. She told him she had missed her period and she became concerned, so she took one of the new tests that had just come out on the market, and it tested positive.

"Those tests can't tell you if you're pregnant," he said as he sat back down. He took her hand in his, "Only a doctor can tell you that," but he knew she couldn't go to a doctor without things coming to light about their affair, so he told her to wait and see if she misses another period. And she did. But by then he had decided what he would do if she had come back with the answer he didn't want. He decided to have her get rid of the child.

"I can't do that!" Abilyn looked at him with eyes of equal horror and disbelief.

"Abilyn, listen to me. If you have that baby, both of our lives will be ruined."

"Your life would be ruined. Not mine," she defended. "And if you don't want this baby, then I'll raise it by myself."

Milton had never seen Abilyn with such determination. He told her to wait while he made a phone call. He called Ella and told her that he would be home a little later, that he was helping a younger pastor prepare a presentation. Then he came back into Abilyn's apartment and they ordered dinner and sat together for the evening. They held each other and they talked honestly about what life would be like if she had the baby. In the end he had convinced her that aside from his life being ruined, that she would have to live as a woman who had an illicit affair with a married man, and the shame it would bring to her and the child. He had convinced her that the mass inside her wasn't even yet a child and that it would be to the best of both their interests if she simply removed the mass. By the end of the evening, she had agreed, and a few days later he sent her away with money, and the understanding that the mass would be removed.

Milton knew why he was having thoughts of Abilyn. It was because of Natasha. He hadn't paid much attention to Natasha when he was first introduced to her or when he saw her sitting out in the pews. He hadn't given her much thought until he she came to the house for the dinner. It was then that familiarity lighted. It was an awareness that was at first vague but that became clearer as he watched her face and listened to her voice. That was when he realized the small similarities Natasha shared with the woman he loved long ago. At first, he found the similarities interesting, but when Natasha mentioned she was from Oklahoma, Milton's heart leapt, and from then on, the haunting remained with him.

The most immediate explanation Milton conjured over the similarities between Natasha's features and her home to that of Abilyn was what he knew about the black Indians of Oklahoma, so he told himself that the two women probably shared features that many black folks might share from that part of the country. He told himself that, but the explanation wasn't enough to keep the past from rising over and over in his head.

Since that night in the kitchen he hadn't seen much of Natasha. She hadn't attended church as often. He was cautious not to ask LaShon why she hadn't been attending because he didn't want to give the appearance of having particular interest in her, but he found out from Ella that Natasha was becoming more involved with working on her degree and didn't have as much time as she had before.

Ella had grown to like Natasha a lot. She saw her younger self in Natasha. Like her, it seemed Natasha was from a good family. She was polite and she had that giving trait, just as Ella had. But it was the appearance of Natasha being alone in the city that struck Ella the most because like Natasha, Ella was once a young lady, alone, in this same city. Natasha had said she was an only child and that the grandparents who raised her were both gone, and it seemed she didn't have much of a relationship to her other kin, at least not enough to stay in her hometown, so it was this shared sense of estrangement that held Ella's interest as well. Those were the things about Natasha that drew Ella to her.

There were other women, of course, who Ella could have formed relationships with, but most of them were the women of the church, women who, in spite of their own pasts, now found it best in their later years to become self-righteous to earn appeasement from God and also to fit into the social order of the church. Ella knew that some of the women in the church already whispered their take on her past (even though they knew little if anything about it), and some were bothered that she would hold the position of pastor's wife, so none of these women made Ella feel comfortable. So it was the sudden appearance of Natasha that gave Ella the hope of having another female friend that she could share her life with.

The one corner of the basement had been cleared, and Milton looked at the pile of trash. He gathered it up and took it out to the bins. They were things he and Ella needed to rid themselves of.

CHAPTER SEVENTEEN

If she hadn't been in the woods that afternoon things would have been different. Ella knew this but she wasn't sure what that difference might have been other than the fact that Damon wouldn't have killed Buddy. Maybe she and Damon would have married and maybe they would still be together. Or was killing in Damon's blood all along? Questions about that day still lay in Ella's head years later and even after the years that had passed she still wasn't sure what her life would have been like if she hadn't gone into the woods that day. One thing she knew for certain and that was Danny would be safer than she believed he was now.

She stood in the bathroom and washed her neck and her face, washing away the sweat that drenched her in her sleep. Then she changed into a fresh nightgown and went back into the bedroom. Milton was sound asleep because he had taken a sleeping pill to get a good night's rest. He hadn't been sleeping well the last few days either. The clock read one thirty-seven and she knew she needed to get some sleep.

The next day Ella went to Mrs. Wexner's apartment. She had set a date to take Mrs. Wexner out for lunch. The lunch would be a special one because Ella had asked Danny to be there. It was something that excited Mrs. Wexner.

Mrs. Wexner was sitting in her living room when Ella got to her apartment. Her coat was buttoned and she had her purse resting in her lap. She sat calmly, looking at the photos on the large ornate credenza. She spoke to the photos in German, her voice coming across with startling intimacy. Her assistant went to the door and let Ella into the apartment and noticed Ella watching Mrs. Wexner talking softly to the photos.

"She's doing that more often now."

Ella watched her for a few seconds more before Mrs. Wexner noticed her standing there. The elderly woman's face brightened. "Well, I thought you had forgotten me."

"I said I would be here at twelve."

"What time is it?" Mrs. Wexner asked her assistant.

Madelyn smiled wryly. "Twelve o seven."

"Mmh." Mrs. Wexner rendered a soft, triumphant grunt.

Ella and Madelyn looked at each other and shook their heads as they helped Mrs. Wexner from her chair.

Ella steadied Mrs. Wexner with one arm while she herself leaned a bit against the wall of the elevator as they went down to the lobby. She was feeling tired from the lack of sleep at night and from her mind dissecting the dreams as she went through her days.

"Are you alright, dear?" Mrs. Wexner asked.

"Me? Oh yeah. I'm fine."

"You don't look it. You need to rest more. There's nothing out there that's more important than a good night's sleep."

"Yeah. You're right."

Danny was waiting for them when they arrived at the restaurant. He stood and smiled as Ella and Mrs. Wexner came in. Mrs. Wexner looked at him, unsure of who he was, and tightened her hold of Ella's arm.

"Hi, Mrs. Wexner," Danny said. "It's me, Danny."

"It's Danny," Ella assured.

"Danny? Oh my!" Mrs. Wexner smiled and hugged him. "Oh my," she repeated. Then she locked her free arm in his and the three of them walked over to their table. "You've grown so," Mrs. Wexner said.

"Yes ma'am."

"And a handsome one, he is," she said, looking at Ella. "Like his father," She said. Then she paused, "Though I never saw much resemblance in them. How is he?"

"My father?" Danny asked. "He's fine," he replied glancing playfully at his mother.

"Good. Tell him I said hello. I have to see him sometime."

"I will."

Ella had reserved a table by a window that overlooked the Ohio River and a park that ran along the riverfront. They took their seats and placed their orders.

Mrs. Wexner was so excited to see Danny that she spent much of her time holding his hand across the table, asking him what his life was like. "So much youth today and I don't know anything about them," she said to Ella. And the three of them talked about their generations.

"We were all so happy back then," the old lady said of her life, "before things began to change. I was a young girl then, around thirteen or fourteen, and I saw it in the eyes of the people around me. I remember how eyes that once looked at me with the brightness of smiles became eyes that were red, and filled with hatred. And the eyes of my family and our friends seemed to diminish into fear and confusion. They became small, as if they sought refuge from the eyes that looked into them."

Danny listened to Mrs. Wexner talk about her life. He felt her hand tighten at times in his hand as she talked about her experience, yet she was able to smile at the good times in her life as well.

"It isn't all bad," she said of life. "You have to dream. Don't become imprisoned by your expectations," she told Danny and Ella, shaking their hands in hers. "And most importantly, live a life of gratitude. That way you find joy in the smallest of things and it makes it all so less burdensome. Grace, my dears. Grace."

Their orders arrived just as a late winter rain came down outside. A large dark cloud stretched across the Ohio River and beyond, joining both sides of the river and everything beneath it in a steady fall of water. Ella watched the rain run down along the window and she listened to Mrs. Wexner talk and watched Danny as he looked at the woman, and it was then that Ella understood why her own story needed to be told.

As they were leaving, Danny went to get Ella's car. He pulled up to the restaurant and raised an umbrella as he got out of the car. He walked his mother and Mrs. Wexner to Ella's car, and just as he opened the door to the passenger side, Mrs. Wexner stepped from beneath the umbrella into the rain. She raised her head and let the rain run down her face and over her body and she laughed before getting into the car.

"Look at you," Ella said as she got into the car. "Now we have to get you home before you catch a cold."

They watched Danny run to his car, and they waved and pulled off.

"Danny is such a handsome man," Mrs. Wexner said. "But his hands. So calloused and scarred."

"He boxes," Ella said.

"The bruises on his hands were not put there by sport, Ella. They were put there by anger," Mrs. Wexner said.

~~~~

"I'm not sure when your father came to New Home. One day he was just there." Ella spoke quietly as she sat in Danny's apartment, holding a glass of water and watching the sunlight bend through the glass.

"One day he was just there?" Danny spoke incredulously.

"Yeah," Ella replied softly. "One day he was just… there," she said with a slight shake of her head.

"Mom. C'mon."

"Everyone knew each other in New Home. We knew who came and who went and we even knew when someone was talking about leaving. That's the way it was back then. But nobody heard about him coming. No talk about 'Old Lady Hogan is bringing her nephew to stay with her' or nothing. And your grandfather would've known because he owned many of the homes there. But I guess that was to be expected with Miss Hogan– I always called her Miss Hogan because your grandmother raised us to be respectful of grownups. But Miss Hogan never interacted too much with other folks outside of the woods."

"The woods?"

"We called them that, and they were in a way. It was the part of town where folks who didn't have much lived. The people who lived there called it Clearwater, because of the lake there, but everyone else just referred to it as the woods. It was all part of New Home though. But Miss Hogan didn't show herself much on the streets in town unless she was going to the store or something and even then she never talked to anyone unless they lived in the woods. It was as if she despised everyone else. So it shouldn't have been a surprise when your father came to live with her without anyone having heard about him coming." She looked up from the glass in her hand to Danny, "So yes, he did suddenly appear."

Ella sat the glass of water on the coffee table. "I would see him walking down the street and I would wonder about him."

"You liked him when you first saw him, huh?" Danny said.

"No. Well, I guess so because I remember noticing how good-looking he was. He was tall and dark-skinned and so lean. Not skinny, just lean. And he would mostly be by himself, going to and from work at the store. I was just about to turn thirteen then, so I was noticing boys, so I don't know why he stood out so. He was much older than me. Eighteen. But I was so attracted to him. We didn't talk until I met him at the store." She looked out into the room and continued to speak. "I think the fact that he was such a mystery made him even more attractive. And the way he moved, so silent and so certain of himself. He was very smart, you know," she said, suddenly looking at Danny. "Really smart. I guess that's what made him even more appealing when I got to know him. He was smarter than what I heard from the other boys in town." She paused before continuing. "I know I was too young, but there was just something about him that told me he had been places and that if I got to know him, maybe one day we would go places together. I wanted to leave New Home, just like a lot of the younger ones did. It wasn't a bad place, but I just wanted to be somewhere else, and in my mind Damon was that somewhere else."

"Where was he from?" Danny's eyes were fixed on his mother.

"Chicago. No one was sure. They talked about him being from Detroit, some said New York City, and some said St. Louis. But he was from Chicago. He never would tell me exactly why he came to a place like New Home to live with Miss Hogan, only that his mother sent him because he was beginning to get into trouble up there. But the first time we met was when me and your grandfather and your aunt were doing groceries. I saw him in the aisle putting up some canned goods, or something, I can't really remember. We started talking, and that's how we met."

She went on to tell Danny how she and Damon dated in secrecy because they both knew she was too young for him and how the people in New Home didn't trust him because they hadn't been given much history about him. And she told Danny about his grandfather and his grandmother, how powerful and rueful Emmanuel was and how much he loved her mother who died of a broken heart because she was so unhappy living in New Home. And how her brother left and her younger sister fell into depression. Finally Ella had begun to tell her story.

It was late afternoon when she finished telling that part of her story. It was a Saturday and she had errands to run and she knew Danny had things he wanted to do as well, so she brought the story to a close. Danny told her he would like to hear more of the story, and she knew what he meant, that he wanted to hear what led up to Damon murdering Buddy, but she told him that was a part she wasn't ready to talk about yet.

She and Danny stood at her car. "Mom, whatever happened, happened. I just want you to know that. Everything will be ok." He held his mother to him.

"I just worry over you. There was so much violence around your coming into this world and, well, I just wonder…"

"Everything's fine. Believe me."

"Ok." She responded with a bit of uncertainty.

Danny watched his mother drive off and went back into his building. As he stepped into the hallway, Mr. Stiggers cracked open his door and peered out. "Who is she?"

Danny looked at the old man half-hidden behind his door, the security chain crossing his face. "My mother."

"I don't want her around here," Mr. Stiggers said.

"What?"

"I don't want her around here!" The old man yelled and slammed his door shut.

Ella sat at the traffic light at the end of Danny's street. She thought about the other day at lunch and about Mrs. Wexner's observation of Danny's hands, *'the bruises were put there by anger'*. That was why Ella had begun to tell Danny his story… their story. She wanted no more bruises for either of them. She hoped that by hearing her words he would understand what happened to him and that he would forgive everything that brought him here. She wanted to end the bruising. Yet she knew that no matter how much she sought to protect him there was probably little he could do to stay out of harm's way because spirits were powerful, and a vengeful one was full of venom.

The Saturday afternoon, traffic along the main thoroughfare had picked up and Ella sat watching people coming and going from stores and vendors selling their goods under canopies that wavered in the afternoon sun. She thought about how fragile the lives were of the people she watched walking along the streets. How at any moment something, a vengeful spirit, could take the light from their eyes or the laughter from their mouths. They had tried it before the day Danny was born. When he slid from the wet flesh between her legs with a cord wound tight around his neck.

The light changed, and Ella moved out into the intersection and waited for the pedestrians to cross the street. One of them, a young man, wove his way through the group of crossers, gesturing wildly with his free hand as he talked on his phone. He was more into his conversation than the business around him and it caused Ella to watch him. Suddenly, as he passed in front of her car, she noticed the birthmark on the side of his face. It was a swath of brown that was broad in the center of his cheek but narrowed as it neared his ear, as if someone had swept his cheek with the stroke of a brush. It wasn't a large mark, but it was visible enough to capture Ella's attention and she couldn't take her eyes off it. She had forgotten about the birthmark. Buddy had had the same type of mark on his face. She watched the young man walk down the street Danny lived on, talking and wildly gesturing as he continued his conversation. The driver in the car that was behind Ella blew his horn, and she drove on.

The first time Ella ever met Buddy was the day he brought groceries to their house. Before then she had seen him working around the store or walking along the road that led to the woods, but rarely on her street because the folks who lived in the woods usually ventured no farther than the center of town unless they were working.

She had been reading a magazine that day and listening to the radio on the back porch, which was to have been turned into a solarium to suit her mother's wishes, but once her mother passed away her father lost interest and the porch was only surrounded by a screened wall. She saw Buddy as he came around the side of the house.

"I got some groceries for you." He spoke through the screen door as he lifted the bag to show her. "Your father ordered it."

Ella looked at him for a second before responding. She wasn't use to boys like Buddy coming around their house. The men who came to their house were usually older and proper looking or they were ones who looked worn from years of neglect, who mowed the lawn or cleaned out the garage. But Buddy stood there under the morning sun, young and a bit spindly, a smile crossing his face.

"Ok." Ella said as she laid down her magazine and walked to the door. "Come on in."

He opened the door and came onto the porch.

"The kitchen's right here," Ella said as she led him into the house.

"Cool," he said as he nodded.

Ella watched Buddy walk ahead of her along the porch. He had become someone with more meaning to her now that she had met Damon. She watched Buddy and thought about Damon and how she had seen Damon and Buddy walk home after work. Ella was reminded of all of this as she watched Buddy standing in the kitchen as the cook went over the list of groceries that had been ordered. It was then that Ella noticed the birthmark along his left cheek. Suddenly Ella felt foolish just standing there watching Buddy, so she went back onto the porch and continued reading her magazine.

Buddy came back onto the porch and headed towards the door, then he stopped and turned to her. "Damon told me to tell you hi." He grinned knowingly.

Ella blushed and felt herself becoming undone. Pulling herself together, she thanked him. "Tell him I said hi," she said with a half concealed smile.

Buddy nodded with a grin. "Ok," and walked off the porch.

Months later, his body would lie on the banks of the lake, with Damon's belt around his neck, the brown birthmark faded against the gray face with the bulged eyes.

CHAPTER EIGHTEEN

Natasha's absence proved to be just as bothersome as her appearance to Milton because they were one in the same. People like her don't just show up and disappear like that unless they got something evil on their minds is what Milton thought as he sat on the passenger side and looked out of the window of the car on his way to church.

Ella drove that day. She talked about something she wanted the women's board to do at the church but Milton only heard pieces of what she said. His mind was still on Natasha. He knew it was more than coincidence that someone who looked like Abilyn and who was even from Abilyn's home would come to Cincinnati, and especially to his church. The more he thought about Natasha and was able to compare her to Abilyn the more bothered he became. He recalled the way Natasha spoke. It was similar to Abilyn's way of speaking, the inflections with the slight downward lilt at the end of her sentences. It was all coming back to him now and it bothered him to the point that he wasn't sure if he missed Abilyn or wished he had never met her.

After opening service Milton got up from his chair and opened the page of his bible, bookmarked by his notes. He thanked the choir for their selections and he looked out over the congregation and remarked how nice everyone looked. Then he looked down and began to speak.

"By now you all know that me and a few more of our ministers are speaking out against the schools here teaching about gay folks." His sign of humility given, he lifted his head and looked at the congregation. "I've even been told that now we should use the term 'same-sex'." He turned to his assistant pastor, who shook his head as some in the congregation moaned their disapproval. "But they're still homosexuals, and I have to call them what they are."

Some in the congregation voiced their agreement, *"Well!"*

"And it doesn't matter if we call them same-sex or, gay, or homosexual, we know it's not the way God wants his children to live."

"Well!"

"It's just why me and my brother ministers have chosen to stand up and speak out against the school board using your tax dollars to support the homosexual lifestyle." He leaned forward and reminded, "You all work too hard for your money and you shouldn't have to see it going towards something that you know ain't right with God."

Many in the congregation nodded in agreement, but some sat quietly and watched him.

"Now, I know what some people have been saying about us hating homosexuals, but the truth is, we love the person who is trapped by homosexuality because somewhere along the road they took the wrong turn. And that's why we as Christians are here. We, the people of God, are here to help them out of their misery. We don't hate them. We're here to help them." He waited until the applause of those in the congregation who agreed with him died down and he continued.

"You know, everyone takes a wrong turn in life." Pausing and looking humbly at his bible, he continued. "I know I've taken some wrong turns in my life. But that's why we have God there," he said, looking again at the congregation. "We have God to turn to when we've lost our way." He went on to talk about those who are lost having a way out of their darkness and about how they might have to endure suffering until they find their way back home, but that anyone who is suffering should know that there are people like the Christ The Redeemer Baptist Church family and others who were there for them, holding a lantern to light the way home for the lost.

He brought the sermon to a close. Finally he wiped his brow with his handkerchief and nodded to the choir to take over.

The sermon went over well with most of the congregation. With those who weren't in agreement with what Milton said, well, they gave him the respect they had come to give their pastor. They remained silent.

Milton and Ella sat in their den that evening, he reading the newspaper, she reading a book. Though Milton read the paper, his thoughts were only half-attentive to what he was reading because much of his thoughts were still on the sermon he had preached.

"A lot of people crossed my mind when I was doing that sermon today." Milton spoke to Ella as he laid the newspaper on his lap. "Like I said, there isn't a soul who hasn't made a wrong turn."

"Mm hm," Ella replied without looking up from her book. "We all need God."

"How is Danny faring?"

Ella looked up from her book. "Ok I guess." She studied her husband's face.

"You know, I think that thing with him and Deacon Samuels was nothing more than teenage hormones on his part, and Deacon Samuels just took advantage of him."

Ella didn't reply.

"Well," Milton continued. "Danny knows the power of God. He was raised on it."

"Yeah, he was," Ella said.

"And I don't want you taking on too much when it comes to what Danny's doing with his life. He's a grown man and he knows about the power of the Lord. He'll be ok if he hangs onto that."

"A mother's always going to worry about her child, Milton."

"I know. I understand that." He paused before going on with his thought. "And Ella. Look, I know we've done a lot of talking about whatever happened to you. Your past."

"Milton, let's not go into that conversation again."

"How can I not? If it bothers you, it bothers me. But I'm not going to go into what it is I don't know, or why you won't tell me. I wish you would, but I'm not talking about that now. I just want you to know that whatever it is, you have to forgive yourself. I keep telling you that. I know you've asked for forgiveness. I know that. But you also have to forgive yourself so you can move on. It's something we all have to do at one time or another."

That night Milton lay in bed thinking about Natasha and Abilyn. Maybe it was best that Natasha disappeared. Maybe she went back home and he wouldn't have to deal with her anymore. He looked at Ella, who was just dozing off to sleep. He kissed her on her cheek.

~~~~

It was late in the evening when Milton drove to the church. Spring was approaching and it had been raining off and on that day but now the rain had turned into a steady downpour, making what would be a difficult situation for Milton even more difficult. He guided his car carefully along the streets in the torrential downpour until he pulled up to the empty church parking lot and sat for a moment in his car, listening to the roar of the rain. His stomach fluttered nervously over what he was about to do.

His phone rang and he answered it.

"You're not out there in that rain are you?" It was Ella.

"I'm just pulling up to the church."

"Stay off the roads if you can. I barely made it home, so much rain."

"I'll be here until the rain stops."

"Alright."

"Ok. Love you."

He opened the car door and dashed through the rain to the church. When he got inside he wiped the water from his hair and his face and went to the restroom to dry himself off as best as he could. The church was dark except for the lighted hallway that led to his office. He walked past Mrs. Hargrove's immaculate desk and into his office where he shut the door and turned on the lamp on his desk. He sat for a while and looked out of the window at the dark sky and the assault of the rain, gathering his nerves for what he was about to do. After a while he turned his computer on and began to search for Abilyn's last name in the city of Tarpley. Sullivan. He found several citizens of Tarpley with the last name, but none that listed Abigail as a first name. He thought maybe she had gotten married and now carried her husband's name. He paused and took a deep breath. He wasn't sure how he would feel if heard Abilyn's voice or how Abilyn would respond to him when she heard his voice. He hadn't heard from her all those years so he figured she had moved on with her life, and that she was happy now, just as he was. Or was the contempt she had for him the reason she never tried to contact him? He wasn't sure, but he had to talk with her to find out who Natasha was.

He decided to go down the list of Sullivans in the directory in hope that one of them would put him in touch with Abilyn. It was the third contact on the list of Sullivans who recognized Abilyn's name.

"Abilyn?" It was the voice of an elderly woman. "Who is this?"

"I'm an old friend of hers from her days here at the university," Milton replied haltingly.

"Oh. Why you callin' for her?"

"Just to check on her—there might be a reunion coming up and we—we're just trying to contact former classmates," he lied.

"Oh, well baby Abilyn is dead. She passed away years ago."

Milton felt his heart stop and he fought to regain his breath. "Oh. She's – she's dead?" his voice weakened.

"Yeah."

"Oh my God," Milton moaned.

"Yep. Died while giving birth. The baby survived, but it left that poor girl without a momma. The poor child had to be raised by her grandparents Nadine and Ernest. My cousins."

"Oh I'm sorry," he moaned. "I'm so sorry."

"Well, it was the Lord's will."

"Yes ma'am. Thank you," Milton said as he hung up the phone. He sat back in his chair and stared at the phone on his desk. Then the pain overtook him and he began to wail, a cry so mournful and so loud, that it matched the roar of the rain outside.

~~~

A chance meeting between Milton and Abilyn couldn't have happened the day that they were first in each other's presence because the university's choir was on stage and Milton was sitting in the audience with Ella. But Milton saw Abilyn. The choir was singing 'To Be Young, Gifted, and Black' when his eyes fell on her. She was standing midway in the first row, swaying from left to right with the choir as they sang the chorus. There was nothing in particular about her that was exciting, but there was enough something about her to hold Milton's attention: her small face framed by a large afro called attention to her even before she stepped up front for the next song. "*I wanna go where the north wind go…*" the words came from her with so much emotion that Milton immediately felt the meaning of the message.

"*Wind go… wind go,*" the choir responded.

By the time the choir had closed the song they were dancing around the stage and had the audience jumping up and down and dancing in the aisles.

"*Right on, Be Free*"

"*Right on, Be Free*"

Even with all of the dancing and shouting Milton kept his eyes on Abilyn, and something in him moved.

After that day Milton found reasons to come onto the campus of the university at least once a week to talk to professors and advisors who he hadn't kept in touch with and to pledge to work more with the black students on campus. When he found out that Abilyn worked in the bookstore, he bought mugs, shirts, and odd little things like paperweights that were in the shape of the school's mascot, and driving gloves that had the school's logo emblazoned across the top of them. Ella was surprised to see his sudden interest in their alma mater and she began to display all of the things he bought along the shelves of their den.

It wasn't until the choir did their spring concert that Milton finally had a chance to really talk with Abilyn. He had made himself known to her from the visits to the bookstore when he would tell her how much he liked her voice and how he appreciated the choir's stand for justice. He would be sincere when he told Abilyn these things because he saw her talent, but at the same time he was bothered that he was telling her these things at all, because he knew he was coming onto the campus just to see her. At times he wanted to walk away before he saw her, but they would smile at each other and he would walk up to the register with an object in his hands.

He told himself he was too busy to take time out to go onto the campus, and he was, but suddenly there was a small opening in his busy life and where commitment to other things would normally fill any open space in his life like church, community activities and time with his wife, oddly he found Abilyn occupying that space. Like a wild flower that had taken seed and just grown in the middle of that space, he found her there.

When they first started talking, Abilyn didn't know she had taken up a space in Milton's life. She saw him on campus and simply took him for an alum who worked with the black student union. Whenever she saw him she would smile and greet him by name because she had come to know who he was and they would exchange pleasantries. However, over time, their encounters and the pleasantries they exchanged happened so often that even she began to wonder if there was something growing between them, and that was when things about him started to stand out to her, like the size and shape of his hands when he put his items on the counter; the size of his knuckles and the veins that mapped his hands; the way his eyes would rest in her own eyes when they looked at each other; and the depth and gentleness of his voice when he spoke to her. Those were the things Abilyn started to notice about Milton that she hadn't noticed before.

As the weeks went on, Milton and Abilyn would step out to get a bite to eat before she headed to class, and they would talk about the school and how things were when he had attended almost three decades ago, and the actions Abilyn and her fellow students could take to effect change. Milton never hid the wedding band on his finger when they had lunch together because he had always had difficulty removing and getting the ring back onto his finger, and besides, he had told himself that the time he was spending with Abilyn was part of his responsibility to the black youth. Nothing more. And for Abilyn, the ring simply became more invisible each time she and Milton met. By that time, though, they both knew what was really happening between them, but the light of just being in each other's company dimmed all of the other things in their lives.

Milton and Ella had been married for eight years when Milton met Abilyn, and while Milton still loved Ella, the sameness of their days made the excitement he once had for her as level and far flung as a field with no mountains surrounding it to inspire it, with no flowers to grace it and no slopes leading down to a lake or a river to make it fascinating. His marriage with Ella was becoming plain. And then there was that boy, her son. The bond she had with her little Danny was so strong and the dislike that Danny had for Milton was equally strong, so strong that Milton already felt like an adulterer whenever he was around them. But more than anything, Abilyn was smart, and she was young and pretty, and most important, she was interested in him.

As for Abilyn, she felt like a woman when she was around Milton. She felt like a woman, but not just in the sense of her sexuality as one might immediately think, but also in the sense of simply feeling mature. Unlike the young men she usually spent time with, her time with Milton was open to conversation that was rooted in experience and wisdom and with the coolness of confidence instead of the coolness of being hip. Even when she and Milton found something funny, it was funny not out of something frivolous, but it was humor, that understanding of something deeper than just the silliness she so often shared with her classmates. All of this came to her at a time in her life when she was on the cusp of adulthood, and that's what made her involvement with Milton so intoxicating that the ring on his finger became invisible to her.

Their lunches together eventually became evenings together. Milton would sometimes leave the church early so he and Abilyn could have dinner at a bistro that was in Abilyn's neighborhood (surely no one he knew went to bistros). To account for his time away from Ella, Milton would tell Ella about a meeting and she would believe him, then he would feel despicable, but the bad feelings would dissipate as thoughts of being with Abilyn came to him and the banality of his life would fade. Sometimes on their walks back to Abilyn's apartment, they would stroll quietly and Milton would feel relief from the always fearful Ella worrying over something from her past, something he still wasn't sure of and that left him feeling detached and unprepared; and of her hands, always busy, moving busily over and around Danny, brushing dirt off the back of his pants or picking lint from his hair or sleep from his eyes. The time with Abilyn even gave Milton a respite from whining church members who hadn't earned a right to a good life because of their perpetual ignorance and their stubborn ways. When he walked with Abilyn, he felt as free as the stars over his head. In the beginning, he and Abilyn never touched. They only talked. But as the weeks went on and after several meetings he gave her a light hug to say goodnight. Then he turned around and left. After that night they hugged each other at the door every time they left each other.

Milton's way with the Lord became uneasy after Milton admitted to himself the true feelings he had for Abilyn. He knew the day he made up his mind to set foot on the campus without Ella, and with no real reason except that he would run into Abilyn, how interested he was in her, but at the time he was convinced that his attraction to her was no more than the attraction he had for some of the women at the church, the attraction he had for the roundness of their hips, or the legs of some of the women that moved from the hems of their skirts to the high heels they wore. He found them attractive, but he never lusted after them; he only had a fondness over seeing them and even then he would ask the Lord to move him from that place his eyes would go to when he saw them. After all, it was Ella that the Lord had sent his way, and in spite of the dying interest he had in her, he loved her nonetheless because she was the one sent to him and she was the one who was by his side, his devout helpmate for the years they had been together.

So the attraction Milton had for Abilyn wouldn't have been bothersome if he hadn't sought her out. His setting foot on the campus that day, and the night before when he considered it, was what made him ask the Lord to move in. However, that night when he asked the Lord for help, it was a tepid cry because all the while he prayed to the Lord, it was Abilyn who was on his mind. At first Milton was confused as to why the Lord didn't move Abilyn from his thoughts. He was worried and prayed more before coming to believe his attraction to Abilyn was a test. He had learned that. The Lord sometimes tests His children and for Milton, living through the attraction he had for Abilyn was no more than having lived through the bitter years with his father without turning away from the Lord. The Lord wanted to see if Milton would hold onto his faith or if he would falter. Milton knew as long as he kept the relationship at arms distance he would survive the test and the Lord would let him go on in his faith.

But it was the evenings he started to spend with Abilyn that exposed the thinness of Milton's devotion. Like a piece of cloth with patches so worn as to lose its opaqueness, Milton's devotion began to wear away. The hugs at the door soon gave way to him going inside of Abilyn's apartment, and the visits to her apartment eventually ended up with him lying between Abilyn's legs.

For a while he and Abilyn spent a few days a week together, and on those nights after he left her apartment, he would come home to Ella, full of guilt, and he would spend much of the rest of the night sitting in the downstairs bathroom, crying and praying, as Ella slept upstairs.

On several occasions Milton and Abilyn tried to end their affair, but after a week or so of not seeing each other, they would end up in each other's arms again, their common sense slipping away into the darkness of the night.

The affair had gone on for almost seven months when Milton gained enough strength to end it. Looking back he would tell himself that. That he had gained strength. But in fact, he and Abilyn had begun to grow tired of each other. Their conversations had lost energy and the sex had become stale, and it was that day, when he went to her apartment to talk about ending their relationship, that she told him she was pregnant.

CHAPTER NINETEEN

Danny held his hand out so the man could undo the remaining glove. "That's it for me," he said, looking over at Littlejohn.

"Same here." Littlejohn lowered his head and removed his head-gear.

Danny and Littlejohn walked past the ring where two other men were sparring.

"You two outta here?" Fletch asked the question as he looked away from the men in the ring.

"Yep," Danny and Littlejohn said as Littlejohn slapped the old man lightly on the back.

Fletch waved his large hand and turned back to the ring, leaning against the ropes that separated from the pressure of his large belly, as he instructed the fighters.

"You hear any more from your mom about your ol' man?" Littlejohn asked as he stood under the shower. He squinted as the water ran down his face.

"Nah. I don't press her though," Danny answered as he turned his back to the spray. "Seems like she got a lot of shit she needs to get off her chest so I let her do it on her own time."

"That's probably best. Hey, suppose your mom was like his Bonnie?"

"What?"

"Bonnie and Clyde," Littlejohn said. "You know, her an' your ol' man worked as a team."

Danny began lathering his chest. "Dude, you know you callin' my mother a murderer don't you?"

"Nah. Well. I mean, it's just a thought," Littlejohn said as he began to wash himself. Then he looked at Danny and grinned. "It would be cool though."

"You crazy. No it wouldn't be cool."

"Yeah it would. I think that would be cool."

"You just fucked up in the head," Danny said.

"Seriously though. I guess it is cool to know about your ol' man no matter what he did," Littlejohn said. "I know I say that shit about my ol' man, but really? I wish me an' him could get to know each other."

Danny and Littlejohn left the gym and walked up the street to Littlejohn's car.

"So what you got planned tonight?" Littlejohn asked. "You know it's rare we get a Saturday off."

"I don't know. Probably take in a movie," Danny answered as he looked out onto the busy street.

"A movie at home or out? You know your ass. You'll spend your entire night off sittin' around your place."

"Maybe out. I don't know."

Littlejohn shook his head. "Why do you do that shit to yourself?"

"Here we go," Danny said with anticipation.

"Well it's true," Littlejohn said. "If you ain't at work or over to Cortez's place you either hangin' around your pad or just hangin' out alone."

"And? What's wrong with that?"

"I know they say we come into this world alone and we leave alone, but damn man, in between we gotta have relationships to make it all worthwhile," Littlejohn declared.

Danny walked on without responding. He knew there was some truth in what his friend said. On the streets he saw people walking together or stopping to talk with someone they knew, or calling out to someone. Even the guy who stood against a building near Littlejohn's car texting was talking to someone, so he knew what Littlejohn was saying was true but it wasn't right for him.

"Me and Azhure was talkin' about going to the movies tonight. Why don't we go together?" Littlejohn continued as he unlocked the car doors.

"Thanks, but I'm cool."

"She wouldn't mind. You know she likes you. You're the only one of my friends she likes."

"I don't know man. I can't promise anything right now. I have to see how I feel."

"Or you have to see if Cortez calls you," Littlejohn retorted. "I'm tellin' you man, you gotta stop that shit," he said as they drove off.

Danny returned to his apartment that afternoon. He stepped into the foyer and started for the stairs, but at the same time he listened for any signs of Mr. Stiggers. It had been weeks since Danny had spoken to him and he was concerned about him. The elderly man had taken to crying a lot and not answering his door and the food Danny would bring home for him would be left sitting by Mr. Stiggers' door untouched. Danny stopped bringing home the gifts of food for him and now stopped to listen for Mr. Stiggers whenever he came in to make sure he was ok. This time there was no sound. No music or crying, and it raised Danny's concern.

"Mr. Stiggers." He knocked on the door but there was no sound.

"He's alright." Danny turned to see Gloria coming down the stairs carrying a load of laundry. "I saw him come from the laundry room a little while ago."

"During the day? He usually goes at some crazy hour when everybody else is sleep."

"Strange, ain't it?" Gloria adjusted the basket against her hip. "I don't know what's gotten into him, but he's acting out of character lately."

"Yeah," Danny said. "He don't even eat the food I usually bring for him."

"I think he's ok though," Gloria said. "At least he looked ok when I saw him. I spoke to him and he mumbled a 'hello' and rushed past me and back into his apartment just like he normally does. But I hear him crying a lot." She looked at Mr. Stiggers' door, then back to Danny. "Strange acting—well, even more so," she grinned. "But he looked ok. I'll let you know if something turns out not to be ok with him," she said as she walked down the hall.

"Alright." Danny looked once more at Mr. Stiggers' door then went upstairs.

Mr. Stiggers' change in behavior bothered Danny. He had a special relationship with Mr. Stiggers that started the day Danny returned underwear to Mr. Stiggers that had been left in the laundry room by him. Danny saw the name 'J. Stiggers' written in the neck of the shirt and in the waist of the shorts. At that time he had only seen the old man quickly shuffling from a cab to his apartment or to take out trash, but Mr. Stiggers let it be known that he wasn't to be approached. When he walked to the dumpster or from a cab, he walked as fast as he could with his eyes straight ahead. It was clear that he wanted no contact with anyone. Danny thought to himself as he read the inscription in the underwear, which was written in the same backward sloping letters as the name that appeared on the old man's mailbox, that Mr. Stiggers was probably the only person in the building who wrote his name on his clothes.

On his way back to his apartment that day, Danny had knocked on Mr. Stiggers' door. There was music coming from inside the apartment. This time it wasn't gospel music like Danny usually heard coming from the apartment. Instead it was a man lamenting a rainy night in Georgia. Danny waited a few seconds and knocked again. The music stopped.

"Who is it?" Mr. Stiggers called out in a voice that was laced with caution.

"Mr. Stiggers, it's Danny from upstairs--"

"Don't tell me my music is too loud 'cause it ain't."

"No sir. You left some laundry downstairs."

Mr. Stiggers didn't reply.

"Um, I can put it in a bag and leave it if you want," Danny continued with uncertainty.

The sound of locks being undone came from Mr. Stiggers' door and he cracked it open leaving the safety chain engaged. "What I leave?" he asked, looking up at Danny then at the clothes in Danny's hand.

"These." Danny lifted the items. Through the opening of the door he could see a large portrait of a matronly looking woman hanging on the wall in Mr. Stiggers' living room. She looked calmly through her spectacles from the frame. The room was brightly washed in sunlight and the scent of disinfectant wafted from inside of the apartment into the hallway. On a table beneath the portrait of the woman was a large knife.

Mr. Stiggers saw Danny look past him into the apartment and pulled the door up a bit. "Thank you," he said as he took the clothes from Danny and closed the door.

That was the first time Danny had ever spoken to Mr. Stiggers.

A few weeks later as Danny was headed out the door Mr. Stiggers called him. "Young man." It was the first time they had spoken since Danny had returned his laundry. Mr. Stiggers stood half hidden behind his door as he called to Danny. "You goin' to the store anytime soon? I'm outta coffee."

"Yes sir, I can get you some," Danny said.

"Here." Mr. Stiggers stuck his hand out and Danny walked over to him. He handed Danny a few dollars that were carefully folded around a small stack of coins.

"What kind you want?" Danny asked.

"The cheapest one. Whatever that can get," Mr. Stiggers said, nodding towards the money in Danny's hand.

Danny came back from the store and knocked on Mr. Stiggers' door. He handed him the bag, and in the bag was a can of coffee, milk and sugar. Mr. Stiggers looked at the bag, at the items showing through the plastic, and he looked up at Danny with mild surprise. "Oh," he said. "You didn't have to do that."

"It's no bother," Danny said.

He handed Mr. Stiggers back the money, still folded around the coins.

Mr. Stiggers slowly took the money then he looked at Danny with eyes full of gratitude.

"Thank you," he said. "Thank you."

After that day Danny began dropping off food to Mr. Stiggers.

That was why Danny was bothered by Mr. Stiggers' sudden change. He mentioned all of this to Littlejohn when they were sitting around Littlejohn and Azhure's apartment, how Mr. Stiggers had yelled at Danny for bringing Ella around the building. Littlejohn had put the movie they were watching on hold and he started to laugh at Danny. He told Danny that Mr. Stiggers was probably into Danny and that Mr. Stiggers was jealous over seeing a woman come from Danny's apartment. Littlejohn assured Danny that there were many older men out there who were like Fletch, and that Danny might as well get used to it. "He don't want nobody gettin' that pipe but him one day," Littlejohn declared.

Danny had never thought about Mr. Stiggers that way. He never wondered at all about Mr. Stiggers except the lonely life he lived, why no one visited him, no kids or grandkids, no friend or even a care-taker or social worker who would stop by and check on him the way Ella did with her clients. No one ever entered or left the first apart-ment in the building except Mr. Stiggers. If Littlejohn were right then the old man would just have to get used to Ella coming over.

~~~~

The moon lighted softly across the grass and the trees in the back of Ella's house. Ella and Damon sat on the steps of the back porch. Behind them the house was dark and silent with everyone inside asleep. Earlier that day Ella had sent word to Damon, through Buddy, to meet her that night. She saw Buddy coming to the house with a delivery and she rushed downstairs to meet him.

"Tell Damon I need to talk with him tonight. It's important," she whispered so the cook wouldn't hear her. "Eleven-thirty," she said as she took the groceries from Buddy.

Now she and Damon sat quietly on the steps and looked out into the distance into the blue-black night, thinking about the news Ella had shared. She had told Damon that she had missed two of her periods. Her periods were one of the things she had learned about from her aunt. When her father gave up trying to keep Ella from becoming a woman he finally turned to Bernice for help. He showed up at his sister's door with his hat in his hand and told her he needed her. "You knew you couldn't raise those girls by yourself," Bernice had scolded before setting out to teach Ella about herself. That was how Ella learned about her menstrual cycles and all of the things she would experience as she became a young lady. And now she had missed two of those cycles. At first Ella didn't pay attention to the absence of her monthly, but it wasn't until she started to feel different and her nipples became sensitive when she bathed and when Damon touched them that she felt something was wrong. She looked up 'menstrual cycle' in one of the books in her father's library, and that was when she discovered what missed periods meant. The talk she had had with her aunt had only prepared her for having her periods, not for missing them.

When Aunt Bernice had the talk with Ella it had been one morning in Ella's bedroom. She told Ella how her body would begin to change, how her breasts would begin to grow and how new feelings would begin to move in her and how she would have monthly discharges. Then she leaned in to Ella. "The main thing to remember is those feelings you're going to start having. The ones I told you about? Make sure they don't get the best of you." Then she put her hand on top of Ella's hand. "And make sure none of these boys get the best of you."

And now, one boy had.

"You sure 'bout this," Damon asked as he looked back up at Ella. When she had given him the news he had unconsciously moved down to the next step.

"No. But if it is true, what are we going to do?"

Damon looked back into the yard. "I don't know." After a while he said, "I guess we can get married."

Ella sat up straight, her emotions piqued, but then reality set in. "My father would never go for that."

"Would he go for a baby?"

She sat back, deflated by Damon's question.

Damon nodded his head. "Right. He wouldn't. I guess we could always elope."

"Where would we go?"

He thought for a second. He had never planned on staying in New Home, yet where he wanted to be never included having a wife and a child along. "L.A.", he said. "I always wanted to see what Los Angeles was like."

That was where Ella would tell Danny his father probably lived when it came to the point in the story where Danny wanted to know. L.A. was the last place she remembered Damon talking about and it was what came to her mind as she listened to Mrs. Wexner talk about her life. The two of them, Ella and Mrs. Wexner, walked through a park arm in arm as Mrs. Wexner reminisced about her youth. She stopped Ella and looked at the flowers that spread before her like colorful hamlets of pink and white, of blue and red and yellow, among fields of green.

"My mother always loved flowers." She steadied herself on Ella's arm. "Throughout our home there would be flowers, fresh flowers that she would cut from her garden. Even in the coldest of winter she would bring flowers into the house from her greenhouse. It was always springtime in our house," Mrs. Wexner said with a smile.

"I bet that was beautiful," Ella said.

"Oh my, it was!" They walked on along the winding walkway, enjoying the mild afternoon. Behind them the city buzzed with the traffic of cars and buses and with people on foot moving purposefully to their destinations, paying only quick mind to the garden in passing.

"My father had a garden too," Mrs. Wexner continued. "But he preferred growing hearty things like beets and carrots and cabbage. Of course my mother made him keep his garden out of the site of our windows so it wouldn't condemn her garden of roses and tulips to a life of the common place."

Coming to a bench, they sat down and continued to talk. "You know, I think of scenes from 'The Sound of Music' when I think of you growing up," Ella said. "I know it might sound silly, but that's what comes to my mind whenever you talk about your life as a child."

Mrs. Wexner smiled. "Kind of," she replied. "But not quite as formal as those damned kids in that movie."

Ella laughed. "Mrs. Wexner!"

"Well it's true." Then she looked out over the plots of flowers that grew under the shade of trees and ones that vibrated brightly in the sun. "Greta and I used to go to a field, not too far from the town in which we lived, and pick wild flowers. We would make the cutest arrangements with them: garlands and bracelets with the entwinement of the flowers. One summer we decided that we would hand them out to the people of our town. They would smile, and thank us. And for the boys who we liked, we made special gifts. We made vests of flowers."

"Vests?"

"Yes," she said. "It was Greta's idea, and we worked hard that summer, painstakingly lacing together flowers with twine in the shape of vests for the boys we liked. For me it was for Helmut—ah, he was such a handsome boy. And for Greta it was Dieter. He was beautiful too, but not as handsome as Helmut. But you know what," she said, pressing her hand on Ella's arm. "They didn't appreciate it. When we gave them their vests, they laughed at us and told us the vests looked silly."

"That's too bad," Ella said. "You know how boys can be."

"It didn't matter, because after that day Greta and I decided we would make our gifts and give them to each other. We would put flowers in each other's hair, and we played by ourselves without those silly boys ever coming to our minds again." She smiled. "Greta and I gave gifts to each other until the day she died. When her husband was alive he didn't like it. He tried to stop it, but he couldn't. I would send her gifts and she would send gifts to me. My Karl didn't care. He understood the emotional depth of love so I think he was simply happy that I was happy with Greta."

"Maybe one day we can visit your home together," Ella said cautiously. She knew Mrs. Wexner hadn't been there since she and her family were taken away.

"Maybe," Mrs. Wexner said. "I'm afraid of what I might find. They took everything from us and trampled the flowers," she said as she looked wistfully at Ella. Then suddenly, with a tap on Ella's hand she remarked, "So. Tell me about your first love."

"My first love?"

"Yes."

"Ok. Well he was older than me. About five years older than me."

"Five? Oh well!" Mrs. Wexner shrugged. "Love is love."

"Yeah. He was a nice boy who invested a lot in love." Ella paused as she thought about Damon and of the tragedy. "He invested a lot in love," she continued, "and it hurt him, so he left… And that's it," she said as she looked at Mrs. Wexner.

Mrs. Wexner watched Ella's face for a second before replying, "I understand." Then slowly, Mrs. Wexner asked, "Was that Danny's father?"

Ella looked at her in surprise. It had never dawned on her that Mrs. Wexner even had any idea that Milton wasn't Danny's father.

"He looks nothing like your husband."

"Yeah," Ella quietly answered.

"Has your husband treated Danny well?"

"It's been difficult at times."

"Does Danny know of his own father?"

"No…"

"Then it will continue to be difficult. Not only between Danny and your husband, but everyone else. Tell him. Tell Danny about his father. Your secrecy only feeds Danny's anger."

"I know."

"Then tell him. Tell him."

As she left Mrs. Wexner that afternoon, Ella thought about Danny's birth and of all the anger, the bitterness and the violence that surrounded it. She stood outside of Mrs. Wexner's building and looked out onto the streets. If only things had been different…

~~~~

Ella's belly had begun to grow and she had done all she could to hide it, but wearing loose clothing and avoiding her father by spending more time in her bedroom promised nothing more than a temporary solution to her situation. There wasn't anything else to do but tell her father the truth. She didn't sleep at all the night she realized that she couldn't keep the pregnancy a secret. Lying in bed on her side, she looked out the window, the same one that Damon had entered so many times to lay with her, and she imagined the ways she could have avoided the place where she found herself. She imagined not having gone back to where Damon was working the day she first saw him in the store, or allowing their conversation that day to become anything more than passing words. She even thought how she could have ended the pregnancy, the way she had read that it could be done. But all of those things, those imaginings projected there against the night sky, languished. Because to have committed to any of them would have meant to regret the joy she had experienced that summer. The baby that was growing inside of her was hers, and it was Damon's. As she saw it, the baby growing inside of her was testament of the love she and Damon had for each other, of the smiles they exchanged, of his large hands holding hers, of the weight of his naked body on top of hers and of feeling him inside of her, becoming one with her. The dream of them being together forever was still there, and so was the baby they had created.

The next morning she lay in bed and listened to her father get ready for work. She listened to him walk down the hall to the bathroom and run his bath water, and she listened as he went downstairs to fix breakfast, and she thought how lonely he was since her mother had died, and how, just maybe, having a baby in the house might bring new life to him. She heard her father and Ren talking in the kitchen beneath her bedroom. Ren's voice was becoming as deep as his father's voice. Soon her father left the house and drove off down the street.

It wasn't too long before she got up and went into the bathroom to get ready. Then she walked quietly down the stairs and slipped out the back door.

Bernice's house was three blocks from Ella's house so it didn't take long for Ella to get there. She had no one to turn to about her condition except Damon, and these days he seemed at a loss for words, so she turned to the only person she felt would have an answer.

As she walked up to Bernice's door, Ella tried to imagine how her aunt would respond to the news she was about to receive. Finally Ella settled on the image of her aunt coming to a point of understanding, after the initial shock. Ella settled on the image right before she rang Bernice's doorbell.

She heard her aunt's voice in the distance, talking to someone, most likely over the phone since her aunt had divorced her second husband and lived alone in the large house, and it was too early to have visitors. Ella heard her aunt tell the person on the phone to hold on and then she waited for her to come to the door.

"This early in the morning!" Bernice grumbled as she came to the door. "Yes?" she asked as she unlocked the door, ready to challenge the early morning visitor, but when she saw it was Ella she became concerned. "Ella. What's the matter? Is everything ok?"

"Yes ma'am. Everything's ok. I just want to talk."

Bernice looked at her for a quick second, trying to glean information. "Ok. Come on."

Ella followed her aunt to the kitchen.

"Have you had breakfast?"

"No ma'am."

"Go 'head and fix yourself something," Bernice said as she picked up the phone. Bernice began to wind down her conversation on the phone when she noticed Ella hadn't moved, but stood quietly near where Bernice was standing. This caused Bernice to look at Ella standing there and her eyes moved down to Ella's belly. "Girl, I have to go," she said to the other person. "I'll call you later." She hung up the phone and turned back to Ella, who continued to stand with her head down. "What have you done?" Bernice said. "Ella. What have you done?" Bernice sat heavily in the kitchen chair and grabbed her niece by her shoulders, shoulders too small and too frail to be part of what was happening. "Ella!" This time Bernice called out her name as she shook Ella. "Ella! No!"

All of the uncertainty that Ella had been harboring came to the surface and she began to cry.

"Who did this to you Ella?"

Ella continued to cry without answering.

"Who?" Looking at her niece, small and broken, her sobbing soft but full of pain against the quiet of the kitchen, Bernice leaned forward and took the young girl in her arms.

Bernice didn't tell her brother why she needed him to come to her house, but that it was dire that he did. She tried to avoid words like 'dire' or 'emergency' because she didn't want to taint what was happening in a bad way, but it was the only way to get him to leave his office.

Emmanuel arrived quickly from his office. Bernice let him in and stopped him in the foyer. "I just want you to know that Ella is here. She's in the kitchen. Emmanuel, she's pregnant."

Emmanuel's knees buckled and he fell back against the door. Bernice held him up. "Emmanuel, she's alright. She doesn't know what to do."

Emmanuel looked around in disbelief. "No," he said softly as he slowly shook his head. "No."

"She's alright," Bernice repeated.

Suddenly Emmanuel jumped up and rushed to the kitchen and without a word he smacked his daughter on the side of her head, knocking her to the floor.

Bernice came running in, "Emmanuel! Stop it!"

But he didn't listen to his sister. He had unbuckled his belt, and in one swift move had pulled the belt from his pants and, raising back, he brought the strap down hard over Ella's back.

Ella cried out from the burn of the leather tearing at her skin. She could hear the swoosh of the belt through the air as it came back down across her back. Her skin burned, but it was the shock of her father beating her that hurt most. He had never hit her, and the shock of his anger shook Ella as she curled up on the kitchen floor.

Bernice ran from the kitchen and returned. She stood with a Louisville Slugger raised past her shoulder, ready to strike her brother. "Hit her again and I swear I'll bust your head open!" she declared. Emmanuel turned around and looked at his sister. His eyes were like razors, and red.

"Hit her again," Bernice dared him. "Now you know I'll do it, Emmanuel. You know I will. I'm not going to stand by and let you destroy what Victoria left behind. And if it comes to that child or you, I'll take the child."

Emmanuel looked at his sister and dropped the belt. Then he slowly walked away. As he left the kitchen he stopped and turned back to Ella. "Come on."

"No," Bernice said. "You go on. She's staying with me until you act like you got some sense."

Emmanuel stared at Bernice and then at Ella. Then he turned and walked out the door.

After he left, Bernice picked Ella up from the floor and sat her in a chair. "You need to eat," she said. "Then go upstairs and lay down." She walked over to where Emmanuel had stood and picked up his belt. Opening a cabinet drawer she put the belt in the drawer and closed it. She never gave him his belt back.

Ella stayed with her aunt for a few days. By the end of the week her father came back to get her. He hadn't spoken to her at all since he left Bernice's house, but he and his sister had talked a lot over the phone. Finally, that Friday night he showed up at Bernice's door. "Come on," was all he said.

CHAPTER TWENTY

Milton walked around the outside of the church with the contractor and Deacon Lewis as the contractor, a stout man who continually cleared his throat as he spoke, showed them the work that needed to be done. The ground was still soft in places from the rain and Milton could feel the earth give way slightly beneath his feet. He listened to the man talk and followed the angle of the man's arm as he pointed to the roof and spoke about the flashing and he listened to Deacon Lewis, who questioned everything the contractor told them before jotting down notes on his pad. Every once in a while Milton would interject a comment or two, or he would ask a question so as to be a part of what was going on; he would strategically place his interjections shortly after the comments of the other two men, playing upon their comments while the words were fresh in his head. He did this because he knew his mind was only half-connected to the conversation, as most of his thoughts were on Abilyn.

In a while, the three men wound back up at the front of the church and stood beside the contractor's truck. Deacon Lewis was correcting the contractor on some numbers that didn't quite add up, shaking his head as he spoke. Milton looked at the pad on which the deacon had been recording the quotes. While he didn't see what Deacon Lewis saw on the paper, Milton nodded his head in agreement nonetheless. They continued going over the numbers as they stood by the truck.

A few minutes later, three girls came down the walkway. They spoke vociferously and their voices pulled Milton's attention away from the conversation between Deacon Lewis and the contractor. As the girls neared the church, Milton saw that one of them was pushing a rickety stroller that held a baby that joyously kicked its feet and waved its hands about from the soiled and tattered seat. The girls couldn't have been any older than fifteen. He watched the girls and the baby, none of them seemingly aware of the possible trajectory of their lives. Just then one of the girls looked over at Milton as she continued to listen to her girlfriends. She kept her eyes on Milton while listening to her girlfriends. This lasted for a few seconds, then the girl slowly turned away, shifting her attention back to her friends as they passed, giving Milton little mind. But it was her look that did Milton in. The girl's look seemed to be one of recognition as if she knew, by looking at Milton, what kind of person he was. Suddenly Milton felt exposed, as if he had been broken open. The hidden things, the things obscured so long ago, the things in him that he had not wanted to think about, seemed to have been laid bare in the afternoon sun, chipped, broken for anyone who looked at him to see, but especially they were things that he himself was forced to see about himself that bothered him. He sought to excuse himself by telling Deacon Lewis and the contractor that he had to make a phone call. As Milton stepped away he caught his reflection in the window of the truck and what he saw caused him to quickly retreat into the church.

The face Milton had seen in the window that afternoon was his father's face. Though the sighting was quick, from his point of view Milton saw all the things about his father's face that he could recall, from the lines of his father's mouth that was usually lax and uncaring, to the eyes that danced with the pleasures he would imagine. Milton saw his father and it frightened him because he was in fact looking at his own face.

Now Milton sat in his car and stared out over the river. After he left the church that evening, he had driven around looking for a place to be alone, and he ended up at a park along the river. He had intended to walk through the park, away from the other visitors, just to walk alone to clear his head; but he found it difficult, for a man emptied of all he believed of himself, to walk, let alone stand or even to breathe. The image in the mirror, news of Abilyn's death, and the consequence of their affair all hit him hard, flushing him of everything he understood himself to be. All of the knowledge that held him fast to his beliefs, all of the moorings that kept him close to shore and all of the priorities upon which he'd built much of his life and his reputation had been scuttled in two acts of humanity: birth and death, and now all he could do was to sit alone in his car and watch the evening as it swallowed the remaining light of day.

Against the fading light he saw images of Abilyn and how she might have appeared as she closed her eyes in final peace, and he found he couldn't cry anymore because the pain had bored too deep into his heart, far from the surface where tears flowed. After a while his phone rang. Ella was calling. She was most likely calling to see when he would be home, but he couldn't answer her because emptiness had no audible sound, but he would have to call her back soon.

People walked along the park that snaked the bank of the Ohio River, enjoying the evening, and he realized he had never done that with Ella. They had never walked along the park by the river, or even eaten at one of the restaurants that overlooked the river. There were so many things he had never done with her and so many things he hadn't told her. He knew he owed so much to his wife, and that in spite of how he felt about what she did when she was younger, he still loved her. But he had never told her this. And now, even if he wanted to tell her these things, they would pale in comparison to what she would come to know about him and Abilyn.

~~~~

The final act of Milton's time alone that day, sitting along the river, was thinking about Natasha. Abilyn was gone but Natasha was there, and even though he attempted to disallow any thoughts of the young lady being the child Abilyn left behind, he couldn't remove the correlations from his mind about the young lady having come from Oklahoma, her age, and the fact that she had said she was raised by her grandparents. Yes, Natasha was his child.

Milton offered his sermon that Sunday, watching the faces of the members that were focused on him. He went on with his sermon, but it was the words of the woman on the phone that told him of Abilyn's death and of the child Abilyn left behind that was on his mind. As he looked across the congregation, he saw his wife sitting up front with her hands folded in her lap, looking calmly at him. He looked at her, and the contentment he usually felt when he saw her sitting there floated about and then slowly descended, pushed aside by the uncertainty in his mind. He knew he had to see Natasha once again to settle things.

After he finished his sermon, he sat down in the pastor's chair, and behind him the choir sang. He closed his eyes and listened to the song and LaShon's voice ringing in front of the choir. He listened as he thought about what to say when he and Natasha met.

~~~~

Bringing Danny into this world was a feat that Ella was unprepared for. Her hips were so small that the doctor wondered if the baby would be able to make it through the birth canal without harm. He had told Emmanuel that Ella might need to have a Caesarean birth and that he might have to transport her to the hospital, but Emmanuel insisted that Ella not have a Caesarean birth and that she would have the child at home. He said the pain that his daughter was going through might serve her as a reminder of what she had done. Then he went to a chair in the corner of Ella's bedroom and waited.

Bernice had wanted to be at the birth, but Emmanuel told her to mind her own business. He never forgave his sister for sticking up for Ella, so Bernice sat in her house by her phone watching it.

The pain was excruciating, and Ella's cries could be heard throughout the house. Her voice rang down the halls causing Ren to finally come out of his room and leave the house. Miriam stood outside Ella's door and cried. She had tried to busy herself with her sewing but the wails were so cutting that she ended up pricking her finger. She stood outside Ella's room, crying, as a tiny pearl of blood grew at the tip of her finger and dropped unnoticed onto her shoe.

Emmanuel had paid a large sum of money to have Ella's room set up to receive the baby and to have a doctor and nurse on hand to deliver the child. He didn't need to make the birth any more public than it had already become by having her deliver the baby in a hospital. He had seen the faces of the folks of New Home after they had found out that one of his children was having a baby. They would never say anything to him for fear of reprisal because everyone in New Home knew that one day they would need him for something, so they would look his way as they often did and speak in a deferential manner to him and move on to their business. But Emmanuel could tell by the look on their faces that they were saying 'see your family ain't no better than none of ours'. It angered Emmanuel that Ella would bring fact to their assertions, how she went outside of anything his family would have done or even her mother's family— God knows what Victoria's family will think once they hear of the baby! In his eyes Ella had shown total disregard for him and of her upbringing. All of this is what added to Emmanuel's bitterness with

Ella's pregnancy. He sat in the room and tried to busy himself by reading a magazine, but he ended up looking at the same passages over and over again because of the screams.

The nurse who was assisting the doctor had grown weary of Emmanuel's behavior. Twice she had asked him to hold his daughter's hand and he had refused, so the nurse went over to him and had asked if he wanted to leave the room. He looked up at her, his stern eyes matching the glare in hers, and he told her no. He said that it was his house and that she was bound by duty to deliver the child.

For six hours Ella wailed on her bed across the room from her father, surrounded by the dolls and dollhouse and the stuffed animals that sat along the pink walls of the bedroom with the white curtains that were dappled with pink flowers. The doctor told Emmanuel that if the baby didn't come soon he would take it upon himself to transport Ella to the hospital.

The light that came through the bedroom window had changed from late morning to early evening before the baby came. The nurse told her it was a boy and they cleaned him and gave him to Ella to hold. No one asked Emmanuel if he wanted to see the baby. In fact, no one spoke to him at all. After the baby had been cleaned, Emmanuel came over to the bed and looked at the baby to see if he could detect features that might give him a clue to who the father was, since Ella wouldn't tell him. Then he took the doctor into the hallway where they talked for a few minutes. The doctor came back into the room with a weary look on his face and pulled the nurse aside. The nurse came over to Ella and told her they would have to put her to sleep. She told Ella she would take care of the baby while Ella slept. When Ella awoke she found the scar along the bottom of her stomach.

Emmanuel paid little attention to the baby after it arrived. For a little over a week Ella stayed in her bedroom with her baby because she was unsure if she and her child were allowed out of the room. Emmanuel would pass by Ella's room and casually glance at the baby lying on Ella's bed to make sure it didn't appear distressed or was in any condition that might bring Emmanuel problems. Every once in a while he would ask if the baby had enough food, or if Ella had cleaned its clothes. He never said the baby's name, Danny, and when Ella and the baby finally left her bedroom, he rarely sat in the same room that the child would be in. The only effort he extended to the child was to make sure it received the things necessary to not bring the law into his home. His sister attempted to shower the baby with gifts, but the gifts were returned with Emmanuel's explicit warning that if she wanted to continue seeing the baby she would have to know her limits, one of which was to keep her gifts to herself. It seemed to Ella that her days after the birth of Danny dragged on longer than the days she remembered carrying him during her pregnancy.

While Emmanuel paid Danny little mind, Ren was crazy over the baby and played with his nephew every chance he got. It was he who finally brought the baby out of his sister's bedroom. But while he adored his nephew he wasn't sure how he felt about his sister. Watching Ella's belly grow during her pregnancy and seeing her chest become full with milk, he slowly lost contact with the person he saw as his little sister. He had lost the ability to banter with her like he used to or to playfully mug her when she said something he found absurd. Holding conversation that was more like brief exchanges was the most he could muster with her after the pregnancy and now with the baby, if even that, and it remained that way until he asked to leave home. For Miriam, having a baby in the house was simply a joy, bringing needed light to the shadows that invaded the spaces of the large house. And to celebrate this new light she sewed clothes for her nephew day in and day out.

In time it was the unbearable sting of Emmanuel's displeasure and the murder that drove Ella to get on the Greyhound that night with her baby in tow and leave New Home.

That was the part of her and Danny's life that Ella had finished telling as she and Danny sat on a bench outside of the store they had come from. It was the sight of an older man playing with a youngster, possibly the man's grandchild, that prompted her to tell that part of the story.

As Ella finished speaking, Danny lowered his eyes. "So that's why you never had any more kids."

Ella didn't answer. Her eyes misted and she curled her lips to hold in the pain.

"What was your father's name?" Danny asked the question after a bit of hesitation, because in the past his mother would never mention his grandfather's name.

"Emmanuel." Your grandfather's name was Emmanuel and your grandmother's name was Victoria. He was a loving man…"

"He turned you away," Danny said.

"He was complicated," Ella defended. "Prideful. He loved us but I hurt him. I let him down."

"But to turn away your own child? Nah, that don't get it, Mom. He chased you away."

"I left on my own."

"On account of him, though."

"No. It was more than that," Ella said quietly.

CHAPTER TWENTY-ONE

St. Gregory Street wound up and around the hill just like many of the streets in Mt. Adams. Milton hadn't been to that neighborhood in so long that he had forgotten about the steep inclines and the twisting streets that made the place. He wondered why Natasha had suggested they meet in such an out of the way location.

For days he had thought about calling Natasha, but the thought of opening up another door had dissuaded him. He had tried to tell himself that Natasha wasn't the child left behind by Abilyn; and even if she was, maybe it was a child Abilyn had by someone else. Day in and day out he thought in that manner: postulating that Natasha could be his daughter before entertaining himself with the conclusion that she wasn't, that Abilyn had gotten rid of the pregnancy as he had instructed. But it was the uncertainty that kept him awake at night, too afraid to toss and turn in bed because it would call attention to his apprehension. So he would sit up long hours into the night staring at the walls of his den. Sometimes Ella would come down stairs to see if he was ok and he would tell her he was fine, that he was thinking about a few things, but he would address the matter as if it was something completely professional so as not to bother Ella. Over time he decided he needed to talk with Natasha, and the only way he could get her was to ask LaShon for her information, which presented yet another problem because Milton feared having someone else aware of the meeting would only complicate matters, but he had to find Natasha, so he went to LaShon and told him he needed to find Natasha to discuss a possible project. When LaShon responded with a look questioning Milton's request, Milton gave him a look of authority and LaShon respectfully deferred.

Milton came to the address Natasha had given him. It bothered him that she would choose to meet in a tavern. As he came through the door he saw her sitting at a table with a drink. *First a bar, and now sitting there with a drink in front of her!* He bristled at what he considered disrespect on her part, then he wondered if it was her way of showing her displeasure of him; it was a thought that crossed his mind, but he pushed it aside. He knew he had to have a level head when the two of them talked. Natasha was looking out the window as Milton walked up to the table.

"Hi Natasha," Milton said.

Natasha turned suddenly to see him. She stood and extended her hand. Her face didn't light into a smile when she greeted him. It was as though her expressions had been distilled, leaving only a look of intent on her face.

"Hi Reverend Pruitt." She spoke politely.

"It's good to see you again," Milton said as they shook hands. Feeling her hand in his felt more awkward than before with what he now wondered about her. Now her hands felt like the hands of a young girl.

"You as well."

"I hadn't seen you at church so I just decided you had found another church home," Milton said as they sat down.

"I've been busy with school and work," she replied as she unconsciously stirred her drink.

"How is school?" Milton asked.

"A lot of work, but it's something I like so it doesn't really seem like work."

A server came to their table and they placed their orders. "One bill," Milton said. The server nodded and walked away.

"Thanks," Natasha said.

"I know how it is pursuing a degree. Short on cash but long on the midnight oil."

"Yeah."

"As a matter of fact, me and my wife both got our degrees from that university."

Natasha listened, not once speaking, as Milton talked more about the university. She watched his face, the anxiety behind his eyes, and she listened.

The server brought their orders and Milton took it upon himself to bless their food. As they began to eat Milton guardedly asked, "What made you choose that school?"

Natasha looked at him with an expression of chagrin. "You know why," she answered. "Or you at least have an idea why. That's why we're here isn't it?" She spoke so matter-of-factly that her words seemed to suspend in the air, waiting to be dissected.

Milton sat still, his breath sucked out of him, unable to respond. He and Natasha sat silently looking at each other before Milton finally asked, "Am I your father?"

"Yeah."

Milton's shoulders slumped as if he had been deflated, and he sat, staring at her.

"I'm sorry," Natasha said.

Milton stared at her for a moment longer before softly saying, "I just wish I had known..." He spoke more to himself than to his daughter as his words trailed with the incompleteness of his thoughts.

"My grandparents used to mention your name every once in a while," Natasha continued. "At first it didn't make much difference. I mean, since I never knew my mother, and as far as I was concerned, my grandparents were the only parents I knew. Any idea of having a father wasn't that important to me."

"Your grandparents used to mention me?"

"Yeah."

"Oh." Milton ate quietly as he continued to listen.

"I would see my mother's picture on the lamp table in our living room, and I wanted to know what happened to her."

"Your mother was a beautiful person," Milton said. He and Natasha looked at each other, realizing the hollowness of his words. Milton continued. "She was so smart and talented. You know she had a really nice voice, don't you?"

Natasha looked at him with a bit of annoyance. "That's what I've been told."

"What about you?"

"Do I sing? No."

"You said your grandparents used to mention me. What did they say?" Milton looked cautiously at Natasha.

"I don't know. Usually it would be in passing that I would hear your name. I really can't say. But if you want to know how they felt, they didn't like you."

Milton fell into silence.

"So what now? That's the question I keep asking myself," Natasha said. "What now?"

Milton shook his head dumbfounded. "I need time to think about all of this."

Natasha looked at him as anger and disappointment rose in her. Calming herself, she replied. "This is crazy. Crazy. I need to get out of here," she said, as she got up from the table.

"Wait. Don't," Milton said as he stood in front of her.

"No, I think we both need to walk away and think about all of this because right now neither one of us knows what we want to do. And it's... I just need to go," she said as she walked to the door.

Milton paid the check and followed Natasha to the door. Once outside he asked Natasha if he could give her a ride home but she told him she wanted to wait for the bus.

"I just need some time to myself," she said.

"Ok. I understand," Milton replied. He raised his arms slightly to embrace her but she leaned slightly away. He turned and walked to his car.

As he pulled out onto the street he could see Natasha in the distance sitting alone at a bus stop. She appeared solemn, with her hands folded in her lap, and her face trained ahead like she was in thought. He watched her for a few seconds, then he drove away, watching her image become smaller and smaller in the rearview mirror.

~~~~

Natasha regretted apologizing to Milton. She regretted it but she wasn't angry over it. That was because she felt no anger towards Milton or over the situation in which she found herself that afternoon, sitting in front of a man who had all the expectations in the world that she didn't exist, that he had planned it as such. In place of anger she felt diminished. Yet she felt it wasn't her place to apologize to him that she was alive, but that it was more in line for him to apologize for what he had done. He was the one, sitting there, looking her in her face, that should have apologized, but he didn't. And for that reason she regretted having offered him an apology.

But that wasn't what she regretted most. What was most regrettable was the feeling that had taken hold of her since she had arrived in Cincinnati. Loneliness had taken hold of her. With both Granny and Paw Paw now gone she was beginning to feel alone in the world.

And even though she hadn't sought out Milton to get him to accept her—she only wanted to know him—she was beginning to feel unwanted and, even more, undeserving of his acceptance. It was something that never bothered her before now. Maybe Paw Paw had been right to be against her searching Milton out. Maybe staying close to the remaining family would have been better, but the interest she had in her mother and father had become so strong that it radiated as she became old enough to understand what happened.

Natasha walked from work to a deli to pick up dinner. With the arrival of spring the evenings were still bright enough for her to walk alone to the store. During the winter, when night came quickly, she walked from work with co-workers who lived close to where she lived, and she would shop on the days she had off during the daytime because she had been told not to go out alone once it became dark. Back home in Tarpley, she would never have been warned against walking out at night. Everyone knew each other and the common history of their blackness wed everyone to each other. But the black folks in Cincinnati were different. They seemed to move in constant opposition to one another, creating a heat and friction that often kept them moments away from conflict. It was why she had found it difficult to make friends since coming to Cincinnati.

LaShon told her that black folks in Cincinnati were so removed from memories of accomplishment (he used the words 'chiseled away from success') that they no longer saw hope. He said navigating disaster and achieving fleeting reward were their only sense of compensation for living in Cincinnati. "All black folks?" she had asked, to which he had replied, "Pretty much."

She didn't believe that, that so many of the black folks in Cincinnati were that way, yet she did miss the men and women she had grown up with; the belief the folks of Tarpley had of sticking together was something she hadn't found much of in Cincinnati, and it made her feel even more homesick, and it was why she buried herself in her studies and work. There had been an inkling of hope that she might form a relationship with Milton, but after that day in the restaurant that hope had begun to dim.

Later that night LaShon came over. They hadn't spoken since she met with Milton and LaShon was anxious to know what the meeting was about.

"Ok, so give me the details," he said as he came through the doorway of Natasha's apartment. "Why did pastor want to meet with you the other day?" He had a bottle of wine with him and waved it in front of her as he spoke.

"Boy, will you please?" Natasha laughed as she walked ahead of him.

"Alright. Hello Natasha. How are you doing this evening? Fine. That's good," he kidded. Then, "Now tell me what y'all talked about."

She had forgotten to prepare for LaShon's interrogation. "We just talked about things," Natasha said, as she took two glasses from the shelf.

"Things?"

"Yeah, things."

"He said he had a project for you." LaShon poured the wine and handed a glass to her as they sat on her couch.

His statement caught her off guard. Milton hadn't told her what he had said to LaShon to get her phone number. "Well, yeah. It's a project, but he doesn't want me talking about it yet."

"Why?"

"Because... he wants to make sure it's worth talking about."

"Hm." LaShon studied her face for a few seconds before moving on to another subject.

Natasha and LaShon emptied the bottle of wine that evening, talking and carrying on together. He had become Natasha's bright spot since coming to the city.

As he was leaving her apartment LaShon stopped at the door. "Damn girl, a whole bottle of wine and you still ain't told me what you and pastor talked about."

"See? You are shady," she said. "Thinking you're gonna get me tipsy and get me to talking."

"Ain't nothin' wrong with a bottle of shade. It can go a long way," LaShon laughed.

"But not tonight," Natasha countered.

"Ok girl. Lock your door," LaShon reminded her as he always did when he left her apartment.

She stood in the window and watched LaShon walk to his car. As he disappeared down the street, she thought how even though she might never hear from Milton again, at least with LaShon, she could leave Cincinnati having made one good friend.

~~~~

The dust that had collected on the dresser had accumulated in small, gray dunes that Milton swept up as he moved his cloth along the surface. He wasn't sure how long the furniture had been sitting in the basement, only that it was there when he and Ella bought the house.

After he finished dusting the outside of the dresser he began cleaning out the drawers. A spider scurried from inside one of the compartments, disturbed by Milton's intrusion as Milton pulled out the drawer. He had begun to spend a lot time in the basement since his talk with Natasha. He told himself that he was going to finish cleaning out the basement but found himself mostly just piddling about. These days the tiniest of things around the house caught his attention and kept him at home, chasing after those little things rather than working at the church.

Ella had noticed his change in behavior, but after having found an unopened letter from Charlotte, she figured that was what was affecting him. When she approached him about what was bothering him, he said he didn't want to talk about it, so she left the matter alone. She would give him time to himself.

Unbeknownst to Ella, Charlotte had become the least of Milton's worries. How to move forward with Natasha now consumed so much of Milton's waking days and sleepless nights that he had lost interest in his sister's problems.

He was still trying to wrap his head around the idea that Abilyn went through with the pregnancy, and after he had asked her not to. He even paid her money that he took from his pockets, added to the bit he figured he could take from the church's coffers and his and Ella's savings without being noticed, to pay for her medical expenses—he was never able to call it an abortion. He did it to send Abilyn back to Oklahoma, where he figured she would live the rest of her life happily ever after with only memories of what happened. That was how he had been living his life.

'*She lied to me!*' Those were the words that went through Milton's mind as he poked and scraped at the corners of the drawers. But he knew that what he had considered a broken promise by Abilyn was irrelevant now. How would he move forward with what was now looking him in the face: a breach of trust in his marriage and a daughter whom he didn't quite know what to think about. That was the weight on his shoulders now. The way he and Natasha had ended their meeting the other day was left with so many possibilities.

Since that day he hadn't heard from Natasha and he hadn't attempted to call her. A part of him felt sorrow over the way Natasha looked at the bus stop when he left her that day; she seemed so alone sitting there. A small figure cast against the background of the surrounding buildings, all of which was swallowed up by distance as he left her there. Sitting. Alone. Sadness came over Milton as it had the last few days, but just as he had been experiencing sadness, he was also wondering what Natasha might do. Now that she had found him, surely there must be something else on her mind. But more than anything, how could he move on without losing so much of his life? Each thought came to him every hour of the day and night, each thought piercing the other, all of them pecking at him for recognition.

He recalled the last time he saw Abilyn. "Are you sure you're going to be ok?" Milton had asked the question of Abilyn as they sat in his car at the airport. She whispered that she would be ok, but he watched her face, hanging with sadness, and her eyes, swollen from crying.

"I just want to finish school," Abilyn said as she looked out the window next to her.

Milton took her in his arms and they cried together. The affair was over and Milton simply wanted her and the baby gone, yet he knew that by sending her away he was destroying her dreams and it made him sad.

"I didn't know this was going to happen," Milton said as he moved his mouth against her face. "I didn't know this was going to happen."

Now he was struggling to handle a situation that he thought had been taken care of long ago.

He finished cleaning the last drawer and shoved it back into the dresser.

CHAPTER TWENTY-TWO

Danny lay in bed thinking about his mother. It was night and Cortez's apartment was dark except for the moonlight that fell through the window. From the bathroom he could hear Cortez taking a shower. It might have been nights like this, Danny thought, that his father visited his mother's bedroom. Surely Damon knew what those nights could bring, and Ella, she was so young that she might not have had a full grasp of the possible outcome of their actions. But it was almost certain that neither one of them would have thought their nights together would have led to murder and a girl assaulted for the birth she had given.

Cortez finished his shower and came into the bedroom. "How come you're laying up here so quiet?"

"Just chillin'," Danny replied.

"Everything alright?" Cortez sat on the side of the bed.

"Yeah. Yeah, everything's alright. But you know, I did promise Littlejohn that I would ask you somethin'," Danny said, changing his thoughts.

Lying on his back, Cortez sighed. "Okay, what is it?"

"He wants to be a part of the business."

"Like partner? Littlejohn?" Cortez raised himself onto one of his elbows and looked at Danny.

"That's what he wants. He keeps buggin' me to talk to you about it."

"A man who can't talk to me himself about becoming partner wants to be a partner. Now how does that sound?"

"I think it was because he thought me and him could be partners. But I told him I wasn't sure."

Cortez thought for a second. "Well I guess it's something we can talk about. How come you're not interested in becoming a partner?"

"I'm just not sure. That's all."

"So what does that mean?"

"Nothin' right now. But I got some things to take care of. Family business, so I really don't want to commit to anything right now."

"Everything's okay though, right?" Cortez asked as he rubbed Danny's chest.

"Yeah."

"Alright. Let me know if it's anything I can do."

"A'ight."

There was never a time when Danny felt he had to protect his mother from anything. It had only been since she started telling him about her life that he saw how broken she was. Until now he thought that whatever his mother went through was something she was able to work out by herself. Her determination to remain silent about her past had led Danny to believe that though what happened was something she wasn't proud of, it was something she was willing and capable to work through on her own. But now he wasn't sure. Watching her, her expressions as she recounted things from her past, the way her body wavered at times like a flame about to be extinguished told him that he had to be there for her. But what was it that he needed to do other than listen to her? Danny was unsure of what his role would be in this awakening. He had never prepared himself for it. All he knew was that just as he had seen his mother's determination that no one would hurt him, her child, the only one she would ever have, how she constantly put herself between him and whatever danger she thought might stand red-eyed with anger to get to her son, Danny told himself that night that he would do the same for her. He committed himself to this as the moon spread its light along the room in which he and Cortez slept.

"Thanks for talking to Cortez for me," Littlejohn said as he and Danny headed down the street. "Azhure said we could put something into the business." He became silent, thinking for a bit as he looked out of the car window. "You know," he said, turning to Danny who was driving, "Now me and her can get married."

"Really?" Danny looked over at him in surprise.

"Yeah," Littlejohn answered. "She's good to me man. I mean, look at me. Ex-con, no real education. And look at her. College educated. A nurse. And she fell in love with me."

"That is true," Danny agreed. "And she coulda gotten any dude, but she chose yo' ass."

Littlejohn smiled and went on. "I never thought I deserved somebody like her. Or a good life period."

"Yeah," Danny said, more to himself than to Littlejohn.

"I wanna do better," Littlejohn said. "I gotta figure out how to do better, and with us going into the business, maybe I can."

"Can't argue with that," Danny said.

"What about you? What are you planning on doing?"

"Right now I'm not sure. But I know I want to do something else."

Littlejohn leaned back in the seat of the car. "Yeah. I know we can't keep doing what we're doing. I done told Cortez that I didn't want to keep doing the side gig anymore."

"What did he say?"

"At first he just looked at me like I was talking some foreign language and shit. Then he just said 'ok'. And that was it."

"You really think that's it?"

"I think so." Littlejohn thought a second more. "Yeah, I think so. And you?"

"I think so too. We can't keep up that kind of shit. So I guess he'll have to get out of that game or eventually find somebody else to do his work."

"Yep."

"Besides, I wanna start spending more time with my mother."

"How's that going?"

"She's still telling me more and more about my father and all the crazy shit that went down."

Littlejohn shook his head. "That must be messed up to carry so much inside of you for all those years. But talking about it is always good."

"Yeah, that's why I want her to get it all out."

"That's probably what my family shoulda done. Man, all we do is hold shit inside of us then let it out by fighting and shit. It wasn't until I got with Azhure that I started seeing that holding all that shit inside ain't good for you."

"Nah, it ain't."

Danny turned down a street and as he did so a guy walking along the sidewalk caught his eye. Littlejohn noticed.

"What about you and him?"

"Who?"

"Cortez? How is that going?"

"Alright, I guess," Danny replied, hunching his shoulders.

"Me and Azhure are always talking about you and him. We don't think it's right how he be doing you."

"The fuck you talking about? Me and him both have a say in what's going on."

"Azhure said you need to find you somebody else, and I agree."

"And how do y'all know that? I mean, I ain't in need or nothing. What me and him got going on is fine."

"I don't know. I think it's not cool the way he brings all those women around you and you just…"

"Just don't care," Danny quickly added. "That's how I see it. I don't care about that."

Littlejohn dropped the conversation as they pulled up to his apartment.

"Thanks again, man," he said as he got out of the car. "And make sure you're there for your moms."

"No doubt," Danny replied. "No doubt."

The stories Ella told and the state the stories left her in made Danny visit her more often. The pain and the sadness in his mother's face as she recounted her past worried him, yet he knew both he and his mother needed the stories so he made every effort he could to visit her to make sure she was ok, even to the point of coming around the house. His visits didn't sit too well with Milton but Milton was reluctant to create a scene because to do so would make him appear the villain and might only embolden both Danny and Ella to having Danny around the house. Besides, Milton was preoccupied with his own problems to bother with any arguments.

The aroma of a beef roasting in the oven drifted into the family room where Ella and Danny sat. The sun had turned a deep orange color and filled the room as it began to retire for the day. Ella sat with a throw draped across her legs. The magazine she had been reading when Danny came over lay open on her lap as the two of them talked and watched TV. On this evening, she didn't tell any stories. She and Danny simply relaxed in each other's company, talking about whatever came to their minds.

Danny noticed the change in his mother's face that evening. Her face had begun to look weary. Even when she laughed her smile had a wan appearance, a weakness that seemed to drain her face of life. Her eyes were the only features that had a sense of vibrancy to them, yet even the brightness in her eyes were dimming as they were now no more than small sparks of light in circles of darkness. Watching his mother, Danny realized even more that he needed to be there for her.

That night as Danny came into his building, he stopped and got the mail from his box. He stood for a moment in the hallway and looked through the letters. He hadn't paid any mind that he was standing near Mr. Stiggers' apartment until the old man hit the door and yelled at him.

"Get away from my door," Mr. Stiggers yelled from inside of his apartment. He struck his door once again, only harder and screamed, "Get away!"

Danny looked at the door for a moment then walked up the stairs to his apartment. From below he could still hear Mr. Stiggers screaming and banging on his door.

~~~~

If only she could tell Buddy she was sorry, maybe then she wouldn't see his face, wet and wrinkled, his gaping mouth and bulged out eyes, and the belt that had been pulled so tight around his neck that it was half hidden in his flesh as his body lay alongside the lake. Maybe the putrid smell of rot and rancid water that rose on the banks of the lake that day wouldn't fill the room in which she now sat talking with her client. Ella had given many days and nights praying to Buddy to forgive her, but nothing seemed to help because the images and the odors came and went at the behest of something greater than her will.

Ella's client was a young man in a wheelchair. His name was Simon, though he hated it when Ella called him by that name. She hadn't seen him in a while because he had suddenly disappeared off the scene and no one knew where he had gone—or at least no one would tell his family or Ella where he was. And now, after weeks of missing, he had suddenly reappeared.

"Simon where have you been?" She asked the question as she sat with her notebook and Simon's records in her lap. She focused intently on her client and past the memory of Buddy.

"Out."

"It's been almost two months. That's not 'out', Simon."

The young man pressed his hands on his wheelchair, lifting his body slightly as he nervously adjusted himself.

"Nobody heard from you," Ella continued. "Your mother, nobody." She figured he had been somewhere with the same guys who were in his gang and that they had taken him out so he could have some fun with them like he used to before a bullet put him in that wheelchair.

"Look, I'm grown," he proclaimed.

"Right. Well, understand this, we were about to close out your case, and if that was to happen then what?"

Simon turned his head away.

"Get this, young man," Ella said. "Those guys you keep hanging around with aren't doing anything for you. Most likely they're going to end up just like you or worse."

Simon looked back at her, "And?"

Ella closed her notebook. "Ok, so here's what we're going to do. I'm going to head for that door and you're going to make a decision about if you want me to work with you. If you want me to work with you, then I'll return. If not, then you let your boys care for you. See how far that gets you." She got up and started for the door.

"You can't just walk out," the young man said. "It's your job to take care of me."

"Now you sound stupid, Simon. You take care of yourself. We work with you, and if you don't care about yourself there ain't nothing anyone else can do for you. So you call me when you get your act together."

As Ella headed to her car she thought about the young man back in the apartment. A bullet had claimed half of his body and he was still willing to push the envelope. It's what worried her about Danny. By the time she got to her car Danny wasn't the only person who crossed her mind, but Damon and Buddy was there as well. She didn't want her Danny to end up like them.

That night dreams of Buddy and the odor of the lake visited her again. She jolted awake and, realizing it was another dream, she looked to make sure she hadn't awakened Milton. But Milton wasn't there.

CHAPTER TWENTY-THREE

The days spent moving things from one corner to another corner of the basement and of bringing forgotten pieces of furniture back to life had settled Milton's shock over Abilyn's death and Natasha's birth. The past few weeks had taken a toll on Milton, but they had also given him time to accept what had happened. Now he began to take walks in the morning after Ella left for work and he had begun to function at his usual pace around the church, but none of this was without having Natasha on his mind and none was without wondering how things would turn out. But at least now the shock had left.

The street Milton and Ella lived on was a street with mature trees and homes that weren't too old. They were mature homes, unlike the modern homes that he and Ella thought were no more than over-sized crates. It was that air of maturity that had appealed to them when they decided to buy their home on the street, and the street had remained that way ever since. The tricycle belonging to the neighbor's daughter sat at the edge of the neighbor's driveway. It had most likely sat there all night, untouched. That's how it was on their street, mature. Mature responsible people.

Milton walked along the street thinking about himself and Natasha. Now that he knew she was real he was able to consider her. He had called Natasha a few times over the last two weeks and they had talked, at first briefly, but over time their conversations became longer. She hadn't come to Cincinnati with her hands out asking for money and she bore no hostility towards him, so it made their conversations easy. By the third time the two of them had talked, Milton actually came away proud of her. Like the trees and the homes on the street where he lived, his daughter was just as mature. They made plans to see each other later that day.

When Milton came into the office, Mrs. Hargrove greeted him before heralding the day's agenda. Even with her stern manner her eyes seemed to say she was happy to see that Milton was back in the swing of things. However, Milton also saw a look of curiosity in Mrs. Hargrove's eyes when they spoke to one another, as if she was waiting for him to confide in her what he might be going through. Milton returned her greeting and took his mail off of her desk, all the while listening to her detail his agenda for the day. He thanked her and went into his office.

After going through his mail, making phone calls, meeting with contractors and signing off on papers, he closed the door to his office, as he usually did, to read the Bible and meditate on the Lord. Then he left the office for the day telling Ella he had to run errands for the church.

Natasha set the cup of coffee on the table and took a seat in a chair to the side of the couch. "Are you sure you don't want anything else?"

"No, no. This is just what I need," Milton said.

"I see you drink your coffee black, just like my grandfather did."

"That's the only way. To me, it's not coffee if you add all of that other stuff to it. Milton shook his head disapprovingly. "That's not coffee, that's dessert."

Natasha winced, "But black. That's too strong."

She had decided to let her father come to her apartment. Over the last two weeks they had talked a lot over the phone, mostly about school and her plans. They had learned some of the things that each other liked and disliked: he loved mystery movies and she liked science fiction films, he only read newspapers and news magazines and the Bible, while she read most things. She had also learned more about his personal life, that he and Ella had been married for twenty-nine years and that they met when Ella moved to Cincinnati from someplace in northern Ohio. Natasha had learned more about her father's stepson and how little Milton knew about him because they had never really been able to bond. And Milton had learned more about his daughter, the fascination she had with life and how she shunned parochial thinking and that after graduate studies she wanted to go into a doctoral program. In many ways she was much like her mother.

One of the things Milton had noticed over the weeks of talking with Natasha was that she had expressed no interest in being a part of his life. It was as though her interest in him was little more than curiosity or a fascination with life and how things turn out. It seemed more inquiry than anything. This bothered Milton to some degree, but to another he wasn't sure if he was ready for her to be that much a part of his life anyway. The sudden appearance of someone who, in his mind, had never existed, required adjustments, and he wasn't sure if he was ready for all of that. Still, seeing her and getting to know her, that she did exist, his life had already been affected.

"Do you have any pictures of your grandfather?"

"Yeah," Natasha said, getting up and going to her bedroom.

She returned with the photo. It was framed in a triptych in which her photo was in the middle frame, flanked on the left by another frame with a photo of her grandparents, and on the right was a photo of Abilyn. Milton took the photos from her and looked at Paw Paw and Granny, their faces inured from years of experience, softened that moment for the click of a camera. He needed to see the faces of the others who were involved in this journey. He looked at them before moving his eyes across the frames, across the history of a family, until he settled his gaze on Abilyn. For a long quiet moment he stared at her photo. Natasha stood over him in the silence that enshrouded both of them, then she reached down and put her hand on his shoulder. It was the first time she was able to feel her father, not just touch him but to feel him, his bone and muscle and his pain.

"I'm sorry," Milton whispered as he looked at the photo. His eyes filled with tears.

Natasha sat down beside him. "It's ok. I know she understands," she said as she looked at the photo. Natasha had wanted to hear those words from Milton that day at the restaurant, but now that she heard them she needed to understand what they meant.

The two of them sat for a moment, quietly looking at the smiling face of Abilyn. After a while Natasha asked, "Why are you sorry?"

Milton looked at her. "What?"

"I need to know why you're sorry," Natasha said softly, but with strong intention. "I need to understand." She took his hand in hers. "I need to understand," she repeated.

"Everything," Milton whispered. "Everything. My falling in love with her, hurting her and your grandparents. Everything."

On his way home Milton thought about Abilyn. The sky had turned a deep violet as he drove in the silence of his car. Along with Abilyn he saw others: his mother, her bloodied face and the tears that intersected the violence but that couldn't stop it; his sister Charlotte and the hopelessness that had taken hold of her; and little Taniya, her life treated so casually and considered so insignificant that it could be extinguished with no memory of the act.

That night before going to bed he opened the letter Charlotte had written him, and he sat alone in the living room and began to read it.

~~~~

Milton's path to the church wasn't an easy one but it was set for him because of the horrific evil he had witnessed in his father, and Milton felt that if there was a place for so much evil surely there must be a place for grace. This is what Milton thought as he grew into a young man.

The first act of grace came when his father died. It took months for his father to die. He had been admitted to a ward for others who had his illness and his condition had progressed to such a state that no one was allowed to visit him, even the doctors and the nurses who took care of him weren't permitted to be near him without having their faces covered with a white mask. During the time Milton's father was away from the house his presence loomed in all of the rooms, rooms that recalled that at any minute a fit of violence could erupt and if it didn't, the shear chill of the revulsion Milton's father had of his wife and children would freeze his family with fear or level them under the weight of self-loathing.

When the phone call came from the hospital that his father had finally passed on, Milton's mother thanked the caller, then she stood with the phone receiver to her ear after the call had disconnected, staring, her eyes focused on an invisible spot on the wall. Milton had been standing nearby and it wasn't until he heard the beeping from the phone that he came over to his mother and took the phone from her and hung it up.

For weeks the family walked in half-silence around the house, their minds in a semi-conscious state of freedom and oppression. They would almost tiptoe from room to room so as not wake their father who might come angrily out of the room and hit one of them for disturbing his sleep, or now, for fear that any sound might bring him back to life. Then one morning Milton woke to the sound of music coming from the radio in the kitchen. It was an especially sunny Saturday morning and the sound of the music coming from the radio pulled him awake. He lay in bed for a while, listening to the music, and calmly, the realization that his father wouldn't be coming back finally set in. When he got out of bed, he went to the kitchen, walking through the living room where the front door and all of the windows were open and the breeze of a late spring flowed through the house. His mother was in the kitchen making breakfast. When he walked into the kitchen his mother turned to him. "I made pancakes," she said with eyes brighter than Milton could ever recall. And in the trash was the small brown sack the woman had given his mother.

His father's passing was a sign of the possibility of good things, not just bad, and from that day on Milton vowed to make sure that the possibilities would lean towards good.

Milton had done the best he could to make sure things went right not only for his mother and his sister, but for others as well. The voice he always had began to speak more clearly and with vigor as he spoke up for his mother, who never overcame her meekness, for his sister, who seemed forever caught up in moments of indecisiveness. And eventually he began to speak for things he thought of as righteous once he discovered his presence while he was in college.

In time, Milton's image as an advocate grew and he became known as a man with a moral conscience who campaigned for the powerless. People would tell him, after having watched him standing on the steps of the campus administration building or speaking in front of City Hall, that he should consider the ministry. They told him that his leadership would have more gravity if he wore the collar of a cleric. He struggled with such an idea because he wasn't sure if he trusted a god that would have allowed his family to go through the suffering they had and why a person like his father would've even been allowed to exist.

Until the dream, Milton struggled with his feelings about God, but it was in the dream where he was told of the war in which God was engaged, and that Milton's father had not been under the influence of the Lord, but of Satan, and that was why it was necessary for Milton to take up the sword to fight in the battle against evil. That dream had told him what he needed to know, and from that day on he set forth to set things right.

CHAPTER TWENTY-FOUR

The past few weeks had been kind to Ella. There had been no dreams about Buddy and no visitations that would awaken her. Even her experiences with Danny and Milton were pleasant, with Danny visiting the house more often and he and Milton beginning to act civil towards each other. Milton seemed to be moving out of his depression and had begun to spend time with her again; though when they did spend time together she felt there was still something on his mind, but that he had become at ease with it. She figured his reading Charlotte's last letter like she had suggested lifted some of his worries. And Danny, there was something new in Danny that brought a light to his eyes and a degree of concern to his voice; Ella believed he was finally realizing he had something valuable to live for. She was sure the stories had something to do with that and she was glad she had finally started to tell them.

More than anything though were the dreams she started to have about Damon. They were different from other dreams she had of him in the past in that in these dreams he appeared to be in the present. There would be things about him—the clothes he would have on and his surroundings—that spoke of the present that told her he was alive. In the dreams his face hadn't aged but maturity had shaped it. The last dream she had about him he was kneading dough in a bakery. He smiled and looked at her as he kneaded the dough. He told her he missed her and hoped she was happy. She told him she was. She could smell the yeast and feel flour gather in her nostrils as she watched him. He told her he was happy too now that he knew she was happy. She watched him wipe his hands on his apron and she told him not only was she doing fine but that he had a son, and with those words he proudly grinned… then the dream ended. The dreams of Damon had been more frequent over the last few weeks and they were what kept Damon on her mind as she went through her day. All of these things over the past few weeks are what gave Ella some relief.

It was late in the day as Ella left Mrs. Wexner's apartment. Along with a few of Mrs. Wexner's family members-- great nieces and nephews-- and caretakers, she had celebrated Mrs. Wexner's ninety-second birthday. Ella had stayed behind to help clean up and to sit with Mrs. Wexner. She couldn't help but wonder with the dementia setting in on her client if it would be the last birthday she and Mrs. Wexner would spend together.

The evening had a calm about it as people walked along under a rose-colored sky. The air was fresh from the fragrance of the grass, the trees and flowers that had left for winter and had now returned. It was too nice of an evening to go home right away.

Ella drove around town with the windows down, feeling the cool air move against her face. A song played on the radio and she hummed along, taking in the evening. It was a little past seven-thirty and she decided to stop by Danny's apartment. She figured he would still be home preparing to go to work that night. She hoped that one day he would leave that job and those people and find something re-spectful to do with his life. Security is what he said he did, but to her, he was just a bouncer, and no good could come from that.

She turned onto Danny's street past the men and women who probably spent half of their lives on corners; past the women who basked in the attention the men gave them as the men sidled up to them or called out to them as the women passed by. Even the young man she had seen some months ago, the one who reminded her of Buddy, took a moment to lower the phone from his ear and call out to a young lady.

As Ella came to Danny's building she saw his car wasn't parked out front so she decided to write a note and put it on his door to let him know she had dropped by. She wrote the note then went into the building. She walked into the hush of the building and looked at the door of the apartment the old man lived in. There was a stillness that seemed to surround it that was so pronounced that it caused Ella's breathing to stop. Suddenly, music started up somewhere on another floor. It was distant and she could barely hear it, but it was enough to dispel the stillness. Ella exhaled softly and climbed the stairs where she affixed the note to Danny's door, then left.

That night Ella hoped she would dream about Damon again, but instead she spent the night listening to what Milton had to tell her when he got home from church.

~~~~

Danny walked through the bar over the broken glass as he, Cortez and Littlejohn checked out the damage. The front window had been shattered and was now covered with plywood and the few tables that had been near where the wheel rim came through the window were overturned and scarred.

No one spoke as they took in the damage. Danny and Littlejohn glanced at each other, but kept their silence to allow their boss to have the first words. They watched Cortez as he quietly assessed the mess, his large frame standing stock still and his eyes moving past the overturned table and chairs to the rusty wheel rim that lay among the broken glass on the floor. He stood quietly, but his face had sharpened into anger.

It was Minnie who broke the silence. "Who the fuck did this?" She came through the door, pointing to the wreckage. Her eyes were wide with a mix of shock and anger. Cortez didn't say anything but continued to look at the metal rim on the floor.

"Cortez! Who the fuck did this?" Minnie demanded, as she confronted her business partner.

"How the fuck do I know?" Cortez suddenly spat, his voice booming.

"What happened?"

He looked at her and blinked in awe of her question. His eyes were rimmed with anger. His response caused her to back down.

The office had been immediately checked and nothing had been taken from the safe but Minnie went through it again anyway.

Danny and Littlejohn sat at the bar and watched Cortez and the investigators go over the site. The police were respectful as they worked with Cortez, with one of them, who seemed to be a rookie, looking in awe of Cortez.

"Look at that shit," Littlejohn said with a laugh. "Just because Cortez was in the NFL they treat him like royalty. If that was you or me they would be treatin' us like any other nigga."

"So you still wanna become a partner," Danny asked.

Littlejohn looked at Cortez and the mess around him. "Yeah," he said thoughtfully. "I do."

The police and Cortez disappeared to the office, where they watched what was captured on the surveillance camera. After the police left, Cortez and the rest of the staff began to clean up the damage as Cortez said they would be open for business that night.

Once the bar had been straightened, Danny headed home. As he stepped into the hallway of his building, he was stopped in his tracks by what he saw outside Mr. Stiggers' door. A pile of clothes and odd items had been dumped outside of the old man's door. Danny stood for a moment, looking at the heap then he walked over to Mr. Stiggers' door and listened. He could hear Mr. Stiggers shuffling around his apartment.

"Mr. Stiggers. You ok?"

There was no reply. He heard the old man mumbling to himself.

"You want me to take care of all of this for you?"

Still there was no reply, so Danny went upstairs to his apartment to get something to put the mess in. When he got to his apartment, he saw the note his mother had left. He smiled as he read it. *Just stopped by. Love you. Mom'*.

Danny went inside and pulled out a large garbage bag and headed back downstairs, where he began gathering up Mr. Stiggers' belongings. Another tenant came through the door.

"What happened?" The woman stood over Danny. "He didn't get evicted, did he?" She looked at the mess on the floor, then to the apartment door. The bag of groceries she carried dangled from her hand.

"Nah. He's just... I don't know," Danny answered as he shook his head.

The woman sighed. "He needs to have somebody look in on him."

"I know. I used to check in on him before he chased me away."

"We all keep our eyes and ears on him. But it's all we can do," she said as she went up the stairs.

Danny finished gathering up the items and took them to his apartment. Once he was inside, Danny set the bag containing Mr. Stiggers' belongings beside the sofa and began going through it. Mostly it was clothes: shirts and pants and shoes; but they were clothes that a younger man might have worn years ago, and some of them had been slashed and torn.

Things went as usual at the bar that night. In fact, there seemed to be a slightly larger crowd, with some who came to see the effects of the break-in. The staff was a bit more vigilant, having been given what little description Cortez had of the man caught on camera. Other than that things went as they usually did.

Cortez stood by a table talking with a group of people. He appeared to be explaining what he thought happened. The people at the table shook their heads pitifully as they listened.

Making his rounds, Danny stopped and talked with some of the patrons. Some of them expressed sadness over what happened, while others simply said it was crazy.

Later that night, Littlejohn came over and stood by Danny. "You see? This is why I still wanna do this," he said as he looked out over the bar. "When people love a place they'll turn out no matter what."

"It ain't about the money?" Danny asked.

"I gotta be able to make a living off this. But nah, it really ain't about the money. I like this business, man."

After the bar closed Cortez, Danny and Littlejohn stayed overnight in case of another assault. The three of them slept in Cortez's office; Cortez and Danny on the sofa bed and Littlejohn on a pallet on the floor.

Danny headed back to his apartment the next morning. As he got out of his car and walked up to his building his phone rang.

"What happened at your job?" Ella asked.

"It wasn't nothin'," Danny replied as he stepped into the hallway and glanced at Mr. Stiggers' door.

"Don't tell me it was 'nothing', Danny. It was something. If it's on the news, then it was something. You weren't there when it happened were you?"

"No. They waited 'til we left."

"You need to let that place go, Danny."

"Yeah."

"I wish you would do it."

"Ok."

Ella listened to what Danny didn't say. Then she sighed. "Danny you need to stop being so bullheaded."

"Mom. I said ok."

He and his mother got off the phone, both of them knowing their conversation had gone no further than it usually did, because Danny set out to do what he wanted to do.

CHAPTER TWENTY-FIVE

Ella watched Milton as he told her. She watched his mouth move, his lips going up and down, his face lower and his head turn to the side in search of more to say. The sound of his voice was a muffled rumble and she could barely hear his words, yet she was able to understand them. The only words she could hear clearly were "I'm sorry," probably because they wavered and they were words that he seemed to choke on. She watched him noticing how different he was from the young man she had first seen when she arrived in Cincinnati, who stood on the steps of the university administration building addressing his fellow protestors, and how different he was from the man that stood in the pulpit on Sundays. All of those Sundays, even when he knew what he had done. And all of the days he sat beside her laughing and talking, right there on the couch where they now sat, like it had never happened. Him and the girl, naked, the two of them. The expression on his face when he was between her legs as he came. Those are the images that raced through Ella's mind as she watched Milton talk, causing the heat in her body that seemed to have erupted in her chest between breaths to rush to her head, and she felt her arm twitch as if she wanted to hit him. But then, slowly, a calm settled over her. A gentle, blue calm that was at first imperceptible came out of nowhere and began to settle over her, replacing her anger with other thoughts, better thoughts, like thoughts of her and Danny and of the feeling of promise left by the dream she had of Damon. Whereas before, Ella had been watching her husband give his pitiful excuse, now she only saw him. He seemed to go on indeterminably long with his explanation causing her attention to drift from him to the window in the room, and it occurred to her that it had been dark for a while. Then she looked back at her husband going on with his explanation. Calmly she stood up. "It's getting late. I'm going to bed." And just as calmly as she stood, she turned and walked out of the room.

Ella heard the phone ringing from the kitchen downstairs. The chime on the phone was supposed to sound cheerful as it usually did, but that day it sounded more like a shriek that pulled her awake. She opened her eyes and lay still, listening to the phone ring. Then it stopped. The half-light of an overcast day illuminated the bedroom where her son used to sleep. The thought of lying next to Milton had been so repulsive that she slept in Danny's old bedroom. She could have slept in the guest bedroom but she needed the comfort of familiar things left behind by her son to help her sleep. The image of Milton telling her about his affair replayed in Ella's mind and she thought how he had suddenly looked like a stranger to her. She thought about how she kept looking at him, trying to bring his face and his physique back to someone she knew, but no matter how hard she looked at him she saw someone different, someone who was so disgusting that she only wanted to be away from him. Even now, lying in the dull light of the bedroom, the only feelings that filled her were revulsion and distrust; where there could have been hurt, she felt those feelings of revulsion and distrust because she had learned that hurt is too expendable and, in time, can lose its value, so it had been instilled in her by experience that she would reserve hurt only for her feelings over Danny. She learned to reserve her hurt the day that Danny was born and she saw the expression on her father's face as he peered over at the dark little boy in her arms before walking out of the room. She learned it then just like she learned that there would be no one else in her life as important to her as her son. Milton was someone she loved, but just like her hurt, he too was expendable, but less valuable. The phone rang again and stopped. After a long silence it began to ring again and she got up and went downstairs to answer it. She knew it would be church members on the line checking in on her and Milton. Milton had the assistant pastor preach that day, giving the excuse that he, Milton, was feeling under the weather. That was what Ella told Sister Ford when she spoke to her on the phone and asked her to pass the word around that they were ok. As for her, Ella said she was just a bit tired from sitting up all night with Milton.

After Ella hung up the phone, she stood in the center of the kitchen and measured the silence. It was too silent and things were too still, so she pulled out dishes and began to cook. She put a pan of biscuits in the oven and took out a pot of stew that had been left over and put it on the range. Then she pulled out fresh vegetables and prepared a salad.

Later she went upstairs to her and Milton's bedroom, and stepping through the doorway she saw Milton move under the covers. He lay with his back to her and the covers over his head.

"I warmed up some stew from the other day."

Milton was slow to answer but quietly mumbled, "Ok," his voice coming from under the blankets.

Ella and Milton ate for a while without saying a word to each other that evening as an almost debilitating stillness hung over the house. Even the radio that normally played during dinner, or the TV that sat on the counter that might be playing had been left off. That evening nothing made a sound.

Finally Ella spoke. "I told Sister Ford that you were feeling under the weather. She said you told Pastor Chenault that and I went along with it."

"Ok," Milton whispered.

"I told her I was a bit tired because I stayed up with you." She looked at her husband, who silently ate his dinner. "That's what you wanted me to say isn't it?"

Milton didn't reply.

"Is that how it's going to be now?" Ella asked. "Is that what we're going to do now Milton? Mislead people?"

"Ella…"

"I'm sorry, but I'm not as comfortable as you are at doing that."

"Neither am I," Milton said.

Ella looked at him for a long minute. "Neither are you? You serious?"

"I made a mistake, Ella. People make mistakes."

"We're not talking about mistakes, Milton, we're talking about lying."

"I never lied to you."

"Then let's call it disingenuous. Is that better for you? Because that's the best you're going to get from me."

"I made a goddamn mistake," Milton suddenly exploded. He glared at his wife. "Like you've never made one. You just cover yours up with silence. You walk around here hiding things from me. I don't know what you're about. Have you ever thought of that? And now you're going to come for me?" He blew a frustrating breath and continued to eat.

"But I've never mislead you, Milton. Never. I told you there were some things in my life that I'd prefer not to talk about. You knew that because I told you before we married. Before, Milton. Not after, and you said you respected that. But I've never mislead you."

"No. Instead you just decided to hide things from me because they're too... I don't know, uncomfortable to talk about? Too bad to talk about? I don't even know. So I just go through the years trying to help you through whatever the hell happened to you. Watching you through all of the sleepless nights and the silent days when the memories hit you. No, you haven't misled me, but you sure as hell haven't made my life easy, Ella."

The both of them looked away from each other.

"And still, I hang in there with you because I love you," Milton quietly said. "Look, the most I can tell you is I messed up and I'm sorry, Ella," Milton looked at his wife. "That's the most I can tell you." He paused before continuing. "And as far as the church is concerned. I don't have to tell them everything about my life. I've confessed to being imperfect. That's all anyone needs to know. I'm just as imperfect as anyone else in that church and it's why I get up there in that pulpit every Sunday. To save them and to save me."

They ate for a while without going any further before Milton got up and turned on the TV to fill the silence.

After a while Ella asked, "What about Natasha?"

"If you mean is she after something, no. I can assure you. She's not that type of person."

"Then why did she come here?"

Milton was slow to reply. "Because she said she wanted to see... who her father was."

Ella exhaled softly and looked at her plate. Then she looked back at her husband and asked him, "How is she doing?" This time her voice was calm and held concern. Having met Natasha she had come to like her and she couldn't blame her for looking for her father.

"She's fine."

"Are you sure?"

"Yeah. I'm sure."

They stayed apart the rest of that evening, Milton sitting in the den and Ella in the living room. When Ella went to bed that night she slept again in Danny's bed, and that night she dreamt again of Damon. She was in the kitchen once again as she had been in the last dream, but this time Damon wasn't there. She called his name but he didn't answer yet she knew he was near because she felt his presence. The kitchen was larger than it had been in the dream she had before, and it was darker and colder. The utensils stood out, looming large around the room, and everything was clean. She looked around and spoke Damon's name, at first self-consciously, then a bit louder, but the sound of her voice quickly dissipated and the kitchen was quiet again. Then, in the distance, she heard a sound like water lapping upon a shore. The sound came from a room that seemed to have suddenly appeared and was lighted by sunlight. When she walked to the room she saw Damon sitting with his back to her, calmly looking out onto a lake. Slowly, she walked into the room and the room became the outdoors. She walked towards the lake, realizing that it wasn't the lake in New Home. Yet the ground felt familiar and the light, the way the sunlight fell across the pine trees that surrounded the lake was as recognizable as it had been when she was growing up in New Home. As she came upon Damon she felt the presence of someone else but she couldn't see who it was, only that it was there and it stood near where Damon was sitting. She spoke to Damon and he turned and looked at her. "Hey," he said softly. He had on a pair of work khakis and a white tee shirt that fit him just like she remembered. Ella sat down beside him and they looked out onto the lake. "What are you doing?" she asked after a while of sitting quietly beside him. He turned to her and smiled, "What does it look like, girl? Waiting." And with that, he turned back to the lake as the odor of rot and sour water rolled upon them.

~~~~

The way the woman straddled his father's lap that evening. She didn't even take off her dress. The bottom of her dress hiked up over her big brown ass and the top part pushed down around her waist. Milton watched her moving round and round on his father's lap like she was bobbing in water. His father's pants and draws were down around his ankles and his was face buried in the woman's breasts, sucking her titties. Milton had seen his father's car as he walked home from a friend's house that evening. His friend had told him that his father came and went from the woman's house often, sometimes late at night, sometimes the next morning, but Milton hadn't listened to his friend, not because he didn't want to but because his friend didn't tell Milton anything new. But that evening Milton saw the car himself, parked on Clemmons Street in front of the woman's house. When Milton first saw his father's car he moved to the other side of the street to pass by it, but just as he had passed it, the image of the car and the small, one-floor house pulled his eyes back and he watched the car, drifting in the waning light of a late winter evening in front of the small shotgun house. He slowly walked back to the house, passing his father's car where his father's felt hat sat on the front seat, up to the house where Milton stood for a minute, his thoughts convulsing. Then, looking around, he walked towards the back of the house. There was snow on the ground and he could hear the crunch of the ice beneath his shoes as he snuck along the side of the house, past the first window where a little girl sat on a bed playing with a doll that was like the one his sister had, and he crept on until he got to the next window, where he saw them. The curtains were only half drawn and he watched them there in the room with his father in the chair and the woman moving across his lap. He watched them until he felt vomit rise in his throat and he ran from the window. Once he got to the street, he looked back and saw his footprints in the snow that led to the woman's bedroom window and he panicked. But then the fear left him and he picked up a stick and carved the word 'whores' in the snow just alongside the woman's house.

Milton hadn't thought about that evening in years, but it came to him as he got ready for work. After he had gotten dressed he walked down the hallway from the room he and Ella used to share, to the room where she now slept. He stood by the door and listened to his wife's breathing. It was just past three a.m. and the hallway was dark enough, the night, still enough, for him to listen to his wife's breath rising from her sleep. After listening to her, he went downstairs and fixed something to eat, then he wrote her a note telling her he was going to the office, and he left.

The steeple atop Christ The Redeemer Baptist Church appeared like a dark thorn thrust against the night sky, and the gray stones of the walls of the church seemed to sulk in the dark as Milton drove into the parking lot. He walked across the lot, listening to the gravel roll and clack beneath his shoes. Once inside the church, he turned off the alarm and went to his office, passing through Mrs. Hargrove's office first, where he picked up his mail and checked for messages.

He sat at his desk and worked, drafting emails that he would send later that morning and reading through his mail. By sunrise he was done and he left the office, after dropping off papers on Mrs. Hargrove's desk.

It was seven-thirty and Ella hadn't called to check on him as he had hoped she would. He figured his having left so early would have prompted her concern, but it didn't. At least it didn't show. So now he found himself sitting in a coffee shop, glancing down at his phone on the table, as if by having the phone in his sight he would be able to summon a call from her. Only one call came in and it was from Mrs. Hargrove, who had seen that he had been in the office and had called to see if he was ok. He told her he was fine and that he would be in as soon as he felt better. After a while of silence, meant to convey to him that she didn't believe him, Mrs. Hargrove finally told him she would pray for him. He thanked her and she hung up.

Outside the window of the café, he watched people emerge from spaces: apartment buildings, cars and side streets, like hatchlings, as they headed to work. Ella would soon be joining them.

The sun rose over the edge of the city and cast a new light that grew in brightness as the day inched towards noon. Milton still hadn't heard from Ella and he was uncertain about calling her. What they went through that night was hurtful, like watching the sneer on the face of someone who once loved you but had now come to despise you. It was just that hurtful and he saw it in Ella's face, her eyes as they looked at him in half shock, and the other half, a look that sought to understand or maybe to deflect what was being said. It was hurtful, not just for her, but for him as well, because he knew no matter how he explained what happened years ago, it wouldn't remove the bite of it. He had had sex with someone else. He had lain naked between the legs of someone else and had emptied himself in her just like his father had that evening in the house on Clemmons Street. It was hurtful and it was something he wished he could remove from his and Ella's life, to make their life as much as it had been, for better or worse, in the past, because he knew that while their life together hadn't been perfect, it had been sustainable, and after all, wasn't that what anyone could ask of marriage? Or maybe that was the problem, he thought, as he stared out the window, that their marriage had become something they both held onto instead of relishing it like they did when they were younger. Maybe, if even then all those years ago, Ella had just given him the right amount of attention the way she heaped it on Danny, that Milton wouldn't have strayed. This is what came to Milton as he sat that late morning, staring out the window of the café.

Once they had been the center of each other's eye. He knew from the day he first saw her on campus, standing in the crowd at the foot of the steps of the administration building, looking up at him as he spoke. She stood out because she was dressed in the uniform the housekeeping crew wore at the university. She had stood with a co-worker, both of them at the edge of the gathering, their aprons weighed down with spray bottles and rubber gloves, and listened to him. He remembered thinking how brave she was to stand there, since she could have been fired for collusion with the kids who were bent on causing trouble. Her co-worker had gotten that idea and had nudged her to step away, but Ella had stood there a bit longer before slowly walking back to work. A few weeks passed before he saw Ella again, but this time it was as he walked by a classroom. He saw her through the window of a door that was closed to a classroom. He stood a bit to the side and watched her, not wanting her to see him. He hadn't noticed how small she was that day a few weeks before. Sitting in the classroom she was the smallest person there and she looked like she could be no more than fifteen or sixteen at the most. He watched her as she looked attentively at the professor and as she scribbled notes in her notebook. It took Milton only a couple of days to decide to approach Ella. He had stayed around campus, studying in the library, until he figured her class would be letting out and he hurried to the building where she was leaving the room. It was an evening class and the students rushed quickly from the room, passing her by. He remembered laughing to himself that her short legs moved so swiftly, but how she was still passed by the other students.

"You gonna need skates to keep up with them," he said, laughing.

Ella laughed. "I'm used to it." She continued walking on.

"My name's Milt," he said before correcting himself, "Milton." He didn't want to sound too casual since they were meeting for the first time. He walked for a bit beside her, but not too close.

"Hi," Ella replied. "I'm sorry, but I have to be somewhere." She spoke apologetically and hurried from the building.

Milton watched Ella a few more times without approaching her. But one day as he was sitting in a study lounge she came in to empty the trashcans. Milton saw her but lowered his face back to his book and waited for her to come over to the can that was beside the chair he sat in. This time it was she who noticed him and spoke.

"Hi."

"Hey. How you doing?" Milton answered calmly.

"I'm sorry I rushed past you the other day. I had to be somewhere."

"Ok," Milton replied with a nod.

"And my name is Ella." She smiled. "I didn't think about it until I got home that you told me your name but I didn't give you mine."

A week later Milton waited for her to come from class. "I'm gonna give this one more try," he said, causing Ella to burst out laughing.

They talked as she walked to the bus stop, and they had been talking ever since.

Milton didn't want to lose what he and Ella had left of their marriage. Even though the marriage had been through a lot and the edges of it were a bit tattered, the seams were still strong. At least he hoped they were. And hoping was the best he could, do besides praying.

A server came over to see if Milton wanted a refill on his coffee and to see if he might want to order something to eat. Milton had been sitting in the shop for so long that the young man thought he might now be hungry.

"Would you like something to eat?" The young man asked with concern as he poured another cup of coffee for Milton. He figured Milton had to be going through rough times since he had been sitting and staring out the window all morning.

"Yeah," Milton replied. "Yes, I'll order something."

The server reached across Milton and pulled a menu from the stand. "Here you go," he smiled. "Let me know when you're ready."

Milton looked at the menu and ordered.

"What type of bread do you want that on?"

"Bran," Milton whispered as he noticed the young man had a ring through one of his nostrils and eyeliner on his eyelids. "Oat bran."

"Alright. Got it." The server smiled and walked away.

Milton ate his meal facing, the window as the day passed by.

Natasha stood in the living room of her apartment with one arm folded across her stomach, while the other was raised to her face as her fingers picked insecurely at her lips.

"How is Mrs. Pruitt doing," she asked.

Milton hesitated before answering, as if a sudden change in outcome would occur during those few seconds.

"Not good," he answered.

"What about me? Did you tell her about me?"

"Yeah." Milton answered with slight bewilderment.

Natasha sat heavily in a chair.

"I didn't want this to happen," she said.

Milton wanted to tell her that it was past that point, that she did show up and now she would have to deal with the consequences, but Milton was a responsible person, so he told her not to take all of this on alone. He had come over to tell Natasha that he told Ella about he and Abilyn. It was late in the afternoon and he still hadn't heard from Ella, and for part of the time he spent staring out of the window of the café, he realized how much he resented the weakness in him that allowed him to act like his father and he resented Abilyn for not being decent enough to turn him away when she found out he was married, and he held just as much resentment for Natasha for coming to look for him. But those feelings were constrained by the thoughts of a responsible man. An honorable, intelligent and responsible man.

"We'll get through this," he said.

It was night when Milton left Natasha's apartment. He had comforted her as much as he could with as much faith as he was able to hold on to. They had talked about things other than the affair becoming known and the future of it being known. He told her more about himself that evening and what he had been through in life and what that same life had done to his mother and his sister Charlotte. The story was so intriguing that after a while, he and Natasha were able to put aside what he had come to tell her. But it was the final part of their conversation that pulled the evening together for them. It was when Milton told Natasha how he had always wanted to have a child and how it was his fear of his infidelity that made him suggest that Abilyn terminate the pregnancy, not the thought that he would have a child. He had always wanted to have a child and now his child was with him.

Milton phoned Ella once again as he walked to his car but she didn't pick up. He put his phone back in his pocket and continued on to his car.

CHAPTER TWENTY-SIX

Ella never had best friends and she always kept secrets. Even growing up in New Home, she had people she knew like Vanessa Travers who lived next door and Coretta Walker, a classmate who, when the three of them were together, would proclaim their friendship. But in truth, to Ella they were no more than people she knew who were almost as close to her as her family, and she even kept secrets from her family. This thing of keeping secrets really wasn't something Ella considered objectionable because to her, it was simply a matter of conducting her own affairs. So she never saw what she withheld from others to be secretive but a sense of propriety, except for the incident that involved Buddy. And this thing of being able to see another person as a best friend, well, she just never quite got it because it required the participation of something she simply didn't recognize as necessary, and that was to share the state of her affairs. That was the way she had always seen things, so it was nothing out of the ordinary that with what she now knew about Milton, she didn't have a best friend to confide in, and even with the person she felt closest to, her son, she kept the matter secret because she knew how unpredictable Danny could be.

A week or so had passed since Milton's indiscretion came to light and it had indeed affected Milton and Ella's marriage. They didn't talk as much around the house like they used to and they tended to spend their time in separate rooms. During those times when they would encounter each other, such as in the hallway or while passing a doorway, they would look awkwardly ahead to avoid eye contact before disappearing to their separate place in the house. It left the house with a sense of vacancy, and if someone were to look at the house from the street at night they would see one light on at one end of the house and another one on at the other end of the house. The only time Ella and Milton came together was for dinner. They still fixed dinner for the both of them because it was quietly understood that the time spent at dinner would be the only way they might heal.

Even at dinner Milton was more likely to seek conversation with Ella than Ella was with him. Her distrust of Milton was just that strong, and any trust she had in him had now been replaced only by the bond she had with Danny. After all it was she and Danny who started this journey the night she sneaked from the house, the night she boarded the bus, the day she needed to find milk for Danny and got off the bus and ended up in Cincinnati. Milton's misplacement of trust only strengthened Ella's resolve to bind herself entirely to her son.

And the honor. While the story of what happened between Milton and the other woman was vile, just as vile was the fact that Milton attempted to terminate the pregnancy, and now knowing that didn't happen, he seemed willing to keep the child in the shadow part of his life. This was beginning to bother Ella just as much.

"Have you been spending time with Natasha?" Ella's question rose from the silence of the kitchen, causing a slight gasp in Milton.

He wasn't sure where his wife's question was leading but he nodded, "yeah."

"She shouldn't have to suffer because of something you did," Ella said, not even looking his way. Natasha had come to Ella's mind over the last few days after what small amount of anger Ella had, had settled, and the resolution that Danny would now be the only person she could trust. It took some time to sort through what she thought about Natasha, because while Natasha had no say in having been born, she did have a say in coming to Cincinnati. Even the way she made herself into Ella and Milton's lives was something Ella mulled over; the way she stood before them at the restaurant, smiling and addressing them as if she was a stranger, and then to even come into their home and eat the food Ella had spent so much time to fix. The subject of Natasha needed considering. The mess that brought her here was done, but who she was to be was something to be considered.

Milton didn't respond to Ella because he was also wondering how he would fit Natasha into his life.

"For God's sake, Milton, at least have some dignity. Even honor," Ella continued. She used the word 'honor' since the word 'morals' had been sacrificed for his actions.

"I want to meet with her, Milton."

This time Milton's gasp was audible and he almost choked on his food.

"Ella…" was all he could get out.

"Me and her need to know where we stand. This is about more than just you, Milton."

"I just don't want no mess, Ella."

"The mess was already made. I'm just trying to clean it up. And you need to clean it up too." She looked at her husband with the sternness of a parent. "You're not going to be able to clean it up by sneaking around, keeping her in the shadows. Folks are going to find out and she might be the only person you'll be able to turn to."

Just as difficult as it would be to accept Natasha, would be not to accept her. Ella understood this because she had lived through hatred and through estrangement. It was hatred that drove her from her father's house. It was hatred and the feeling of being estranged more than anything that made her steal past her father's bedroom at two in the morning balancing her son in one arm and a suitcase and diaper bag in the other. She had fallen out of favor with her father when she became pregnant, and over time his disfavor had turned into pure hatred of her and the bastard she had by that boy.

So much had happened that year as Ella's baby made his way into the world: Buddy had been murdered and Damon had left town; Ren had left home and Miriam had taken to her mother's sewing room for most of the day. And as for Ella's mother, Ella wasn't sure what her mother thought because she hadn't heard the voices coming from her father's room anymore. So for Ella there was nothing left to do but leave.

She walked quietly down the stairs, praying that none of the planks on the stairs would creak, and then she went into the kitchen where she gathered up the bottles of water and bottles of baby formula for Danny and placed them in the diaper bag. She looked down at Danny to make sure he wasn't about to wake up and she headed for the door. Once she was on the porch, Ella put Danny in the carrier on her chest, which was one of the last gifts her Aunt Bernice had given her before Emmanuel made her stop bringing over gifts for the baby. Then, leaving her key under the doormat, Ella started down the street without looking back, because she knew everything that mattered was with her and before her. The bus was scheduled to leave the station at three a.m. and she figured she could make it over to Stratford in time if she hurried, so she walked quickly along the quiet streets of New Home, listening to the soft breathing of her sleeping child against her chest and the low roar of the wheels of her suitcase rolling along the sidewalk. She was about to cross the bridge over the creek that separated the two communities when she saw a car coming toward her. The car startled her because she had planned her departure at a time when she didn't expect anyone to be up, but there came the car crossing the bridge from Stratford into New Home. The car slowed a bit as it passed. She could see the figure of a man behind the wheel looking at her as he rolled by, but Ella continued to walk towards the bridge. A few feet away the car turned around in the road and came back. The man slowed down and rolled alongside her.

"You ok?" the man asked. He wore a fedora and Ella could barely make out his face.

"Yessir," Ella answered as she continued walking.

The man continued to drive slowly alongside her.

"You on your way to the bus station?" He nodded his head towards Ella's suitcase.

"Yessir."

"If you tryin' to catch that next bus, you ain't gonna make it. Get in."

"We can catch the one after that," Ella said. She didn't recognize the man, but since he was black she figured he was from New Home.

"Sun'll be up the time the next bus leaves out. If you runnin' away I figure that won't work in your favor."

She knew the man was right. Once the sun rose and her father saw she was gone, he would come looking for her. Maybe. But she didn't want to risk it. She slowed and looked at the man. Buddy's murder and Danny's birth had served to bring an understanding of consequence to her, so she wasn't sure if the man could be trusted.

"I don't know you."

"Mr. Maxberry, from over on Lindsey Street," the man said as he raised his hat slightly. "I'm Mr. Maxberry," he repeated. "If you don't need a ride I'm fine with that," he said as he started to turn the car around.

"Ok," she called out suddenly.

Mr. Maxberry stopped and she got in.

"Where you on your way to," Mr. Maxberry asked.

"Los Angeles. I have an aunt who lives there," she lied.

"L.A.? That's a long way. You and that baby will be on the road for a couple days or more."

"I know. My aunt told me."

They rode for a while as she listened to Mr. Maxberry sing under his breath to a song on the radio. Finally they arrived at the bus station. Ella thanked him and got out of the car and pulled her suitcase from the backseat.

"Here," Mr. Maxberry said as he pulled out a few bills from his wallet. "This'll help you out."

Ella looked at him for a minute.

"Look you better take this money so you can make that bus," Mr. Maxberry said, pushing the money through the air.

She took the money from him. "Why are you doing this?"

"'Cause I don't like yo' daddy," he said. Then he touched the brim of his hat. "You take care of yourself," he said and drove off.

Ella watched the car as it pulled away then she looked in the terminal and saw that passengers were already boarding the bus. She purchased her ticket and rushed to get in line. Soon she was on the bus and New Home was moving away into the night.

Ella understood hatred and she knew how it felt to be disowned, and it was why she now waited for Natasha at the coffee house near the campus. They had agreed to meet at twelve thirty and it was already a little past that time. Ella looked towards the door as another person came into the shop. It was a sunny brisk day and the light and the rush of the wind every time someone entered or left the shop caused her to squint and shiver slightly, but she didn't move to another table because the brightness and the cold invigorated her. The night before had been another sleepless one.

It was ten minutes later that Natasha came through the door. Ella raised her hand to get Natasha's attention. Natasha hesitated as if a second thought had come to her, then slowly she made her way to the table.

"Hello Mrs. Pruitt," Natasha said. She spoke softly as she tried to mask her uncertainty.

"Hi," Ella replied. She stood as the two of them briefly clasped hands before sitting down.

"Thanks for coming," Ella said.

"You're welcome. I'm glad you asked to see me."

"Well, if Milton had it his way we probably wouldn't be meeting at all."

Natasha sighed slightly. "I'm sure that's something we can all understand."

"No, not really," Ella remarked before signaling for the server. "Let's order. I really need some coffee. And lunch is on me."

As the server left with their orders, Natasha offered an apology. "I'm sorry for all of this Mrs. Pruitt."

Ella looked at Natasha for what seemed to Natasha like the longest stare in her life. Then Ella replied, "As long as your intentions are good you shouldn't have anything to be sorry for. That's why I wanted to talk with you. I understand that you had no control over what Milton did, but I do need to know what your intentions are."

Natasha shook her head as she looked at Ella. "Intentions? Mrs. Pruitt it's like you've already painted me as a villain."

"Well it's just that everyone has intentions. And, well, come on now, you did travel almost a thousand miles with what I'm sure was some idea that you might stir up conflict once you arrived here. And then you sidled up to Milton knowing what you knew. I don't think anyone wants to make you out to be a villain, but you do understand what all of this conjures up don't you? I mean, none of this is coincidence."

"Ok, wait." Natasha raised her hand a bit. "Nobody sidled up to anyone, Mrs. Pruitt. I didn't even come here with the thought of getting to know Reverend Pruitt personally."

"Then why did you come?"

"I'm not someone who's out to vindicate an act. I have way too much to do with my life than to wallow in mess like that."

"Then why did you come?" Ella repeated.

The server returned with their orders, causing Ella and Natasha to sit back quietly. Then they thanked the server, who looked apologetically at them and hurried away.

"Listen to you, Mrs. Pruitt," Natasha said. "Instead of me being the bad person, maybe you should look at yourself as being paranoid. Like I told you, I am not interested in vindication. Look, I'm the person Reverend Pruitt didn't even want to live," Natasha continued. "And in the process of it all another life was lost. My mother's. Don't you think that's enough of a story that warrants attention? I wanted to see this man who was at the center of that story—my story. I needed to see who Milton Pruitt was."

Ella fell silent. She took a sip from her cup and set it back on the table. "You're right. It's something that does warrant attention, and I'm sure it'll get it. But none of this removes my need and even Milton's need to know what your intentions are." She raised her hand to stop Natasha who was about to speak. "And it's not about painting you as a bad person." She paused before continuing. "If anything, he's the villain…" She heard her voice trail as she spoke life into the awareness she had of her husband. "So it's not about anyone being a villain, but of concerned parties needing to know how to deal with all of this."

"I only wanted to see him," Natasha said as she moved her food around on her plate. "I would have left that Sunday after I saw him at church if it wasn't for LaShon latching onto me. He was the one who wanted to introduce me to the two of you."

Ella looked at her, waiting for Natasha to understand what she had just said.

"I know. I could've just declined his invitation," Natasha admitted. "But… after I had seen Reverend Pruitt and had listened to his voice he became real to me… more real than just imagining him. He was there and I was too, and I…" She put her fork on her plate and looked into Ella's eyes. "You know, I thought all I needed to do was to see him. To see who this man was and then just walk away. It's not like he ever played a big part in my life other than what we both know, Mrs.Pruitt. And my grandparents did a good job raising me, so it wasn't like I needed anyone else's attention. But…" she paused and slowly shook her head. "But when I saw him I found that I couldn't just walk away."

Ella quietly listened to Natasha.

"And when he looked at me," Natasha continued, "It was like, 'he sees me'." She looked into Ella's eyes. "Mrs. Pruitt, you might not know how that feels, but it was like…" she looked a bit ahead, past Ella before repeating, "He finally sees me. And when he shook my hand…"

"All without knowing who you were," Ella finished.

"Yeah," Natasha replied quietly.

"Natasha I apologize," Ella said. "I can't right what Milton did."

"I know. But it's not about righting anything."

"So what now?" Ella asked. "How can we make this situation better?"

"I'm hoping you and Reverend Pruitt can help answer that question."

"We're going to have to work through this together. That's a start," Ella said as she began to eat her lunch.

~~~~

There were more than just clothes in the pile that was outside of Mr. Stiggers' door. Lodged between the discarded pants, shoes and shirts were torn photos, memories dispersed among the refuse. Had it not been for Danny's preoccupation with the past he wouldn't have dumped the clothes from the bag and he wouldn't have found the pieces of photographs. When he got up the morning after he had taken the clothes to his apartment, he found he could barely keep his eyes off of the bag. Sitting there in a corner of his living room, the bag seemed to radiate a presence, as if there was something living inside of it. He walked past the bag a few times that morning as he got ready to leave, and each time he felt it, the life that was holed up inside the bag. At one point he thought he saw the bag move slightly, as if whatever was inside of it shifted positions. That's when he made up his mind that he would go through the clothes when he returned home.

That afternoon he took the bag to his bedroom and emptied its contents onto his bed, and that's when he saw the first bit of paper, half-hidden in the fold of a shirt. It was about half the size of a dollar bill and white in color. When Danny turned it over he saw that it was a black and white photo that showed the upper part of a tree. Danny set the piece aside and began going through the rest of the clothes searching for the rest of the photograph, and ended up finding other pieces of other photos. He continued rummaging through the pile, removing piece-by-piece, torn photographs and setting them on the bed with the other torn bits. In time he ended up with a pile that was large enough to fill several shoeboxes. Scooping up the fragments, he did just that. He put them in shoeboxes and took them to his kitchen table where he spread them along the tabletop. He stood there, looking at the pieces scattered across the table, his mind filling with wonder, then he sat down and began sorting out the pieces and as he did so, the photos began to come to life: first an arm, then half of an image of a car, and more images of trees. He could tell by their content that the images were from different photographs and he put each piece in line with what he thought would match the other piece. It was a process he knew would take him some days to complete but he was willing to go just that far to learn what Mr. Stiggers sought to forget.

Hours passed as Danny sorted through the scraps of photos. The sun had gone down and now he sat under the kitchen light watching faces emerge. One of the photographs had been pieced together, and in it a young lady with a beehive hairdo sat on the hood of a car with her legs crossed, posing coquettishly on what appeared to be a summer's day. Her dark skin stood out from the white, horn-rimmed glasses on her face and the bright sleeveless blouse. Danny had decided that he would run strips of clear tape across the front and back of each photo once he assembled them to keep them intact. He finished covering the front of the photo of the young lady and turned it over to cover the back and that's when he saw the inscription, 'Murlene 1962', written on the back. Danny smiled and turned the photo back over to look at the young lady. Now she was someone. She was Murlene.

That night at work he told Littlejohn about the photos as the two of them sat in the back room of the bar. He told Littlejohn about the time he had spent that day putting the photos together and how he had finished one with a young lady named Murlene in it and the year the photo was taken.

After Danny finished telling what he had done, Littlejohn stared at him for a second then asked, "So what's it to you what some old man did with his pictures? What are you going to do with them once you're finished? Take 'em back to him? He don't want 'em."

"Maybe he does."

"He threw 'em out."

"I'm thinking he set 'em out. You know, so somebody could find 'em."

Littlejohn cocked his head slightly. "Oh now you gettin' all psychological and shit. But hey, maybe you right. Just don't let that crazy ass throw the whole box of shit back in your face when you hand it to him." He laughed.

"Nah. I don't think so," Danny replied.

"Detective Danny," Littlejohn said jokingly. "'ey, maybe that's somethin' you can become if you ever leave this place. A private eye."

Danny respected memories. He respected them in all their forms, even as fragments of colors of pink, blue and white; and of voices that were light and gentle and of ones that was dark and angry.

Heavy voices that came and went in Danny's memories like mist. And he would feel a distant despair that would rise and settle, then dissipate. In time, he came to name those colors and sounds and those feelings as memories and in time, he hoped his mother would bring them to light. And while he couldn't get a handle on those memories, he respected them, whether they came as the wisps of memories he had or in the rush of memories his mother had. Even in the memories that Mr. Stiggers sought to toss aside, Danny saw them as important. Danny had come to respect the hunger of those memories, so when Littlejohn asked him what he was going to do with the photos once he had put them back together, he couldn't say right away, but he knew he wouldn't destroy them.

Eventually, Mr. Stiggers would reject the photos, and they would end up along the wall of Danny's bedroom; faces of people Danny never knew and of a place and time he had no knowledge of; looking out on him during the day as he moved around his room, and at night as he slept.

CHAPTER TWENTY-SEVEN

Ella drove to what would be the last of her appointments that morning. She looked for a place to park so she wouldn't have to walk too far in the neighborhood. The streets were so narrow that she could barely fit her car through them, and on both sides of the street the old apartment buildings rose high and gathered shoulder-to-shoulder, blocking out much of the sun, casting a shadow over the men and women who sat on the stoops and that congregated on the corners. Children playfully ran along the sidewalks, their tinny voices rising over the calls of adults as Ella rolled up her windows and locked her car door. She spoke to some of the people on the stoops that had gotten to know her, and played with a gleeful baby cradled in his grandmother's arms, then walked into the building.

"He ain't up to no good," she heard the grandmother say to her as Ella let the door close.

As she climbed the stairs, Ella thought how difficult it must be for Simon to get up and down them and how he definitely needed help. It was where she knew he needed the help of his buddies. Once on his floor, she walked down the hall to his door. From inside the apartment she could hear young men talking boisterously and someone calling out to get the door as Ella knocked.

Simon expected her and rolled in his wheelchair to meet her as another young man held the door open.

"Hi Miss Ella."

"Hi Simon." Ella stepped into the apartment as the young man closed the door. "Didn't you know I was coming?"

"Yeah," Simon said as he and Ella went over to a table along a wall.

"We should be talking in private," Ella said as she brushed crumbs and cigarette ashes off the table. She sat down and glanced around the living room at the other young men that sat on the sofa and at one lounging in a chair in the corner of the room. Two of the guys on the sofa played a video game, while a third one stared at the floor, twisting his locks. The guy in the chair in the corner was asleep with his legs hanging over the arm of the chair.

"They ain't doin' nothin'," Simon said as he rolled closer to the table. "They my niggas."

"We live here." One of the young men had overheard Ella and called out from the living room.

"Is that true?" Ella looked to Simon for an answer.

"Nah. Nah, that nigga lyin' his ass off," Simon said, giving his buddy the eye.

Ella stared at Simon until he turned back to his buddies.

"'ey y'all. Why don't y'all head out so me an' her can talk?"

The young men left out cussing.

"You know you could lose your aid," Ella warned.

Simon slowly nodded his head.

"Look, this is crazy," Ella continued. "I'm here to help you and you don't do anything to help me out. Why is that?"

"I don't know," Simon said, clicking his tongue.

"You have to start doing better, Simon."

Simon threw his head back. "Damn. You always tellin' me that."

"Because you don't seem to get it. And watch your mouth," Ella said as she opened her notebook.

They talked for a while, with Ella going over Simon's needs and trying to get him to not give up on himself. After they had finished, she began gathering up her papers when another young man came out of the bedroom in his boxers and walked to the bathroom.

Ella looked in shock at Simon, and he addressed her expression.

"He don't live here either. He just needed to crash for a while."

From the bathroom Ella could hear the young man peeing. "Ok you need to get it together before you lose your aid." She spoke sharply as she got up from the table and started towards the door.

The woman was still sitting on the stoop holding her grandson as Ella came out of the building.

"You would think one bullet would be enough," the woman said.

Ella blew an exasperated breath and shook her head. "How do you get them to change?"

"I don't know," the woman said as she looked down at her grandson. "I really don't know."

The evening sky was blue and violet and ended in a blaze of orange at the edge of the city where the sun set as Ella drove home from work. She glanced up and noticed how even the clouds seemed to race towards the sunset, and for a quick moment she saw herself racing with them over the horizon. Those were thoughts that came to her more and more since Milton's confession and with the dreams she was having of Damon.

When she got home, Milton had already prepared dinner. She thanked him and they sat down and ate with only a few words being exchanged. Conversation between them had been something the both of them had worked on, but Ella's feelings of betrayal and Milton's shame would drift between them like an oily stain on water, and they would find their conversations fading to silence. After she finished dinner she went to Danny's old bedroom, which had now become her room, and read a book while Milton disappeared into his office. As she read, her mind kept going back to the way the sky looked that evening as she drove home. The way everything, the colors of the sky and the clouds, seemed to move towards the horizon made her wonder if Damon was somewhere where the clouds and the shifting light ended. He had broken her trust too, but there was a child between them so he would always be a part of her.

Later that night Milton knocked on her door.

"Ella? Can I come in?" His voice came cautiously through the door. She invited him in.

"I'll be going back to work the day after tomorrow. I just thought I'd let you know." He stood still, waiting for Ella's reply.

"Are you ready for that?" Ella looked over her glasses at him.

"Yeah, I think so."

"Well you better be sure."

"What else am I going to do?" Milton asked. He looked at his wife, hoping she would have a better solution.

"I guess you're right," Ella said. "Why are you just now telling me?"

"I didn't decide on it until tonight. I can hold off if you want me to."

"No. Do what you have to do."

After a moment of silence, Milton started to leave the room. "Ok. Well, just thought I'd let you know."

Ella didn't reply but turned back to her book. Milton quietly left the room.

Tonight would be no different than recent nights in that Damon would visit Ella while she slept. The two of them would walk along a path in the woods just as they did when they were younger and they would study each other's faces as they sought answers. He even appeared to Ella in dreams she would have of other things. He would appear as someone in a crowd whose face stood out to her, or simply as someone passing along a street. Seeing Damon in dreams had become something that Ella had come to expect, and tonight it was something she needed.

These days, Damon's face was coming to Ella much more. Even the sound of his voice and the way his skin felt, like smooth, taut leather laid thin over muscle, were becoming more and more present with each dream at night and at times with memories of him during the day. But while the dreams and the memories warmed her, they worried her as well because she wondered if Damon's sudden continued presence was a warning that she should do more to protect Danny. She knew there was more to the dreams and those possibilities were what stayed on her mind many nights as she fell asleep.

~~~~

The rain had been falling that morning and had left the ground a shimmering green carpet. Ella had told Buddy to have Damon stop by at a time when she knew her father would be at work and now Damon walked across the back lawn and up the stairs of the back porch. He looked at her and smiled and asked if she was feeling ok. She told him except for some sleepless nights when the baby would kick she was doing fine, but she told him she needed to tell him something. Damon looked at her, his face taking on a worried look.

Ella sat on the steps and Damon sat beside her.

"What's the matter?" he asked.

She was about to answer him when Ren came through the yard. He looked at them then turned his attention away and went into the house. Ella looked up at the house and saw the curtains to the sewing room slightly apart and Miriam's face peering past. Suddenly Miriam's face disappeared and Ella heard Ren scolding her.

"What's wrong?" Damon held her hand. And that's when she told him about Buddy.

Damon leapt from the steps and began to walk in circles, talking under his breath, cussing to himself. The rain began to fall again and she called to him, but he didn't hear her, he continued to walk in circles talking to himself. Suddenly he bolted from the yard, with Ella calling to him, but in a moment he was gone.

~~~~

It was the feeling that someone was in Danny's bedroom that brought Ella awake that night. The sudden closeness of the air and the narrowing of sounds caused her eyes to open and look around the room, but she didn't see anyone, yet the feeling of a presence was there in the bedroom. She didn't think it was Milton standing there in the room, so she whispered, "Damon?" but her voice faded into the blackness of the room. Hearing her voice fade into the darkness told her she was only imagining things, so she pulled the covers over her shoulders and started back to sleep and that was when she heard it, a slight rustle as if someone moved in the dark. She reached over and turned on the light, but no one was there. She turned off the light once again and began to pray as the smell of the lake drifted throughout the room.

CHAPTER TWENTY-EIGHT

"You know why I became a minister?" Milton asked the question as he watched the cup of coffee that he held in his hand. He sat on a windowsill in Natasha's apartment that looked out onto the street below.

"To spread the word of Christ, I guess," Natasha said. She sat on the couch looking across the room at him.

Milton smiled and turned his face to the window. "Well, that would be the most convenient answer," he said, looking out onto the street below. He turned to Natasha. "And in the end, yeah... at least to some degree. But mostly, it's personal. You see, we all have a personal stake in this whole heaven and hell thing no matter what we say. Ministers, just like everyone else, we have those things that bite at us and drive us while we're standing up there in that pulpit. Personal things. We all do," he said as he lifted his cup to his mouth then lowered it without taking a drink. "Mine was thinking I could change the things I saw around me. All of the craziness I had experienced." He paused before continuing. "All of the monsters around me... And I knew it would take something bigger than me to make a difference. A black man trying to make a change. Now how do you think the best way to do that would be?"

"The church," Natasha replied. She listened to him and waited for him to say what was on his mind. She was uneasy with what she thought might be his summation and yet she wanted to get it over with so she could tell herself she had done all she could do, and then move on with her life.

Milton nodded in agreement as he came from the window and sat beside Natasha. "Of course you don't know anything about my father, your grandfather. He was one of the monsters I never wanted to see again. He was a man without a conscience. I mean, he would do the nastiest things to your grandmother and to us and he wouldn't think anything of it. Despicable things… vile," Milton said as he shook his head and set his cup on the table. "It was like he was the Devil himself."

"You don't really believe that do you? Maybe he was struggling with unresolved issues." Natasha spoke as she watched Milton staring across the room.

"What. You don't believe in the Devil?" Milton asked as he turned back to Natasha.

"I don't know. But I do know people mostly act out of things that have happened to them."

"The Devil is real, Natasha. He's real. I've seen him many times and I've had to challenge him many times. He's real."

Natasha didn't reply.

Milton went on. "My father was a womanizer. No, a whore." He shook his head. "A whore," he repeated softly. "He slept with every woman who would let him in, and then he would come home and beat the mess out of my mother and me and Charlotte, your aunt. I hated my mother for letting him get away with all of that." Milton shook his head sharply to clear it. "Look, I shouldn't be telling you all of this. I'm sorry."

Natasha looked down at the cup of coffee Milton had set on the table so she wouldn't see him in his pain. "People have difficulties," she whispered.

Milton continued, barely noticing her comment. "And I saw that monster again, but this time it was me. I guess I got so caught up in trying to clean everyone else up that I forgot about myself." His eyes filled with sorrow as he looked at his daughter. "Natasha, I did Abilyn wrong. And I did you wrong."

Natasha and Milton sat for a moment in the silence of her apartment. Finally Natasha spoke.

"Well," she sighed. "If it helps, I tend to not let things like that catch me up. Good and evil. I try to understand things and make them work out for the better."

"That's good," Milton said softly. "That's the best way to look at things I guess."

"It is."

"Natasha?"

"Hmh?"

"Even though I'm ashamed of what I did, I'm not unhappy to have you here."

Natasha looked at him, stunned.

"You're my child."

"Oh," Natasha whispered. "I never thought I would actually hear those words from you. I—I wasn't prepared for it."

"Prepared?" Milton repeated.

"Yeah."

"Well it's true. I'm sorry for what I did and I hope God forgives me for what I did. But it's true, I'm happy to have you here."

Natasha sat in silence for a moment, then, "Okay…" was all she was able to say.

Later that evening, as Milton was about to leave, Natasha walked him to the door. Milton asked her if she and Ella had any plans of seeing each other again and Natasha told him they had said they would.

"Good," he said with a smile. Then, "One more thing. Would it be ok if you stop calling me Reverend Pruitt?"

Natasha looked at him for a second, "Not at this time. Maybe as time goes on."

"I understand."

They hugged each other.

"I'll see you later," Natasha said. She felt Milton squeeze her closer.

"Ok," he whispered.

She watched Milton from her apartment window as he walked to his car and for the first time she saw someone different than the man she first met some months ago, and as she watched him drive away, for a brief second she saw her father. The evening spent with him had left a lot on her mind. She had indeed expected to see more of Milton, but she hadn't been prepared to cross over into stories of his life. His family, his past, his pain, she hadn't prepared herself to know that part of him and now that she did, she wrestled with where to go. The man that was talked about when she was growing up had now become more than just talk.

Later that night as Natasha was studying, her phone rang, and she took a break from her studies and talked with LaShon. It wasn't long into their conversation when LaShon told her he had been on her street earlier.

"I was about to see if you were home and then I look up from my car and I see Pastor sitting in your window. That caught me by surprise," LaShon said. "Why was Pastor at your place?"

"He just stopped by."

LaShon listened quietly. "But why," he asked.

"To talk. Why are you asking me all of these questions?"

"Girl I've only asked one question."

Even though LaShon replied lightly, Natasha could hear the heaviness of the curiosity in his voice.

"Pastor hadn't been to church because he was feeling under the weather and then I see him sitting in your window. With a drink of some kind in his hand, no less. Were you and him working on your project?" LaShon dangled the question before Natasha.

"Yeah," Natasha answered. "Yeah, we were working on the project. That is ok with you, isn't it?"

"Maybe. But he is my pastor, you know."

"Child, believe me, I do know."

"Ok. I was just wondering. It does look strange to see your pastor sitting up in the window of someone he barely knows. You might want to tell him to not sit up in your window next time he's over there."

"Why? If he wants to sit in a window he can do so."

LaShon sighed. "Girl, I can see you don't know anything about the church. No one wants to drive down the street and see their pastor sitting up in someone's window."

"That's silly."

"Silly or not, it's true." LaShon hesitated before continuing. "And especially if it's the window of a pretty young woman and the pastor is already married. Mmh," he exclaimed.

"Ok, you need to shut up right now, LaShon. Don't insult me like that."

"I'm only giving you the facts of how it would play out. Girl I'm bein' real."

"Well thank you."

"Ok."

They changed the subject and continued to talk on into the night, but Natasha knew the question LaShon asked hadn't been answered enough to quell his interest.

~~~~

All of the ministers at the meeting welcomed Milton back, but none of them asked him about his illness. It was out of respect that they didn't ask and most likely out of caution, because to know of someone else's problems could very well make them your own, so an official welcome was in order from Reverend Harris as he convened the meeting and from individual well-wishers as the morning went on, all without note of the challenge Milton might be going through. Milton understood the reluctance of the other ministers to get into his business and he was grateful for it because if anyone had asked him about this thing that had him 'under the weather,' he would have to lie to avoid telling them his illness was spiritual and not physical.

Milton listened to Reverend Harris speak and to the other members who had been set to speak. He listened as much as he could, but his mind drifted to the phone call he had gotten from Natasha. She had told him that LaShon had seen him in her apartment and was now curious. Natasha told Milton she hadn't told LaShon what was going on, but she was concerned over what to do. Natasha didn't want to hurt Milton, however she didn't think she should have to go through any mess that he created. She didn't come straight out and tell Milton this, but he could tell by the sharpness of her words that she was bothered. He would tell Ella about it when he went home.

"She should be," Ella said. "She shouldn't have to go through any mess. And I shouldn't either."

Milton stood in the doorway of Ella's room as he told her about the call. He shook his head, "I know. You're right."

"The thing to do, Milton, is to tell the congregation about Natasha. You knew you would have to do that sooner or later, didn't you?"

"Yeah."

"Well then…"

"This is going to be crazy," Milton heard himself say. "You know this is going to affect you too."

Ella looked at him like *he* was crazy. "You don't think I know that? Everything is about to change. I just think whatever happens will depend on how well you tell your story."

Milton closed the door to her room and had started down the hallway when Ella called him. He came back to the room.

"Yeah?"

"I don't think you should mention how you tried to abort your child. That would be something most folks might not forgive you for."

The last speaker at the meeting had finished speaking and was looking at Milton to see if he had anything to say.

"Reverend Pruitt?" Milton heard someone call him, pulling him back to the meeting.

"I'm fine with it," he responded after assuming the posture of authority and discernment that was expected of ministers.

After the meeting he drove with the car radio off as he headed back to his office, something he rarely did when he was driving, but he needed the quiet in order to process what was happening without worrying over what might happen. He told himself that morning as he got ready for work that worrying wouldn't help anything, and that he would focus on being aware of what he needed to do instead of what others might think and how others might act. Such thinking, though, was proving difficult for him.

"I'm glad to have you back," Mrs. Hargrove said as she handed Milton his mail.

"Thanks, Mrs. Hargrove. It's good to be back."

"Things just haven't been running as smoothly with you not around." Mrs. Hargrove glanced around and leaned over her desk. "Reverend Chenault. Just isn't as good as you when it comes to making the right decisions."

"Now Mrs. Hargrove. Let's not start that. I'm sure any decisions he made were within the church's charter."

"It still doesn't mean they were the most sound decisions," Mrs. Hargrove said as she went back to her work.

"Ok. Well, we'll leave all of that behind us," Milton said.

"Alright." Mrs. Hargrove replied in a tone that seemed more like a warning than agreement.

"I'm going to close myself off while I catch up on things."

"Like the Nixons? You have heard about what Sister Nixon did. Word got out and now it's all over the church."

"What ever it is we're going to leave Sister Nixon to herself and God, Mrs. Hargrove. That's what we're going to do. We can only extend a counsel of love to her. And that's what I expect you to do too," he said as he closed the door to his office.

"You just need to know that LaShon is really curious about whatever secret you and I might have… I just wonder if he knows that I'm the secret…"

Those were the words Natasha had spoken earlier and they played over and over Milton's head as he started work.

~~~~

The afternoon sun filled the apartment and the new air of spring stirred the draperies as Ella and Mrs. Wexner sat at an open window in Mrs. Wexner's living room. Neither of them spoke. Mrs. Wexner's caretaker, Madelyn, had told Ella that Mrs. Wexner rarely spoke these days and mostly sat before the open window. She said it was only that particular window that Mrs. Wexner asked to be seated in front of each day, and that she would sit for hours, staring out the window. Now Ella observed her. In the background, the sound of dishes being moved around came from the kitchen as Madelyn went about her duties. Mrs. Wexner sat still, silent and still, respectful. Her silver hair was pinned back, leaving wisps of hair that glinted in the sunlight, framing a pale face that had been etched with time. There was nothing catatonic in Mrs. Wexner sitting there. Rather, it was as if she was waiting on something. Ella could tell, because the elderly woman's eyes held tiny sparks of anticipation in them and her mouth was relaxed into a subtle crescent.

Madelyn came from the kitchen carrying a tray with two lunches. Ella stood to take the tray from her.

"Let me help you with that."

"She won't eat it," Madelyn said. "Even when I feed her she only takes a few bites. That's why I make sure she gets her protein drink and vegetables first."

"Yeah," Ella said softly as she looked at Mrs. Wexner. "I'll see what I can do."

Ella gave Mrs. Wexner a small spoonful of mixed vegetables and watched caringly as Mrs. Wexner ate. She dabbed at the sides of Mrs. Wexner's mouth as the old lady continued to stare out the window.

"What do you see?" Ella whispered as she fed the woman. "Who are you waiting for?"

As Ella was about to leave, she and Madelyn talked about what was to become of Mrs. Wexner, and they agreed that no matter her condition, Mrs. Wexner should remain in her home. Ella had arranged to have hospice take over if it was needed. Just before she left, Ella looked over at the table that held Mrs. Wexner's photos, just as she always did. It was as if she expected a sign of some sort from one of the persons framed on the table, but as usual Frank and Greta smiled back from the photographs. Patiently.

After leaving Mrs. Wexner's apartment, Ella stopped by home. The presence she felt in her room the night before had stayed on her mind. It all seemed so real that she couldn't pass it off as something she had imagined.

When she got home, she came in through the back door and entered the kitchen. The house was quiet except for the small mechanical clicks and whirs of the house, and the rooms were filled with afternoon light and shadow. She walked through the house and started down the hallway. As she neared her bedroom she slowed to a stop and listened to hear if anything would move. Then slowly, in the silence of the hallway she walked to the room where she slept. She stood just outside of her room and looked into it. Feeling safe, she slowly walked past the doorway into the room and it was then that the smell of the lake met her. She stepped back, frightened, and as she backed to the doorway she noticed the book she had been reading the night before was open on her nightstand. She walked over to the book and saw that the pages were open to where she had left off reading that night, but she was sure she had closed it. She always closed books once she finished reading them. She stood for a second, staring at the pages of the book, then she closed the book and hurried from the room and the house.

That evening Ella prepared a large meal. The busyness of preparing the meal relieved her mind. The aroma of the food and the sight of Ella setting the table caught Milton off guard as he came through the door.

"Hi." He greeted Ella cautiously as he closed the door.

"Dinner'll be ready in a minute." Ella spoke without looking at Milton as she continued to prepare dinner.

When dinner was ready they sat down to eat.

"I baked the pork chops," Ella said to break the silence. She gave her husband a half look then focused back on her meal. "We have to start taking better care of ourselves."

"Yeah," Milton replied.

"Have you decided when you want to talk to the congregation? You shouldn't wait too long. The longer you draw it out the worse it'll look."

"I know. I'm working up to it. Ella? Are you sure you're ready for this?"

Ella hesitated before answering. "I've been through worse and I know you have too. We'll get through it. You just have to make sure you let them know how sorry you are."

"That should be understood anyway." Milton set his fork down hard onto his plate. "I'm no different from anyone else. Why can't people see that?"

"Things are the way they are, Milton. You of all people should know that."

"What about you? Do you know what you're going to say? It won't be just me talking, you know."

After a second of thinking Ella replied. "They'll see me as a victim. I'll let them know that I'm disappointed. That's it."

"You can't just leave it at that."

Ella wanted to tell her husband that she could leave it at that, but instead she replied, "I'll let them know I forgive you. It's the only way to move forward."

Milton began to eat. His expression relaxed a bit.

"But don't think I'm there yet, Milton," Ella continued, suddenly causing her husband to look up at her. "Don't think I've forgiven you. We've worked too hard to build what we have and I'm trying to hold onto as much of it as I can. So don't think for one minute that I forgive you. I'm working on it, but I don't know what's going to happen."

Milton nodded and quietly ate dinner.

What Ella told Milton at dinner was true. She had begun to work hard on forgiving him. But it wasn't only her husband who needed forgiving. She thought this that night as her room began to fill with the odor of the lake.

CHAPTER TWENTY-NINE

"I want to tell you something and I don't want you flying off the handle," Ella said. She and Danny sat out on a plaza, having lunch.

Danny looked cautiously at his mother before replying. "Ok."

"Milton found out that he has a child." Ella measured her son's silence and watched his expression darken. At that moment he looked like his father after she had told him about Buddy. The fountain on the plaza splashed and the waters behind Danny danced in the sun.

"How old is she?" Danny asked the question as he looked down at his hands that were now clenched together into a large, ragged knot.

"Twenty-two, twenty-three, I'm guessing."

Danny continued to look down at his hands. He tapped his clenched hands against the top of the table a couple times. Then he looked at his mother. "You ok?"

"I'm getting used to it, but yeah, I'm ok."

"Really." Danny looked skeptically at his mother. "How come?"

"I didn't say I wasn't hurt, but it's nothing I can't adjust to. People make mistakes and they learn from them." Ella paused as she continued to think about her own past. "We ask for forgiveness and we move forward, understanding what caused us to stumble."

"He ain't learned nothin'. He messed around on you and went all this time with this self-righteous shit all the time knowin' what he had done."

"That's something he has to live with. But I do know he's sorry for what he did."

"How are things around the house?"

"A little tense, but it's settling down a bit. He's getting ready to tell the church."

"Good. I kinda hope they kick his ass to the curb, but I know that would affect you. I'm guessin' you're gonna stay with him."

"I'm not sure."

Danny exhaled and sat back in his chair. He looked out onto the plaza a while without speaking.

"Things happen, Danny. And I'm ok. I'll get through this. That's all you need to think about," Ella said as she ate. She told him about Natasha and how he had met her at the Christmas dinner, and how neither she nor Milton knew who Natasha was then. She told him how Natasha had come to Cincinnati to find Milton and how it didn't seem like she wanted anything more than that.

"She's a nice girl," Ella said. "And I think her heart is in the right place."

"You sure about that? Ain't she from Oklahoma? She came all the way to Cincinnati from Oklahoma to find Milt?"

"She's also going to school here. So I don't know if one follows the other, school first and then to look for Milt while being here, or vice versa."

"Doesn't matter really. She's here. Don't be surprised if somethin' does go down," Danny said as he began to eat.

Danny knew his mother didn't want to escalate what she and Milton were going through, but Danny needed to talk to Milton. After he left his mother he drove to the church. As he drove into the lot he saw Milton standing outside with Deacon Lewis and Mrs. Hargrove. They were looking over the work that had been done on the church.

Danny knew the people who were with Milton because he had grown up around them, but when he left home, he left Christ The Redeemer Baptist Church, so now, Deacon Lewis and Mrs. Hargrove were no more than distant ghosts, images from a past life.

Danny got out of the car and called to Milton. Milton had seen him come into the lot and now stood looking at Danny as Danny stood by his car and called to him.

"Milt. Man, we need to talk."

Milton continued to look at him. Deacon Lewis and Mrs. Hargrove looked at Danny, a growing concern showing on their faces.

"You want me to call the police," Mrs. Hargrove whispered as she pulled out her phone.

"Put that damn phone back in yo' pocket ol' woman. Ain't no-body talkin' to you!" Danny yelled from where he stood.

"No," Milton said to Mrs. Hargrove. He walked over to Danny. "Don't get yourself in trouble."

"I just wanna talk," Danny said, staring at Milton.

"Ok…"

"Now you know I would knock yo' ass out right here if it wasn't for my mother. So I just need to know how you could do somethin' like that to her? She been there for you and all this shit." He waved his hand towards the church grounds.

"Watch your mouth, Danny."

"Or what? What'chou gonna do?"

"It's not necessary. All you're going to do is get yourself into even more trouble than you probably already are in."

"Man you don't know nothin' about my life. You made sure you didn't and I don't give a fuck anyway."

Danny and Milton glared at each other.

"She been there for you, man," Danny repeated. "And you go out there and do some shit like that."

"I'm not proud of what I did and your mother knows that. We just want to get on with our lives, with whatever happens."

"You know, you make shit sound so sweet. Like 'hey, shit happens, let's move on'." He pointed to Milton. "Look, if my mother gets hurt anymore than she already is, I'ma fuck you up." He got in his car and drove out of the lot. Deacon Lewis and Mrs. Hargrove hurried to Milton's side.

After he left the church Danny went back to his apartment. He wondered how much more could his mother take. He knew she had been through a lot. He lay across his bed thinking about his mother, and about Milton, and about secrets. He now realized that secrets catch up with you sooner or later, just like Danny knew his secrets would. Secrets are vindictive because they've been pushed into the shadows and they resent it, so they come after you. And when they do, then what? Do you face them like Milton is doing, or do you try to run from them like his mother had done for so many years? Or like Mr. Stiggers was doing?

The photos that Mr. Stiggers had thrown away had been put back together. Afterwards Danny put them in a box. He thought about the box of photos and went to the kitchen to get them off of the table. He had been hesitant to return the photos to Mr. Stiggers, but that afternoon he made up his mind to do it. He went down to Mr. Stiggers' apartment carrying the box of photos. When he got there he knocked on Mr. Stiggers' door. As usual these days there was no sound coming from inside the apartment. Danny wondered how could Mr. Stiggers keep any sounds, even any hint of sound, from coming through the door.

"Mr. Stiggers?" Danny knocked on the door.

Still there was no sound.

"I don't know if you want 'em, but I brought your pictures back." Danny waited to hear something. He continued. "I put 'em back together for you. They're nice. You really should keep 'em."

Suddenly a very loud bang came from the other side of the door that caused Danny to jump back.

"Get away from my door!" Mr. Stiggers screamed and hit the door from the inside with what sounded like a hard object. "Get away!" he screamed and hit the door again. "Get awaaay!"

Two other tenants opened their doors to the ruckus.

"Danny! Leave that man alone. You know he don't want nobody botherin' him." The lady across the hall stood in her doorway with her hands on her hips.

"He crazy as fuck!" One of the neighbors on the next floor yelled out to whomever he thought was at Mr. Stiggers' door, before slamming his own door shut.

"Yeah," Danny said to the woman across the hall. "Yeah," he repeated as he went back upstairs to his apartment. He sat the box back on the table and wondered what he should do with them. The photos were more than just frozen images. They represented something that was still alive, and as long as what was in the photos spoke of time and place and consequence, then they too would always be alive. Danny picked up the box and went to his bedroom and spread the photos across the bed, then stood back and looked at them: a laughing man and a dog playfully engaged in a tug of war with a rope; three young ladies standing together dressed in nice gowns, each with corsages pinned to their dresses; a men's baseball team posing proudly under a bright sun. One of the men on the team was a younger Mr. Stiggers who stood in the center of the photo smiling beside an older, stoic looking man who might have been the team's coach, and to the right of the line was a boy who held up a jersey with the team's name, 'The Scorchers,' emblazoned across it; and the photo of Murlene who continued to look confidently from the photo over the years. Those were just a few of the many photos Danny had been able to salvage. The others still had missing pieces. The photos were too relevant to a place and time to throw away, and Danny had taken them to heart after having spent so much effort piecing them together, that he now took the photographs and began taping them to the wall in his bedroom. Faces and moments that would tug at his curiosity whenever he looked at them.

~~~~

Danny watched Littlejohn and Azhure's faces as the three of them sat on the balcony of Littlejohn and Azhure's apartment, having drinks. He had just told them about Milton and he measured the stunned looks on their faces.

"Damn," Littlejohn said after Danny finished telling them.

"Are you sure you should be telling people this," Azhure asked.

"He's going to put it out there anyway," Danny said.

"And he's supposed to be a minister," Littlejohn said with a laugh.

"Ministers are people too," Azhure said before adding, "But he is supposed to be a moral conscience."

"That's what I'm talkin' about. Moral conscience," Littlejohn parroted.

"How is your mother taking it?" Azhure questioned.

"She said she's adjustin'."

"So she's going to stay with him?"

"I guess. Looks that way."

"And his daughter don't want nothin?" Littlejohn asked the question as he leaned back in his chair and put his arm around Azhure.

"My mother said it don't appear that way. His daughter even came to their house for a Christmas dinner. And get this, at the time my mother and her husband didn't even know that the woman was his daughter."

"Whoa!" Littlejohn sat straight up.

"Wow. Now that's bold," Azhure said. "Are they sure she doesn't want anything? Sounds a little shady to me."

Danny hunched his shoulders. "I don't know. She seem cool though."

"So you met her," Azhure said as she emphatically pointed her finger.

"Yeah. I was there. She seem cool."

"This some soap opera shit," Littlejohn laughed before taking a swallow of beer.

"Oh," Azhure said as she nudged Littlejohn. "No it's not."

"I don't know. I think Littlejohn's right," Danny agreed.

"Stuff like this happens," Azhure said. "As long as it doesn't go too far over the top it's just, it's just… life," she said, raising her hand.

"Still, he's a minister though," Littlejohn persisted. "And he's supposed to be part of that whole school board thing with them other ministers too."

"Yeah," Danny said. "That's some crazy shit anyway."

"It's the Twenty-First Century, and they're trying to keep us back in the dark ages," Azhure agreed.

"Kids nowadays know the deal. Them ministers and folks like them need to let folks live they lives. The kids know that. Them ministers need to learn that too," Littlejohn said.

"Which brings me to another topic," Azhure said with a sly smile.

"Aw c'mon Azhure," Littlejohn begged.

"Me and Cortez, right," Danny said as he lifted his glass.

Littlejohn laughed. "You knew it was comin' with her around."

"Well… How is that going?" Azhure asked.

"You know how it's goin'."

"Shouldn't it be more?"

Littlejohn jumped in to deflect his girlfriend's question. "C'mon girl. That's their business."

"It's just, I've been knowing you for a while," Azhure continued, "and I've never heard you talk about anyone but Cortez." She turned to Littlejohn. "And I've never heard you talk about Danny having anybody since you've known him, so I was just wondering."

"You act like that's a crime or somethin'." Danny laughed as he self-consciously traced his finger through the frost along the side of his glass. "Me and Cortez are cool. We friends."

"With benefits," Littlejohn added.

"So… that frees you up to see other people," Azhure said.

"Aw man. Look she got this dude on her job she thinks you might like." Littlejohn jumped in with a grin on his face. Then he took a drink as he waited for Danny's response.

"I'm good." Danny gave a quick reply to end the conversation.

"He's a gay activist," Littlejohn added.

"That's not so much it," Azhure corrected. "He's just not in the closet," she said, glancing at Danny.

"Like Cortez is," Littlejohn said with a grin.

Danny laughed. "I'm good," he repeated.

"Ok. Just looking out for you, brother-in-law," Azhure said before sipping her drink.

"Danny got other things on his mind, like those pictures that old dude threw away. How far you gettin' with them?" Littlejohn asked the question to change the subject.

Danny told them about the photos and Mr. Stiggers' reaction.

"Ah! Told you!" Littlejohn said, pointing at Danny.

"Man, he went off," Danny said.

"Why?" Azhure looked inquisitively at Danny. "What's in them?"

"Nothin' out of the ordinary. Photos of people and things. Oh and one of the pictures show him when he was on a baseball team when he was younger," Danny said, suddenly recalling one of the photos. "'The Scorchers'. That's what the team was called."

"The Scorchers," Littlejohn repeated. "I like that."

"It was early in the evening when Danny left Littlejohn and Azhure. Instead of going home he went to Cortez's apartment to spend the night. The next morning when he went home he started up the stairs to his apartment. Suddenly Mr. Stiggers opened his door slightly.

"Boy?" He spoke to Danny through the cracked opening of the door.

"Sir?"

"You get rid of them pictures?"

Danny stopped on the stairs and looked at the half-hidden face. "No sir."

"Get rid of them pictures. Throw 'em away." He closed the door and the sound of locks came from inside the old man's apartment as Danny continued up the stairs.

CHAPTER THIRTY

Natasha walked quietly in a park alongside LaShon, listening to him speak. She bowed her head slightly so she could concentrate more on what he was saying and not be distracted by the expression of distress on his face or by their surroundings. She knew his having seen Milton in her apartment had stayed on LaShon's mind because he hadn't called her at all since he told her he had seen Milton. It wasn't until she called him that he asked if they could talk.

"Seeing Pastor sitting up there in your window shook me up," LaShon said as they walked along a path that wound away from the streets into a shade of still green.

Natasha watched LaShon's hands, his fingers moving nervously through the keys on his key ring.

"It just didn't look right," he continued. "Like he was somewhere he wasn't supposed to be. It was like he was in a place—not just a physical place but… I guess you could say a spiritual place, but a darker place, a space that was working against him."

"But all you saw was him sitting in my window. That's all," Natasha said.

"Yeah." LaShon stopped and looked at Natasha. "You don't think that looks strange?"

"No. I don't know, I guess we're seeing things from different perspectives," Natasha said. "LaShon, look, you know there's nothing sexual going on between Reverend Pruitt and me if that's what you're implying."

"That's what I keep telling myself. And I wouldn't insult you like that. I know you well enough to know that that's not the type of person you are. But the questions keep crossing my mind. I mean, you've only been here a few months and already he's coming to your apartment? Sitting casually in your window like he's supposed to be there?"

They walked farther along without speaking. Natasha had tried to not look into LaShon's face but the silence between them had grown so full of uncertainty, so buoyant with unspoken words that it lifted her head and she looked in his face. It was then that she saw his mouth, how the corners hung under the weight of disillusionment. And the eyes that usually blazed with mischief were now dim and seemed to look more into the concern that was within him than outward onto what was before him. She reached over and took his hand.

"LaShon. It's ok. Things will be ok."

"I depend on Pastor being right. I need him to be a righteous man."

"We should expect that in everyone, LaShon," Natasha said, squeezing his hand as they continued to walk.

"No. You don't understand, Natasha. If I lose faith in Pastor, I lose faith in myself."

"LaShon…"

"He saved me, Natasha. There were times he hurt me but it was for my own good."

"You don't have to talk about this."

LaShon looked at her and smiled. "It's ok. I still got a ways to go but to be honest I would be worse off if Pastor hadn't stepped in. Natasha, Pastor has been there all the way. Trying to help me… he even gave me a prayer that he wrote just for me," LaShon said, before stopping under the canopy of trees and reciting the prayer."

"Oh Lord, Highest of High
Please hear the cry of my voice
And feel the pain in my heart.
I come to You as a sinner who is in search of cleansing
I want to walk with You in Your light.
Please cleanse my mind and my heart
Of the darkness that courses through me
So I might be of service to You."

When he finished, he turned to Natasha and spoke in a way that was at once solemn and wistful.

"That's a prayer Pastor wrote for me. He told my parents to make sure I said it at least three times a day. That was after my parents started noticing that I was interested in boys."

They walked on in silence for a bit before LaShon continued. "I always thought that maybe the prayer didn't work because I hated it. Oh I hated that prayer," he said as he shook his head. "But to be honest though, I guess it wasn't the prayer I hated, but how it made me feel. Like I was a mess."

"But you're not."

"I don't know. Maybe not," he said, squeezing Natasha's hand. "But I can't help feeling that way so I keep saying that prayer." Suddenly he burst into laughter, bringing back that spark of mischief to his face. "But not as much as I used to because girl I have so many thoughts going on in my head. I would be out of breath saying that prayer over and over." After his laughter had died he continued to speak quietly, thoughtfully. "But it's a good prayer though," he said as his expression became solemn once again. "That's why I need him to be righteous. I need to see that."

Natasha watched LaShon as he pulled away from her building that afternoon after dropping her off. That night she called Milton and told him about the time she spent with LaShon and how LaShon was bothered to see Milton in her apartment. She told her father that LaShon didn't press her for answers but that he expected them soon.

"Who is he?" Milton spat indignantly. "Of all people…" he went on before hearing himself and calming a bit. Natasha listened, not stunned anymore by his reaction, after having spent the day talking about Milton with LaShon.

"How bothered did he seem?" Milton asked.

"Bothered might have been the wrong word," she replied. "I think worried would be more like it."

"Worried?"

"Yeah. Worried. Like you might not be who he always thought you were."

Milton fell into a long silence.

"You ok?"

"Yeah," Milton replied. "Yeah. I'm ok."

Natasha didn't want to spend the entire time on the phone talking about Milton coming clean because it left her feeling like the culprit, so she led the conversation on to other things. But she knew her father going public with what he had done was still foremost on his mind. As she hung up the phone she thought about the prayer Milton had written for LaShon and wondered if he recited it when he met Abilyn.

~~~~

Danny walked up the driveway past Ella and Milton's cars and knocked on the front door. He knew his coming around irritated Milton, but he didn't care.

Ella answered the door and they went into the den where Ella had mounds of clothes and large plastic bags all in a half-circle.

"We're giving away some of this stuff." She walked into the center of the half-circle and sat on a footstool.

"All of this? Want me to help?"

"You can put them in the bags after I put them in that pile near you."

Danny brought a kitchen chair into the room and sat beside his mother.

"This is a lot of stuff, Mom."

"Some of it is your clothes from when you were a boy. I don't know why I didn't give them away back then."

"Where's Milt?" Danny began gathering up clothes.

"In the basement like he always is." She saw how Danny was stuffing the clothes into the bag and slapped his leg. "Boy fold those clothes before you put them in that bag."

As Danny folded the clothes he noticed how quiet the house was, as if sadness had snuffed out everything. When he grew up there the house was never sad. It was filled with energy: lively conversation between Ella and Milt or Ella and Danny, the sound of the TV playing and of music from a stereo. Even when there was a disagreement between Danny and Milton the house seemed to have moved with activity. But now it suffered under a cloak of sadness and seemed caught between breaths for what was to come.

"Mom."

"Hmh?"

"Are you and Milt working on things?"

Slowing the sorting she was doing, Ella answered. "Yeah. Why? I would think you wouldn't want us to."

"I think it's crazy to stay with him. But at least I said what I needed to say to him."

"So I hear. Why would you go over to the church and confront him like that?"

"He needed to hear me."

"But Danny…"

"I know. I guess I could've handled it better."

"Yeah. I've been telling you all of your life to think things through when you get angry."

"Well, he got the message."

"He already had the message, Danny. He knows what he did was wrong. You need to stop reacting to things without forethought. Consequences. Think of consequences."

"You're right, you're right," Danny replied.

They continued talking and sorting. Milton came up from the basement carrying more clothes.

"Ella." Milton called out as he walked through the kitchen. "Do you think we should keep these or…" he stopped when he saw Danny. "Or just throw them away," he continued. "Hi." He spoke to Danny with little emotion.

"'sup," Danny replied as he picked up another piece of clothing.

"What are they?" Ella looked at the things in Milton's arms.

"Just clothes I use to work in."

"Then keep them."

"Alright," Milton said as he walked from the room.

Danny continued to fold after Milton left the room. After a while he spoke. "You know folks are gonna come down hard on him because he always going around moralizing… All that stuff on TV he been talking about."

"Let's not get started," Ella said.

"I'm just preparin' you."

"We know what people are going to say."

"Why are you defendin' him so much?" Danny put a piece of clothing in the bag.

"Defending him? I'm not defending him. I just think we need to find a way to move on."

"He can start by apologizing to all the people he done hurt over the years. He been bullyin' folks with that bible for a long time."

"Stop talking foolish."

"You don't think he hurt people? Bad mouthing folks for not being what he think they should be. And like I said, joining those other preachers."

Ella went on with her work without replying.

"I've been thinkin' about it more and it's wrong how he's been doin' folks."

"Everyone has their beliefs," Ella finally said.

"The way he did me," Danny went on. "He hated the fact that I wasn't into women."

"He rarely brought it up, Danny. You were the one who broke the rules. I mean, why would you bring someone into this house and have sex with them? That was the final straw, Danny."

"You know, Mom. That might sound right, but I really don't think that's it. I don't think I woulda been kicked out if it was a girl he caught me with. Yelled at? Yeah. But kicked out? Nah. I don't think so."

"It was all coming to a head. You and Milton never got along."

"You're right about that. I still say he needs to apologize though. Especially to all the folks sittin' up there in Christ The Redeemer scared as hell of what might happen if he ever called them out on anything *he* didn't like. A lot of them people done been there for him —and might even be now if he tells 'em he's sorry and he means it. He wouldn't be the first minister to change gears on things."

"That'll be his decision."

"Guess you're right." They continued working. After a while Danny asked, "How do you feel about me? You know that I'm gay."

"Don't be silly." Ella sought to deflect what she considered to be an imposition.

"Nah, I'm serious. How do you feel?" Danny's question startled himself just as much as it did his mother. He had chosen to live his life without any sparring over it. And Ella, she had chosen to close her eyes to it just as she had to other things she felt she had no control over. "How did you feel when you found out?"

"Surprised—but not too surprised," Ella said. Then she added, "Look, I know it's part of life."

"Yeah," Danny answered.

"Now let me ask you," Ella went on. "How did you feel when you started to understand it?"

"Pissed. To me it was like one more thing against me."

"One more thing?"

Danny looked at his mother for a bit before answering. "Yeah."

Ella looked at him, understanding the full meaning of his words then went back to sorting through the clothes.

"I always wondered why you didn't stand up for me when Milt told me to leave," Danny went on.

"What are you talking about? Danny, you attacked him."

"He kept going on about me. I was like, 'ok', but he wanted more, something I wasn't able to give. That's what pisses me off now, how he was trying to come down on me to change who I am, but he was out there doing his own..." he started to say the word 'shit', but caught himself. "His own mess."

"I know. You have a right to be angry," Ella said. "That whole thing stayed on my mind for a long time, but not only because I think I could've done more to keep him from harassing you... It's stayed with me because when all of that happened I didn't want to deal with any of it. I was angry at you too," Ella admitted. She stopped working and continued. "I was just as angry about what you did as much as what you were, and I'm sorry. I was wrong."

Danny stared at his mother. He hadn't prepared himself for what she was saying.

"But I don't feel that way anymore," Ella said. "Now I'm more concerned about the type of people you keep company with."

Before Danny left, Ella asked him to go up to his old bedroom with her.

"Do you smell anything?" she asked as they stood in the doorway

Danny raised his head and sniffed. "Like what?"

"Something wet, sour... something rotting."

"Which smell is it? Wet and sour, or something rotting?"

"Both. Sometimes one, sometimes the other."

She continued to stand in the doorway as Danny walked further into the room.

Danny stood in the center of the room and turned his head from side to side, taking in a few deep breaths each time. "I don't smell anything," he finally said. "But I can look around. Maybe something died in here."

After Danny left Ella sprayed the room with disinfectant and opened the windows further. Then she sat on the bed and began to cry.

~~~~

"Why are you crying?" Ella's father glanced at her as he drove them from the lake.

"Why are you crying!" He demanded as he slapped the steering wheel. His anger rose and he pressed his foot on the accelerator, causing the large sedan to speed along the road that led from the lake.

Ella tried to answer but her throat was choked and caused her to cough and to heave. She leaned against the door of the car sobbing, her body rocking from the movement of the speeding car over the unpaved road.

"Don't you throw up in my car." Her father pulled off the road. "I told you not to come," he said as Ella opened the car door and leaned out. She coughed and heaved but didn't vomit.

"Now close that damn door."

Her father sped off and Ella sat on the passenger side, crying softly.

"Ella, I told you not to come. No girl should see anything like that. I told you."

"I—I had to see," Ella said.

"Why? You thought it was the boy who got you pregnant?"

Ella didn't answer.

"Answer me!"

"Yeah," she replied in a weak voice.

"Was it? Was Buddy the one?"

Ella turned to her window and sniffled.

"Girl you better answer me! You don't know, do you? You been out there doing it with more than just one!" He backhanded her and caused her mouth to bleed.

She began to sob, "Daddy! Daddy, no! No I haven't!"

Her father pulled out his handkerchief. "Here. Wipe your mouth."

Ella began to wipe her mouth with the back of her hand.

"Here! Take the handkerchief!" He thrust the handkerchief to her and she took it.

He drove for a while before he spoke again. "Your mother will be so heartbroken," he said.

Ella looked at her father as she wiped her mouth.

"She's gonna be so… heartbroken…" her father repeated as he drove along. "I wish all these niggers round here was dead," he said, as he looked at the ramshackle houses that dotted the woods.

CHAPTER THIRTY-ONE

Milton rested his chin against the backs of his hands, which were folded in front of his face. He watched Sister Lawson as she read the church announcements. Her hat, that was of a powder blue color, moved serenely in the light of the sanctuary as she spoke softly and with great diction. His eyes were set in half-moons and his lips formed a subtle smile. His face appeared no different than on most Sundays. From his vantage point, he looked out over the church at the congregation. It was a gathering that was larger than usual, and Milton noticed that most eyes were on him instead of Sister Lawson. There was great anticipation in the air as word had gotten out that on this Sunday Milton would make an important announcement and that it would most likely be about his private life. It was what everyone waited for and why even those who hadn't attended in a while showed up.

At first Milton's disappearance from the pulpit fueled speculation that he was suffering from an illness, but when word spread about the confrontation in the parking lot between he and Danny, speculation mounted to plain old tongue wagging about what might really be going on. Milton continued to smile and nod as he looked out across the sea of observers. His eyes finally rested on Ella, who sat up front with an expression that was at once remote and ensuring.

"Amen," Milton said, expressing his approval after Sister Lawson finished the reading of the announcements. The church joined in, "Amen!" but kept their eyes trained on him. The more astute members also tossed quick looks Ella's way to measure her demeanor.

Now the chords from the piano filled the air as the choirmaster stepped out front and raised her hands, summoning the choir to its feet. Immediately, members sitting in the audience began craning their necks and tilting their heads in order to whisper among themselves because now, they noticed that LaShon wasn't up front with the choir. Instead he sat in the audience, watching Milton. His face was dark and his eyes were filled with uncertainty as he looked up at his pastor.

The choir rose and began to sing a selection of songs. The choir ended its selection with a song that Milton had requested:

"I've had many tears and sorrows,
I've had questions for tomorrow,
There's been times I didn't know right from wrong
But in every situation,
God gave me blessed consultation,
That my trials come to only make me strong.
Through it all,
Through it all…"

When the offering of songs ended, the choir members took their seats, and Milton stood.

"Amen," he said as he stepped up to the podium, to which the church replied, "Amen." Milton praised the choir for its offering and spoke of how important they were in lifting the spirits of anyone who might have come through the doors of the church with sadness in their hearts or malice on their minds. He spoke of the importance of seeking light when times are most dark and that the light, the light of Christ, is within each heart, and how it lies in wait for each person to come to it.

After he concluded his sermon he slowly closed his Bible. He leaned forward on the lectern, his hands gently holding both sides.

"There are so many of you here today," he said. "Most of you I see each Sunday and some I see once in a while." He paused and took in a face. "Brother and Sister Barnes, it's good to see you here today. And the Turnbow family", he said, addressing an entire gathering of family members who rarely attended. "I'm so blessed to see all of you together. We've missed your faces and pray you come more often. To all of you," Milton continued as he raised his hands towards the congregation, "Christ The Redeemer Baptist Church welcomes you, and to all of you, may you fill your hearts with the light of

Christ that we've been talking about today. It's a light that should never dim, even when times are most trying."

A few voices murmured 'amen' but most of the members sat intensely silent.

"Times can be trying, as we all know," Milton continued. "But with that light we can always see our way through, and that light is what I stand in today, here on this Sunday afternoon as I speak to you." He became quiet to allow his words to set in and his eyes moved across the faces of the congregation before he continued.

"You see, we've all done things, acted in ways that we know are wrong but allow ourselves to fall prey to the devil who is always waiting for those moments of weakness. That's when the devil steps in and can sometimes grab you. When you are at your most vulnerable and your heart is unaware." He paused again and looked sternly into the faces locked on him. "It happened to me. Some years ago what I had intended to be a friendship turned into an affair."

A sudden gasp came from the audience, then an eruption of voices, murmuring and a cascade of nodding and shaking heads moved throughout the congregation. Milton gave the members a few seconds to take in what he had said before he went on.

"It's something I'm not proud of." He looked at Ella who sat with her head held high as he spoke. "The love I have for my wife, the woman God gave to me, is the gift He gave to me, and for a moment I let it slip from my hands. But never out of my heart." He smiled at Ella as some of the members sitting near her smiled as well, gently nodding their heads as they looked at her. "When I saw what I had done I immediately asked God for his forgiveness… and out of shame, I never told my wife." Many of the women then gasped and adjusted their bodies under the sting of that insult. "And that was the second sin," Milton confessed. "You see, in my most human condition I experienced shame. So much shame that I sought to shield myself from my deeds and also to spare my wife any pain. I promised God that the frailty that befell me would never happen again, and it didn't, but that I needed to spare my loving wife of any pain because I love her so much."

Now he looked down at the Bible in front of him. He slowly opened it once again and moved a few pages past his eyes. "Sisters and brothers, I went for so long keeping what I did a secret." He spoke with his eyes on his Bible. "But secrets always come to light. They come to light because they are you. Not something to be forgotten, but to be recognized and to be lived because they are your actions… they are you." With those words he lifted his face once more and with eyes that had acclimated themselves to his deeds he spoke. "From that affair, unknown to me, I fathered a child."

The revelation was so much that a loud "Oh!" came from the church. The congregation had erupted into a sound of dismay that rang to the walls and the ceiling of the church. LaShon stood up and walked out.

After the shock had settled to awe, Milton went on to talk about Natasha and how she sought him out, not with malice, but with a loving heart, the longing of a child to find her father. He spoke of how he and Ella had come to accept Natasha as part of their family and how, in spite of the wrong act he committed, he was blessed with a child, because, he reminded them, a child is never a burden, but always a blessing.

Milton and Ella stood outside of the church after service ended, where they greeted and talked with the parishioners. It was something they usually did before going to the restaurant for Sunday dinner. Milton wanted to go home after service, but Ella insisted that they do as they had always done. She said to do otherwise would allow folks room to gossip at dinner. She told him they needed to be there so their presence would be felt.

Out front of the church Milton and Ella were greeted mostly by the same parishioners that usually made their way past the others to stand near he and Ella. These were the members of the church who had attained authority within the congregation because of their esteem and because of the money they gave to the church. But there were a few of those heralded members who walked on to their cars without saying anything to Milton and Ella, and a few who stood back in a group talking among themselves.

Sunday dinner didn't go as usual. Not as many people showed up, and of those who did, most of them crept around the restaurant carefully avoiding Milton and Ella. They crept along the food bar, to the restrooms and even to each other's table, anyplace but to where Milton and Ella sat. And if they did have the misfortune of passing Milton and Ella's table, they greeted them with an awkward smile before plotting and executing a retreat.

The day hadn't been all bad though. At least that was the way Ella saw it that evening as she and Milton recounted the day. There had still been a nice turnout at the dinner and there were those who did sit with them and those who came to them with conversation as if nothing had changed. Some people even told them they had them in their prayers. Bits of good news like that was something Ella and Milton knew they would have to hold onto in the face of what might come.

"You know Arlin Jeffries and his bunch got something going on," Milton said. One of the things the day's trials had succeeded in doing was bringing Ella and Milton closer, for matters of defense. They sat on the sofa in the den watching TV, and for the first time in weeks, they talked like two people committed to the same life.

"They made sure they stood away from us, but not out of sight of the rest of the congregation," Ella said.

"Yeah."

"Just something to deal with when it comes."

"If it comes," Milton said. "Who knows? Maybe they were just talking about what they heard and that'll be the end of it."

"I doubt it," Ella replied.

Milton's phone rang and he saw that it was Natasha.

"Natasha," he said to Ella as he picked up the phone.

"Hi," Milton answered.

"Is everything ok?"

Milton could hear the worry in Natasha's voice. "Everything's ok," he said, looking at Ella.

"I hadn't heard anything from you and I became worried," Natasha said.

"I should've called you," Milton replied, again glancing at Ella. He went on telling Natasha how things went at church and at dinner.

Ella listened and as she did, she realized how it wasn't right that Natasha should have to take all of this on herself. No one asks to be born, we're just put in circumstances that we have to make sense of. The other day at lunch with Natasha, Ella understood her. Ella tapped Milton's arm. "Let me talk to her."

"Here, let me put you on speaker," Milton said.

"Natasha, everything went well," Ella said.

"This is just so crazy," Natasha bemoaned. "So crazy."

"Look, don't take all of this on yourself."

"It's hard not to."

"Why don't you spend the night here? Milton will come over and get you." Ella signaled Milton and he began putting on his shoes. "Go ahead and pack your things."

"Thank you," Milton said to his wife as he left.

"When I decided to come here it was mostly because of school. Granny had talked so much about the University of Cincinnati—it was like she wanted me to finish what my mother didn't," Natasha said as she, Milton and Ella talked that night after Natasha had come over to the house.

"That's understandable," Ella said. "I can understand how your grandmother felt."

"I know we talked about this, but it's true, meeting you wasn't what I had in mind," Natasha said, looking at Milton. "The entire time leading up to coming here my mind was on school, my program and my future. Seeing who you were was the only thing I had in mind, not meeting you."

Milton moved uncomfortably in his chair.

"I had it planned. I would see you and that would be it. I would go my way. Take care of school and then move on with my life. But that didn't happen." She sat for a second more, in thought, before continuing. "I was so nervous when I saw your church. It was like, 'he's in there'. It was so scary. And then a thought came to me to turn away, to go back to campus and just forget about it, but I couldn't. Something told me to keep walking up to the door and before I knew it, I was inside. I guess I got there a bit early because the church was pretty empty. Only a few people, so I sat in back and waited. That's when LaShon spotted me. He introduced himself and we talked. He didn't know it, but he calmed me a bit. He told me to sit closer to the front of the church. I told him I was fine and that I would probably leave before the service was over and he asked why I would come if I didn't intend on staying."

"That's LaShon," Ella whispered, looking at Milton.

Natasha continued. "I sat there watching you, Reverend Pruitt. And I kept thinking, 'that's him! Oh my God, that's him!' I don't know if I was happy to see you or if... or if I was just excited over my discovery. I don't know. Like I said, I really only wanted to see who you were, but the more I looked at you and heard your voice, I found that I couldn't just leave you."

Natasha finished her story and quietly closed down.

Ella looked at Milton, who sat in awkward silence, and then she spoke up. "It's only natural for you to want to get to know who your father is."

"I didn't mean for all of this to happen," Natasha said again.

As she was about to go to bed Natasha asked, "How is LaShon doing?"

"We don't know," Ella said. "We'll check on him."

The next morning after Milton left for work, Ella and Natasha sat at breakfast.

"How do you think things will turn out?" Natasha asked.

"To tell you the truth, I'm not sure and neither is Milton. I don't think the entire congregation would want him to resign, but who knows?"

"He seemed confident as he left out this morning," Natasha said.

"Might as well be," Ella said as she poured two cups of coffee.

"How is your son taking all of this?"

"Danny? Well he and Milton never did get along so it only made matters worse. Well, in some ways. At first Danny was angry, now he seems like he's willing to deal with it. I think he's finally maturing. Finally."

"That's good."

"Yeah," Ella sighed as she lifted her coffee. "We'll just have to see how everything goes."

Ella gave Natasha a ride to campus as Ella headed for work. They sat in traffic as they approached the university.

"Lord this campus has changed so much since I went here," Ella said. "So much larger," she added as she looked out of the window.

"You know, sometimes I wonder what kind of person my mother was," Natasha said, her face to the window. She turned back to Ella, who looked quietly ahead. "I want to think of her as a good person, the way she looks in the photo I have of her—and I hear she was, but... to do what she did makes me wonder just who she was?"

"Well," was the only reply Ella gave.

"I'm sorry," Natasha said, catching herself. "It's just that I wish I knew more about her."

"That's to be expected. You know, we all do things out of character. We do it more often than we want to admit. Especially when we're young," Ella said.

Ella pulled up to one of the gates on the campus.

"Thanks for letting me come over last night," Natasha said.

"Thanks for coming over. We all need to figure out how to move forward."

"Yeah," Natasha said. "Well, thank you."

As Ella watched Natasha walk onto the campus she felt sorry for her, and it only widened the chasm that had grown between Ella and Milton. She wondered if she and Milton could ever fill that space between them.

~~~~

"LaShon. Boy, call me. I'm worried about you." Natasha hung up the phone and went back to her studies. Ella told her earlier that day that she had spoken with LaShon's parents. They told her that LaShon was definitely bothered by what Milton did, but they didn't think it would be anything to worry about. They said they felt he would continue serving the Lord.

But that didn't sit well with Natasha. They hadn't been with her and LaShon that day in the park. They hadn't listened to the pain and the confusion in LaShon's voice, the way he wrestled with words about himself, or seen the discomfort in his face. It's why when she got home that afternoon that Natasha began calling LaShon.

She sat at her computer, doing her studies. Every once in a while she would find herself staring at the screen, thinking about the damage Milton caused in people's lives. She wondered why she even wanted to be around her father.

An hour went by and she picked up her phone and called LaShon again.

She was beginning to trust Ella and to feel more comfortable about her. Even less than thinking she would ever get to know Milton, the thought of getting to know his wife had never crossed Natasha's mind, and now she was being invited to join Ella and Milton's family. It was clear Ella was reaching out to Natasha, but with the scorched earth Milton left, Natasha only hoped Ella was right, that they could all just move on.

Milton had been made out to be a despicable person in the eyes of Granny and Paw Paw. Growing up around them, Natasha rarely heard Milton's name mentioned until the subject of Abilyn came up, at which point her grandparents' faces would become a mix of pity and disgust, or during those moments when Paw Paw railed against the church. But in spite of hearing these things about her father, Natasha had never been fully swayed to hate him. Since she never knew what he took from her, there was little, if anything at all, for her to make him out to be some kind of monster. So instead, what she was left with was more curiosity than hatred. But curiosity had never been enough for her to envision becoming a part of her father's life, let alone a part of his family.

"We'll just have to see," she whispered, as she went back to work.

CHAPTER THIRTY-TWO

Milton looked over the bills once again before signing off on them. Sister Grambley, the church's bookkeeper, stood across the desk from him and waited for him to finish. She didn't stand behind his desk alongside him as she usually did and she didn't have much to say when she came into his office.

"Is that how much we're paying for gas and electric?" Milton asked the question, hoping he could spark conversation out of Sister Grambley.

Sister Grambley frowned a bit and replied, "It's the same as it's always been."

Sighing, Milton signed off on the last of the papers.

"Start looking at other companies. I've been seeing other utility companies vying for our business. Don't you think we should start looking at them?"

"I've been thinking that for some time now." Sister Grambley's face brightened a bit as she became engaged in the conversation.

"Ok, then let's start looking around."

"Ok," she said. "Now let me get these bills ready before the mail carrier comes."

Sister Grambley left the office and closed the door behind her.

Milton went back to work. Outside of his door he could hear the activities of the church: Mrs. Hargrove talked with someone who came into her office—it sounded like a vendor, Deacon Lewis could be heard giving instructions to the custodians, and outside, the voices of the contractors talked loudly to each other over the sound of their tools. Every once in a while someone would stop into the outer office and talk with Mrs. Hargrove, but they never asked to speak with him. In fact, only a few people had really spoken to him. The others who encountered him gave cursory, respectful greetings, before making their way to their duties around the church.

By mid-morning Milton had done little work and it was now time to meet with Reverend Harris. Milton turned off his computer and put his papers away, and as he walked out to the front office, he saw Mrs. Hargrove talking with another member of the congregation. They became silent when Milton came out of his office.

"Good morning, Pastor," the woman said. She attempted a smile but was only able to muster a grin.

"Good morning, Sister Patterson. Is everything ok?" Milton asked the question as he locked his eyes on hers.

"Oh yes! Yes, everything's fine. I was just on my way from the store and thought I'd stop by and see Sister Hargrove. How are you this morning?"

"I'm well. Thanks." Milton turned to Mrs. Hargrove. "I'm on my way to a meeting. I should be back by two."

"Ok, Pastor," Mrs. Hargrove said.

"Glad you stopped by, Sister Patterson."

"Oh yes!" she answered suddenly and with a great degree of awkwardness.

Reverend Harris blew a sharp breath and sat back in his chair. "I was hoping what I heard last night wasn't true."

Milton shook his head slightly, unable to speak.

"Milton, you know we can't have this, don't you?"

"Yeah," Milton said resignedly.

"Who is this girl? Why did all of this have to come out now, Milton?"

"She's my daughter." Milton bristled from the tone of the minister's question.

"I know. I'm sorry. But Milton, you have to wonder why she suddenly showed up. She's been here all this time and suddenly, when we're gaining steam against the school board, she just shows up?"

Reverend Harris' question made sense to Milton and they looked at each other for a brief moment before Milton replied. "She didn't grow up around here. She came here from Oklahoma."

"Oklahoma?"

"Yeah."

"Oklahoma?" Reverend Harris whispered to himself, to preface his next question. "And you don't think that's strange? That someone would come all the way from Oklahoma to Cincinnati at this particular time?"

"Bernard, I don't know," Milton said, calling the reverend by his first name. "Look, it might and it might not sound conspiratorial, but it's done."

Reverend Harris tapped his desk as he contemplated Milton's situation.

"Yeah. You're right," he sighed. "It's done, Milton."

"So I want to step down from my position," Milton offered. "Take more of a back seat."

Reverend Harris sighed. "You know this is something I'll have to run past the other board members."

"I know."

"Look. I'll do what I can. And you're right, you should step down from the board." He curled his lip as he thought about things. "But I'm wondering if that would be enough?"

"What do you mean?"

"We need as many members of the faith community behind us and Christ The Redeemer is definitely needed. So we need you to continue your work. But I'm thinking, when all of this hits the media—and it will, believe me—they'll come looking for you, Milton. The press. They'll search you out and work on you. You know how the news media is, half news, half entertainment. And you've given them just what they need."

"It's not out there, my having a daughter from an affair."

Reverend Harris scoffed. "You don't think it is? Come on, Milton. You're too smart and too seasoned to believe that."

"So what are you saying?"

"To be honest with you, I don't know. Like I said, we need Christ The Redeemer Baptist behind us, but what we don't need is to have you in the news. So we have to figure out how we can, one: keep Christ The Redeemer Baptist Church, in alignment with what we're doing, and two: keep you out of the spotlight—or at least keep this…" he waved his hand, "matter, out of the spotlight."

"You want me to be invisible."

"Truthfully? Yeah. But like I said, it's not up to me to make these decisions. I'll meet with the other members of the board and run this past them. I'm sure the word has gotten out already and they'll be calling me very soon to have a meeting."

"I guess that's that, huh?" Milton said. "Keep me apprised."

"We will."

As Milton stood to leave, Reverend Harris asked, "Are you still able to work with your congregation, Milton?"

Milton hesitated, then replied, "I think so."

~~~~

A dragonfly flitted about the yard under the hot June sun, its wings fluttering so fast that they appeared as a line of gray color vibrating from the dragonfly's back. Danny watched the dragonfly as he sat on the patio with his mother. They didn't have much to talk about since Ella said she didn't want to go on talking about what Milton had done and she hadn't offered more of her own story that day, so they sat silently for a while with Danny watching the dragonfly and Ella gazing off into the distance. Danny watched the dragonfly as it moved about the yard and as it went to the far corner of the yard where the dead bugs were buried. He wondered what was left of their wingless bodies under the ground. Ella stirred a little and brought Danny's attention back to her. He wasn't used to this, to seeing his mother lost in a gaze. He was used to seeing her in constant movement, whether she was moving pieces of furniture around the house, or something as small as plucking away a speck from atop one of her plants, she was always in motion. So for her to be sitting, caught up in a distant gaze, bothered him. But he didn't know what to do.

But what Danny didn't know was his mother's gaze was full. Far from empty. It was full of questions about the young lady Milton slept with—she didn't want to know Abilyn's name because to know her name would give more life to her even though she was dead. From seeing Natasha, she had an idea about Abilyn's face: soft, light complexion-- isn't that the way black men usually go? She thought about this to herself, with a slight shake of her head. And she wondered if she could ever trust Milton again, what would it take for her to lower her palms from her face and see him as she once did? Then her mind went to her own problem, the one she was finding more and more difficult to live with, that was beginning to haunt her more and more each day. Buddy had returned and she knew she would have to face him. The smell of the lake and of rot, the book that lay open in her room, he had definitely returned and she knew he needed reckoning. But to face him she would need Damon because he needed to ask for forgiveness just as much as she did. So while Ella's gaze seemed aimless, it was far from it.

"Have you been looking for another place to work?" Ella finally asked, breaking the silence.

"What? No. No. Not yet," Danny answered.

Ella turned her eyes back to the yard. "Why not?"

"I don't know. I just haven't gotten around to it."

"And you won't will you? Not until something else goes wrong. What is it that makes you stay around that place anyway?"

Danny didn't give her an answer.

"Lord have mercy," she whispered.

"You making too big a deal over all this."

"No I'm not. Don't tell me that. You worry me. You got your father in you and it worries me."

"Mom, you have to stop hanging onto the past."

Ella looked at him then turned away.

"And this thing about me being like my father. If anything, you made me more like him."

Ella quickly turned to Danny. "What?"

Danny nodded his head. "Yeah."

"How in the world…"

"Because you treated me like I was a threat."

"A threat?"

"Yeah, a threat. To you and anybody you thought I might come across. It was like you made it so real for me that eventually I started believing it. I started believing I was a threat to everybody. And it wasn't fair. I mean you didn't even give me a chance."

Ella sat for a moment, thinking about what her son had just said. Then she looked at him. "I guess I can't say I didn't do that", she said quietly. "But what have you done with what you think about yourself? What have you done with it?"

"Nothing," Danny lied.

Suddenly the dragonfly darted from the place where the dead bugs lay and hovered before Danny's face.

CHAPTER THIRTY-THREE

Ella's father scooped her up in his arms and hurried to his car. She felt the blanket around her that he had wrapped her in. It was the wool one that he kept in the garage. She could feel the scratchiness of the wool and the smell of mildew. She was wrapped to her head with only her face exposed and she saw the trees overhead and the breaks of light from the sun as her father rushed her through the woods away from Damon's house. She could hear her father's breath, panting as he carried her and she heard the voices. There was someone, a man, running alongside her father.

"I found her just layin' there and I knew it was yo' little girl. That's why I called you."

"Thank you."

"She was bleedin'. Blood all over that tub over there."

"Clean it up."

"Yessir."

"Mr. Stallworth?"

"What!"

"Mr. Stallworth, is there some kinda reward? You know, for me findin' her and callin' you?"

"Yes, yes," she heard her father say as he laid her in the backseat of his car. "Yes. Now clean up that mess and don't you tell anyone. You hear me?"

"Yessir. Thank you Mr. Stallworth."

As the car sped through the woods all Ella could think of was Damon. Where was Damon?

~~~~

Ella drove along the street as she looked for a place to park. She watched the men on the corners as she drove past. They were loud and crude and they appeared to be lost, so far removed from where they came. Wrenched from a place and left at no place. She understood the history that put them there. She knew they had come from a lineage much greater than they knew. She parked her car, retrieved the suitcase and walked up the street to where Simon used to live.

The neighbors parted along the sidewalk as Ella came to the building, everyone knowing what happened and allowing Ella the rite to what was left of Simon's life there.

"A shame what happened to that boy," the old woman who sat on the stoop in her usual spot said with a shake of her head.

"I know," Ella said as she came up the steps.

"They said those boys stomped him 'til he was almost dead in that park. I hear that now he's all the way paralyzed. Can't even feed hisself. Now why in the world would people do that kinda mess like those boys did? Drugs, that's why. Greed."

"We definitely have a problem."

"Mm hm," the woman said. "What nursin' home is he in?"

"I'll let his family tell you. I'm not allowed to give out his information."

The woman looked at her with a degree of indignation.

"I'm sorry," Ella said again.

"Well… Guess it's better than him bein' out here in these streets."

"Yes ma'am. I agree."

"The super up there right now. He'll let you in," the woman said as Ella walked past her.

"Thank you."

Ella had the key to Simon's apartment. She had been given permission to collect some things Simon would need and a voucher to purchase what was needed. When she got to the apartment she saw the super working on the door. He was a thin black man who appeared to be in his mid to late fifties. His hands worked busily on the plate of the door.

"Hi," Ella said, introducing herself. "I'm Ella Pruitt, Simon's caseworker. I'm here to get some of his things."

The super stood up and shook her hand. She noticed his hands were large for someone his size.

"Mr. Coston," he said as he introduced himself, peering over his glasses that sat low on the bridge of his nose. "Whatever's left," he continued with a nod towards the apartment. "They broke in and took what they wanted. Left the rest."

"Who?"

"Friends. Family. They all wanted something." He stepped back and allowed Ella entry.

She shook her head and sighed as she stepped into the apartment. From where she stood just inside of the living room she could see what was missing. The TV and stereo were gone as well as one of the living room chairs. The living room closet had been left standing open and had been stripped bare. She was sure the other closets in the apartment were the same. She walked to the bedroom and went through Simon's bureau. Much of his outerwear had been taken, so she began to remove his underwear and put them into the suitcase. She went to the nightstand by his bed and took out his remaining prescriptions and put them into the suitcase as well. She would just have to buy everything else he needed.

"My daddy worked on construction." The woman on the stoop continued her conversation as Ella left the building. "But ain't nothin' like that around much anymore for these men." She looked sorrowfully at the street before continuing. "What makes it bad is things my daddy and them knew done got lost. Skills and knowin' how to make things work, they got lost 'cause they weren't used no more. No place to use 'em."

"Skills and the knowledge," Ella agreed.

"Yeah. They got lost when the jobs went out there where the white folks went. And you can't just tell them kids what should be if it ain't much chance for it to happen."

"But we can't give up," Ella said.

The woman looked up the street to one of the corners. "No, we can't."

Ella and the woman talked a while longer, then Ella said her goodbye and made her way to her car. As she walked up the street she felt the sense of loss from those who remembered and the ignorance of those who never knew and a sense of despondency came over her, a despondency that suddenly seemed at home along the streets where she walked, and she was reminded of all of the things she had lost in her life: her mother, her family, the life she knew back in New Home, Damon… and yes, Buddy. And now it seemed she might lose Danny and quite possibly Milton. It did seem that loss had become her constant companion. What Danny said to her the other day when they were sitting on the patio bothered her, and maybe he was right. Maybe. Maybe it was true that she saw him as someone who was damaged, but she never thought of it that way. It was inheritance that she feared. Not him. After all, everyone believed in legacy, that the sins of the fathers shall be visited upon the sons. Call it payback, justice, karma, whatever, everyone believed in it. God could be a vindictive something... or an equalizing force, she quickly corrected herself, and that is what she was most cautious of. So maybe Danny got it wrong that she made him into a hateful person. Maybe he was simply meant to be that way so his death could be used to punish her and Damon. In any case, she would be there to fight off that corrective god if it happened to feel it necessary to destroy her only child.

Danny hadn't always been hateful. He was the prettiest baby Ella had ever seen (though she hadn't seen many), dark skin like chocolate and wide wondrous eyes that looked constantly about as if even at birth he was assessing the people around him and his place in their world. But always, always those wide wondrous eyes would go back to Ella and he would smile there in her arms. Since her father didn't want her anywhere around the house with the child, Ella pretty much stayed in her room and she would sit by the window and rock her baby from sunrise to sunset, looking down at the son who constantly smiled at her. The people of New Home would walk down the sidewalk in front of Ella's family's house, hoping for a glimpse of the baby that brought Emmanuel Clinton Stallworth to his knees in shame and that came into the world on the wake of such violence. The interest in Danny became so intense that it became a source of desperation for some, and what started out as casual passes by became an almost steady flow of passersby who would look up at the large house for a glimpse of Ella and the child. Sometimes people would bump into each other in passing and they would chuckle, knowing why each one was there, and they would continue past the house with their eyes looking up at the windows. And all people would see when they passed the Stallworth house was the girl, not much older than a child herself, rocking back and forth in front of the window, smiling and talking to something in her arms.

No, Danny wasn't born hateful, and Ella swore that she would fight any angel God sent to take him from her. She would even fight God himself if He came to take Danny away from her.

~~~~

Charlotte had asked Milton once if he thought there would ever be an end to their misfortune. It was just after she had been arrested for her daughter's murder. Charlotte had looked so worn from the abuse she had gone through in her life, and so small as she sat behind the window holding the phone to her ear. She was so much smaller than Milton remembered her being. The drugs and alcohol had stripped away what little life she had left, leaving her looking small and incidental. Milton recalled having startled himself when he thought his sister looked incidental. He startled himself because he realized that was probably how their father saw them: incidental to a life he had chosen to live that didn't really include his children or his wife. Since then, since those years under his father and his father's passing, Milton had forgiven him. At least that's what Milton told himself. But if he really wanted to forgive his father he would have tried to understand why his father was the way he was. But each time Milton tried to look into his father's past, each time he started to take a step towards going into his father's past to understand what might have happened, something would hold him back. This something was fear, because Milton feared what he might find and he feared having to revisit what he, his mother and Charlotte had to endure under his father. It was this fear that left him feeling incomplete, things unresolved, and it was this lack of resolution that left him dangling over a pit of uncertainty and anger. So that day he looked at his sister sitting behind the glass of a jail, and all he could do was stare at her, in all of her confusion and from all of his anger, and tell her to trust in God and that misfortune was only relative to what God had in store for them if they believed in Him. Telling her that had been enough then, because he wasn't ready to confront her question.

Now Milton sat in his car, staring out into the street. The misfortune had continued, but not because he lacked belief in God, but because of his own actions. He knew this and he understood that he would have to bear responsibility for them. But it was dealing with what was to come, the uncertainty, except the certainty that there will be hard times that had him frozen at the wheel of his car lost in the street. It had become known now that the board of Christ The Redeemer Baptist Church was sending him a letter to appear before it to discuss his possible resignation.

After a long spell of sitting in his car, he headed home.

CHAPTER THIRTY-FOUR

Littlejohn was dead. Danny had gotten the call from Azhure, who was crying so hard that he had to ask her, "Azhure, what? Azhure, what?" as if between the sobs and the gasps of air the story would change, that she wasn't saying Littlejohn was dead. But he was. He had been murdered. Azhure said they were about to go out to a movie and Littlejohn forgot his phone. He told Azhure he had to go back to their apartment and get it. On his way back to the car a man walked up to him, raised a gun to Littlejohn's head and shot him.

Danny rushed over to Azhure's sister's apartment to sit with Azhure. Her sister had gone to the police station, picked Azhure up, and brought her back to her place. Danny held Azhure as she cried. The blood from where she had cradled Littlejohn's head left tiny ellipses of red stains beneath her fingernails and her skin still had a slight ferrous odor left from Littlejohn's blood, even though she had showered and changed clothes. Danny listened to her as he breathed in the odor, realizing it was all he had left of his friend.

Danny stopped by a liquor store on his way home that night. He passed the men and women who hung around the store, their thin bodies situated so close to the walls of the building that they appeared to be part of the very structure itself, an iron railing or such. It was as if they were clinging to the last ship that threatened to set sail without them. As Danny passed the women and the men, their faces shining like smears of grease in the light that came from the store, their expressions seemed to say they knew what happened, 'oh baby, I'm so sorry', 'damn man, that's fucked up', or 'wow' (expressed with a pitiful shake of the head), that's how the faces appeared to Danny. But there were some faces that seemed to know more than just what happened, those were the faces that seemed to say they knew who killed Littlejohn. Danny stopped in front of one of the faces that told him it knew and peered at it. Azhure said the guy who shot Littlejohn was young, and the face Danny was looking into was younger than the others in front of the store.

The young man leaned back, slightly startled. "Damn man!"

Coming to himself, Danny walked on into the store. He got a pint of gin and headed from the store. As he walked out the young man whose face he had studied came up to him. "What's up?"

Danny looked at him without speaking.

"We can hook up if you wanna." The young man spoke, grinning through yellow teeth as he kept his eyes on the bottle in Danny's hand.

"Nah man," Danny replied.

"We can get a bottle and chill, you know, kick it," the young man said as he licked his lips and looked at the bottle, then to Danny's crotch.

"Get the fuck outta my face." Danny snarled at the man.

"Man fuck you," the young man replied as he retook his spot in front of the store.

As Danny turned down his street he looked out of his car at the darkness around him. His street was never well lit but it never bothered him. But tonight the street seemed more like a gullet than a street. Long, pitch black and leading to something he was unsure of. He slowed down as he approached his apartment and took in everything around him: trees and spindly branches reaching out from the bushes, the roofs and eaves of houses that jutted sharply into the night sky, and the liquid pools of light that fell from the few working street lamps. He checked things out. He wasn't sure why Littlejohn had been murdered, but he understood the world he and Littlejohn traveled and even cultivated, and that it could come down to his own death. He turned off the car and sat for a few seconds as he continued to scope things out before going inside his building.

Once inside his apartment, he sat on the side of his bed, drinking and staring at the wall. The nights had never seemed so silent to him and things had never moved so slow. He thought about Littlejohn and how Littlejohn was the only friend he had ever had. He had been the only person Danny could turn to.

Danny continued to drink, thinking about the times he and Little-john had, then he began to cry and drink more.

A furious noise woke Danny. It was like someone was fighting and all hell had broken loose. He turned over in bed. He was still dressed and his bedroom was dark except for the TV that played. He didn't remember turning off the light or turning on the TV at all. There was someone banging on his door, and from below he could hear a bothered Mr. Stiggers screaming for the person who was banging on Danny's door to leave. The neighbors had joined in threatening to call the police if the person at the door didn't quiet down.

"Danny! Danny!"

Danny could hear Cortez calling him. He got up and went to the door. When he opened it he saw Cortez standing there, his large frame filling the doorway.

"You ok?" Cortez asked as he studied Danny.

Danny shook his head and let Cortez in.

"I didn't know what to do," Danny said. He stood in the middle of his living room and cried, "I didn't know what to do."

Cortez came to him and hugged him.

That night they slept curled up in each other's arms.

"We have to check on Azhure." Danny spoke as he watched the gentle waves move across the water in the tub. He and Cortez had made it through the night, each one lying awake in thought at times, listening to the silence and feeling the sadness in their hearts. Now it was morning and they sat in the tub together with Danny lying back against Cortez's chest.

"I'll call her," Cortez said.

Danny watched a drop of water gather at the tip of the faucet before falling into the tub, creating another wave that traveled across the water and disappeared around their bodies.

"He was kind of short," Azhure said as she looked down at the tissue she was holding in her hands. "At first I just thought he was some young guy passing by. Even then I became aware," she said, looking at Danny. "You know how these young boys can be. And then," she paused, then began to cry. "And then he just raised this pistol and… and he shot Julius." She began to cry so hard that her sister put her arms around her as they sat on the couch. Danny and Cortez were sitting in chairs across from her on either side of her. They looked at her as they sought to find the words to comfort her.

"I know you talked to the police, but, can you tell me how he looked?" Cortez spoke softly to Azhure.

"Like I said, a young guy. Somewhere in his early twenties. He had on a dark green hoodie but he didn't have the hood up. Either he was stupid or he just didn't care who saw him. I don't know."

Cortez and Danny glanced at each other.

"And you gave a description to the police, right?" Danny asked her.

Azhure nodded. "Yeah. I have to go down today so they can do a sketch of him."

"She said she doesn't think the guy saw her, but she's not sure," Azhure's sister said. "But to be safe, she's going to stay here with me."

"Yeah," Cortez said. "Look. I'll take care of all of the arrangements. And if it's anything you need just let me know."

He and Danny stood to leave.

"I can't help but think none of this would've happened if he wasn't around you." Azhure spoke quietly, but matter-of-factly as she looked at Cortez. She spoke with such clarity and with a lack of enmity that her words stopped Cortez in his tracks.

"I don't know. I hope not," Cortez said. He looked at Danny, who started for the door.

Danny and Cortez walked out to Cortez's car under a gray sky. Danny could feel Littlejohn walking beside him.

When they got in the car Cortez sat staring ahead. "Is Azhure right?" He spoke as he continued to look out of the window. Then he turned to Danny. "Do you think this wouldn't have happened if he wasn't around me?"

"I don't know," Danny said. "I really don't."

~~~~

Ella wasn't sure how to feel when Milton told her the board intended to remove him from the pulpit. Just like when he told her about the affair he had, she watched his mouth move while her mind skimmed through a mix of thoughts and her heart wrestled with a host of feelings. It wasn't that she didn't care about Milton's predicament, because she did. They had invested too much to get him to where he was for her not to care. But he didn't care, did he? He didn't seem to care when he decided to run after that young woman, and he didn't seem to care when he decided to drop his pants and put his thing inside of her. Ella pushed that thought out of her mind like she had been doing for the last few weeks. Still, by pushing it out of her mind she was left with the taste of betrayal, and that was something she wasn't able to put aside, and it was what made her listen to Milton's plight without the concern she once would have had. As she sat in the dining room under the chandelier, the chandelier that she had chosen when they moved into the house, it became clear that the things she built would most likely disappear. That's what she realized more than her husband's pitiful fall from grace. And yet things had already changed. In fact, it was so obvious that things had already changed that it was almost laughable watching Milton speak, seeing his face, so sad, and his body, slumped, diminished in the light of the dining room. She watched his hands clasp, then unclasp, and move across the table to her, and she wanted to laugh. Things had changed and things were threatening to change even more with all of the other things that were going on in her life. She wanted to ask Milton what in the world did he expect? But she didn't. Instead, she listened and she let his hand fold around her own hand as he continued to talk. She had other things going on in her life that didn't include caring what happened to Milton's position in the church and his image in the community. She didn't care, but she did.

"That's just something you've heard," she finally said. "You haven't gotten a correspondence from them have you?"

"No."

"Then how do you know for sure?"

"Talk."

"Well you know how talk can be."

"Even then, there must be some truth to it," Milton said. "There's always some foundation when people talk. Somewhere. If it's not the board then it's parts of the church that want me out."

"But there are parts of Christ The Redeemer that don't want you out. I'm sure of that. And you know that." She locked her eyes onto him. "You know that," she said. "So you need to make your case with them."

Milton gently shook his head. "Yeah."

Over the weeks Ella had begun sleeping in her bed again. It came to her that this was her bed as much as it was her husband's bed, even though it might never be their bed again. But it was hers.

That night as they were in bed, Milton turned to her, "Ella?"

"Huh?" She answered from where she had been lying with her back to him.

"When we were talking this evening. You told me I need to make my case. It sounded like you weren't going to be there for me."

Ella didn't reply.

Milton waited a while before continuing.

"I know I brought all of this on myself, but I need you to forgive me."

"I do."

"It doesn't feel like it."

Ella rolled onto her back and crossed her wrists at her stomach. "What do you want from me? It's only been a few weeks, Milton."

"I understand. It's just that, well, it'll look and be much better to have you by my side."

Ella hesitated before continuing. "Right. It looks good to have the pastor's wife by his side. That's what you're saying. Like everything else, Milton, it's about you isn't it? Whatever," she said, turning her back to her husband. "You should've thought about that long before now."

The women in Ella's life knew what to do to make things work. From her Aunt Bernice, who knew she had to dispose of husbands when they fell out of favor with her; to Mrs. Wexner, who understood the virtue of patience when waiting for love; to her sister Miriam, who discovered the solace that lies beneath insanity; and even to Ella's mother, who knew when it was time to leave when life became most bleak, the women in Ella's life knew what it took to make things work. But the men, well, that was a discussion of a different sort. The men. They seem lost from the day they come into the world, roughing about, breaking things, tripping aimlessly through life and hurting loved ones. And most likely they leave this world not even understanding the trouble they've caused while the women are left behind to clean up the mess they created. That's why women lived longer... to clean up the mess. And all because in truth, men belonged to women.

This is what Ella mused over the next morning as she cleaned the breakfast dishes. She half-listened to the morning news show that was playing on the TV that sat on the kitchen counter, while the other half of her mind was on the mess of men. Like Milton. He had the nerve to ask her to be by his side because of the mess he created. She grunted softly to herself as she ran water in the sink and washed her plate. Like she should just naturally be there for him. Her face stiffened as she thought about it all, but also because she knew she would be there by his side. As much as it bothered her, she knew she would be standing there beside him, putting aside, momentarily, what he had done to her. What he had done to create the mess. Even in the case of her father, people pitied him when his wife took the notion to not wake up, but Ella knew there was more to it than that. She knew her mother *chose* not to wake up because of the mess her father had created, imprisoning her in that town her mother had always likened to an outhouse. She knew it when she heard Aunt Bernice during a moment of anger say to Ella's father, "You're the reason she didn't want to wake up, Emmanuel. You!" It was then that Ella knew it. So in spite of all of the pity Ella's father received, Ella knew that it was the mess he had created that led her mother to not wake up. And Damon. If he hadn't done what he had done she wouldn't have done what she did and Buddy would still be alive. Maybe. Maybe…

In the background, the TV continued to play when suddenly the half-part of her mind that was on the messiness of men was pulled away by the news as the newscaster mentioned the murder of a 'Julius Littlejohn'.

Ella dropped the dish she had been holding into the sink and looked at the TV. She didn't recognize the face on the screen of the man who had been murdered, a face that was framed in an old mug shot, but she recognized the name. Danny had mentioned it a few times in conversations when she fished around for knowledge of the somethings or someones in his life. He had mentioned a Littlejohn as his friend, and though Ella had never met Littlejohn, she didn't care for him because of the way Littlejohn's name would dissipate from Danny's conversations when Danny thought he was giving away too many details about his life. She knew this must be *the* Littlejohn. And now this. At first she stood transfixed as she waited for the voice coming from the box to say 'and a second man…' but the voice didn't mention Danny's name. Ella let out a long breath and leaned against the sink in relief.

She began dialing Danny's number. It didn't matter that he might still be asleep. She needed to talk with him.

Three rings went by before Danny answered.

Danny's voice was thin as he answered. "Hey."

"What happened?"

"I don't know."

"You weren't there were you?"

"No. He was coming from his apartment."

"And you don't know anything about what happened? You're not involved in anything…"

Danny sat quietly at the other end of the call. Ella could feel his exhaustion through the silence.

"I'm tired, Mom."

"Boy you need to tell me if there's something wrong."

"I don't know… Look, I'm tired. We can talk later. I'm tired. I wanna go back to sleep."

"Call me when you get up."

"Yeah."

"I mean it Danny."

There was no reply.

"Danny."

"Ok. I said yeah. Ok." He hung up the phone.

For most of her day at work Ella checked in on the story about Littlejohn, listening to the news as she drove to appointments and reading news stories at her desk, looking for anything, a phrase or a construction of a thought that might direct her to worry even more over Danny. In time she found herself in her office staring at her computer, but her mind was no longer on Littlejohn or his murder, but it was on the jagged path her own life had taken. She told herself that she was done with wrestling over guilt and that she needed to change the course of that jagged path. To clean it up. To finally clear some of the shards from that path.

The evening had become cool, more like an autumn evening than a summer one, and the sky had fallen from a deep blue that afternoon to a bitter gray. Ella called Danny to let him know she was on her way to his place. She drove up the street under stubborn black clouds that gathered in conspiracy over the city. A deep concern weighed on her mind and fear plucked at her heart. A distant rumble of thunder rolled across the sky as she got out of her car and walked up to Danny's building, entering the vestibule and the stillness of the hallway. She glanced at the old man's door on the first floor as she started up the stairs. Once she got to Danny's floor, she found him standing in the doorway. He had on only a pair of jeans that hung loosely from his hips, no shirt, socks or shoes. It looked as though he hadn't slept or eaten in a few days. Without a word, Ella walked past him, taking his hand in hers as she went into his apartment. She closed the door and led him to the couch.

"You need to eat."

Danny looked at her. His eyes were empty.

Ella thought how she should have brought over some food. She got up and went into the kitchen to look for something to make for him and to not see the sadness in his face. She fixed up a quick meal from the eggs, sausage, butter and bread. The milk was sour, so she poured it out and made coffee, then went in the living room and sat by her son.

"Eat."

Danny sat for a moment, looking down at the food on the coffee table before him. It was as if he was trying to connect the notion of food, and of eating, to loss. Slowly he began to eat.

Ella watched him eat. She had come over to talk to him, like she always did, about getting his life together. And this time she had pre-pared to engage him with a sense of urgency. That's what she had planned to do. But when she saw him, she knew that all she had planned should be set aside, and that she should wait for him to speak. She knew she had to listen to his pain. Danny ate without speaking for a while, halting between lifting forks of food to his mouth. Lingering in thought and memory. Eating.

"I never had a friend before." Danny spoke quietly, but it was sudden enough to rupture the stillness in the air. "All those years," he said, looking at his mother. "And he was the only real friend I ever had. I always thought you would be the only person I could turn to."

Ella put her hand on Danny's thigh and waited. She listened without speaking as Danny told her about Littlejohn. Recounting sto-ries that were sometimes funny enough to make him and his mother laugh, but mostly he told his mother how Littlejohn was there for him when he needed someone to talk to. Littlejohn met him in places that no one would dare go to of their own will, places that were dark, where fear and confusion spoke as anger, where spit and semen overpowered love, places where animals, with their limbs torn from their bodies, lay. But those are the things Danny didn't tell his mother about his friendship with Littlejohn. They were things Ella didn't need to know even though, in fact she had always assumed as much. She knew he saw the ugliness of life even before he came into it.

"The best you can do is to hold onto the good things he left behind," Ella said.

Danny nodded in agreement. "Yeah," he whispered.

The two of them continued talking, with Ella doing most of the listening. Though she listened to Danny, in her mind she sought a moment when she might be able to move the conversation away from the death of his friend. After all, it was Danny who she was there for. Finally, she excused herself to go to the bathroom. She felt she had shown enough sympathy for the death of his friend.

Danny sat back on the couch without finishing his food and waited in the deepening light of the evening. He had said all he wanted to say to his mother and had started to retreat into silence when he heard his mother cry out and the sound of her falling against the wall. He jumped up from the couch and ran down the hallway where he found his mother half slumped against the wall, her eyes wide with terror as she looked into Danny's bedroom.

"Mom! What's wrong!" Danny ran to his mother.

Ella tried to speak, but her voice had left her. She put one of her hands to her mouth and shook her head.

"Oh, oh…" she moaned as she recaptured her voice. "Where…" She stopped speaking and backed away from her son. "Where did you get those?" She yelled at Danny. "Where did you get those?" She screamed louder as she looked across his room in terror.

It was the photos. Danny looked at them then looked back to his mother. His expression was at once of confusion and fear. He reached for his mother, taking her by her shoulders. "Mom. What's wrong?"

Ella broke away from him and walked into his bedroom, shaking her head. Then she walked up to one of the photos and covered her face with both of her hands and began to cry. There in the photo was the baseball team and in the middle of the photo, looking stoic and proud, was her father. And to the far right was the batboy. His name was Buddy.

~~~~

The baby was beginning to move more often, and with each yaw, each kick that Ella felt in her belly, the more she thought about Damon. She hadn't seen him in a while, ever since her father had put out notice that no men could come to their house and had told the neighbors to keep an open eye on his house. He put the word out, and since it was Emmanuel Stallworth who declared the decree, it spread quickly throughout New Home, partly because of his importance, but mostly because it pleased most people to see that Emmanuel Stallworth had a child who was willing to throw open her legs to the first guy to come along, showing she wasn't much different from the people he looked down his nose at.

No men were allowed to come to the house because Emmanuel wasn't sure which one of them might have gotten his daughter pregnant. There was an exception to the decree and that was the man who cared for the lawn. But he was an elderly man who took so long to mow the grass because of arthritis and just plain age, that Emmanuel knew he couldn't possibly be the father of Ella's baby.

Ella spent her days sitting in her room, feeling the baby kick, and thinking about Damon so much that one afternoon she decided if Damon couldn't come to her, she would go to Damon.

The sun was high that afternoon when Ella rocked herself up from her chair and started down the hallway. As usual, Ren had left out by then and was off somewhere with his buddies, so he wasn't around to stop her from leaving the house. That left Miriam and whomever the woman was who was downstairs cleaning to stop her, and Ella knew Miriam would be no problem.

Ella walked as soft as a young girl could who was carrying almost a third of her own weight. She paused and listened for the cleaning woman. She heard the woman singing to herself as she went about her chores. She was sure her father had told the woman to not let Ella leave the house, so Ella went back to her room and got her wastebasket. If the woman saw her, Ella would tell her, whatever her name was, that she was going out to empty the wastebasket.

As Ella was at the top of the stairs for a second time she heard the sound of the vacuum cleaner coming from the study, so she figured that would be the time to sneak past the woman and go out of the back door. She set the wastebasket down and started down the stairs. Just then Miriam came up the stairs, carrying a new garment she had just sewn. She saw Ella and stopped. They looked at each other for a second or so and Miriam quickly dropped her head and rushed past Ella where she went to her bedroom and shut her door.

It didn't take long for Ella to escape from the house and she quickly walked the path across the backyard and through the thicket she had seen Damon take so many times when he came to visit her. She wasn't sure if the neighbors saw her, but she was so desperate to see Damon that she would take her chance.

The heat of the sun bore through Ella as she walked along the back roads of New Home, sapping her strength and her energy from her, but just as she would feel her energy and her strength drain, she would find another reserve of energy, and she continued on.

She finally made it to the back road that divided New Home from Clearwater. She smiled to herself in spite of the fatigue that gripped her and continued along the dirt road that took up once you entered Clearwater. Since it was the middle of the day, there was no one around, as most of the people were at work or just staying in the house to escape the heat. Taking a path from the road that led her to the shack where Damon lived, she began walking through the woods. She had come to know the place well because it was where she and Damon spent a lot of time alone. She smiled to herself as she imagined how she would go to Damon's house and knock on his door, and he would come to the door and they would laugh from the surprise of her being there, and Damon would say something like, 'Girl, whatchou doin' to my baby? It's too hot out here,' and then he would take her in his aunt's house and give her some water and a place to rest, and he would hold her in his arms as they sat together and they would just sit, quietly enjoying each other's company.

The thought of being alone with Damon made her giggle with excitement as she walked through the woods. Suddenly she heard what she thought were voices nearby. She stopped and listened. She thought it might be Damon and almost called out to him, but then decided against it since it might not be him. She decided to continue on to the shack where Damon and his aunt lived when she heard the voices again. One of the voices was Damon's. She couldn't tell what he was saying, but she could tell it was his voice, so she walked in the direction of where his voice was coming from and she saw him. Damon and Buddy were together. Their pants and their shorts were down around their ankles and Buddy leaned face forward against a tree and Damon was behind him, in him. Ella stood, looking in horror as she watched from the woods. Damon was inside of Buddy and he was moving in him the same way he moved inside of her and they were talking to each other, moaning and groaning things to each other until she watched the muscles in Damon's behind tighten into a knot as he thrust forward into Buddy's behind. Then he held Buddy close, and the two of them stood, breathing heavy, in the shaded woods. Ella covered her mouth to keep from crying out, and she ran from the scene as fast as she could until she made it back home.

That night Ella found it difficult to sleep. She was weak from the sadness that gripped her and she cried softly into her pillow.

The baby began to move and she put her hand on her belly. She turned onto her back and stared out of her bedroom window at the moon that shone, like a white pearl promised to her, and thought about how things would never be the way she thought they would be, that the white pearl moon's promise was nothing at all. And it was then that she considered killing the baby inside of her. Damon wasn't who she thought he was and the baby shouldn't be either.

She cried herself to sleep as the baby moved inside of her belly.

By morning the thought came to her. The only reason Damon probably did what he did with Buddy was because he couldn't do it with her. Now she understood. A comforting warmth came over her as she told herself that she understood. They say that to sleep on things is to understand them and she had, and now she understood what she had to do. And it was then that she sent word to Damon to come to the house, and it was then that she told him the lie, that Buddy had sexually assaulted her.

~~~~

Ella finished telling Danny the story as she cried and told him how sorry she was to cause Buddy's death.

"It's why I've spent so many nights asking God to forgive me and it's why I'm so scared that He'll take you from me."

"Who?" Danny held his mother in his arms.

"God. I'm afraid that he's going to ask for you in return for what me and your father did to Buddy."

Danny pulled his mother close. "Mom. I don't think that's going to happen."

"How do you know?" Ella asked, between sobs.

"I don't know, but I just… I don't think it's like that."

Danny walked his mother to her car. It was dark now, and she had stayed much longer than she had expected. He had fixed her something to eat and talked to her, to calm her fears, but he knew nothing he said would bring her peace of mind. As they walked down the stairs they passed Mr. Stiggers' apartment. Ella stopped and looked at the old man's door.

Who are you?' she thought to herself as Danny walked her to her car.

~~~~

Milton held the letter, weighing it between his fingers, feeling the lightness of it. He considered the irony of the lightness of its weight considering the message it contained. Mrs. Hargrove had kept the letter behind her desk to make sure no one else saw it before Milton came in that morning, and as he did Mrs. Hargrove looked closely at him after telling him about his appointments for the day.

"Pastor." She spoke with concern.

"Huh?" Milton was looking through the other mail she had given him.

"It's from the board." She whispered her reply as she handed the letter to him in an inconspicuous manner, keeping it low so anyone who might be passing by wouldn't see it.

"Thank you," Milton said, taking the envelope from her and walking into his office.

The letter was a request that he appear before the board to discuss his position at the church. The letter wasn't something he was unprepared to receive yet he hadn't prepared a defense. Ella had given him a strategy, though she seemed to have taken an almost non-committal stand, and that was just as hurtful as the request he was now reading.

After Milton finished reading the letter he told Mrs. Hargrove he didn't want to be disturbed and he spent the rest of the day in his office making phone calls to church members.

"She doesn't even seem to care." Milton sat beside Natasha in her apartment as he told her about the letter and about Ella's behavior. Outside the window, the low rumble of thunder rolled through the night over the sounds of the streets below.

"It's a lot for her to take," Natasha said. "I think she'll come around. She's a good woman."

"I know," Milton said.

"Frankly, I think she's handling all of this with as much grace as she can muster. She didn't have to tell you to have me come over the other day. And when she dropped me off to work - -"

"Ella? She did?" Milton looked at Natasha with surprise.

Natasha nodded her head. "She and I talked and she was... she's a graceful woman."

"I know," Milton said. "I know." He looked at Natasha and continued. "I'm not only worried about her, but you too."

"Me?"

"Yeah. I don't want you to feel like you're responsible for any of this."

Natasha sat for a second before replying.

"I don't. Not anymore. I like my life and my living it doesn't have anything to do with Christ The Redeemer Baptist Church."

"And it shouldn't. It's just that I didn't want you feeling responsible in any way."

Natasha looked at her father with a hint of anger in her eyes. "Believe me, I don't. I can't let what someone else has done affect me to that point."

"No, I'm just saying…"

"I think I understand what you're saying."

Milton spoke after a while of awkward silence. "How do you feel about all of this? I mean… I really don't know how you feel."

Natasha thought for a minute or so before answering him. "Well, you're human, first and foremost. And we all do things that we regret. You and my mother could've used a little discretion… especially you since you were older. But hey, things happen, right? And the fact that that 'thing' happened is what's allowing me to have this conversation with my father. So…"

Milton dropped his head. "Thank you," he whispered.

That night, Milton came home and found Ella sitting on the side of the bed in Danny's old bedroom, staring into a corner of the room.

"Ella, you okay?" Milton stood in the doorway.

"Yeah," Ella whispered.

Milton started to come into the room.

"I need to be alone," Ella said.

Milton stopped. "Alright," he said, and left the room. As he walked down the hall, he could hear Ella crying and telling someone she was sorry.

CHAPTER THIRTY-FIVE

Danny watched his mother as she slept. She slept curled in a fetal position, her body so small that she looked like a petal that had been placed on his bed, but for a quick second she looked to Danny like one of the wingless butterflies that were buried in the back yard. He sat in a chair by the bed in his old bedroom, watching her to make sure she was okay. She was so distraught when she left his apartment that evening that he couldn't sleep, so he went over to her house to stand guard over her, and now he sat, noticing just how small his mother was, and he was amazed at how such a body could have endured the challenges it had been given. His stepfather stood in the doorway of the bedroom, careful not to cross over into the space that Danny and Ella were in.

"What happened to her?" Milton spoke quietly, his voice coming from the doorway into the darkened room.

"It's something she needs to talk about. Not me," Danny said, without taking his eyes off of his mother.

Milton sighed. "All of the secrecy," he said.

Danny turned to him. "Hers or yours?"

"All of it," Milton said. "All of it," he repeated as he closed the door and walked away.

Danny and Ella slept that night, Ella in his bed and he in a chair. Later that night, Danny was awakened by Ella's voice. She talked as she slept, mumbling words Danny couldn't understand. He only understood the sorrowfulness of her voice, and when she began to cry in her sleep he got up from his chair and went over to the bed and sat beside her. It was then that he was able to understand some of her words.

"You know what you did… No, it wasn't supposed to happen…"

She began to cry even more and Danny reached over and put his hand on her shoulder and whispered to her.

"Mom. It's ok."

His voice must have reached her on some level because she quieted and fell back into a deep sleep. Danny watched her for a while longer with his hand on her shoulder. Then he pulled the covers over her and went back to his chair. Soon, he heard his mother once more.

"I'm sorry," Ella quietly mumbled. And as Danny listened to her he thought he heard another sound in the room, a sound that was like the rustle of clothing, or movement, in a far corner of the room. He turned on the light and looked around, but no one was there.

The next morning, Ella and Milton sat in the den and talked. Bright morning light filled the rooms, yet there was a feeling of uncertainty in the house. The uncertainty wasn't the kind that causes a person to hold their breath. It wasn't so much a cautionary uncertainty, but an uncertainty that begs the simple question of how to fix something. And that's what Ella and Milton talked about that morning in the den, with the doors closed to the hallway, together, just the two of them. Milton needed to hear the whole story of what Ella had done and she needed to know the extent of Milton's dilemma. It was a complicated morning in spite of the cheerful light that came through the windows.

Danny sat in the kitchen with Natasha, who had come over that night when she heard Ella wasn't feeling well.

"I hope your mother's okay," Natasha said as she looked at Danny, who sat across from her at the kitchen table.

"Me too."

It was their first time sitting alone with each other and an awkward silence drifted, but never took hold.

"Your mother's a good person."

"I know." Danny's reply came out more like a confession than an agreement.

"She really is. I mean, she took me in, when she didn't have to," Natasha said.

Danny didn't say anything.

Natasha continued. "Because what my father did was wrong. Your mother could've been like a lot of other wives and kept me away. She could've hated me because I reminded her of what he did. But she didn't."

"Were you prepared for that?" Danny asked. "To be turned away when you came here?"

"To be honest. I didn't intend for it to go this far. I just wanted to know who my father was."

"What's the verdict?"

Natasha thought for a second then said, "Well, I have to make room for him in my life. And you?"

"Me? What do you mean? Is there any room for him in my life?"

"Yeah."

Danny thought for a second, looking down at his hands before answering.

"Me an' him never got along. But, I don't know…" Then he looked at Natasha. "That's a crazy question, though. I ain't never been asked that."

"Really?"

"Nah," Danny said, shaking his head. "But I guess," he continued. "I guess if he can accept me then I can accept him. He ain't the easiest person to please, you know. You sure you ready for all this? I mean, and not just dealing with him, but if you wanna be a part of this family, considering all the shit that's happening?"

"I guess it's family," Natasha replied. "Who knows? Maybe you and I can end up making the difference."

"Hmh," Danny softly grunted.

"With everything that's happening," Danny went on, "I guess it's good it's all coming to light so we can see it better. Understand it better."

"And then start fixing it," Natasha said. "My grandmother used to tell me, 'mess always need fixin'. But it can make you strong'."

Danny looked at Natasha and nodded. "Yeah, I guess you right. And it ain't going nowhere until it does."

~~~~

Ella and Milton had prayed that morning in the den. After they ran out of apologies, and words meant to comfort each other, and found themselves looking at each other in the aftermath of their deeds, they turned their troubles over to God. They prayed that God would forgive them with the understanding that they were fallible. They had prayed that God would see them through what they knew were hard times ahead. Yet when they walked away from the room, neither of them was comforted because they knew the reality of all the things they were about to encounter.

Ella went on to work the next day, but things weren't the same. Whereas before, she carried her past like most people do, set up and arranged somewhat haphazardly in those spaces in their lives that kept the troubles of the past out of the way of everyday living. Arrangements that sometimes come more as agreements, that the things done will, for periods of time, allow the perpetrator some respite. But now, the agreement Ella had was broken. Before, the agreement was that her past would only seep into spaces of the present and bother her every now and then. That had to be the agreement, because she hadn't settled her account. But now the agreement fell apart, splayed to show the blood red reality it had held for so long. And it was all because of the photos on Danny's wall. The photos that brought the past to the present, within reach if it needed to cause her more suffering. Danny told her that he would take the photos down, but she told him to leave them on the wall so she could visit them every now and then. It was something she needed to do.

That morning at work, Ella sat in her office, where she had been processing notes on her clients. She sat, cordoned by her thoughts. From her office she could hear the morning busyness of her co-workers, but she didn't join them like she usually did. Instead she sat alone, her hands resting alongside the keyboard of her computer, staring at the computer screen. Her mind was crowded with memories, memories of New Home, memories of her mother's death, memories of hiding in her bedroom with her baby to escape the hatred of her father towards her and her baby, memories of Damon and Buddy before the horrible lie, the images of all of those events and the people gathered solemnly in her head, assuming the place that was rightful. Once or twice a co-worker stopped into her office to see if she was ok. She told them she was just busy and that she was ok, before giving in again to the platoon of memories that now stood at the forefront of her thoughts.

~~~~

Danny found it hard to leave Azhure after the funeral. Azhure sat in her mother's living room, surrounded by family and friends who talked among themselves in measured words and measured tones. Every so often someone would reach out and touch Azhure lightly on the arm, or a well wisher passing through would touch her shoulder as they spoke to her, eliciting a weak smile from Azhure as she acknowledged them. There were a few of Littlejohn's relatives there and they sat awkwardly by with expressions on their faces as if they were trying to understand how Littlejohn had found a decent person like Azhure. She was educated and productive, more than the women they were used to, and it confused them that Littlejohn had found her and more than anything that she loved him. It was confusing and it showed on their faces.

"It's sad, ain't it?" A woman spoke to Danny. She had come out of nowhere and stood beside him, sucking on a breath mint.

"Yeah," Danny said. He could smell the faint odor of stale liquor on her breath.

"She really loved him. Look like they were goin' somewhere together. He was even gettin' his life together. Sad."

After a while Danny decided to leave. Cortez was waiting for him outside. Cortez had given his final respects and then told Danny it was all he could do and that he would wait for Danny outside. Cortez had paid for the funeral and the repast afterwards. He held Azhure as she wept in his arms and comforted her, talking softly to her before excusing himself. He told Danny he would be waiting for him in the car.

Danny and Cortez didn't speak much after they left the repast. Cortez drove from the house towards his place. Reaching down, he turned on the stereo. "That ok?" He asked Danny as he turned the volume down.

Danny nodded his head, "Yeah. It's cool."

They rode along for a while in silence before Danny spoke.

"I still can't believe he's gone."

"Yeah. I know," Cortez said. "When I'm at the bar I keep expecting him to come walking into the office laughing and saying something he damn well knows is stupid."

Danny laughed softly. "His crazy ass. And I keep expectin' him to call me. I catch myself thinking about calling him and then think 'shit, he's gone'."

"Yeah."

"You ever lose somebody before?" Danny asked.

"My mother. It was hard. Took me a long time to get over it. Or so I thought, because you never really get over it. You just adjust to it."

When they got to Cortez's apartment, Danny went out onto the terrace and called Ella to check on her.

"How is your mom doing?" Cortez asked as he and Danny changed out of their dress clothes.

Danny shook his head. "Not too good. She's dealing with some stuff and it's got her down. Shit is crazy," he said with another slow shake of his head.

Cortez fixed drinks and they went into his den where they turned on the TV.

"On the way back I kept watching people going on with their business," Danny said as he looked at the TV. "And I thought to myself, 'damn that's how it is, dawg. People come and go and life goes on to the next event."

"Yeah, that's about the size of it," Cortez agreed. "But it don't mean we forget about the people we lose or the things that happen to us. We learn from it all."

"Right. I guess the answer is always the next step along the way, huh."

"Yeah," Cortez answered quietly. He curled his lips and looked ahead at the TV screen. "You know, what Azhure said the other day… it might be my fault." He spoke softly, keeping his face forward.

"What?"

"My fault what happened to Littlejohn."

Danny picked up the remote and muted the TV. "What do you mean?"

"The nigga who trashed the bar. I think it might've been him who capped Littlejohn." He looked at Danny, who was staring intently at him. "I didn't tell anybody this, but the nigga left a note telling me he was gonna fuck me up and anybody else who had something to do with his brother."

"His brother…" Danny spoke the words, trying to piece things together.

"Marcus. The one you and Littlejohn put in the trunk of the car. The one whose shoulder y'all dislocated."

Danny sat back on the couch. "Oh."

"The note said his brother told him why it was done and that it was probably you and Littlejohn who did it."

"You didn't tell the police?"

"And incriminate us? No. I tore the note up and got rid of it before the police came. I guess I didn't take it that seriously."

"You didn't take it seriously? He said he was coming for us. How come you wouldn't take it seriously?"

Cortez shook his head. "I guess… I guess I just thought it would be some shit like breaking our car windows. Some shit like that. I never thought…"

"You really think it's him?"

"I don't know. Seems like it might be unless Littlejohn was involved in some shit we didn't know about."

"Nah," Danny said, shaking his head. "He woulda told me. He told me everything." Danny paused then continued. "He was even talking about getting his life together. Said it was why he wanted to buy into the bar, because he was over doing what we were doing. Azhure was a good influence in his life."

"I'm sorry, man," Cortez said.

"That ain't gonna bring my friend back. You and me, we might have caused all this shit. I need to know how he looks. The one who trashed the bar. I need to know how he looks. You got the video back from the police?"

"They got a copy of it."

"I need to know how he looks so I can find his ass."

"Azhure gave a description to the police. They should be posting it soon."

"Yeah, well I still wanna see the video of this nigga."

The letter had come marked 'confidential' and was bound with a seal across the opening. Mrs. Hargrove had laid it on Milton's desk, and now he read it as he sat in his office behind closed doors. The church was quiet as a cold silence lay over the building. A cardinal chirped and played on a tiny branch outside of Milton's office window. He listened to it sing and then turned just in time to see it fly away. He wasn't surprised that he had been pulled from the pulpit, but what bothered him just as much was that he wasn't able to get enough support from the congregation. There had been a few words of support for him to remain pastor, but the words were meager, the words of weak-minded individuals who couldn't find it in themselves to stand up for him. Aside from the weak-minded in the congregation, most of the others in the church weren't about to have talk going around town that Christ The Redeemer Baptist Church's pastor had done what Milton had done. He had brought disgrace to the church and they weren't about to stand for it. In passing, some had mentioned to him that it wasn't about him, but that it was about the church. They said they simply couldn't let him lead the church. In the pantheon of ministers he was too much of a distraction (though what they really meant was 'an embarrassment') to represent their congregation. Milton was angered by their hypocrisy and he wanted to tell them that. The things he knew about some of them. He wanted to consider them all hypocrites, but those thoughts hissed and deflated, like a balloon, each time the thoughts crossed his mind.

No one came by his office that day and his phone didn't ring at all. It was as if everyone knew what was happening, or had in the least waited in expectation of it. By late noon he called Ella and told her, then he left the office. Mrs. Hargrove asked him if there was anything he needed her to do. He wasn't sure what she meant by the question: if she meant packing up his office or helping him ward off the board. He looked at her for a moment, then said 'no', and left the office.

When he told Ella about the letter she didn't have much to say. "Well… Just have faith." That was all she said, but she said it with an air of resignation that didn't do much to encourage Milton. Maybe it was because she had her own problems to deal with, or maybe his problems were too much for her. Maybe she felt he was getting what he deserved, or maybe she just didn't care. That always seemed to be the way things were with her. Too caught up in her own problems to take time out for him.

He had often felt that way, that he was nothing more than a coincidence to Ella, a side note in her life. That her life really revolved around New Home and Danny and Danny's father. Damon. That was his name. Damon. Now that Milton knew Damon's name, he found himself hating him more. Before, Milton's feelings about the young man who got Ella pregnant left a bad taste in his mouth and a wandering jealousy, a jealousy too vagrant to lay in his chest and eat at him every day. But now that he knew Damon's name, the jealousy and the hatred had found their places in Milton's heart.

That was Milton's thinking as he sat in his car on a side street in a forgotten part of the city. The name of the street was Harbor Lane.

Milton wondered how such a ragged little street that didn't lead to a river or a bay could have such a name. The street was jagged, as if over the years it had been searching for a way out of the neighborhood, with broken asphalt and old apartments and houses that seemed to lean to one side or the other, or that threatened to crumble face first to the street under the weight of age and disrepair. Milton remembered the street that late afternoon after he left his office, even though he had only driven down Harbor Lane once some years ago when he was trying to get to a church member's home to pray with her. He wasn't sure why the street stuck in his mind, but it did. He remembered this street and it was where he found himself that day.

He sat in his car and watched the main street that ran at one end of Harbor Lane, the cars and buses that rolled up and down the busy avenue and the rush of people along the main street. Older men stood along the curbs waiting to taxi people coming out of the stores. Younger men and women, and the older ones who had squandered what little fortune life had given them, lounged languidly on benches at bus stops.

The hot afternoon sun bore down on Milton's car and came through the open windows. The letter from the board lay open on the seat beside Milton, bright and fresh in the sunlight. Milton had opened it to read it once again, but lost interest in the letter and sat it on the seat of his car. What was done was done. Now he only needed an idea of what to do to fill in what had just been taken from him, so he sat, thinking.

As he continued to watch the scene at the end of the street, a young woman came walking by. She was carrying a bag of groceries that hung loosely from her hand and swung side to side as she walked. Milton saw her and watched her coming his way. She was a large-breasted young lady with full hips, which told him she was probably a mother of one, no, more than one child. Only two, he thought, because she wasn't that old. Hopefully no more than two kids, he thought to himself.

The young lady passed by his car and looked at him, gauging Milton. She spoke to Milton as she assessed him. "Hi," she said.

Milton quickly looked down at the letter on the seat beside him and pretended to read it.

"You know you lookin' for somethin'."

Milton kept his eyes from her.

"Apartment 3 if you're interested," the young lady said. She laughed and continued down the sidewalk. After she had passed the car, Milton looked in his rearview mirror to watch her. She went up the steps to one of the buildings and just before going inside he saw her look back to see him watching her through his mirror, and she laughed once again as she went into the building.

~~~~

It had been more than an hour that Ella sat before the photos on the wall. She sat alone in Danny's bedroom, watching the photos as if she was waiting on one of them to come to life, a tiny movement of a head of one of the persons in one of the photos, or even a hand reaching out to her from a photo. She half-expected it to happen because the photos were there. Somehow they had found their way to her over the years so yes, of course, there was something else that should happen, and so she waited. She had started visiting the photos almost every day since she discovered Danny had them.

Every once in a while, Ella would get up from the chair and look closely at the photos that were lined along the three walls of Danny's bedroom. She was frightened that they were there, yet she welcomed them, a link to home, and she would smile as she looked at some of the photographs, remembering a place and time. There was the photo of Lora Nell's Fish Bar. On Friday nights her father would pick her mother up from the salon and they would all go across the street to Lora Nell's Fish Bar for a dinner of catfish, or whiting, with biscuits and buttered grits, and a large drink. Miriam didn't like fish and would always eat chicken, which bothered Ella's mother because Ella's mother was raised Catholic. Ella stood in front of the photo of the fish bar and smiled, remembering how pleasant the times were before her mother left them. Things were better then but everything seemed to go wrong after her mother left them. After she died, the world they all knew began to slowly unravel exposing gaps that allowed the space for anything that could go wrong to make its way into their lives. Ella always felt if her mother hadn't left them, if she hadn't decided not to wake up, that Ella wouldn't have given herself to Damon. It was the loneliness her mother left behind that Ella needed filled. If only her mother had chosen to wake up that morning things would have been different.

Danny sat in another room, leaving his mother alone with the photos. He knew she needed to be with the photos in a place where

Danny would only circle the periphery, like a satellite, connected with a shared, but brief time, to the inextricable story the photos told.

There was more on Danny's mind that evening than the photos, though. He was still dealing with losing Littlejohn and the recent discovery that Cortez had an idea of who might have killed Littlejohn weighed on Danny. He sat in his living room, half-hearing his mother down the hall moving around his bedroom every now and then and every once in a while letting out a sigh or sometimes a soft moan. For Danny, her visits were becoming common. What gripped Danny that evening was the footage he had seen of the guy who wrecked the bar and left the note, the one who Cortez felt might be behind Littlejohn's death. He had watched the video with Cortez: an empty bar, a still frame suddenly exploding in shattered glass, and a tire rim coming from outside the window, a man stepping in and hurrying to the bar, slamming down the note, taking two bottles of booze, and running from the bar. It was when the man went behind the bar that the camera, meant to watch the bartenders, caught view of the man's face. A young man no older than his early twenties. Average height and build.

"That's the little nigga," Cortez said. "We shouldn't have a problem finding him with that mark on his face."

Danny nodded his head. "Got 'im."

There had been something about the young man caught on camera that seemed familiar to Danny. He hadn't told Cortez that at the time, but as he watched the video, Danny felt he might know the man. It was that sense of familiarity that was so slight that it rose from the bottom of Danny's throat and lay there, waiting to come out. To be spoken suddenly when things were quiet. It wasn't until that night that Danny remembered who the guy was, causing him to gasp, almost waking Cortez. He recalled the man. He hadn't noticed the birthmark on the guy's face that day, but it was the same young man who been standing near Littlejohn's car as Littlejohn and Danny left the gym.

The question of who Mr. Stiggers might be rattled Ella. That he would have possession of things from her past and that he would be in the same city as her, the city to which she fled to escape her past bothered her, and more, that all of these things would be only a few feet from Danny. It was enough to unnerve her. She wondered if the old man who was invisible to her, holed up behind that closed door knew what she had done. Was he standing behind his door watching her? Planning his next act? It wasn't that she was afraid he might know, in fact she had come to secretly welcome someone knowing what she had done. She was tired of carrying things around. But she had to know what the old man might know so she could decide whether or not to breathe in the air of freedom. And most importantly, so she could do what she might need to do to keep him or an angry spirit he might represent from harming Danny if that was his intention. The first day she came to look at the photos Danny had to escort her away from Mr. Stiggers' door. "I need to know who he is," she had demanded as Danny pulled her away from the door. Since then she had accepted that in order to visit the photos she would have to pass by the door on the first floor without confronting the man that lived beyond it. Now she quietly looked at the old man's window that night as she was leaving the building.

"Don't worry about him," Danny said as he noticed his mother looking at the dim light that bled along the edges of the drapes in Mr. Stiggers' apartment.

"I just wonder who he is. We're both from New Home."

"A place you and him left - - you scared, and him crazy. Just leave it alone."

CHAPTER THIRTY-SIX

The only person who visited Milton on his last day at Christ The Redeemer Baptist Church was Mrs. Nixon. She had called that morning and asked if she could stop by and see him before he left. And while Milton figured her visit would be a contentious one, he was willing to see her because she would be the only person to hear him before he left his position at the church. Mrs. Hargrove was there to hold down the office, not hear him. She asked every now and then if he needed her to do anything, and each time he told her no. He knew she was against him. Mrs. Hargrove was fine with not helping him because she felt all that Milton was dealing with was his own fault. And what made matters worse for Milton was talk of an abortion, that Milton didn't even know he had a child because he asked the mother to end the birth. This bit of gossip surprised Milton. He wasn't sure where folks had gotten the information, if it was something they knew for sure, or if it was one of those stories that grow out of other stories, something purely speculative that took root in the craw of their gossip. Even if no one knew for sure that he had asked Abilyn to end the birth, it was realistic enough for many folks to grab onto such a twist and run with it. And it was enough to judge him. It's why he figured Mrs. Nixon stopped by, to look at the man who lashed out at her for choosing to abort her birth.

Milton was in the middle of packing away books when Mrs. Hargrove knocked on his office door. She chose to knock on his door instead of calling him on the phone when Mrs. Nixon arrived. It was as if she took pride in presenting another spectator. She looked at

Milton, then to Mrs. Nixon, then back to Milton, before closing the door behind her as she left the office.

"Come on in Sister Nixon," Milton said as he pointed a book towards a chair.

"I'm not going to stay long," Mrs. Nixon said as she sat. "I just want to see how you're doing."

"Thank you. I'm well," Milton said as he put the books into a box.

"Pastor, I just want you to know, I understand."

Mrs. Nixon's comment caught Milton off-guard, causing him to pause for a second before he reached for another book on his bookshelf. It bothered him that she would compare the two of them. But that was why she came, wasn't it? To get one final dig at him. He suddenly thought it was she who probably started the gossip about the abortion. To spite him.

"Understand?" He put the books into the box.

"Yes."

"I'm not sure how you can understand—how anyone can understand when they don't know the whole story, Sister Nixon."

"It's like no one wants to hear the whole story," Mrs. Nixon added. "They only hear what they can frame for their own interests. Yes I do. I understand that. I also know that the decisions we make might never be understood by someone else. It's the way things are."

"We do have to frame our actions in a moral conscience, though, Sister Nixon. And that's where we have to take responsibility."

"So you think you're not taking responsibility?"

"No. I think I am taking responsibility but no one is seeing that, and that's what bothers me."

"It's in their best interest not to see it. That's what I'm saying, Pastor." Mrs. Nixon watched Milton put another bundle of books into the box. She put her purse on the floor and began helping him.

"Sometimes we make wrong decisions. Probably more often than we might want to admit," she said as she took books from the shelf. "But I do believe more often than not we make those decisions in the hopes of committing the least heinous acts and the least amount of damage to others. Sometimes we get it right and sometimes we don't. None of us are perfect."

"It's why we have forgiveness," Milton reminded.

"Of ourselves even if no one else will," Mrs. Nixon said as she put books into the box.

Milton loaded his boxes in his car and turned to look one last time at the church. He was flooded with memories, and sadness came over him that he was saying goodbye to the family he had known for so many years. He stood by his car, letting his eyes travel over the outside of the building, and that's when he saw Mrs. Hargrove looking sternly out of the window at him. Milton got in his car and drove from the church he had called home.

Milton hadn't heard anything from Ella. But given what she had been going through the last few days he wasn't surprised. He sat in his car along Harbor Lane. Alone. After a while, he got out of his car and went into the building where the young lady lived.

Two calls had come in from Natasha after Milton left the church, and one from Ella. Milton saw them listed when he returned to his car. The one from Ella came while he was with the young lady. He listened to the call from Ella first. She wanted to know how his day went and how he was feeling. Her voice sounded a bit strained, as if there was an effort to piece together words. She sounded tired and labored from other thoughts that were on her mind. Then she asked why he hadn't called. The call from Natasha had been much of the same. But to call them back in the state he was in made him feel uncomfortable, because in his mind the young lady's thighs were still around him and one of her nipples was still in his mouth. He had left the young lady in her apartment but she stayed with him. 'You can't put it in 'cause you don't have a condom', she had said, 'but I'll jack you off.' It was quick, to the point, and all done in a matter of minutes, but she was still with him and he needed to let the warmth that was left from his excitement cool some more before he called.

A few minutes passed and he called his wife.

"Hi."

"Where are you?"

"I'm just sitting here in the car. I needed to be alone."

"I called to check on you and Mrs. Hargrove said you had already left."

Milton listened to the exhaustion in his wife's voice. "I left early," he answered.

"Are you sure you're ok? You don't need to be by yourself, Milton."

"No. I'm fine. It's just… a lot happened and I need to process it. I don't want to come home in a muddle so I'd rather process some things before I get home so we can talk with some understanding."

"You shouldn't be by yourself."

"I'm fine," he repeated. "I'm ok. I'll be home in a little bit."

"Alright."

After he hung up from Ella, he called Natasha and assured her the same.

Milton hadn't lied to Ella and Natasha about being ok. At least that was how he felt. In time, as he sat alone in his car looking out of the window, out at the lives of the women and men that came and went along the streets, at a world he had sworn off, a growing sense of belonging rose in him. It opened, deep and bright as a waiting day, and it summoned him, calmly with that sense of knowing a place, a familiar something. A familiar place. A place to belong. He felt that a burden had been lifted from him. It was a burden he hadn't recognized. The years of protecting his sister and his mother from his father, of standing and declaring in public spaces and yes, even taking charge of the often convoluted lives of the members of Christ The Redeemer Baptist Church had all been weight he had borne for much of his life. Yet none of it had he ever known as a weight that he had grown tired of. He had never known the kind of freedom he now felt, not since that morning he found out that his father had died, and he left his mark of that freedom as a trail along the inside of the young lady's thighs.

~~~~

Danny wasn't used to having the fight knocked out of him and this time was no different. The fight in him had been clipped by Littlejohn's death, but it wasn't enough to defeat him. What Littlejohn's death did do, however, was to cause Danny to think about the turn he and Littlejohn's life was beginning to take before Littlejohn was murdered.

"I wanna do better… I gotta figure out how to do better… What are you plannin' on doin'?"

"I wanna start spendin' more time with my mother."

Danny was angry and confused that Littlejohn would be struck down at a time when Littlejohn was trying to get his life in order. It seemed it didn't matter that Littlejohn was becoming a better person because instantly, without warning, he was still taken away with the commission of a single act.

Maybe it was his time to go next, Danny thought as he lay in bed watching the sky grow bright over the city. Maybe his mother was right, that you have to pay for your sins. After all, his mother had spent so many years trying to usher him to a safe place, even to out-run what she had done, or to possibly receive forgiveness, was something she had been doing for many years, but all of it seemed to have found her. Everything seemed to be coming full circle with Mr. Stig-gers and the photographs. And with this, Littlejohn's murder, Danny was beginning to wonder if his mother was right to concern herself with past sins. It just might be his time to go next.

And the guy who Danny and Cortez believed might be behind Littlejohn's murder, thinking about the guy made Danny's stomach knot. The guy had stood so close to him and Littlejohn outside the gym. So close…

The day after Littlejohn's funeral, Danny and Cortez spent most their time away from the bar and from people who might want to know what happened. To answer what happened to Littlejohn would prove too clumsy for both Danny and Cortez to speak on because the answer was something they still wrestled with.

"We all made the wrong decision," Cortez said. "You can't just blame me for what happened."

"I'm not blaming you. I know me and Littlejohn coulda made up our own minds." Danny stood on the terrace of Cortez's apartment overlooking the city that arched out like an unending dialogue, the streets and the people walking along them parables to be reckoned with.

"Then why do you act like it's all me?" Cortez asked.

Danny turned to Cortez, who stood in the shadow of his living room out of the light that came through the window. "We gotta do things differently, man. I gotta do something else," Danny said. "That's all I know. I gotta do something else."

CHAPTER THIRTY-SEVEN

Events were taking their toll on Ella and Milton, stunning them both to near silence. An abiding despair rose every night they tried to sleep, leading to days full of concern and feelings of hopelessness. Neither one of them wanted to talk about what they were going through and neither one of them had enough interest in the other to ask how the other might be doing. That was just how consumed they were with their own problems, so the house fell into a stultifying silence, with Ella and Milton mostly staying to themselves in different parts of the house, passing each other every now and then and looking into each other's eyes, too afraid to talk and too afraid of wanting to know the difficulties of the other.

Ella had taken leave from work, which was probably best in order to save her job since she had begun to overlook the needs of her clients.

"Miss Ella? You ok? You didn't write down what I tol' you my doctor said."

"Oh. What was it again he said?"

Some of her clients had even started to treat her as a client.

"Baby, what's on your mind? You can talk to me."

Ella would smile and tell them there was nothing on her mind.

"There ain't never nothin' on a person's mind. Maybe you need some time off. Clear out whatever's botherin' you."

Ella did need time off. It became clear the afternoon she sat in her office, staring at her monitor without putting in her notes from visits with her clients. That was it. She needed time off, so she took a leave of absence.

Milton had taken to the basement again. Most of the straightening up there had been done, so he sat in a chair and looked off into space most days. Once in a while he would move something he had moved before back to the place it had been, then he would sit and stare off into space until the things he was feeling about himself would become so ugly that he would grab his keys and go out. There weren't many places he could go where people didn't recognize him, places where folks would look at him and talk to each other out of the side of their mouths, or with eyes that said 'I'm sorry for you', or ones that lighted with laughter, 'You ain't no different from the rest of us, fuckin' hypocrite,' so Milton would mostly drive around or find out of the way places to sit.

Natasha checked in on Ella and Milton every day. She called them on their phones and struck up what little conversation she could from what information she could glean out of them. Sometimes she would get on the bus and go over to their house, where she would cook and clean while continuing to pull words from them. She didn't like seeing them in their condition and she did whatever she could to pull them out of their despair, their lull, as she saw it, because she knew with her and Danny's help Ella and Milton would be up and at it in a while. She had even gotten Danny's phone number from Ella and had begun to engage him more.

At first Danny was reluctant to comfort Milton. "He's your father, not mine," he told Natasha.

"So I guess that means I shouldn't care about your mother. You know how ridiculous that sounds?"

"But she ain't never done nothin' to you, but Milt has to me."

"Look, I know all about your relationship with my father. Your mother told me, and it's nothing you can't overlook."

"Yes it is."

"No it's not. Holding on to all this mess is toxic. That's the problem in this house. And if you have any intention of making your life worth something you're going to have put all of that mess aside and be a bigger person." She paused to listen to Danny's response and when he didn't reply she continued. "Now what I see are two people who love each other, two people who made mistakes like we all do, suffering in silence. What are you going to do about it, Danny? You coming over here and checking on your mother while overlooking your father - -"

"You don't get it, do you? He ain't my father."

"He's the one who took care of you, messy as it might have been. That's the way it is sometimes with parents. But he is the one who took care of you. Now you can call him whatever you want. But you have to understand that right now all of that mess should be left behind so all of us can get back to living our lives. And hopefully, out of all of this, that means better lives."

Eventually Danny came around to seeing things Natasha's way. Watching her run between his mother and her father, fixing lunch, cleaning the house and talking with them brought him around.

Natasha understood how difficult it might be for Danny to deal with her father. Milton was an unforgiving person. He expected to be forgiven, but he wasn't given to acts of forgiveness. He had known little forgiveness when he was growing up. His father never forgave him for being whatever that thing was about Milton that kept his father from looking at him when his father spoke to him—in fact, he rarely spoke *to* Milton, but *at* him, and Milton's mother never forgave herself for having two children who his father never approved of, so forgiveness had never been much in Milton's life. And with that lack of a sense of forgiveness, Milton became a person so hardened, so bitter towards others who didn't meet his approval, that he became a person who was more likely to persecute those who fell out of favor with him than to forgive them. But his form of persecution had been gloved in the velvet touch of righteousness, and of a mythical love, so it was soft to the eye and to the ear, but it scarred the heart as persecution does. His mythical sense of love had gotten him far, and had rooted in him a strong sense that what he did was right, and that the suffering he actually caused others were the fault of their own unrighteousness. Natasha saw this about him in the few months since she had come into his life. She listened to him preach, she listened to him when they sat around her apartment talking into the late hours of the evening, she learned this about him from stories she had gotten from Danny, and she had seen it in the pain he had caused LaShon.

She still hadn't heard from LaShon, and when she went over to his apartment, she saw that his windows were bare, so she figured he had moved. She told Danny about it and Danny told her that since LaShon moved she at least knew that LaShon had enough sense to not kill himself. Then he told her that either LaShon had gone in search of another minister and that more than likely it would be someone who was just like Milton, or that maybe LaShon had finally decided to get on with his life. "Shit. I know I would if some hypocrite had kicked my ass like Milton did his," Danny said. But Milton's take on LaShon's disappearance was different than hers and Danny's. His feelings were that LaShon had seen the path life could take and that he finally started to do something about his own. Milton had told Natasha this one night as he drove her back to her apartment. "I might have done some wrong, but what I did for that boy only helped him," Milton told her. And he had said it with such conviction that she knew to end the conversation. So yes, she understood Danny's feelings towards her father.

Now with Danny and Ella it was different, because Danny simply didn't know what to say to get his mother to forgive herself. And the photos made things even worse. Since he came across them he had been spooked himself so he really didn't know what to say. He wasn't afraid like his mother was because fear was something he wasn't prone to, but there was concern that she might be right about her having to requite for what she did. After all, the photos were there, weren't they? The very people his mother had sought to escape, or at least appease, had found their way back into her life through images displayed on his wall-- the wall of Ella's firstborn. It was enough to spook Danny, but not frighten him. But he did what he could to distract his mother from what she feared by engaging her with conversation about her clients, or other things. He did all of these things while trying to keep the concern he now had from showing in his own eyes.

In all, Natasha and Danny did what they could to keep their parents afloat.

~~~~

Danny walked up the street from the store to his apartment. The nighttime sky was deep and speckled with stars flung along the vast blackness. He walked along thinking about things. His life was in a place it had never been before, and it was a crazy place to be in, a place of having concern so sharp that it edged on fear, of having his mother slipping even more between the past and the present, of not knowing just how large the monster might be that waited for him around the next corner and of knowing the weight of loneliness since Littlejohn left him. It was all a crazy place to be in, but he was there and he tried to deal with it. Whatever awaited him or his mother, Danny told himself he would be there and he would die fighting if it came down to it. He took in a deep breath and let it out. *Little-*

john. Man where are you?' he thought to himself as he walked up to his building.

He came through the door and walked towards the stairs. As he started up the stairs, he heard Mr. Stiggers call him from behind the door of his apartment.

"Boy?"

"Yessir?"

"I need to talk to you."

Danny hesitated before replying. "Ok," he said, stepping back from the stairs. He stood in front of Mr. Stiggers' door and waited for him to open it. He wasn't sure if Mr. Stiggers would talk to him through the door or open it, but tonight he felt Mr. Stiggers would open the door, and if he didn't, Danny told himself that he would ask him to.

It took a few seconds for Mr. Stiggers to open the door, as if he was reconsidering his offer, but Danny waited, and as he waited, he recalled the rage coming from the old man's apartment and the large knife he had seen on the table that day when Mr. Stiggers had his door open. But something told Danny none of that, the rage and the knife, were meant for him, so he waited. Knowing about the photos was more important. Soon, the sound of locks being undone was heard, *clack, clack, clack*, and the door slowly opened, with Mr. Stiggers standing behind it. Danny stared ahead through the doorway into the brightly lit apartment at the mismatched furniture, at the table where the knife had been that day, and at the portrait of the woman on the wall, then slowly, he walked in.

~~~~

Harbor Lane looked even more forgotten at night. Milton watched it and its narrow crooked sides and the single houses and apartment buildings leaning, almost falling onto each other or into the very street itself until the street disappeared into the darkness. It was the first time he sat along the street so late in the night. He had visited the girl a few times since that first evening in her apartment. Each time, she opened the door with a feigned smile, as if she was surprised to see him, then she would lock her two kids in their room and she and Milton would sit in the living room, and they would talk about nothing in particular before she would let him play with her breasts and suck on them. At times she would sit and watch TV with her breasts out, watching TV contently as Milton sucked her nipples like a child. Every once in a while she would look down at him and grin, "That's what you want, ain't it?" she would whisper. Once when he wanted to fuck her she straddled his lap, but he told her not to do that. It made him think of his father and the woman he had seen through the window so the girl would lie on her back and open her legs and let Milton in her. He usually left before the evening became night, but now it was late and he sat and wondered if she would let him in at this hour, or if she was even alone.

He had driven around the city since he dropped Natasha off. As he was about to leave Natasha's apartment, Natasha told him she would feel better if he went straight home. She said it wasn't good for him to go driving around and walking to places by himself as the sun went down. She told him it wasn't good to feed his feelings with detachment. Milton knew she was right, and he told her she was right, but after he left he went back to driving around the city and sitting for long moments alone. Natasha had called him, and he had told her he really needed time to himself. He could tell she wasn't comfortable with his reply, so he told her he would call her when he got home. He understood her worry because he knew what worried her was true. That he felt insignificant, and that such feelings in a man who had great pride could break him. She was right, but it was too late, he was already broken, and now he sat along Harbor Lane deciding whether or not to go up to the girl's apartment. Every few minutes, a late-night bus would lumber down the main street and a voice would ring out as someone called someone from a corner. Milton looked up at the girl's window and saw the lights on. He got out of the car and went up to the girl's apartment.

The sound of the phone ringing seemed so distant to Ella, as if it was coming from another time, yet in her mind's eye, Ella could still see the phone. It was a beige Princess touch-tone. She recalled the brightness in her mother's face when her father came home that evening as Ella's mother demonstrated the new phone to him, lifting the receiver to her face, the light of the buttons illuminating her coral complexion, her eyes, and her smile.

The first ring stopped, ending in what seemed to Ella like a long, dead silence, before the next ring. After the second ring ended, someone answered the phone just as Ella's mother had taught them. It was Ella's sister who answered.

"Hello?"

"Miriam?"

Ella's sister seemed unable to speak, so Ella repeated herself. "Miriam?"

After the second time Ella called Miriam's name, she heard Miriam set the phone down and whisper loudly to her brother, "It's Ella! Ren! It's Ella!"

It had been years since Ella had spoken with her brother and her sister, not since Ren had called her to inform her that their father had passed. It had been a very formal call out of duty, nothing more, and he had quickly instructed her of that and that there was no need for her to come to the funeral, he had added. In fact, he had instructed her not to come. The call had been just that formal, and they hadn't spoken all the years since.

Ren came to the phone. "Ella." He announced her name.

"Hi Ren."

"How are you, Ella?"

"Fine. How are you and Miriam doing?"

"We're fine."

Ella and Ren sat in silence for a moment, before Ren asked, "Is there something you need, Ella?"

"No. I just wanted to call to see how you and Miriam were doing."

"Oh. Well we're fine."

"How is Aunt Bernice doing?"

"She's doing as good as she can do."

"Is she still in her house?"

"Yeah. We take care of her."

"I'll call her."

"Don't. We've been doing fine." After a brief pause, Ren continued. "Well look, if you're sure you don't need anything then I have to go."

"I've been thinking about you all."

After another brief silence Ren repeated himself. "If you don't need anything, I have to go."

"Ok."

"Bye Ella."

"… Bye."

It was the living that needed each other. That was what a client had told Ella once when Ella visited a nursing home. The woman had told Ella how important it was that Ella continued to help people who needed her. "Dead folks don't need no help. The living do, and that means you too." The woman had told Ella this, years ago when Ella was starting out in her field, and now the words came to Ella as she sat by the phone after her brother had hung up. But maybe it was the dead that needed help just as much, she thought. Especially the ones that needed the living to understand their story.

Ella walked through the house, making sure the doors and windows were locked. It was late and Milton hadn't returned. She knew he wouldn't be home any time soon after he dropped Natasha off because his disappearances were becoming expected. She turned off the last light in the hallway, leaving only the porch light on and a lamp on in the living room.

CHAPTER THIRTY-EIGHT

Daylight had just arrived when they found Milton in his car. Two women going to catch the bus for work found him slumped behind the steering wheel with his head against the window. His eyes were half-open and his shirt was wet from the saliva that ran out of the side of his mouth. He saw the women as they walked past the car but he wasn't sure if he wanted them to stop. His shame wanted them to walk past him without seeing him. He had been there since he left the girl's apartment and had watched the night pass as he lay slumped against the window of his car. He had heard the buses roll by and voices call out as he lay there until the buses had stopped and the voices stopped. He saw a cat cross the street in the moonlight and disappear between buildings. He heard the sound of an animal scruffling through a garbage can, and then he saw his father pass by, whistling and quietly singing to himself, wearing that damn hat he always thought made him look good. He passed by Milton without even looking at him and disappeared, the singing, the whistling, and the stupid hat. At that same time Milton lost consciousness.

But the women did stop when they saw him that morning. They stopped and turned back around to look at him. Then they rushed up to the window and looked in and when they saw what had happened they called the police. As Milton was taken from the car, he was covered and placed on a gurney. He was grateful that the paramedics covered him because he had peed on himself during the night. He only wished they had covered his face from the onlookers who stood by gawking and recording the event on their phones.

He awoke later that day to find Ella and Natasha by his side. His hand was resting in Ella's hand and Natasha had her hand on his shoulder. The room was bright and he could hear the soft purr and beep of machinery. He looked into Ella's eyes and then at Natasha. "I'm sorry," he muttered out of his twisted mouth. "I'm sorry." Tears formed in his eyes and ran down the side of his head along his temple.

"It's ok," Ella said as she squeezed his hand. Her eyes looked at him as if she was studying him.

"Yeah. It's ok Dad," Natasha said as she wiped away his tears.

He could tell by the redness of Natasha's eyes that she had been crying as well.

"Do you want me to let the church know you're here?" Ella asked. "I think they would want to know."

Milton thought for a moment then slowly nodded his head.

A nurse came in and checked on him. She told him what had happened and that he was doing fine. Ella and Natasha thanked the nurse as she left the room.

"Don't let them know where they found me," Milton said. Then he turned his face away and the room fell into silence.

The house was hot and the air was damp from the wet clothes Milton's mother had hung to dry. It was too cold to hang the wash outside. Milton sat at the desk in the bedroom and tried to do his homework, but the image of his father and the woman was still with him. When he got home that evening he had tried to eat, but the food was tasteless and stuck in his throat. He had seen them and it made him sick and angry not only towards his father, but at his mother for her complicity. Charlotte came into the room to get a book and crayons. She was singing a silly song she had heard somewhere or had made up in her head. Milton wished he could be as naïve as Charlotte was.

"'Good Times' gonna be on soon," Charlotte said as she picked up her book and crayons.

"I know," Milton said.

"You better hurry up and finish."

"Alright."

Charlotte walked towards the door and stopped by the desk where Milton was sitting.

"What's the matter?"

"What do you mean, 'what's the matter'?" Milton spoke without looking at his sister.

"You actin' funny."

"You bein' nosey."

"So."

"So leave me alone."

"Well you better hurry up so we can watch 'Good Times'," Charlotte said as she left the room.

It wasn't long after his sister had the left the room that Milton went to the kitchen where his mother was putting away dishes.

"Momma?"

"Hmm?"

"I saw Daddy."

His mother stopped for a second, then, as if catching herself, continued putting the dishes away. "That's good," she said as she put the plates on the shelf.

Ella and Natasha didn't speak much about where Milton had been when he had his stroke. They got his car from Harbor Lane and Natasha drove it back to the house.

Natasha watched Ella fixing an overnight bag to take to the hospital.

"Do you think he's going to recover?" Natasha asked.

"I don't know," Ella replied as she folded an undershirt and put it in the bag.

"Looks like you were doing some work in the dining room. I saw all of your paperwork. Are you thinking of going back to work?"

"Yeah. I was. But with all of this, I'm not sure when."

"Just remember that I'm here too, so if you need to go back to work I can take care of things."

After Ella had finished fixing the bag, she and Natasha sat in the kitchen and talked about things they needed to do. Neither of them spoke about Milton and Harbor Lane.

~~~~

"Milton had a stroke."

Danny listened to his mother over the phone and gauged her emotions. He wished she had given him a little more of a statement than the fact that Milton had a stroke because it would give him more time to find the words to say to convey his concern. After all, it was his mother's state of mind that mattered more to him than his stepfather having a stroke.

"A stroke?" He replied.

"Yeah."

"How is he doing?"

"He has paralysis over most of his body, but the doctors say he might recover. Me and Natasha were with him most of the morning. I'm just getting some things ready to take back to the hospital for him."

"Is Natasha ok?"

"She's shaken up, but I think she's ok. She took his car so she could go home and get some things together. She's going to stay here."

"I'm sorry to hear that, Mom."

"Yeah."

"How are you holding up?"

Ella sighed before answering. "I'm holding up ok. It's just—it's just unexpected."

"Things like that always are. What hospital is he at?"

"University."

"I'll stop by to see him. Is he conscious?"

"Yeah."

"Ok. I'll stop by."

"He can't speak well. I just wanted to let you know that."

"Alright. Do you need me to bring something?"

"Not that I can think of right now."

"When are you going to be out there?"

"I'm going right back, so I'll be there probably most of the day."

"I'll stop by later on this afternoon."

"Ok. Danny, are you really going to visit?"

"Mom, yeah."

"Good."

"I'll talk to you then."

"Danny."

"Ma'am?"

"Make sure you visit. You should do it because it's the right thing to do for both of you. It's time to move on."

"Yeah. I know."

Danny hung up the phone and walked over to the photos on the wall. He looked at each of the photos, stepping from one photo to another, realizing more that what he was seeing was in his mother's memory and among the weight in his mother's heart. He moved slowly along the wall of his bedroom, studying the photos, imagining his mother walking along the streets of New Home past the drug store, hardware store, shoe store, Lora Nell's Fish Bar, the tree lined avenues with the large homes, the small streets lined with gunshot houses and the back roads that led to the park and the lake, the passions she must have felt, the joy and the pain she must have carried, and the fear and the confusion that caused her to run away. He walked along the wall until he came to the photo of his grandfather posing with the team members. He reached up and began to peel the edges of the photo from the wall so he could have it ready for his mother to inspect. But he decided to leave it in place because he understood that it was part of the overall narrative that his mother would need. He had called his mother so he could tell her what he had learned from Mr. Stiggers. He wanted to be in his mother's presence when he told her the story. It was something he wanted to tell her face to face, but now, with what was going on with Milton, he decided he would wait a day or so to tell her, if he could.

His grandfather's face looked back at him from the photo, set in place over the years, his grandfather's face etched with the arrogance, the impatience, and the sense of disdain appearing as a slight sneer on his face that Danny had heard about from both Ella and Mr. Stiggers. And he studied his grandfather's face, now knowing what his grandfather knew.

CHAPTER THIRTY-NINE

Milton's mouth had been twisted, as if some god, surely not the one that favored Milton, had taken its divine finger and snatched one of the corners of Milton's mouth to one side of his face. Danny had expected to see his stepfather's face frozen into a scowl when Ella told him Milton had been paralyzed. But it wasn't that way at all. Instead of a scowl it looked as if Milton was crying. The corner of his twisted mouth pulled to one side of his face and then down towards his chin. He looked as though he was sobbing instead of scowling.

Danny sat in a chair on the side of the bed across from his mother and Natasha, watching them as they held Milton's hand and stroked his shoulder and dried the drool that gathered at the corner of his mouth. And he listened to them talk: how they spoke low and cheerful with the assumption that their cheerfulness would aid Milton in his recovery and mask the possibility that things might not change or might even get worse. Danny didn't have much to say, just as he rarely had much to say to Milton. He had come to see Milton. See him. To see *what* had happened to Milton, not how he was doing. In fact, Danny wouldn't have come at all if Ella hadn't asked him to. He had said a few assuring words after he entered the room and he knew both he and Milton didn't expect much else, so Danny sat by and watched his mother. And he watched Natasha. Natasha. She was suddenly in their lives, having come from nowhere it seemed, but definitely from somewhere. Possibly a place as lonely as the place Danny himself had spent most of his life, wondering who she was and why she had been kept a secret. Then Danny laughed to himself. 'Two bastards!' Yet Natasha was sitting right there talking with the man who didn't expect her to be at his bedside. 'Shit, he didn't expect her to be anywhere!' Danny thought to himself. And there they were, talking and consoling each other, and her smiling and talking with Ella—not her mother, but his mother. She was there and the three of them formed a cluster while he sat on the other side of the bed. And as he looked at them, he saw that his mother was becoming Natasha's mother and that, in spite of what Natasha and Milton had endured, that Milton was her father.

"Nobody likes being in a hospital, Dad," Natasha said. "So what's your point?"

"What's my point?" Milton slurred. He struggled to get his words out, so he used the inflections of his voice to drive home his feelings. The sound he created, a high-pitched, almost tinny sound, was so comical that it made everyone laugh, including Danny.

Milton looked at Danny with laughter in his eyes and a joy that he and Danny could laugh together.

Danny continued to laugh and he shook his head as he sought words to say to his stepfather.

"Maybe if you stop complaining and just do what they tell you, you'll be out sooner," Ella said.

Natasha nodded in agreement and looked over at Danny for confirmation.

"Yeah," Danny heard himself say. He sat by, quietly watching his mother, Milton and Natasha. The memory of a day when he was a boy, standing alone in the back yard came to him. It was after a hard rain had fallen. A tiny stream had formed where their yard ended in a thicket of trees, and in the stream a tiny bird lay its eyes closed and its mouth open, lying still. Danny figured the bird had fallen from a nest that was hidden in one of the trees and had died. He watched it as the water rolled around the small gray body. Suddenly a gush of water came along and pulled the bird along the stream. As the water carried the bird away a sudden shudder went through the bird's body and its small wings fluttered before it disappeared into an opening in the ground. The memory of the bird left him, and Danny found himself looking into Milton's face. Their eyes joined in a silent stare, a silent stare filled with a mutual understanding.

Ella, Natasha and Danny stayed with Milton the rest of the morning before Danny told them he had to leave. On his way out he told his mother to call him when she was leaving. Then he hugged Natasha and took Milton's hand. "I'll be back to see you," he said.

"Ok." Milton could only mumble the word, but his eyes were filled with gratitude.

"I always knew they was close." Mr. Stiggers shuffled slowly through his living room with his hands clasped behind his back speaking in the exhaustive manner of someone who was finally confessing his behavior. He had asked Danny into his apartment so he could talk with him, but it was Danny who was just one of the persons in the room to whom the old man spoke. Danny sat on an old but sturdy living room chair and watched Mr. Stiggers walk back and forth across the living room, his steps shaky with age and his eyes fixed straight ahead as he recaptured the past.

"Before Damon came to town Buddy was just your average boy," Mr. Stiggers said, with a slight nod of his head. "Hangin' out with the rest of the boys his age. They would go blackberry pickin', go fishin' and swimmin' in the lake." He paused and looked at Danny. "Buddy could swim, you know. He knew how to swim," Mr. Stiggers said as he looked away. "And they would all just hang out on Sumpter Road like everybody did in Clearwater. And Buddy was our batboy." Mr. Stiggers fell into momentary silence before continuing. "But when Damon came along," Mr. Stiggers stopped his pacing as he began to talk about Damon. "When Damon came along, Buddy started to be around him more than anybody else. I never knew what control Damon had over Buddy, but Buddy started goin' over to ol' lady Hogan's shack everyday. Almost nobody went to ol' lady Hogan's shack. She was too mean. Didn't want hardly nobody comin' into her little raggedy piece of land. But Buddy started goin' over there everyday."

"What kind of person was Damon?" Danny asked the question as he looked up at the old man.

"Different. Nothin' bad that I know of, though I did hear tell he came to New Home 'cause he got in some trouble back where he was from. I never knew what it was, though. I was older than them and didn't know them that well. But he didn't do too much runnin' around like the other guys his age. He always seemed like he was older than the rest of 'em but he wasn't. Maybe it was 'cause he came from a bigger city. You sure you don't want nothin'?"

"No sir. I'm fine. I ate a little while ago. Where was he from?"

"Who?"

"Damon." Danny had asked the question in order to pull Mr. Stiggers back to the story.

"I don't know. Just some place that was supposed to be bigger than New Home. Chicago. Detroit, maybe."

Mr. Stiggers sat in a chair by a table that had a large lamp on it. Like everything else in the apartment it looked as if it belonged in another time, another century. It was large and heavy and the porcelain was yellow with age. The light from the lamp lit the living room in a warm glow, exposing the large knife on the table beside Mr. Stiggers. The blade of the knife was long and pointed with a razor sharp edge, but it had lost the silvery shine it once had.

"Him and Buddy became fast friends. And Buddy got him a job at the store in town where he worked. That's where I figure he met Ella."

"My mother."

"Your mother," Mr. Stiggers said before becoming silent once again.

Danny watched the elderly man sitting quietly in the glow of the lamp. The knife on the table beside the old man and the portrait on the wall of the woman staring out into the room were all framed in Danny's view. Danny wasn't concerned that the old man might attack him in the rage that Danny would hear coming from the old man's apartment. The man was too old to make any sudden moves that Danny couldn't handle. Danny only wanted to hear what the old man had to tell him.

"Ella's daddy, Mr. Stallworth, didn't want nobody comin' close to his family," Mr. Stiggers said finally. "'specially nobody from Clearwater. They all looked down on us," he said, as he looked at Danny with a look in his eyes that held a resentment he had just recalled. "So I figure that's where Ella and Damon met, at the grocery store."

Mr. Stiggers folded his hands in his lap and looked down at them before he continued. "You know your Momma got pregnant, don't you?"

"Yeah."

He looked up from his hands back to Danny. "Word got around quick about it. Quick, 'cause she was Mr. Stallworth's daughter and she was so young. Nobody ever knew who the daddy was. We knew some of the boys from Clearwater used to sneak over into town and meet up with some of the girls there. I never could find no girl in town that liked me. But some of the other guys did and they would meet up with the girls and, you know…"

Danny nodded his head.

"Then one day Damon and Buddy got into a fight. We was all sittin' around on Sumpter Street. Buddy was comin' from the store and Damon came runnin' up to him and slammed him against a car. He started yellin' somethin' about Buddy puttin' his hands on Ella. That's when we all knew who the daddy was. Buddy was tellin' him he never touched her. He kept sayin' 'you know I wouldn't do that', but Damon told him what he would do if it ever happened again. Then Damon stormed away, all mad."

Then a heavy silence fell over the room as Mr. Stiggers stopped talking. He seemed to fade in the light of the room, becoming almost a faint image. Danny stared at him and waited.

Finally, in a quiet voice, Mr. Stiggers continued. "Maybe I shouldn't a done it, but I told Mr. Stallworth who the daddy was." Mr. Stiggers spoke as he watched his fingers wrestling in his wringing hands. "I told him I thought it was Damon."

"Why?"

"I don't know," Mr. Stiggers said, shaking his head. "I just thought. Maybe I could get in good with him. Be somebody he might like. He owned almost half of New Home and all of us paid him rent. He was a powerful man." Mr. Stiggers shook his head remorsefully. "I need some water," he suddenly said, and got up and went into the kitchen. He returned with a glass of water he'd gotten from the sink. He set the glass on the table and slowly lowered himself back into his chair and sat looking down at his hands.

Danny sat with impatience, but he didn't let it show.

"How did my grandfather take it?" Danny finally asked, in an easy voice.

"Mr. Stallworth was mad. He went out lookin' for Damon. He got a few of us from the baseball team together and took us with him. And we went lookin'." Mr. Stiggers paused and looked over at Danny. "I didn't wanna to go. But he made me."

"My grandfather?"

Mr. Stiggers reached over and raised the glass of water to his lips and took a sip.

"Yeah," he said, setting the glass back on the table. It was clear that he was hesitant to go on with the rest of the story.

"How many of them were you," Danny asked.

"Five. Six countin' Mr. Stallworth. He was so mad. And when—and when we found your daddy, he was sittin' on a old bench. Him and Buddy. They was sittin' on a old bench like the ones you see on a porch, but it was out in the woods. Like it was a place they took that bench so they could sit. Like it was a place they had made up just for them. And they was sittin' and talkin'. It looked like they made up and became friends again." He paused and searched his memory. "But they was holdin' hands…" He fell silent to make certain of the memory he held. "They was holdin' hands," he said with a slight nod of his head. "When Mr. Stallworth saw 'em. Saw 'em holdin' hands, he became even more angry. And he told us to get 'em."

Suddenly Mr. Stiggers' eyes welled with tears. "He told us to get 'em. And we surrounded 'em. I didn't wanna to go," he said as he took in a breath and a tear rolled from his eye.

Danny cautiously reached over and patted Mr. Stiggers' knee. "It's ok."

"Nothin' woulda happened if they hadn't started fightin' back, your daddy and Buddy. But they did," Mr. Stiggers went on. "Especially Buddy. He was the one who swung around and hit Mr. Stallworth in the face. And Mr. Stallworth…" Mr. Stiggers began to cry. "He told some of us to hold Damon and then told the others to beat Buddy. I wanted to hold Damon, but he made me one of the ones who beat Buddy up. Oh God… I didn't wanna do it, but he told me if I didn't want me and my momma kicked out of our house, I'd better do what he said. So we beat Buddy. We beat him and beat him until his whole face was just… It was red, bloody and soft, and bone. And the blood, it was all over my hands." Mr. Stiggers raised the back of his hands and looked at them, remembering the blood. "Oh God." He cried and covered his face. "Oh God."

"Ok. You don't have to go no further," Danny said as he rushed over and stooped by the old man. "You don't have to go no further," he repeated as he rubbed Mr. Stiggers' shoulder.

But Mr. Stiggers needed to go on. He needed to tell what he had been carrying inside for so long.

"Damon was screamin' for us to stop. I could hear him. And I wanted to stop, but I was scared. I was scared for my momma and I was scared for what I had already done to Buddy so I just kept on hittin' him and hittin' him until he stopped movin'." Mr. Stiggers let out a heavy sigh. "And then your grandfather told Damon, 'See that? That's what's gonna happen to you if you and that filthy aunt of yours don't leave here'. Then he told us to take off Damon's belt and he… he told us to put it around Buddy's neck and he made Damon drag Buddy into the lake. Damon drug that poor boy and all the while he was cryin' and callin' Buddy's name."

Mr. Stiggers couldn't go on, and he sat in his chair and cried.

Danny was stunned. The only sound he could hear coming from his body was his own breath.

After Danny had calmed Mr. Stiggers, he told him everything would be ok. He told him that he wouldn't tell the police and that he would only tell his mother if she promised not to tell anyone else. He said she needed to hear what happened.

As Danny left Mr. Stiggers' apartment, Mr. Stiggers called out.

"Boy. I'm the only left. I know he's gonna come for me. But I got somethin' for him if he does." And he lifted the knife from the table.

Danny looked back at the old man, then to the portrait of the woman on the wall, before closing the door.

Ella's legs gave way and she fell to the floor of Danny's bedroom as he recounted Mr. Stiggers' story. Danny stooped to lift his mother but she waved him off and remained on the floor on her hands and knees. Her breathing was deep and rapid as she stared at the floor of her son's bedroom.

"Mom. Mom, you gonna be alright?" Danny was crouched by his mother's side with his arm around her.

But Ella didn't answer him, only her panting on all fours being her response. Then quietly, her breathing coming under control, she looked up at the photo on the wall.

"You gotta get up, Mom," Danny said as he lifted Ella from the floor.

They sat on Danny's bed in the deepening evening, surrounded by the photos of New Home. The photo of Ella's father, with his stern expression, and the images of Mr. Stiggers and Buddy and the rest of the team, looked out at her as night lowered itself over the room.

~~~~

Ella attempted to fold the clothes she was going to take out to Milton, but she found the simplest of acts like folding clothes diffi-cult, and her hands became tangled in the clothing. There was too much on her mind. She thought about Damon, and Buddy, and her father and what she now knew about that fateful summer in New Home.

Mr. Stiggers had told Danny the story and Danny had told it to her, but not before making her promise to keep it between the three of them. Danny said he didn't want the old man to get into any more trouble than he already had gotten himself into. And while Ella had agreed to the promise, she struggled with her agreement because of her part in what happened. What she knew didn't free her and she still needed to bring it all to light. It was her lie that had set everything in motion that summer.

After Danny told Ella what happened, she wrestled with it that night. She had tried to convince herself that what she now knew relieved her, but it didn't. She had tried to conceive the reasoning that if Damon had been true to her, things wouldn't have gone as far as they did. But her mind spun and she found herself blaming Damon for being in the store that day when she first saw him, for the nights she let Damon between her legs, and for his coming to New Home. And she blamed her mother for having died and leaving her alone with a man who rarely spoke to his children, except to scold them or to instruct them. Her mind spun wildly that night, but it all came back to her part in what happened, and the lie she told that day. Hearing what happened did little to lift the weight from her heart. Instead, it created a tear, a tear that pulled apart every fiber in her heart. She imagined Damon dragging Buddy's body through the woods, the sound of Buddy's lifeless body being pulled over the ground: the rustle of weeds and the breaking of twigs, the snap of vines that tangled around Buddy's body and were pulled from the ground as his lifeless body was dragged through the woods, the woods opening up, the woods she, Damon and Buddy knew so well. And more than anything, she heard Damon cry as he pulled Buddy's body through the woods. Buddy, the only person he probably loved as much as he loved her.

She finished packing the bag as best as she could and left the house.

On her way back from the hospital Ella replayed what Danny had told her. She didn't want to hold onto the secrets any longer. She thought of the elderly man in Danny's apartment. Sitting alone, being eaten alive because of what he had done. Going crazy. She didn't want to be like that. Before she left the hospital, she told Milton that they would talk more when he came home. He told her he would like that. He told her everything would be ok. She could only wonder.

Danny walked along the walls of his bedroom and removed the photos, carefully peeling each one from the wall and removing the tape from the backs of them. He placed them in one box. He had watched enough of them and he now knew what they were about. He didn't need to see them anymore, or at least for a long time.

The last photo he took down was the one with his grandfather and Buddy in it. He looked at the faces of the men in the photo, his eyes moving along the line of faces from his grandfather's face, along the faces of the other team members, past the face of the young Mr. Stiggers, before coming to the face of Buddy, smiling happily. None of the men in the photo had any idea of the ugliness that would come to them.

Once Danny put the last photo in the box, he put it back on the floor of his closet. The only person he didn't see in any of the photographs was the man he wanted to see most, his father.

"How are you feeling?" Danny studied his mother as they sat at a table that was away from the other diners in a restaurant. He watched her as she stared at the menu.

"He actually knew. All that time, and he knew," Ella said, speaking about her father. "He knew about Damon and everything. That day when we got to the lake, I remember him telling me, 'I'll signal you if it's him.' … He knew." She shook her head as she continued. "To be honest I don't know how to think about my father. I guess I shouldn't be too surprised that he would chase your father out of town, but… to have someone killed. To have them kill Buddy. I don't know how to think about him now."

"Cold hearted and a killer."

"Those words aren't easy for me to say, Danny. I mean, how do you say that about your parent?"

Danny didn't reply to his mother. He just looked at her.

"You're thinking 'because it's true'," Ella said. "And I guess it is--"

"You guess? Mom, it is true."

"But I can't think that. It's like, it's like…"

"Destroying everything you been taught a parent should be."

"Yeah," Ella said.

"The only thing though Mom is he already did it. He did it, not you. You've been letting all this stuff eat away at you little by little over the years. And it's had an effect on people around you. Including me."

"I wanted to keep it from you."

"What you ended up doing though was making me feel like something was wrong with me."

Ella looked at Danny. "No."

"Yeah. I grew up knowing something was wrong and that it had something to do with me. That was all I knew."

"That's not the way I wanted you to feel."

"I never knew how to feel or how you even felt about things. Even me, you know, liking guys. We never even talked about that."

"There was nothing to talk about."

"And when I found out what happened with my father and Buddy, I figured that was why you never talked about it."

"That's not it."

"Then how come we never talked about it?"

"Because it is what it is. I know it's not that big of a deal."

"Except when you're living in a world where half the people hate you. It is a big deal. I needed somebody to talk to."

They ate a bit before Danny asked, "How did you feel when you found out about my father and Buddy?"

"Shocked. Shocked and frightened because everything I thought was going to happen between me and your father suddenly fell apart when I saw them. And I—I didn't know what to do." Ella paused before continuing, "But it wasn't anything someone should've gotten killed over."

The sun set a violent orange hue over the city as Ella and Danny headed back to Danny's apartment. Ella drove slowly along the busy streets and long shaded avenues that were buttressed at each end with people gathered on the corners.

They came to Danny's street, where people stood on the corner and around the shops. As she turned the corner and started down Danny's street, she saw the young man she had seen some months ago, crossing at the intersection and gesturing wildly as he talked on his phone. That day he had reminded her of Buddy, and this evening he reminded her even more of Buddy as she watched him leaning against a building alone, talking to no one, his eyes watching the streets. Sadness rose in her.

Once they arrived at Danny's building and started up to his apartment, she slowed in front of Mr. Stiggers' door. Danny gently put his hand on her back to move her forward.

"Poor man," Ella said as she came into the apartment. "And it's all my fault."

"But your father didn't have to take it that far. Kids lie all the time, but he didn't have to take it that far, so don't put it all on yourself, Mom."

"Nothing was done out of love on his part," she said about her father as she sat on the couch. "Nothing. Ever. It was always about control. That's why he did what he did. Control. He was angry that he had lost it."

"You think so?"

"Yes," Ella said. "He was bothered when my mother passed away. Hurt, but angry too. She had the nerve to leave him. And the way he handled us after my mother died… he went on with that way of telling us what to do, what he expected of us. Never once did he sit with us and just talk with us. He never took the time to know his own children. We were like a commodity to him, something he needed to hold onto his stature. My mother's leaving was the first peg pulled out from under him and then…"

Danny sat beside his mother and looked at her hands, her fingers that tapped at the top of her thigh.

The two of them sat for a while talking about Ella's mother and father, her sister and her brother. They were the grandparents and the aunt and uncle, the family Danny had always wanted to hear about. As Ella talked she watched Danny's face, the expression he held of interest in her life, their life, they were the eyes and face that she had forgotten to see, the expression that became lost to her over the years, and much of it she was to blame for not seeing. Not Danny, or what happened to her so long ago, but it was she who forgot to see the eyes, and the face, and the expression of her son. They were the things that got lost.

It was night when she finished talking to him. She called Natasha to see how Milton was doing and to let her know she would be leaving for home soon.

"Natasha's moving in to help take care of Milton," she said to Danny when she got off the phone.

"That's good."

Ella smiled. "It's good to hear you say that."

Suddenly from the hallway someone screamed. "Oh shit! Oh shit!" And the sound of an alarm went off, followed immediately by shouts of 'Fire! Fire!'

Danny jumped up and immediately grabbed his mother by the arm and ran to the door. Already he could feel heat rising through the floor and once he opened the door to the hallway, the heat and the screams of tenants running past him and down the stairs met him and his mother. Someone fell over something at the foot of the stairs and yelled, "Aw fuck!"

"Come on Mom! Come on!" Danny led his mother down the stairs and there it was, the thing that people were stumbling over, the body of the young man Ella had seen that evening on the corner and who she had seen crossing the street that day; the young man who Danny had seen near his car the day when he and Littlejohn left the gym, and who he had seen on the surveillance camera, there he was, the young man, lying at the foot of the stairs, dead, with a knife buried deep in his chest. Ella stopped and screamed, frozen by the sight. Danny swooped her up in his arms and ran past the body. He could hear the roar of the fire and see the smoke coming from beneath Mr. Stiggers' door.

The orange and yellow flames cracked and split the floors and beams of the building and lit the nighttime sky. Danny stood across the street with his mother and watched the building turn into one large flame. He thought about Mr. Stiggers, who was still inside of his apartment, how he most likely sat in the chair beneath the portrait of the woman on the wall as the flames engulfed him. Then Danny thought about all of the photos and he imagined them curling in the heat of the fire before turning to black ash. It was all gone, just as Mr. Stiggers wanted it.

CHAPTER FORTY

The tape around the building had been changed. For the first few days the yellow tape had read 'crime scene,' and once the officials had done their research about the crazy old man and the 'bad' street thug, they recorded their findings and went about their business, allowing the tape to be changed to one that warned of caution instead of crime.

"A mess." A woman stopped to look at the building.

"Yeah," Danny said as he looked at her, then back to the building. "I used to live there."

"Were you there when the fire broke out?"

"Yeah."

The woman shook her head, correcting herself. "Broke out ain't the right word. They said it was set."

"Probably so," Danny said.

"Did you know the crazy man who did all that? Killed that boy and burned the place down?"

"I used to live right over him." Danny motioned to where his apartment had been.

"They still don't know why he killed that boy. They did say the boy had a gun on him and that he was the one killed that guy a while ago. What do you think that was all about?"

Danny shook his head. "I don't know." He lied because he did in fact know. He knew enough about the young man and about the ghosts that haunted Mr. Stiggers.

"Well, you never know when you got evil and crazy mixed together," the woman said. "Guess we'll never know. You take care."

"Thanks," Danny said.

The woman continued down the street.

Danny walked back to his car and with each step he thought about Mr. Stiggers and about Ella and what he and Ella were now prepared to do. He called Cortez once more and thanked him for taking him in. He told him that they would talk about their relationship once he was done with what he had to do.

He looked back at the building for a final glimpse and saw the morning mist that had gathered along the ground and the building lifting as the sun rose from beyond the trees. Then he got in his car and drove away.

~~~~

Ella dialed her aunt's number without giving it any thought. Ren had told her not to call Bernice, but Ella knew she had to speak to her. It was as if talking to her aunt was, after so many years, requisite to everything Ella had lived through, coming now, full circle.

Ella glanced down at the small, tattered book of phone numbers she had packed away when she left New Home. The pink cover was dog-eared and gray around the edges. She had turned to her aunt's number and dialed.

A voice came over the phone. "Hello?"

"Aunt Bernice?"

Bernice hesitated before finally replying, "Ella," releasing the name from a place where it had quietly been stored. A place where Bernice knew that one day she would be able to release the name once more to air and to light.

"Yes ma'am."

"What took you so long?"

The two of them talked at length that morning. Ella sat in the den, watching the morning light fill the corners of the room as she told her aunt everything that had happened. Her aunt listened to her and she listened to her aunt, and every so often between their words each one shed the tears that were needed to bring up and push away the pain, but not the memories.

Finally it was time for Ella to go. She promised her aunt that she would see her as soon as she did what she needed to do.

Bernice told her she understood. "I hope you realize now that all of that running you did only brought you back to where you were," Bernice said.

"Yeah," Ella replied. "Thank you. We'll talk."

"Yes we will."

Just as Ella was about to hang up, her aunt spoke again. "One more thing before you go. I understood why you left. You were doing it to protect yourself and your baby from that crazy ass brother of mine and all that mess that was going on around here. Nobody else understood, but I did, and you made it through."

"I know. Thank you, Aunt Bernice."

"Well. I said what I needed to say and you said what you needed to say. So I'll see you when you get here."

Ella carried a bundle of clothes to the bed and began sorting through them. Milton sat in a chair by the window, watching her.

"How much clothes are you taking?" he asked, as he rested his arms on the walker in front of him.

"I'm not sure," Ella said as she laid the clothing out on the bed.

Milton watched her a bit longer before continuing. "I'm glad you're doing this." He paused then went on, "I—I just wonder if you're ever coming back."

Ella stopped what she was doing and looked at her husband. She hesitated a moment, then answered. "I'll come back."

"I guess it's something you need to do," Milton said. He watched her and spoke with uncertainty.

Ella sat at the foot of the bed across from her husband and took his hand in hers. "Milton I can't take what I've been going through any longer. You've seen what it's done to me. And now that we know what really happened…" she shook her head. "I have to bring some closure to it."

"Can you? I mean, nothing you do will bring that boy back."

"I know that. Nothing can bring him back, but I can start healing wounds. There're only two of us left that knows what happened. And what Damon went through, he must have as much pain as I have. I have to bring some healing to all of this. When I talked to him on the phone I could tell how much he had gone through over the years."

"So Danny's boss really found him," Milton said.

"Yeah. Once I finally told Danny Damon's last name and that Damon had often talked about going to L.A. Danny's boss found him some way. Danny says his boss has connections."

From down the hall, she could smell breakfast being made.

"You and Natasha will be just fine here."

"Ella, this is our home. You're supposed to be here."

Ella looked at him and gently squeezed his hands. "I thought so too."

Milton studied Ella's face and saw that she did belong somewhere else.

"I got some work to do too," Milton finally said. "I know I do."

Danny arrived and they all sat down to breakfast. Once they were done, Danny began to load the car. He came back in and hugged Natasha.

"Take care of him," he said.

"I will," Natasha replied with a smile as she looked at her father.

Then Danny hugged Milton. "Everything will be okay."

"I know," Milton said as he hugged Danny.

Ella sat beside Milton and they held each other. They began to cry softly.

"Danny's right," Ella said. "Everything will be fine."

Danny had loaded the last of the luggage in the car, and called for his mother.

"Go ahead," Milton said. "He's waiting for you."

As Ella walked to the car, she felt someone move alongside her and she knew it was Buddy. She smiled and whispered, "Yes, he's waiting for us."

****

ABOUT THE AUTHOR

Doug Cooper Spencer is the author of six books. His novels are: *This Place of Men*, *People Like Us*, *Leaving Gomorrah* (which are books of a trilogy), and *Ella Pruitt*. He also authored an epistolary work, *A Letter to a Friend*; and a collection of stories, *Gather the Bones*. He is currently at work on his seventh book.

www.ingramcontent.com/pod-product-compliance
Lightning Source LLC
Chambersburg PA
CBHW030602180626
46816CB00005B/1648